Praise for

Saving Vincent

"Art history buffs—like me—who never learned how van Gogh's paintings survived will welcome *Saving Vincent*. Drawing on voluminous research, Fernandez brings to life the unexpected story of Jo van Gogh Bonger. I found it tremendously gratifying to discover the vital role she played at a time when women were virtually excluded from the art world."

—Jude Berman, author of *The Vow*

"Fernandez's immersive rendering of Jo Van Gogh Bonger's real-life efforts to rescue Vincent Van Gogh's art from obscurity is a story of such substance readers won't want to miss a single word. By outsmarting the art world controlled by men who did everything to thwart her efforts, Jo rises as a heroine for the working class, the very people for whom Vincent Van Gogh painted. Fernandez's finesse in capturing Jo's spirit as a woman coming into her own at the beginning of the twentieth century is considerable. Readers will be equally thrilled to find Vincent on the page as well, speaking to Jo through excerpts from the letters he left behind."

—NJ Mastro, author of *Solitary Walker: A Novel of Mary Wollstonecraft*

"[This is] . . . a great story . . . and timely application of advocacy principles for women, especially. Jo's experience demonstrates agency in a man's world and holistic fulfillment. Each chapter exemplifies a bend in the road, a triumph and pitfall, in the process of creating a successful marketing campaign."

— Penelope Schmidt, gallery owner

"An intriguing art- and history-filled tribute to an oft-overlooked dynamic woman."

—*Kirkus Reviews*

"Joan Fernandez is a remarkable author; her latest book is an invitation to delve into the captivating story of Jo van Gogh. . . In this delightful read, Fernandez not only uncovers Jo's significance but also enlightens us about the crucial role she played, weaving a rich tapestry of storytelling that underscores the profound importance of art in our lives."

—*Midwest Book Review*

"Joan Fernandez has brought to vivid life a truly remarkable person in tooth, claw and sinew that perhaps the world in general knows too little of. The writer has made her own and not inconsiderable contribution to a necessary and fuller understanding of the contribution of a truly steadfast and courageous individual."

—*Historical Fiction Company*

"*Saving Vincent*, like the art of its eponymous demiurge, brilliantly evokes both the dignity of the mundane and the fire of revolution at the turn of the 20th century."

—*IndieReader*

Saving Vincent

SAVING VINCENT

*A Novel of
Jo van Gogh*

———✦———

JOAN FERNANDEZ

SHE WRITES PRESS

Published 2025
Printed in the United States of America
Print ISBN: 978-1-64742-870-9
E-ISBN: 978-1-64742-871-6
Library of Congress Control Number: 2024925818

For information, address:
She Writes Press
1569 Solano Ave #546
Berkeley, CA 94707

Interior design by Stacey Aaronson

She Writes Press is a division of SparkPoint Studio, LLC.

*For the dissidents and rebels and dreamers who
challenge the status quo.*

*This is a historical fiction parable.
Based on documented fact and told through a modern feminist lens,
this biographical retrospective of Jo van Gogh's life celebrates her defiance
of patriarchal norms, her enduring legacy,
and the compounding power of love.*

ALMOND BLOSSOM

---◦---

Work was going well, the last canvas of the branches in blossom, you'll see that it was perhaps the most patiently worked, best thing I had done, painted with calm and a greater sureness of touch. And the next day done for like a brute.

—VINCENT VAN GOGH, *on or about March 17, 1890*

Winter
1891

ONE

---·---

PARIS

Jo

JIMMYING OUT THE CLOSEST CANVAS, JO VAN GOGH RECOGNIZED one of the sunflower paintings. Pretty golds and yellows, yet the drooping blossoms looked a little forlorn. This was not the one she wanted. Gritting her teeth, she wriggled it back into the crate.

Morning sunbeams highlighted scattered dust across the flat stretch of wooden boxes shoved against every wall of the stuffy salon. Some were stacked on top of each other, blocking the settee and upright piano Aunt Cornelie had given them as a wedding gift, while other crates jutted out into the narrow room so that she had to edge sideways to cross it. The only free chair was squeezed under Theo's tall oak writing desk with its piles of mail and stacks of old *Le Figaro* newspapers.

Her fingers fluttered along the rough edge of the next crate. She had not looked inside this one. Yanking it open, she pushed the rough wooden top aside to peer into the slapdash row of paintings for a glimpse of a white sprig from *Almond Blossom*, Theo's favorite painting. If her husband came home—she jerked back—no, *when* he came home and saw it, he'd be comforted, reassured.

She thumbed the canvases. Stormy grays, speckled oranges, goldenrod yellows, but no fairylike pale blossoms. Frustrated, she slammed the top down.

This was just like her. She'd always doubted herself, always assumed others knew best. Pa had taught her to beware of errant female thoughts running contrary to common sense. So she'd gone along with her brother Dries's insistence to organize the paintings, not realizing he intended to hide them away in unmarked crates. No list, no record. She knew better; Theo would be very unhappy.

She sneezed, hugging herself as a chill flickered up her spine. A lingering odor of turpentine and sawdust hung in the stale air. She'd dressed in Theo's favorite gown. Never mind that the thin silk was for evening opera outings, the pretty violet would delight Theo, especially paired with the fashionable, dainty boots she'd brought from Amsterdam. But her feet must have grown when she'd been pregnant, for the shoes pinched, and now she had to take care that the gown wouldn't snag in the cramped aisle between the crates.

She couldn't give up. *Almond Blossom* was a good-luck charm, the ideal homecoming for Theo. She wanted his return this morning to be perfect.

She needed it to be.

Because once Theo was back at his desk, sipping a glass of his favorite merlot as Vincentje's feet kicked from his lap, he'd be content, relieved to be through his ordeal. That was when she'd seek his reassurance on her decision to send out Vincent's drawings to the Vingt exhibit in Belgium. A jittery staccato rose in her stomach. She shoved aside a crate top and riffled through the row. It was too late to withdraw the Vingt submission, but Theo had a way of calming her agitation. If her decision was a mistake, he would make it right. His comforting words always made her feel safe. He might even be proud of her. Then they'd unpack the paintings and resume their work for Vincent together.

She shoved another lid aside, and her fingers flew through the artwork.

It had been three long months since Theo had left. Their most prolonged separation ever, longer even than the vacations she took to visit her family back in Amsterdam. Dr. van Eeden telegrammed regular reports that Theo's headaches were easing, but she couldn't help worrying he wasn't telling her everything. Didn't the doctor remember *she'd been here* when the asylum men had struggled to get Theo into a straitjacket? And *Theo had screamed her name*. Over and over as they'd scuffled. Surely Theo understood now that she had needed to call them for relief from the helpless nights when he'd writhed with agonizing pain, strangling on screams that had terrorized her and the wailing baby. Shuddering, she willed the images to fade, but she couldn't shake the shame of hiding as they had dragged him away.

The doctor's telegrams gave her hope. But when she; Theo's sister, Wil; and Mother van Gogh had taken the train to Utrecht to visit last month, the doctor had blocked their way, saying the hypnosis treatments for brain disease needed more time. She'd left without even a comforting glimpse of him.

Or the chance to explain. Ask his forgiveness for summoning those men.

Tiredly, Jo cocked her head to listen for the baby, but he was still sound asleep in their bedroom. Her aching eyes swept over the sea of boxes again. Theo would not like this at all. Twenty-seven crates, ten or more paintings in each, carelessly stowed away.

It didn't feel right. The paintings were the heart of their life together and always would be, even though Vincent was gone.

Seeing *Almond Blossom* again would remind Theo of their perfect union.

The canvas of delicate white-and-pink blossoms was her favorite too. She and Theo had married while Vincent recovered from his latest episode in the Saint-Paul-de-Mausole Asylum. Vincent had painted it a few months after Vincentje's birth. Though Theo assured her his brother approved, she'd known their marriage had inserted a wedge into the brothers' close relationship. *Almond Blossom* had felt like an olive branch.

For the hundredth time, she pulled from her pocket the thin telegram Dries had sent last night. She read aloud: "I have news. Arriving nine tomorrow." Closing her eyes, she pressed it to her chest. Dries had always been clumsy at keeping secrets. It made perfect sense that he would escort his best friend back home and want to surprise her. He'd played matchmaker before.

For from the first moment he'd introduced them, Theo had slid into a space alongside her, filling a gap she hadn't even known she had. As if, in some past life, they'd made a compact to find each other in this one. Agreeing to marry and follow Theo to Paris hadn't even been a choice. More like a foregone conclusion. A dream that had come true. For by being Theo's soulmate, she was blissfully, utterly complete. When she burned the roast, instead of scolding as Pa would have done, he laughed and claimed a cold supper of bread and cheese was exactly what he'd hoped for. When he woke at midnight, unable to sleep worrying over whether one of his artists could pay rent, she rose to console and listen. Theo had none of the abrasiveness of Pa's rough ambition. In the privacy of their home, Theo was a husband who shared his hopes and fears and wanted to know what she thought.

Because of him, she was the mother of a beautiful son. The first of many children they'd planned together.

She and Theo had a pact etched in their hearts.

Partners forever.

Outside the still apartment, cité Pigalle's clock-tower bells began to ring. Nine o'clock. With her heart in her throat, she'd already turned to the entry as a sharp knock reverberated through the flat.

Rushing to the door,, she flung it open. Dries stood in front of her.

She tried to chuckle—the tease. Pushing him aside, she peered behind him.

No one.

"Where's Theo? Dries . . ." Jo's words fell away, silenced by her brother's red-rimmed eyes.

"I need you to sit down." He caught her arms. With numb steps, Dries pushed her through the crate path and dropped her into the desk chair. He knelt in front of her. "I have news—"

"Theo's worse," Jo babbled, frantic. She grabbed at his coat sleeves. "He was so thin. Is he even thinner? He's stopped eating, hasn't he? I hear they force-feed—"

"No, Jo . . ."

"They turned me away!" She jerked from him. "I must go to him! He'll respond to me!"

"Jo!" He clasped her shoulders, his voice suddenly a whisper. "Theo's *dead*."

"N-no. I was just there! Just tried to see him." Her chest pinched.

"I'm so sorry, Net."

At the sound of her childhood nickname, Jo's breathing stopped.

Theo couldn't be dead.

She'd just gotten started being a wife, married only twenty-two months. Madame Smethe was coming this afternoon for Jo's next cookery lesson. Just yesterday, their new gas cooker had been hooked up in the kitchen. She felt swindled. She'd planned to fry the first steak on it for him.

She sucked in a breath.

Vincentje will never know his father.

Twisting her arms from Dries's grip, she picked up the miniature double portraiture with single photos of her and Theo side by side. His dear face gazed from the oval frame. Even though she'd tried to tame his unruly bangs by wetting them down, his hair had rebelled, swooping in a wild wave above his laughing eyes. The image blurred. Dropping the portraiture, she gripped the chair for support.

"I'm not ready for this."

Dries pressed a handkerchief into her hand. "Do you feel faint? Do you need to lie down?"

She shook her head. What difference would taking to her bed make?

"The asylum sent me the telegram yesterday."

She blinked. "Wait . . . you? Why not—"

"Come now! Remember how depressed you were after the baby. Pa insisted that I be their contact."

"But this news . . ." It was true that she'd struggled for a time after Vincentje had been born. Theo hadn't even seen fit to tell her Vincent had died until the day after. Wasn't this just like Pa to take over? Wanting to protect his favorite daughter. Shielding her from bad news.

Fresh tears welled up. But no one could protect her from this.

Swiping at her eyes, she whispered, "Some part of me knew it, Dries. I couldn't sleep last night. And the baby. He was fidgety. He felt it too."

"Theo had a seizure. Fell unconscious. He died in his sleep."

She stared at the crumpled handkerchief twisted in her hands. She should have been with Theo. How could she have let him die alone? A rivulet of tears slipped to her jaw.

"Pa sent me his instructions this morning." He reached inside his coat for a telegram. "Funeral at Soestbergen Cemetery in Utrecht on Monday. Jo's train ticket. Moving arrangements," he read.

Jo's stomach churned. "So far away . . . Utrecht must be four hundred kilometers from here. How will I visit . . . ?" She couldn't say it: *Theo's grave*.

"It's Pa's decision."

"Wait . . . Pa knows?" She looked at Dries, confused. Theo had only just died.

"I sent a telegram as soon as I heard."

"Last night?"

Dries frowned. "No, I told you *yesterday* morning. Come, Jo. This is a shock. You need to lie down." Dries reached for her, but Jo stood up, pushing him away. He was the one confused, not her.

"I do *not* need to lie down. You *kept* the news of Theo's death from me? You told Pa before me? I am Theo's *wife*." She was shaking.

"Theo was my best friend! You're not the only one who is grieving here."

She blinked down at him, eyes streaming. "Oh, Dries. *Was*. I *was* Theo's wife."

"Net . . ." He stood up to reach for her again, but she stepped back.

"Wait. You took the time to send a telegram to Pa before telling *me*?" Her anger surged. She jerked her hand back to slap him.

Dries caught her wrist. "Don't you dare scold! We're looking out for you. You know we had to make arrangements. You know how you are. It's a wonder you're standing. You always take to bed at the earliest sign of . . . upset."

Jo yanked out of his grip. Her thoughts tumbled. "I . . . I . . . need to contact Theo's mother."

"Calm down. It's done, of course. And Pa secured the gravesite in the Van Gogh plot last month."

Last month?

Jo's chest tightened. Of course Pa had. With grim efficiency, he'd planned for her husband's *death*. Jo collapsed into the chair, splayed her fingers across her face, and sobbed.

Later that afternoon, Dries set a cup of steaming tea in front of Jo on a cleared desk area. She fiddled to straighten the edges of the nearest stack of mail. The letters were hers now.

"Take a sip?" Dries leaned against the edge of a crate. He peered at her. "I need some information, Jo."

She nodded, reaching for the cup. Instead of giving her the

useless cookery lesson, Madame Smethe had taken the baby out for a walk in his carriage. She and Dries should talk before they came back. Feeling drained, Jo struggled to take hold of her shame. All this time, she'd been unaware of how delusional she was. Her distraction—no, her ignorance—had squandered time with Theo. She should have insisted on seeing him, stayed in Utrecht, kept a closer eye, and asked more questions. She had acted like a little girl. No wonder Pa and Dries had taken over. She dropped the teacup untasted back into its saucer. She had failed to be there for Theo when he'd suffered. The least she could do was to pull herself together now.

Her voice was rough. "Who . . . who do I pay for the gravesite?"

Dries cocked an eye at her. "Pa took care of it . . . Jo, do you have any idea how much money Theo had?"

She hesitated. Of course, she posted their daily housekeeping expenses in their account book and had helped Theo track sales, but it hadn't occurred to her to tally them up. Theo always did that. She shook her head.

"As I expected."

Blinking, Jo willed her tears not to start again. "Theo had investments." She hesitated, trying to recall. "I've been living off of Theo's paychecks—Boussod's continued them even while Theo's been . . . sick." It was the one decent thing Boussod & Valadon could do after making Theo's life so miserable managing their Montmartre art gallery. Theo had been forced to use his own funds to buy paintings he believed in, despite the disapproval of his director, Georges Raulf. So disdainful of Theo's taste. There must've been at least a dozen paintings from Theo's own collection there—works by Camille Pissarro, Edgar Degas, Claude Monet, and a sculpture by Auguste Rodin. She pressed a handkerchief to her eyes. "And there's Theo's personal collection at the gallery."

"And you've inherited all of this . . ." His arm swept across the salon.

The rough containers squeezed in on her, crowding her up and out of her chair. At least three hundred paintings here. Drawings and lithographs too. All unsold. Theo had left these to her care. The realization sent a shock. These containers didn't hold even half of Vincent's work. Panicked, she furrowed her brow, fighting to concentrate. The paintings Vincent had done in Auvers-sur-Oise were stored at Père Tanguy's in the attic above his paint shop. A café in Arles had the work Vincent had done in the south of France. Where else? At least half a dozen other small art dealers across Paris. Were there one hundred more paintings? Two hundred? What had Theo been thinking to die like he had? She couldn't be responsible. Theo had known where all his brother's artwork was. She had no clue.

"Steady, Net." Dries pulled her back into the chair. "Theo's inheritance is split equally between you and Vincentje. He'll get his portion when he turns twenty-five." He scanned the wooden crates. "Not that there's much here. Vincent painted so much—and poor Theo never made a sale."

"A few. One last winter."

"What's that?"

"Theo sold *The Red Vineyard* to Anna Boch, Eugène Boch's sister."

Dries looked blank.

"He's the artist who became Vincent's friend when Vincent first came to Paris. There's a portrait of Eugène Boch . . . somewhere here." She cast about the crates. ". . . a poet." She recalled the portrait's otherworldly background of twinkling stars. Her racing pulse began to slow. Theo had commented that it suggested Boch's imagination, but she hadn't needed the explanation. The painting's feeling of transcendence was self-evident.

"Not a *serious* collector, then," he said.

"What do you mean?"

"His sister bought it."

Dries didn't know what he was talking about. Theo had had his share of society ladies come to the gallery, one hand on their husband's elbow, acting demure while shrewdly selecting some of the better art to coax their husbands into purchases. Theo had liked to say his sales were apolitical—the value of a franc was the same whether an aristocrat or member of the bourgeoisie paid it, whether a man or woman. Every sale had counted toward his annual bonus.

His bonus.

"Theo's bonus is paid in the spring. I need to contact Boussod to see if I can get the payment now."

"How important . . . ?"

"It was double Theo's salary last year."

He swallowed. "Well then, I'll have to take care of it."

"Let me do it."

"Absolutely not, Net. Art traders are bullies. And of all the top dealers, Boussod is the worst."

"I know how horrible they are. Theo tried to break from them, remember? When you backed out of owning a gallery with him?" She couldn't stop the taunt. She wanted him to hurt.

"You have *no clue* what it's like to be in commerce."

"In fact, I do." Her mouth suddenly dry, she reached for the tea. "I—I sent some of Vincent's drawings to the Vingt's annual show."

"In Brussels? The deadline was months ago."

"I wrote to Director Maus, asked if we could send pen-and-ink drawings."

"You can't have. Theo was too confused. He couldn't possibly—"

"I sent the drawing titled *Fountain in the Garden of the Asylum.* Theo loved that one. And others." Her head bent. How ironic that Theo had been in an asylum.

"It's an annual show for *paintings*, Net. The Vingt men pride themselves on being at the forefront of avant-garde art."

"*I know that.* Theo told me how they showed Vincent's oils in the past. That's why I reached out when I realized we missed the entry date."

"Come on. You shouldn't have gotten involved with that. And in the middle of Theo's breakdown!"

How could she explain that the notion had come out of the blue? The thought had been vivid even in the whirlpool of frantic worry over Theo. The idea had been impetuous, uncharacteristically spontaneous, scribbling a quick telegram to Director Maus without consulting anyone. It was a little concept—inconsequential, really. Nothing to get so wound up about. But she'd counted on Theo's assurance—his confidence in her acting on her own—when he returned.

Now she'd never know if she'd been right.

She picked up the portraiture at her feet and stared at her innocent face. How naïve she'd been. Even in the terrible months as Theo's illness had worsened and she'd struggled in constant exhaustion caring for him and the baby—even then, she'd never imagined their beautiful partnership could end. But now . . . Vincentje's parenting. Their cozy Paris apartment. Theo's lifelong work to showcase Vincent's art. Her tender companionship with Theo—all of this would dissolve once she moved under Pa's roof. Dismay rose from deep within her, yet for once, her eyes were dry. It was time to face the fact that her fairy-tale life had come to an end.

Still, she craved to take hold of one thing, just one last thing, before she said goodbye forever to her life with Theo. The bonus proved Theo's love for her and Vincentje. It was hers.

With sudden ferocity, Jo grabbed her brother's arm. "I'm claiming the bonus."

He tugged at her grip. "My god, you're impossible." He paused. "Braver than me."

"I'm Theo's wife."

"Theo's . . ." His eyes softened. "Oh, Net, let's get through the funeral first."

He caught her when she let go. She'd misspoken again.

TWO

UTRECHT

Jo

THE STONE TOMBSTONES OF SOESTBERGEN CEMETERY DOTTED
the uneven, scrubby grass in languishing cold white rows. Bare tree
limbs bent and jostled, offering no break from the gusts of icy January wind. In front of Theo's grave, Jo leaned into Dries's comforting
arm. Swirls of loose hair flew across her face. Her throat throbbed,
choked with unspoken words.

She hadn't thanked Theo. Never told him how he'd helped her
come alive. How she'd had no idea, no clue of who she was until
she'd met him. He'd been the one person she trusted to give her
permission—more than that—*courage*—to follow her own ideas.
Without him, who was she now?

Not enough.

In front of them, a minister pressed his index finger against
Bible passages while he struggled to read aloud from the riffling
pages.

She stiffened. The toneless recitations grated at her. Theo
would have hated this funeral. He and Vincent had discarded their
heartless upbringing as soon as they'd left home, yet Mother van

Gogh had put her foot down. She had God's ear. Theo would have a Christian burial.

What did Jo expect? She was the dutiful daughter-in-law. Trapped under parental wings from both sides of the family. Of course she would have no say at her husband's grave.

Jo glanced around the empty graveyard. Just three of Theo's friends—artists Émile Bernard and Paul Signac plus paint merchant Père Tanguy—had made the trip to Utrecht. Pa's scheduling had been so efficient; they were the only outsiders here.

Dries squeezed her shoulder as if the tighter his grip, the better it would fill in for her absent family. Pa had forbidden their travel. Train tickets to the funeral were an unnecessary expense. She'd be back in Amsterdam soon. Plenty of time to receive condolences in person then.

Dries's steadiness on her left offset Wil's trembling on her right. Impossible that her sister-in-law's waiflike profile could seem even thinner. The coal-dark shadows under her blank eyes looked translucent, ghostlike. Theo's death had struck like a hammer blow just six months after Vincent's. Jo worried Wil wouldn't make it through the funeral without fainting. She slipped an arm around her.

Her mother-in-law stood on the other side of Wil. Even shorter than Jo, her silvery gray-haired head could only be seen beyond Wil's elbow. She stood statue-still, chin tilted straight up as if in a direct line to her God.

At the end of their sad row, Theo's twenty-four-year-old brother, Cor, shuffled his feet, eyes on the ground. Jo's heart reached out to him. How must he have felt? Bewildered? Crushed? In six months, he'd gone from the youngest carefree son to the single Van Gogh male survivor. All familial responsibilities dropped onto his shoulders. His dreams of the future were now razed to the ground by Theo's death.

Like hers.

For now, instead of visiting Amsterdam on vacation as the indulged youngest daughter, she was returning as a burden. Widow with a baby. Another dependent woman for Pa to support along with her two unmarried sisters and youngest brother, Wim. She could feel Pa's grim resignation all the way from Amsterdam.

A half hour later, when the minister closed the Bible and Jo tossed a chunk of dirt into the grave while Cor half carried Wil from the site, Dries asked her a question, but she didn't catch it. She didn't care.

"Madame van Gogh?" Émile Bernard stood before her, forcing himself into her focus.

"What?" She wanted to be rude.

His eyes were moist though. Père Tanguy stood behind his shoulder, crushing the edges of a soft hat in clenched hands. They'd loved Theo too.

"Don't worry, Madame. We'll take care of everything," Bernard said.

Tanguy dropped his head. "First Vincent, now Theo. I'll stand by them yet."

Behind them, Signac nodded, wiping his eyes with a handkerchief.

Dries shook the men's hands. "We'll count on you."

Wordlessly, Jo watched the men walk away. How strange that she'd get to know them without Theo now. She didn't want to.

Dries took her elbow. "Everything's under control. We'll have your affairs squared away in no time."

"I just wanted to be happy," she rasped.

The pity in Dries's eyes was almost more than she could bear.

THREE

------◆------

PARIS

Raulf

THE NEXT DAY, IN FRONT OF THEO VAN GOGH'S PLAIN wood-paneled apartment door, Georges Raulf fought to steady his breathing as he knocked frozen horse manure from his boots. Leaning over with his hands on his knees, he sucked in great gulps of air. He glanced out of the adjacent window overlooking the courtyard where the snowstorm from yesterday had already churned into slippery blackish slush. The same type of mess he'd stomped through leaving the Académie des Beaux-Arts's meeting an hour ago, where those weak-kneed directors had practically whimpered when delivering the devastating news that the biennial Paris Salon—the beloved standard-bearer of Parisian art superiority—had been canceled. Canceled! After centuries of revered art-world authority, the Paris Salon had been discontinued, all because the old fools didn't grasp the opportunity of the hour. Not since Napoleon had France secured this chance to extend its influence and take its rightful place as a world-class republic.

Père—God rest his soul—would have been livid.

Paris's art world could be the point of the spear. Its superiority had even surpassed Rome as the center for classical art. Paris was the glittering jewel of Europe thanks to the foresight of financier pioneers like his father. The Académie directors were soft, removed from the iron-fisted street fighting between Paris art dealers. They had no idea who shaped progress. After years of scoring deals, cut-throat tactics, and behind-the-back stealing, his appointment to the Salon's coveted jury had been a critical rung on the political ascent he'd mapped out with Père. Now the Académie's unbelievable cowardice burned. He clenched his jaw, furious. What would Père have said?

Walk over the fools.

Raulf drew a steadying deep breath. He'd take care of this errand and be on his way before opening the Boussod & Valadon gallery on boulevard Montmartre. He arranged his face in a sorrowful expression, yanked off his thick leather gloves, and knocked. News of his manager's death had traveled quickly. Yesterday his latest junior protégé, Antoine, had tentatively sidled up to his marble desk to stammer out the gossip and then slid a note in front of him that unwittingly confirmed the rumor. The curling handwriting on the linen envelope looked like a schoolgirl's: *Monsieur Georges Raulf.* His annoyance with Antoine drained away as he read the simple-minded note. Theo van Gogh's wife wanted her husband's bonus.

Manager bonuses were based on 7.5 percent of their gallery profits. He'd looked up the Montmartre branch. Last year Van Gogh had been paid eight thousand francs—twice the manager's annual salary—and this year's sales had been even better. With Theo dead, he wasn't about to pay it, and he smiled at her innocent request. Doubtless, the widow would be moving home to her father's care. Raulf needed those funds more than she did.

Especially after this morning's meeting.

Dead or not, Van Gogh owed him for the headaches he'd caused. Theo van Gogh's stubbornness had turned the Montmartre

gallery into some celebrated outpost for independent art, relentlessly exhibiting troublemakers like Edgar Degas and Claude
Monet, not to mention his brother Vincent's maniacal painting. It
was cruel. It gave false hope to the thousands of impressionable
young men who poured into Paris from across Europe, leaving
small towns and villages mesmerized by the fantasy they could be
discovered in Paris, as though their meager talent would ever
bring them riches. If anything, Van Gogh should have been arrested
for fraud. If those damn directors had any teeth, any integrity,
they would have shut down these imposters years ago. Idealistic
young men like Raulf's brother, Raynaud, wouldn't have caught the
artist's sickness and wasted their lives.

Raulf would start with the Montmartre gallery, scrubbing it
clean of avant-garde art. Not only was it the right thing to do for
France, but it would elevate him in the eyes of Boussod & Valadon's
partners. Since the Académie had abandoned its role as standard-
bearers, there was a vacuum. His fingers itched. He already knew
which paintings he'd secure to hang in Montmartre. William-
Adolphe Bouguereau. Gustave Moreau. Within Boussod, *he* would
finally be acknowledged for his singular patriotism. Being named a
partner would surely be a foregone conclusion.

He swept his bowler hat off his head. The door swung open as
he smoothed his hair.

"M-monsieur Raulf." Van Gogh's wife greeted him solemnly
and extended her hand. She was short—her height only just reached
his chest—and took a step back to regard him with tired eyes. "I'm
Madame van Gogh," she trembled. "Pl-pleased to meet you."

Poor girl. His manager had married a young one. He bent over
her hand. "Your husband was one of our best managers." Oddly, the
cloying odor of a paint dealer—or a carpenter's shop?—tickled his
nose. He looked up into the apartment behind her.

The girl nodded, accepting his condolence. "Please excuse the
disorder."

Raulf trailed behind the widow's slight figure down the hallway, awkwardly sidestepping packing cartons. He peeked inside each doorway as they passed—a kitchen, a box room turned into the dining room—he was surprised to see those areas, too, crowded with crates. Their apartment must have been jammed with household items.

"Coffee?" she said over her shoulder, waving him toward an armchair squeezed between two wooden cartons.

"No, thank you. I won't be staying." He fought the temptation to pull out a handkerchief to block the heavy turpentine musk. It dawned on him that these cartons weren't all household items. Some boxes must've contained *paintings*. How extensive was his manager's collection? The wooden crates were closed shut, but they must've all followed Van Gogh's preference for wanton modern art. What a colossal waste. No wonder the widow was begging for money. It was sad to see another victim of the avant garde destined for the trash bin.

The girl perched on the edge of a chair and pulled a heavy ledger onto her lap from a desk behind her. She quivered. "I appreciate your responding to my note so quickly, Monsieur Raulf. I want to start by thanking you for continuing Theo's paychecks this fall after he fell ill."

Raulf drew a blank. It must've been a carryover from Van Gogh's uncle, "Cent" van Gogh, a former Boussod partner who'd died three years ago. The old fool's spineless sentimentality still lingered. "It was the least we could do," Raulf murmured.

The widow lifted her chin. "We . . . I have a young son—almost one year old." Her hand fluttered. "He's . . . napping." Her short fingers found a ledger page. She grasped it. "I . . . I'm getting our finances in order . . ."

Surely she wasn't asking about the bonus? Raulf was caught off guard. He glanced around. He'd assumed a brother, cousin, or another male relative would be here to discuss the money. He held back a laugh. These provincial Dutch didn't understand how good business was done. He tugged on each jacket sleeve, smoothing out the fabric ripples. "You're moving back to the Netherlands? To your father's?"

Startled, she looked up. "We're moving soon, which is why I sent you the note about Theo's bonus income."

Persistent as an annoying fly.

She ran a finger down the page. "Theo's records show you owe him eight thousand francs." Her voice was stronger. She looked up at him. "Or more."

Or more? Raulf sat back. Who had done the percentage calculations for her? Her earnest gaze perplexed him. He was used to Parisian high society in which women fluttered fans and flirted nonsense. Van Gogh's wife had an unsettling gravity. A strange determination. He would need to cut off this twaddle.

"You're mistaken," he declared.

She flushed and tapped her finger at the end of a column of numbers. "Another . . . amount?"

"Another *time*. Our policy is to do our inventory now, then pay out bonuses in the spring, and . . ." he improvised quickly, ". . . the *chèque* we sent you came from the sales Theo made earlier in the year. Boussod and Valadon has already done all we can."

The widow flushed deeper. "But four months' pay is only twelve hundred francs. That's . . . that's hardly close . . ."

What blather. Raulf pulled out his pocket watch. He'd done what he'd come here to do; he'd given his condolences on behalf of Boussod. Irritation rose. "Where is your father, Madame? Or another family member . . . a brother?"

"My brother Andries Bonger is a broker here for George Wehry."

"The importer?"

"Yes."

Relieved, Raulf nodded. He would handle the brother and be on his way. "I'm surprised he's not here." How long would he have to wait? He winced at a headache's first twinge. Fresh air would do the trick. He stood up, but it appeared the room's only window was blocked in. "You're ready to move already?"

"Our things need to be packed." She followed his gaze. "These are my brother-in-law's paintings."

"*All* the cartons are his paintings?"

She nodded.

Van Gogh's half-wit brother! Raulf laughed out loud. He took a few steps down the path between cartons, giving each crate a crisp knock as he passed. "Unbelievable, Madame. I had no idea. Your husband tried selling some of his brother's work in the gallery, but . . . so many boxes . . . the waste." He turned to face her. "It's all . . . clutter."

She sprang to her feet. Her cheeks flamed. "You're mistaken."

Raulf spun around in one spot. "I can get rid of these for you," he said. "The École is always looking for practice canvases."

"You mean painted over? But they'd be . . . erased!"

"The École des Beaux-Arts is the best art school in Paris. They'll be put to good use."

"I'm keeping them."

His laughter died. Gad, how he hated female sentimentality. He'd wasted enough time. Placing his bowler hat onto his head, he tapped it into place. Let the Dutch keep their Dutch painter.

"Madame," he dismissed himself.

Her small hand clasped his arm, shocking him. "But Monsieur, you're *sure* about the bonus . . ."

He pried off her grip. "I'll show myself out."

What a pity, but he couldn't afford to get sentimental. The girl was emotionally attached to an amateur. He had to stay focused. Take the lead in ridding Paris of all the upstart modern painters. And one thing was for sure: Theo van Gogh's death gave him the perfect opportunity to make his mark on Paris.

—◆—

FOUR

PARIS

Jo

FOR THE FIRST TIME SINCE THEO'S FUNERAL A WEEK AGO, JO awoke rested.

Sunlight cascaded from the window across the salon and highlighted the thick coat of dust in each cubbyhole of Theo's desk. She'd cleared a small work area by shoving the teetering stacks of mail and newspapers into taller piles. Each day the post delivered notes of condolence. The initial trickle had become a deluge, especially after Theo's obituary had appeared on page six of *Le Figaro*. She'd been piling up the notes unopened, fearful of ripping open the paper-thin covering she'd sealed around her grief.

But today she'd awakened with a new resolve to face them.

Dries had taken the day off and come by early. After the baby's breakfast and an extra-strong cup of coffee, she'd shoved the boxes into a makeshift blockade around Theo's desk to keep Vincentje contained next to her. After stacking the sympathy notes into a pile, she'd tucked Theo's loose papers into a single drawer to sort through later. Dries had picked up the widow's stationery with the wide black border for her.

She opened a note; a pale thumbprint was smudged on its top right corner.

"Sara de Swart . . . she's the sculptress?" she asked Dries, who had appeared in the dining room doorway. She gently pressed her thumb over the print.

He leaned against the doorjamb and bit into a kipferl. Flakes of pastry floated onto the floor. "Rodin's lover." He took another bite.

Jo fingered the note. Auguste Rodin. Theo owned one of his sculptures. She remembered Sara now. She'd met her with Rodin at the party in the World's Fair Dutch Pavilion last year. Jo nudged the edges of the envelopes to straighten their edges, thinking hard. She vaguely remembered a dark-haired woman with a forceful laugh, but she'd possessively clung to the arm of a female companion, not Rodin. Were they lovers? Jo flushed. So flagrantly brazen! She imagined Sara bent over a desk, long loose hair masking her face, fingers scrunched around a pen trailing a trace of powder. The grayish print must've been from molding clay. The word "sculptress" sounded sensual, foreign on her tongue. What would it be like to be as bold as Sara?

Or Suzanne Valadon. Another woman who had chosen to be an artist. She remembered Theo chuckling over the rumor of her scandalous affair with Pierre-Auguste Renoir after she'd posed as his model. Or was Henri de Toulouse-Lautrec her lover?

These women were so different from her. Taking lovers. Living independently.

Trusting their own ideas.

Jo pictured herself walking through Paris on her own. A little shiver raced up her spine.

Not her.

She knew better. She had always been the dependent one in the family. "Babied," her sisters whined. So, when Pa had granted permission for her to marry, she'd moved from her father's care to her husband's. She was safe that way.

Jo bent her head to scratch out a few stiff, pacifying sentences. Too formal. She crumpled the note paper into a tight ball. Picking up the envelopes, she fanned through them, skimming the names on their return addresses.

"I had no idea of all the things Theo did for his artists," Jo said to Dries.

"Why would you?" He broke off a tiny piece of kipferl and dangled it over the crate to Vincentje, who clambered along the inside of the enclave. Teetering, the toddler grasped the bit of roll, then plopped to the ground.

Jo waved a note card. "Camille Pissarro wrote that Theo gave him money for rent once. Claude Monet remembered Theo paid out of his pocket to repaint the entire gallery for his first solo show."

"Annie would kill me if I spent money that way."

"I have a note from Albert Aurier. He and Theo had planned to publish some of Vincent's letters."

"The art critic? Why?"

"Honestly, I'm not sure." She scanned the desk's cubbyholes stuffed with yellow envelopes. "Theo saved every letter from Vincent since they'd started writing to each other at least ten years ago. He read a few aloud to me." She looked down at the note in her hand. "I'm not sure why he'd publish them. Vincent could be so insulting."

"He was mad."

"Theo didn't think so. Vincent suffered from episodes, but there were times he was quite lucid."

"If you say so. Doesn't matter. They're both gone now. Oh, Net . . ." His head jerked, regret in his eyes. "I'm an insensitive brute."

Eyes shining, Jo shook her head. Underneath his bumbling, Dries had a heart of gold. How could she explain how unnerving it was to read about a side of Theo she hadn't known?

"I thought Theo shared everything with me." She steadied Vincentje as Dries placed the last of his pastry into the baby's outstretched hand. "He used to lie with his head on my lap and tell me about his day—every insult, every ignorant comment, every snub. He wanted to help his artists *so much* it gave him headaches."

"That was the disease."

She shook her head. "He truly cared, Dries. And I wanted him to release the burden of it, allow me to carry it for him."

"Why?"

"Isn't that what a wife does?"

A look crossed Dries's face. "I wish Annie . . . At any rate, you no longer have that duty." He patted Vincentje on his head and disappeared back into the dining room.

Over the next hour, a parade of names and faces passed in front of her—Émile Bernard, Isaac Israëls, Odilon Redon, Edgar Degas, Meijer Isaac de Haan, Paul Signac, Père Tanguy —all people she'd met through Theo but now realized she'd never truly known, never been inside their world. She was the wife. At dinner, the woman behind the scenes, on Theo's arm for outings. Why didn't she know their stories? Paid more attention?

It was too late now.

Sighing, Jo picked up another letter. *Mevrouw Jan Veth* leaped off the return address. Anna Veth. Her dear childhood companion. Pressing the linen paper to her nose, she breathed in a light lavender scent. The lovely detail was so like Anna, her ladylike, thoughtful friend. Just last year she and Theo had traveled back to the Netherlands to visit Anna and her husband, Jan, for a peaceful weekend getaway to see their new home in the small town of Bussum. The trip had put such color in Theo's cheeks, Jo had made him promise they'd make it an annual affair. But in addition to Theo's improvement, she cherished how she and Anna had rekindled their friendship. On a stroll, dawdling behind the men's loud arguments about art, she and Anna had linked arms, recalling silly little girl antics until they'd doubled over laughing and gasping for breath. When the men had scolded *What's going on?* they could only shake their heads and wipe their eyes before bursting into giggles again.

How impossible that trip had only been nine months ago.

Vincentje pulled at her skirt, breaking her from reverie. Smoothing back his silky blond curls, Jo planted a kiss on his crown. She couldn't dwell on the past. Her focus was raising Vincentje now.

Wiping her eyes, Jo picked up the baby. "Dries! Would you take Vincentje?"

The opening of cupboard doors squeaked from the dining room.

"Stay out of my things," Jo said when he appeared. Dries had a way of making a mess even when he thought he was helping.

"Come here, young Vincent." Dries lifted the baby from her.

"Vincent-*je*."

"He's the man of the house. Shouldn't we call him a man's name now?"

"*No!* He's still my baby." But without a father, her son's future had changed forever. Soon enough, he would find out how different, how singled out and deprived he was with only a mother as his parent. The last thing she wanted was to rush his growing up.

Dries jiggled Vincentje until he giggled. "Let's go do men's work."

"I don't want you meddling," Jo called after them. She stretched her arms over her head to ease her tight shoulders. Pa had arranged for the movers to come in two days. She already had a plan for how to pack—which items to go to Pa's (Vincentje's crib, two trunks of clothes) and which to send into storage (nearly everything else since her childhood bedroom had been untouched since she'd left). Over Pa's objection, Theo's clothes would be stored too. She wasn't ready to get rid of them yet.

Turning back to the notes, Jo read the name Octave Maus. The faint pulse of a headache threatened. She still needed to answer his telegram. Vincent's drawings had been so well received in the Vingt exhibit that instead of returning them, Maus had taken the liberty to send them directly to the Museé d'Art Moderne in Brussels to include in a show next week. She still hesitated at the news—Theo had been so careful about where he'd placed Vincent's artwork—but if the Vingt reception was as good as Director Maus claimed, surely Theo would have approved—wouldn't he?

And there was another problem. Director Maus asked what prices to put on the drawings.

She fingered the note.

Theo had done all the pricing.

She had no idea.

A crash sounded in the dining room.

"Dries!" Jo shoved aside a crate to scoot out of the barricade. "Don't make a mess!"

A dozen silver spoons lay scattered under the dining table. A sunburst of white sugar crystals fanned across the floor next to sugar tongs and an upturned sugar bowl. An open velvet-lined box leaned against a chair leg. Dries crouched to pick up the spoons as Vincentje crawled rapidly toward the sugar. "I'm counting the silver," Dries said, looking up.

She grabbed the baby by both legs and pulled him back. Scooping up the box, she turned it upright onto the table. "Honestly, Dries! Whatever for?"

Dries swept up a few spoons and dropped them, clattering, into the open box. "These could be sold."

"Spoons? Sugar tongs? They were a wedding gift from Ma."

"Pa told me to calculate your wealth," he said. Jo opened her mouth to retort, but before she could comment, he said, "You were wrong about Theo's bonus."

Holding her tongue, she grabbed Vincentje, who was making a determined beeline back to the sugar. He wailed and kicked as she pulled him onto her hip. Struggling with the baby, she still couldn't fathom how her calculations had been so far off, but there was no way she was asking Dries for help. She shook her head slightly. The math must've been beyond her somehow. But Dries—the blunder-head—certainly didn't know more than she did.

He cleared his throat. "Jo, I'm directing your affairs now. Pa has agreed to appoint me as your guardian."

"Guardian?" Jo started to laugh. Annie had to remind him to put his socks on in the morning. Her laugh died at his solemn face. "You're not serious?"

"I am your older brother, Jo," he said, raising his chin. He pulled the box of silver toward himself. "I'm in charge of your affairs now. Besides . . ." His voice faltered. "I thought you'd be pleased. We've always looked out for each other."

"This isn't make-believe! It's my life!"

"You'll still move home, of course. But the artwork will remain in Paris." He patted a crate next to him. "I've arranged for the mess to be stored in Père Tanguy's attic. He already has Vincent's paintings from Auvers."

She'd never seen the last paintings Vincent had done in Auvers-sur-Oise. Theo had come back so shaken by Vincent's suicide, she hadn't thought to ask.

Jo gazed at the crates lining the dining room walls. Dries spoke as though the paintings were a nuisance, pitiful relics from a dead man's life. Dead *men*. A lump formed in her throat. Was it all over, then? After so many years of supporting his brother, Theo's passion had turned out to be futile. His brother's lifework would be shut away in the dark attic of a second-rate paint shop.

She couldn't swallow.

Dries continued, "And Émile Bernard is coming by this after-noon to select paintings for his exhibit."

"Exhibit?" Jo shifted the baby to her other hip and cleared her throat. "What exhibit?" Bernard was planning an exhibit. He was such a good friend.

"Bernard promised Vincent," Dries explained. "On his deathbed, no less. Of course, now he wants to dedicate it to Theo too."

"Theo would have been pleased!" she said. The depression threatening to drag her down had sprouted wings and taken flight. "Will Monsieur Bernard use the same apartment downstairs?" Bernard and Theo had unsuccessfully tried to stage a show for Vincent in their building a year ago. Before Dries could answer, another idea occurred to her. "Or he can use this apartment. Once the furniture's gone, the rooms will be perfect. The bedroom is especially spacious, with good light. And the rent's paid for six months."

Dries grimaced.

"Let's do it here," she confirmed in a rush of memories. "Theo and I talked about how to improve the next one." She paused. "I read Monsieur Bernard's note. It's strange he didn't mention it."

"Why would he have told *you*? I didn't tell you when the Indépendants planners contacted me."

Delighted, Jo bounced the baby. Exhibiting at the Société des Artistes Indépendants show was more excellent news. His friends were rallying. Vincent wasn't being shut away at all. Relieved, an idea struck her. "Wait, Dries . . ." Plopping the baby onto the floor, she wrestled off the top of the nearest crate. "Last year Theo showed ten of Vincent's paintings . . . but which ones?" She concentrated, carefully flipping through the paintings, peering at each one. The Indépendants annual exhibition had become the most prestigious national exhibit for unknown artists to get their work in the public eye. Some even claimed its popularity had brought about the collapse of the preeminent Paris Salon.

Hastening to the next crate, she spoke over her shoulder to Dries. "I'm looking for the fishing boats Vincent painted at Les Saintes-Maries-de-la-Mer. The blue and purple in the waves are so vibrant. Oh . . ." She pulled out one of Vincent's self-portraits. The yellow straw hat reminded her of a farmer. She stared into Vincent's blue eyes, accentuated by the random blue brushstrokes in the background. Her voice softened. "Even if Theo showed this last year, we must include a self-portrait. It can be a sort-of tribute—"

"Stop, Jo!"

"If it's an *homage posthume* show, shouldn't it contain a picture of Vincent?" She couldn't help scolding a little. "I really wish you'd made a record of the paintings as you put them away. We'll have to be very careful looking through them."

Dries yanked the portrait from her hands. His face was red. "*We?* Choosing paintings is none of your concern, Jo. You're moving back to Pa. *I'm* in charge of these affairs now."

She took a step back. Dries knew very little about the art world, and frankly, neither did she. But she did know what Theo had wanted for Vincent. Better than anyone. Relief flooded through her. That long list of people in the Parisian art world might have known Theo, but not in the way she did. She'd *lived with* Theo's love for Vincent, that devotion to his brother so all-encompassing it had been an unspoken part of their marriage compact.

Dries shimmied the portrait back into the crate.

Hands on her hips, she came to a decision. She would not allow Dries to take over her affairs. He would have to prove his manhood to Pa in some other way. Not with her life. And as for Pa . . .

Suddenly, Jo couldn't move. A realization hit her. As for Pa, she would no longer be that favorite doting daughter. She couldn't squeeze herself back into a mold she'd outgrown.

A movement caught her eye. Vincentje sat in the middle of the white crystals, contentedly pinching sugar between his fingers and licking them. If she moved back to Pa, her son would be raised learning to be a man in her father's image. She glanced at Dries fidgeting at a crate, thumbing through paintings. Like her brother, Vincentje would struggle against his grandfather's impossible demands. No, she would not move home. Vincentje had to become the man Theo had wanted. It was her duty, her obligation to Theo. She would raise their son in the way Theo had wanted.

Dropping her voice, Jo said, "I don't need a guardian, Dries.

And I'm not moving back. Tell me the truth—Pa put you up to this."

His face twisted into a scowl. "You can't live in Paris by your-self!"

Sara de Swart does, she thought but bit back the retort. She had to agree with Dries on this. Paris didn't feel right.

"You've never lived on your own!" he argued.

"I have! In London."

Dries laughed bitterly. "When you were a student? Oh, *certainly*."

Jo bit her lip. The London trip had been Pa's gift after completing her university studies. She'd stayed in a guesthouse with two other women. Delicious days surrounded by books in the British Museum reading room and losing herself in Shelley's romantic poems. Giddy late nights out when they'd snuck past the humorless widow manag-ing the guesthouse. London had been a final burst of freedom from under Pa's tight rein before she'd taken her teaching job.

She'd changed so much since then.

Jo paused, a thought taking hold. Of course. *She'd changed so much since then.*

"Dries," she said slowly. "I know this sounds crazy—and I know Pa will react with fire and brimstone—but I don't want to move home. I've grown up since I got married. I can handle it." Fear rippled through her. She forced herself to continue. "I . . . I owe it to Theo. We shared life in a way I never dreamed marriage could be. And he gave me a son. You knew Theo as your mate. Dozens of people knew him as the Montmartre art dealer dedicated to modern art. But I am . . . was . . . his wife. I knew him differently."

She traced the top of a painting next to her. "And I know that Vincent was never far from Theo's thoughts. How Theo looked at every painting in his gallery in relation to Vincent's. How he saw every painting through the lens of his brother—did it indicate something beautiful? Something *beyond* the paint?"

Clarity flooded through her. She faced Dries. "I know what Theo thought about every single one of Vincent's paintings. What color frame each should have. Which paintings should be shown together."

"How would you know that?"

"I've lived and breathed Vincent's art. When I fell in love with Theo, I fell in love with *all of him*. His devotion to Vincent too."

Dries shook his head. "You're not making any sense. Annie knows nothing about my being an importer. Art dealing is business. You think you understand, but you can't. Theo was Vincent's brother, but he was also his patron. Look how he sent Vincent money every month. For years. Theo talked incessantly about selling Vincent's work. He wanted his money back."

"No, you misread him. He didn't care about the money. Theo believed in the people he was close to. He believed in Vincent."

Just as Theo had believed in her.

"I'm not going to argue with you about whether Theo was a fool," Dries retorted. Jo's cheeks flushed, but he held up a hand before she could object. "None of this changes the fact that you're not equipped to live on your own. Pa won't send you money. What will you live on?" Panic crossed his face. "Theo may have supported Vincent, but Jo, I *cannot* support you! Annie would kill me. Remember, Pa was the one who gave you money in London."

The face of the London-guesthouse keeper came to Jo's thoughts. "Dries," she said as an idea took shape. "I can run a guesthouse! It's a perfectly acceptable occupation for a widow."

"For a crone."

"For *all* widows," she rebuked. Her thoughts skipped, forming answers. "I have the funds to rent a place. I'll get one with a large enough attic for the paintings."

"What—"

"All of the paintings are coming with me."

"*No*, Jo. Bernard and I are *both* doing exhibitions—"

"We'll make the selections before I go," Jo planned. "And we won't move the paintings already stored at the Tanguy paint shop.

They're safe enough, and I know Père Tanguy exhibits them in his window sometimes."

"No one cares what you think."

"Maybe not, but that doesn't change the fact that they belong to me, and it's my decision. And Dries . . . I'll explain everything to Pa. This is my idea. I can speak for myself. Better than you."

He closed his eyes. They both knew—no matter what Jo wrote—Pa would blame him. "Well then . . ." he sighed. With the release, Jo's heart surged. They were still childhood best friends. He still had her back as she had his, despite Pa's wrath. "And where will this mythical guesthouse be?"

As though it was the most natural thing in the world, the location tripped off her tongue. "Bussum."

His eyes snapped open.

"Anna Veth lives there," Jo explained. Then, seeing his grimace, she said, "Oh, Dries. It's what Theo would want me to do."

She paused—noticing her newfound lightness—and murmured as if to convince herself, "And it's what I want to do too."

Just past midnight, Jo slipped into the bedroom and sank onto the bed. Every muscle ached, especially her arms. Earlier that afternoon, she hadn't felt tired when lifting painting after painting from their crates to consider for the exhibitions, but now her limbs felt like lead. A knot of worry fluttered in her stomach.

Had she picked the right images? Dries had stomped away after just half an hour, exasperated at her second-guessing his decisions. But he didn't know anything about art. Couldn't he see that?

She kneaded her muscles through her sleeves.

Neither did she. Not really.

If she was being honest, the hardest part of the afternoon hadn't been in the physical effort but in composing the telegram to Pa. No matter how she'd worded it, his angry face had risen in front of her. His duty to bring her home was inarguable. She'd seen herself through his eyes: Youngest daughter. Widowed with a baby. Helpless. Burden. In the end, she'd surrendered pretty language for a few blunt sentences.

She couldn't stop him from being angry. She couldn't soften her decision.

Now in the dark, Jo's eyes adjusted, and as usual, she searched the crib shadows for Vincentje's silent form. He lay motionless. With a sharp bolt, fear struck. She jumped up, pressing her palm on his back. The gentle movement of his breath rose and fell under her fingers. Relief flooded her body.

But right on the heels of reassurance, worry cascaded: What had she done? Instantly she saw a vision of herself with Vincentje in torn clothes and dirty faces, stranded on a strange street amid indifferent people who shoved by, ignoring their distress. They could be penniless. Had she made a terrible mistake? How could she care for her son alone? What was she thinking? She was crazy.

Sliding her hand under Vincentje's warm body, she gently pulled him up onto her chest. Stirring, he nestled into his familiar spot on her shoulder and sighed in sleep. Tears glistening, she kissed his soft hair and began to gently rock, back and forth, in the comforting cadence they'd swayed in thousands of times before.

"I love you," she whispered. "Your papa loved you." Now tears ran down her cheeks. She would have to try. She would do this thing. This plan to move to Bussum. Take the paintings with her. No, Vincentje would not remember Theo, but she could try with all her heart to keep him in their lives. Theo would come to Bussum with them. Vincentje would know his father. He would know his work; he would know his father adored him.

Vincentje's small body had heated her chest. Her fingers traced a line of dampness along his hairline. She moved to a window, aware of the lingering odor of turpentine. Wresting the sill ajar, a soothing thread of cold air slid into the room. She took a deep breath.

"We'll do this together, won't we?"

She sniffed and used her cuff to wipe her nose. *Wash your face.* Bussum awaited.

POTATO EATERS

⸺◦⸺

These folk, who are eating their potatoes by the light of their little lamp, have tilled the earth themselves with these hands they are putting in the dish, and so it speaks of MANUAL LABOR and—that they have thus honestly *earned* their food. I wanted it to give the idea of a wholly different way of life from ours—civilized people . . . I'm convinced that in the long run, it produces better results to paint them in their coarseness than to introduce conventional sweetness . . . You'll hear—'WHAT A DAUB' be prepared for that as I'm prepared myself. Nonetheless go on giving something *genuine* and *honest*.

—Vincent van Gogh, *April 30, 1885*

Spring 1891
to
Winter 1893

BUSSUM

Jo

THE FIRST DAY OF MAY WAS A QUIET TRIUMPH FOR JO: moving day. With Anna's help, she had found a boardinghouse to rent in Bussum, down the road from her friend. The walnut furniture she and Theo had bought in Paris fit nicely in the salon. She found spots for their linen cupboard, bookcase, dining room set, and sideboard. Theo's desk was tucked into the end of the room. The bed was moved into a back bedroom she shared with Vincentje.

That left purchasing three wooden beds for the guest rooms upstairs, plus rugs to lay on top of the linoleum. In the back of the house was an extension overlooking the back garden. Jo envisioned buying a few tables and wicker chairs when she had the extra funds.

But of all the rooms, the most important was under the roof's peak, where an attic extended over the entire house. The perfect storage for Vincent's artwork. She'd swept it free of cobwebs and dust herself, then carefully unpacked Vincent's paintings from their shipping crates and—with the help of a hired boy who'd carried them one by one up the attic stairs—arranged the three hundred or so paintings into rows. She hadn't had time to put them in any order yet; that would have to come later. Several portfolios containing Vincent's drawings had been placed there too. She'd purchased an "art cupboard" to store drawings and graphics once she sorted them. Seeing the familiar, colorful paintings out of the crates had given her the subtle sensation of settling in. A new home was taking shape.

After posting a notice in the local paper, Jo hired a young maid named Marta and a cook who insisted on being called Cook.

As expected, Pa had denounced her plans and sent her a flurry of angry telegrams demanding she return home. No doubt Dries had received his share of insults. But since Pa didn't bother to travel to Paris, or to Bussum, she could make the move despite waking up full of fear night after night, pushing away images of the baby and her shivering and homeless and out of money. When she did sleep, she wandered blurry streets looking for Theo.

But today she was happy to feel relief. Her very first boarders, the Baas family, were arriving next week. A family of five. Marta was giving the guesthouse floors the last mopping.

The overgrown back garden was one of the final tasks. She knelt in a dense bed of iris. Weeds nearly overtook the sturdy green shoots. As she yanked deep-rooted thistles and thick vines out of the damp earth, she drew deep breaths of their pungent objection. The garden had cinched her decision to rent the guesthouse. It reminded her of a favorite thicket of purple iris in the Luxembourg Garden, where she and Theo had sipped merlot and torn off chunks of crusty bread between kisses a year ago. Above her now, boughs of cheerful white apple blossoms splashed their bright color against the cloudless blue sky. For all its fashionable splendor, Paris could not match a glorious Dutch morning in May. A deep contentment filled her. If she hurried, she'd have just enough time to clear this last flower bed of weeds before putting the baby down for a nap.

Vincentje tottered up to her, two handfuls of sticks clenched in his fists. Jo sat back on her heels to pry open one of his hands. No insects. As she reached for his other hand, he jerked away and slipped a twig into his mouth. Jo froze. She saw a vision of him choking. As if on cue, the baby spit the twig out, then bent to pick up another. Exhaling, Jo smoothed his blond curls. What else was out here he shouldn't get into? She scanned the garden. She didn't know the first thing about country living.

Or the first thing about running a guesthouse or raising a son alone.

Being a widow.

Abruptly, she sat up, tried to stop the tears from coming.

She would never get used to Theo being gone.

"I knew I'd find the country girl out here!" a familiar voice teased. Gratefully, Jo turned to the greeting. Anna cheerfully stepped into the garden from the kitchen doorway. One arm carried Saskia, who sucked on her fingers, nestled comfortably on her mother's hip.

Jo swept her arm across her eyes. "Just in time! You always make the world a little less lonely." She smiled at her dear friend. Anna had taken to coming by every afternoon at one o'clock like clockwork.

She stood up, wiping her hands on her apron. "Vincentje's eating twigs."

Anna teased. "City girl! Thank goodness I live nearby to save him." She plopped her daughter down with a grunt. "Though Saskia's getting heavier by the minute." She watched the toddler stumble toward Vincentje, then smoothed her dress to reveal a bump in her stomach. "By the end of summer, I won't be able to carry her."

"Another baby? Congratulations!" Jo pulled Anna into a hug to hide her face. Anna was well on her way to a house full of children when she could barely keep up with one.

"It feels like old times to have you close. Sometimes I forget Theo's gone." Anna's voice was muffled against Jo's shoulder. Stepping back, she surprised Jo by hastily wiping away a tear.

"You're my family here, Anna." No family member had visited her yet. Only Wil had a good excuse. Theo's funeral had upset her so much that her mother-in-law had sent her to a sanatorium for rest.

Anna pulled away. Drawing a newspaper from under her arm, she cautioned, "I know you wanted me to bring this—"

"Jan's review!" Jo grabbed the paper. "What did he say?" Jo flipped through the pages without waiting for a response, searching for the byline *art critic Jan Veth*. Anna's husband had promised to reconsider a review he'd published on Émile Bernard's exhibit of Vincent's work.

It was a silly misunderstanding. Eager for news on how the exhibit was going, Jo had pleaded with Jan to make the long trip to Paris to see the show himself. It had irked her that after sending Bernard six hundred francs to cover expenses, she hadn't heard a word about how well the exhibit had done. In Paris, she and Theo had read from *Le Figaro* and *Le Mercure de France* regularly. But in Bussum, news from Paris was frustratingly slow.

Without talking with her, when Jan had returned from Paris, he'd published a column in *De Amsterdammer* making the ridiculous statement that Bernard did not think Vincent had been a unique painter and considered much of Vincent's work unfinished.

In protest, Jo had dashed down the road and confronted Jan at home. His column couldn't have been more wrong. She reminded him that she'd been there when Theo and Bernard had coordinated every detail of their first exhibit for Vincent. Jan had misread Bernard's feelings somehow. For heaven's sake, he thought of Vincent as a brother and mentor. She'd insisted that Jan write a correction. Stone-faced, Jan had refused, saying only that he stood by his opinions.

Jo had seen no recourse but to write a letter to the editors herself, correcting the misunderstanding and quoting Bernard's own remarks about Vincent's work.

Then Anna had told her Jan had written a rebuttal.

Heart racing, Jo scanned the article. It was a rebuke, all right—but not about Bernard's opinions, but *hers*. Cheeks flaming, Jo read Jan's veiled reference to *those biased individuals who have little understanding of art criticism*. He claimed the artist's intention should not be confused with what he *actually* achieved. The criticism ended with one last sarcastic slap: *It was unfortunate that Mr. V., in his search for someone who would share his opinion on Vincent, had to end up with one of Vincent's greatest admirers.* Stung, Jo reread the sentence slowly. Jan was *mocking* her.

She raised her eyes to Anna. "Your husband is criticizing me."

"No . . . Yes . . ." She placed her hand on Jo's arm. "Listen, don't misconstrue. Jan simply feels your opinions are a little too . . . enthusiastic."

Guilt overwhelmed her. She'd thought correcting Jan was the right thing to do. Instead he was irritated. She chastised herself. Theo would have been so happy to have Vincent's name in a public newspaper.

A throb began to pulse behind her left temple. She pressed it gently. "Enthusiastic?"

"*Emotional* is a better word. Or *tender-hearted*." Anna squeezed her arm. "It's to be expected! You've suffered quite a shock. I reminded Jan that to lose a husband at our age would make anyone act irrationally. Don't worry—you're forgotten already."

Jo couldn't help thinking his reaction shouldn't be about her. She had intended to make a point about Vincent. Sighing, Jo reread the review closely. "No sales at Bernard's exhibit?"

"Well, poor Vincent never did sell any paintings, did he?" Anna's musical voice carried a note of pity.

Jo held her tongue as Anna turned toward the children. Had Vincent gained a reputation for not being salable? The newspaper articles around his suicide and then Theo's death hadn't outwardly stated it. Still, they'd fanned a flame that Vincent had been another promising failed artist, dying too early to realize his potential. Yet

Bernard had done all this work to hold an exhibit. He believed in Vincent. And Albert Aurier had written wonderful reviews about Vincent's work in *Le Mercure de France*. So why would she be criticized for coming to Vincent's defense? She closed the newspaper. She didn't understand it, but she could enlighten her best friend.

Anna picked up Vincentje and began to tickle him.

"*I* did," Jo insisted. Her voice rose. "I sold a drawing at Museé d'Art Moderne in Brussels. For two hundred francs." She felt a twinge of satisfaction. Her pricing had worked. She'd told Director Maus to price the drawings between one hundred and four hundred francs.

Vincentje squealed. Wrestling with him, Anna glanced sideways at Jo. "Not *you*, Jo. The museum did."

Jo bit back a retort. In fact, she had sold it. She'd owned the drawing, then she'd set the price, and an art admirer had bought it. She wouldn't tell Anna that she'd found out in an odd way. A letter from Père Tanguy had preceded the note from Director Maus. Tanguy had claimed she'd stolen a commission from him by agreeing to the sale.

More confusion had arisen when the artist Paul Signac had also approached Director Maus to buy Vincent's paintings. Three for five hundred francs, or four for eight hundred francs. All paintings held at Tanguy's.

An offer made without her knowledge.

It was confusing.

On the one hand, Signac had been a good friend of Vincent's and undoubtedly was acting out of loyalty by trying to sell the paintings. But on the other hand, the paintings Tanguy held were a part of Vincentje's inheritance now. Shouldn't Signac have asked her? Or Tanguy? And how had they set prices? Did Signac and Tanguy already have some sales arrangements?

Her son's inheritance was most definitely her responsibility. Theo counted on her to protect it and, God willing, increase its value.

She hadn't realized how being so far from Paris would make it so difficult to know what was happening.

What she did know was that her errors had been innocent. Theo had never talked about his agreements with other dealers and how business was conducted between Boussod and artists and buyers. She'd assumed purchasing a painting was like buying a loaf of bread—a simple exchange of an item for a price. Before responding to Tanguy's accusation, she'd written Director Maus to ask if she owed anyone else a sales commission, but he'd responded no and included a copy of the Vingt's latest magazine, *L'Art Moderne, Revue Critique des Arts et de la Littérature*, with a placemark at a generous article about Vincent.

She didn't understand why Père Tanguy—Theo and Vincent's friend—would be so angry, claiming a sale that wasn't his, when a virtual stranger, Octave Maus, was so generous. She was out of her depth. Theo had complained that art dealing was political, but he'd never explained how he'd navigated between all the parties.

"I can see you're upset," Anna said. "Pay this review no mind! I know you loved Theo dearly and only wanted to help, but you don't want to look foolish. You have a guesthouse to run! And from what I can see, it will be the best Bussum has to offer!"

Fatigue swept through Jo. Anna didn't get it. If Jo was looking foolish, it wasn't all her fault. She was being kept in the dark.

Her sale was not accidental.

"Anna, there's more to it. Director Maus came up with the idea to do the museum show *because* of the interest I created in Vincent's drawings in the Vingt show last fall. The Vingt group prides itself in being advocates for modern art. Vincent's drawings created a stir for them."

"I don't understand."

"Vincent's work cast a positive light on the Vingt group. The drawings I sent reflected the modern art image they want to convey. I helped them; they want to help me. It's reciprocal."

"But it's not *you*, dear. Jan explained it all to me. It's *business*." Anna tilted her head sympathetically. "You can't be doing this. Besides, this sale must be sentimental. Vincent's work is vulgar. Jan says so. Other artists may tolerate him. Not art collectors."

"Vulgar?" Theo had hated that word. Jo's heart started to race. "Other artists didn't *tolerate* Vincent, Anna. He was *known* among artists. Many admired him. I'm trying to get others to admire him too."

"You?"

"I'm getting other people's names connected to Vincent's art. Respectable people."

"You're speaking in riddles."

"I asked Director Maus if he would include two paintings I gave to Doctor van Eeden in the Vingt museum show."

"Frederick van Eeden? Our neighbor?"

Jo nodded. "He was so wonderful taking care of Theo that I gave him a painting called *The Sower* and an ink drawing of a country road bordered by trees. Actually, the road in front of this house reminded me of that drawing."

Anna bit her lip.

Encouraged, Jo continued, "Doctor van Eeden loaned them to the museum exhibit. When people read in the exhibit catalog that a *doctor* owned Vincent's painting, I hoped buyers might give Vincent a second look." Jo couldn't help but smile. The simple idea had come to her so easily, like a bud easing into a blossom.

Looking dubious, Anna said, "You're saying that Vincent having a private collector would make him more appealing?" She separated Vincentje and Saskia's squabble over a twig and then turned back to Jo, a new light in her eyes. "Like a child who wants a toy because another one has it."

Relieved, Jo hugged Anna's shoulders. "Exactly!"

Anna pulled away. "But you *gave away* the paintings, Jo. Isn't it dishonest to call the doctor a collector?"

Jo shook her head, sobering at the memory of her last conversation with the doctor. "I don't think so. He was fond of Theo and tried so hard to help him. He got an inkling of Theo's devotion to Vincent before Theo became . . . confused." Jo swallowed, willing herself to push away her last image of Theo's angry blank face, then continued, "I wanted to show the doctor my thanks in some way. Besides, it makes me happy to think of Vincent's paintings being with people who love them. And he's not the only one."

Shrugging a shoulder, she recalled, "Let's see. I've given Director Maus a beautiful painting of fishing boats Vincent painted in Les Saintes-Maries-de-la-Mer. I also sent him the portrait Vincent did of Eugène Boch to give to him. Monsieur Boch loved Vincent. He traveled all the way out to the museum in Brussels to see the exhibit and asked the director about his portrait. Director Maus agreed to find Monsieur Boch in Paris and give it to him." Jo smiled to herself. The skinny poet would treasure it. He was the type of collector she'd love to have own Vincent's work.

"Whoever is feeding you these ideas is wrong. It sounds like you're giving away Vincentje's inheritance piece by piece."

"Absolutely not. These gifts will make a difference in the long run. Each person has agreed to loan their paintings to exhibits if I ask them to."

"Then they're not exactly gifts, are they? You want to take the paintings back?"

"They *are* gifts. Private collectors *own* the paintings now. I guess it's more accurate to say that the gifts are an investment for me. I'm banking on the idea that private collectors will help create sales in the future."

"Jan was right. You *are* one of Vincent's greatest admirers."

"Anna!"

"It's a compliment from me! Theo would be proud of you. Of course, if he were here—"

"I wouldn't be doing any of this." Jo swallowed back a lump in her throat. Where had her outburst on art collectors come from? Sometimes she didn't know herself at all. Remorse flooded her. Poor Anna had put up with her tongue-lashing. "I'm sorry, Anna. It's . . . it's up to me now. I need Vincentje's inheritance to amount to more than a mountain of sentimental keepsakes. That's all."

Anna snatched the newspaper and wadded it up. "You know what we Dutch like to say: 'The nail that sticks up gets knocked down.' I don't want you hurt."

Before Jo could answer, a sudden gush of water splashed from the house; a bored-looking Marta poured a bucket of cloudy water onto a cluster of purple crocuses.

"Don't waste it, Marta," Jo scolded. Shouldn't that water have been dirtier? Her landlord had promised he'd install running water and gas before her first boarders arrived. Heaving water up from the well had made each bucketful priceless. Without a glance, the girl disappeared into the house.

"You need a firmer hand, Jo," Anna said, frowning. "Remember, you're the mistress!"

"You sound like my mother."

"You'll learn! Maids are lazy. You must supervise Marta more closely. She was lounging when I walked through . . . and you do have lots of work left to get this place ready." She scooped up her toddler. "Poor Jo. Remember, this will all be over soon. Jan said Vincent's memorial exhibits should only last until the end of the year. All these reminders can't be good for you. Soon things will be back to normal."

With a quick smile and a few steps, Anna disappeared through the door. Jo stared after her.

What exactly was normal?

That afternoon Jo held Vincentje against her hip with one hand as she gestured with the other. "Here are the paintings." She directed a local worker Cook had recommended, a broad-shouldered and quiet decorator named Bouwman. During Vincentje's nap, she'd carried the paintings down from the attic into the salon herself. Thirteen in all. She was looking forward to this final task of hanging the paintings. It would be the last touch to make the boarding-house feel like home.

"The three flowering orchards go in my bedroom," she instructed.

Jo plopped the toddler onto the bed. Their back bedroom would be cozy, a place to escape the noisy busyness she imagined the boardinghouse would become. And with the blooming trees just outside their windows, it felt natural to extend the garden into the room. She centered *The Pink Peach Tree* on the long wall opposite her bed and placed *The White Orchard* and *The Pink Orchard* on either side for Bouwman to hang. All had been painted when Vincent had been in Arles. Light brushstrokes blurred the white blossoms so that they seemed to glimmer and stir in a warm spring breeze. It was as if she could smell the warm earth, hear the buzz of busy insects, catch glimpses of darting birds building nests.

A new beginning.

Next she fetched *Almond Blossom* to hang over her son's cot. As in Paris, Vincentje would look up at the large branches of white almond blossoms and know his uncle had welcomed him.

She set *Pietà (after Delacroix)* and *La Veilée* across from the window. The mothers' bent heads and protective bearing for their children felt like a benediction. As though she wasn't the only mother here caring for her child.

Bouwman let Vincentje play with the picture-hanging cord as he measured the walls, giving Jo a chance to bring in the last painting, *Small Pear Tree in Blossom*, another one of Theo's favorites. The lovely flowering sapling would be hung in her dressing room alcove.

Standing clear of the swinging hammer, Jo sat at the foot of her bed, pulling Vincentje into her lap and smoothing the soft blue blanket she and Theo had slept under in Paris. She looked around the room. "Feels less lonely in here already, doesn't it?"

"Mevrouw," he grunted kindly.

Back in the salon, Jo picked up *The Potato Eaters* to hang over the fireplace. She remembered the catch in Theo's voice when he'd showed the painting of the family gathering to her. *I can hear the clatter of the sitters' clogs.*

Behind her, Bouwman cleared his throat. He pointed his hammer at the painting. "I like that one."

They stood together in front of it. Five figures sat around a table sharing a simple dinner of potatoes and tea. Tired eyes, rumpled clothing. A lit lamp indicated it was late. At first glance, the subtle shades of grays and browns made the family portrayal drab, but leaning closer, muted touches of reds, greens, blues, and yellows ingeniously deepened the understated portrait.

"Laborers," she said.

"Proud."

While he centered it, Jo positioned *Irises in a Vase* to its right, then angled *The Harvest* opposite it on top of the large cupboard. She leaned *Boulevard de Clichy* against the doorjamb leading into the dining room. Even without the paintings hung yet, the purple in the irises drew out the blues in both the landscape and city scenes.

Leaving behind the hammer blows, Jo dragged *Fountain in the Garden of the Asylum* around the corner into the downstairs hallway. She'd been half glad that the Vingtistes had returned it to her unsold. It was one of the drawings Vincent did while in the asylum at Saint Rémy de Provence. She wanted to pair it with a similar pen-and-ink. She'd chosen *Garden of the Hospital*, drawn when Vincent stayed in the Arles hospital.

The monochromatic drawing of the serene fountain complimented the busier sketch of the garden's lush courtyard with its abundant beds and pathways. They were perfect together. Both soothing, yet skillful. Their tranquility refuted Vincent's troublesome reputation as volatile and unstable. And side by side, their different approaches demonstrated how versatile he was. In the fountain drawing, Vincent had scraped away the ink so that the paper's surface made the water jet shine brightly. And in the garden scene, Jo loved its playfulness. She remembered spotting a few figures in the lines and the elfish signature he'd hidden on a watering can. Delight warmed Jo from within. Right inside the front door, visitors' first impression would be to see how rapidly Vincent's talent had advanced.

Theo would have loved this pairing. She was sure of it.

It was only later that she realized both pictured confinement.

SIX

BUSSUM

Jo

THE NEXT AFTERNOON, JO SAT AT THE DESK SURROUNDED BY stacks of documents. Organizing Theo's papers had to be prioritized. In the meantime, she'd instructed Marta to leave her mail in a small wicker basket on the desk, her corner of order until she could sort through Theo's.

Right on top, she spotted two envelopes with Paris postage. News about Vincent's work? Heart fluttering, she tore them open. Sure enough, one was an inquiry to buy Vincent's *The Sower (after Millet)* and the other requested a price on *Good Samaritan (after Delacroix)*. Jo stared at the buyers' names; she didn't recognize them. But somehow they had found her and the Villa Helma address. Who had directed them to her?

She reread the notes, looking for clues, but there was nothing. Surely no art dealer would send a note. Wouldn't he simply make the sale? If only she'd paid more attention to Theo when, or if, he'd explained how art dealing worked.

And there was no way it was Dries. He still wasn't speaking to her. Pa had dressed him down so fully for disobeying his instructions and allowing her to move to Bussum, she expected he was staying as far away from her affairs as possible to avoid any more blame.

Meanwhile she'd extended an olive branch to Pa by appointing him as Vincentje's guardian. If being the favorite daughter had taught her anything, it was that Pa loved control. Asking him to be a legal steward gave him an opening to influence his grandson's future. Even more important, it gave her peace of mind. If anything happened to her, her son would be looked after.

Jo tapped the letters in her palm. Had Director Maus given the buyers her name? Maybe, but it seemed more likely that he would have taken care of the transactions himself as he did at the Brussels museum.

The only other dealer she knew was Georges Raulf. In contrast to the patronizing she'd put up with from Theo's friends, in hindsight, Raulf's visit to the apartment had been refreshing. He'd acted distracted, indifferent. Not even very sympathetic. But besides the confusion over Theo's bonus, his manner had been a relief. More honest than chafing hypocritical sympathy.

Jo dipped a fountain pen into an ink bottle. She would offer Raulf the opportunity to earn a commission on these sales on the condition that he give her a small business lesson: advice on how to work with dealers. For Vincentje's sake—to do right by Theo—she had to learn more. Surely selling a few paintings couldn't be any more complicated than taking on the running of a guesthouse. Raulf had already said he couldn't care less about Vincent's art. She'd take a chance that she could ask him for this one last good deed—a final favor on behalf of his former employee—with a promise not to cross his path again.

Plus, after painstaking review of all her finances, she was convinced Raulf had withheld Theo's bonus. Any objections from her would fall on deaf ears. Still, if he had a single ounce of guilt, maybe his meeting with her would assuage it.

Her hand paused above the writing paper. With any luck, she'd be on the train to Paris before the end of the week and back before the Baas family arrived on Monday. She understood running a guesthouse; it was the art business that mystified her. She was making mistakes and getting rebuffed. The year was nearly half over. What had Anna said? Jan told her Vincent's memorial exhibits should only last until the end of the year. Time was passing fast. She couldn't afford to ruin any chances for sales before Vincent's posthumous memorial exhibits ended for good.

Jo spotted Marta swinging a rag as she shuffled down the corridor. "Marta! Take this to the telegraph office. Right away!"

As the maid sped toward town, Jo stood on the front stoop. Turning back inside, her eye caught the plaque, *Villa Helma*, above the front door.

Villa Helma meant Home of the Determined Protector. When she'd first seen the sign, she'd read it as an affirmation: a home where she was determined to protect her young son.

Now a new idea made her wonder, *Can I somehow defend the artwork too?*

The plaque felt like a good omen.

PARIS

Raulf

HIDDEN BEHIND HIS NEW ELEGANT GREEN MARBLE DESK IN the back of the Montmartre gallery, Raulf watched for Madame van Gogh's arrival, curious to see her reaction to the transformation he'd made of her husband's former workplace. He ran his hands along the smooth surface. The expensive tabletop was a rarity. A symbol of the prestige within his grasp. He hadn't told the partners yet about the purchase—why should he? They'd see his wisdom soon enough in more sales than they'd ever dreamed coming from Montmartre.

Madame van Gogh entered the gallery. As he expected, she was transfixed.

It was a reaction he'd been waiting for. A month ago, he'd thrown out her telegram requesting his expertise. He'd been done with her long ago. And he would have continued to ignore her even as she'd persisted by sending a second and then third telegram, except that one of the Boussod partners had called him *ruthless*. As if it was an insult. Fine. The widow gave him the perfect opportunity to show them otherwise. Theo was the nephew of a deceased partner. They'd admire his compassion for indulging her.

Over the past six months, since he'd met the widow in her apartment, he'd worked feverishly. For every Signac painting in the Montmartre gallery, he'd replaced each with a Robert Lefèvre. For every Monet, he'd hung a Benjamin Constant. Like playing a card game, discarding one card for another, he'd expertly exchanged and cajoled and bargained his way into a winning hand of impressive traditional French paintings. All painted by graduates from the very best instruction the École des Beaux-Arts had to offer. All faithful followers of the Old Masters. The Montmartre gallery—once an embarrassing sore spot among Boussod & Valadon's collection of European galleries—was now the very definition of high French art and the partners' pride and joy.

A testament to his skills. Naturally, he'd been awarded a promotion. Becoming a partner was a foregone conclusion.

If only Père were still alive to see him manipulate the old guard.

"Stunning, is it not?" Raulf said, smoothing the front of his jacket as he rounded the desk. The widow jumped. Ah, the fine art absorbed her. "I do beg your pardon, Madame. I thought you heard me approaching."

"I scarcely recognize the gallery," she said, still looking startled even as she extended her hand.

He beamed and bowed over her fingers. It pleased him that his new cufflinks peeked beyond his jacket sleeve, the requisite inch and a half for the gold to glint.

"I've made a few changes," he demurred. "As though you're visiting the Louvre, is it not?"

She stopped in front of a painting of two children fishing for frogs. "The image is flawless. They look . . . a bit staged."

"Exquisite detail."

"I can't say I *feel* anything." She tilted her head. "I mean, it's very . . . exact. Like one of those new photographs."

"William-Adolphe Bouguereau is the very best of our French academic painters. He was at the top of his class at the École des

Beaux-Arts. He was rewarded with a three-year residency at the Villa Medici in Rome. He is very selective about which galleries sell his work."

"I don't know that name."

Raulf was shocked. Bouguereau was quite famous among his clientele. Madame van Gogh didn't seem a bit embarrassed by her ignorance. "He's quite popular and is being studied in the best art schools."

"I studied music at my university."

"You're a pianist?" Typical female training.

"A poor one, I'm afraid." She smiled at him. "I grew up in a family of amateur musicians. Sunday afternoons playing little concerts in the salon." Jo turned back to study the Bouguereau. "Does he paint from a photograph or a live model?"

"A live model, of course! A classic artist would never use a device like photography for art!"

"I don't see how you can tell."

"I have a trained eye." As she moved on to the next painting, he peered closer at the Bouguereau. He'd have to ask the artist the next time he saw him.

The widow strained to smile. "I've seen enough. Shall we sit down?" Her voice carried a tinge of hesitancy.

Raulf nodded, waving her toward his desk. She'd seen what might have been if only her husband hadn't been so stubborn, focusing on local Montmartre artists and ignoring his counsel to represent works exclusively from the École.

"Would you like a cup of tea while you wait, Madame?" Raulf asked. She'd come ahead of her inconsequential importer brother. Inquiries at the men's club had revealed that Andries Bonger, George Wehry's junior associate, was a typical Dutch conservative nervous of his own shadow. Nowhere near Wehry's partner track. Certainly not a Frenchman.

"No tea, thank you." Madame van Gogh ran her hand over the

top of one of the new leather armchairs facing the desk. Then, without waiting for his assistance, she slid her woolen coat off her shoulders and folded it onto her lap as she sat down. She swallowed. "Where do we start?"

"Start?" He looked toward the gallery's front door. "Your brother . . . ?"

With a flash, he recalled meeting alone with her in Van Gogh's apartment too. The poor girl must have had some family estrangement.

"Or your father?" he asked.

"I'm on my own."

"But . . . the paintings you wanted to sell?" He glanced at the front door. Had she placed them there when she came into the shop?

"Oh, I didn't bring them. I simply need your *advice*."

"*You're* selling them?"

She sat up straighter and gave him a flickering smile. "You were going to explain how sales transactions work?"

Smothering a chuckle, Raulf pulled out his pocket watch. He liked to use the gesture to signal he was an important man whose time was valuable, but the watch slipped, and he juggled it, realizing he had unwittingly agreed to a meeting just with her. He wasn't in the business of wasting time. He was disappointed there was no man to spar with. Still, he could take half an hour—enough time to elaborate on later to the partners—then send her on her way. He flicked away a bit of dirt on his lapel and tucked away his watch. "Very well, then."

For the next thirty minutes, Raulf explained how art was sold. At first, he kept his commentary simple and brief. Still, the young woman followed up with so many questions that before long, he found himself showing her blank sales contracts, examples of shared commissions, informal letters of agreement, bid negotiations, the percentages dealers typically took from painting sales, even examples of exclusive sponsorships art dealers offered to painters. He relaxed, reveling in her admiration. Indulgently, he gave her copies of the various documents. No wonder Van Gogh had been so much happier after he'd married. Men needed feminine adoration, and this young woman was exceptional at it.

"How do you determine a painting's price?" Madame van Gogh asked.

He held back a laugh. She really enjoyed flattering him. "First I established the standard of quality I choose to represent. In Paris, the gatekeeper reputation of the dealer is even more important than the painter, for the art dealer is responsible for guiding the public toward the right art. My clients depend on me to discern truly exceptional art from the wasteland of amateurs. I can drive higher prices for the painters I represent because of my reputation."

Madame van Gogh was admiring him, hanging on to every word.

He preened. "But an art dealer's role goes beyond selling. We're not simply merchants. We have a critical responsibility to define France's cultural identity, the very heart of this great nation, and, therefore, the very heart of the civilized world. Our navies are doing their part for France's imperial expansion and conquests of new colonies. Now culture must ascend and guide the French to take its place as the pinnacle of taste. Art dealers have this sacred duty; this gallery is now a standard-bearer."

A frown wrinkled her brow. "Theo never talked about France."

He settled back into his chair. "Of course not. He was Dutch."

Her frown deepened. "Theo wasn't a fan of politics. He didn't speak about art as you do. Art was more personal to him."

"Art is personal to everyone. It's a reflection of an individual's refinement. Personal taste that's nurtured and matured over time."

She shook her head. "Theo said art succeeded when it gave the viewer a glimpse of themselves."

"Glimpse of what?"

"A glimpse of what you've truly lived. What you truly know." She paused. "Who you truly are."

Who I truly am. Raulf felt a chill shake through his body as though he'd been stripped naked of his fine suit. With shock, he saw what it was to be married to her. She was someone who could help bear one's burdens, comfort one's loneliness. Shed one's fakery. Raulf was flooded with an overwhelming desire to confess all his shortcomings to her, all his faults. To share how difficult it was to get others to see the world as he knew it was. To reveal how the world was hard. The world needed tough men; yet how he longed to let down his guard sometimes.

He'd glimpsed how Père's brittle shell must have been softened by his mother. If she hadn't died giving birth to Raynaud, perhaps Raulf would have known how a woman could be.

A hard lump had formed in his throat.

"Good art reveals soul," her soft voice affirmed. She held his gaze for one beat longer, then dropped her eyes to her clasped hands.

Raulf fought to regain his composure. The woman's naked grief had somehow gotten to him. Women! He cleared his throat, took a deep breath, and shoved his chair away from the desk. Van Gogh's widow was wrong. Art was not personal; art was absolutely political.

"The French Revolution was fought for Frenchmen to be freed from the tyranny of kings so that *all* may be uplifted. It's up to us to establish that model."

She looked up, her eyes distant. "I remember Père Pissarro saying one night at dinner that we should abolish all capital—"

"Camille Pissarro? The Impressionist?" He snorted a laugh. "Of course Pissarro would make that statement. His work can't support him, can it? He should recognize that modernism is a dying trend. Impressionism doesn't have the permanence of the classics like Delacroix or your Rembrandt and Vermeer." The Dutch did have a Golden Age after all. Too bad their best artists lived two hundred years ago. "You would do well to embrace your past," he added.

"I prefer to think of us *learning* from the past. It's impossible to repeat the past, isn't it?"

Irritated now, Raulf took a deep breath. Her argumentative nature was probably why her father had refused to accompany her. He changed the subject. "In your letter, you said you had two paintings?"

She squared her shoulders. "One painting is called *The Sower (after Millet)*. The other is named *The Good Samaritan (after Delacroix)*." She glanced out into the gallery. "I believe Vincent's *Good Samaritan* hung here for a while. Did you ever see it? I thought it was quite a different take on Delacroix's. Brighter. Very poignant."

"It's common for art students to copy classic paintings. That's how they train, dear. By studying the Masters."

The widow flushed. "Yes, I'm aware. My brother-in-law did several renditions of the classics."

"At least he admired the right artists. Boussod has been honored to sell the *real* Delacroix work. Now *he* is an example of a true artist. His father was a minister of foreign affairs and later an ambassador during the French Revolution. Most of Delacroix's work is historic. He painted classical battles. And Biblical stories, of course. Aspirational. Inspirational," said Raulf, dismissing the subject.

He pulled out his pocket watch again. Astonished, he saw that an hour had passed. He'd wasted enough time. "I'm afraid I must ask you to leave." He would tell the partners that she'd wept a little. How she'd been grateful for his comfort. It made him feel solicitous. "You've had a difficult go of it. I trust the exhibits will be over soon?"

"There are final farewell exhibits planned at the Pulchri Studio in The Hague in December. Another at the Arti in Amsterdam."

Raulf nodded, but he'd already stopped listening. Art societies were second-rate hobby clubs; the only shows that mattered were in Paris. "You will be relieved when the exhibits are finally over, then. It can't be good for you to be reminded so often of your husband."

"Why must everyone assume I should forget Theo? If anything, I am trying *not* to forget him."

Startled by her unladylike annoyance, he hesitated, but before he could respond, she was standing and extending her hand.

Scrambling, Raulf prepared to bow over her fingers when her small hand grasped his and shook it.

"You've been generous with your instructions. I must catch my train." She slid her arms into her coat as he hurried around the desk to assist her. "Au revoir, Monsieur."

She slipped across the gallery and was gone.

He stared as the swinging door shut.

He would have refused to sell her brother-in-law's paintings anyway, but it bothered him that she hadn't asked for his help. He missed the satisfaction of snubbing.

EIGHT

BUSSUM

Jo

RAISED VOICES ASCENDED THE STAIRCASE LIKE AN INCOMING flock of birds, shattering the morning quiet. Jo placed the breakfast tray outside the door for her guest and raced down the stairs and back to the kitchen.

"You're ruining my grandson's breakfast!" Mother van Gogh brandished a big wooden spoon, taking a stance between a bubbling kettle of barley porridge and Cook, who looked like a sentry, legs wide, hands on her hips.

"You think I don't know how to make a good porridge? I've cooked since I was a child. The only girl in a home of ten big laboring brothers!" She huffed and then made a dive for the spoon. With a quick sidestep, Mother whacked Cook's hand.

"Mother! Cook!" Jo forced herself between them.

As if to make up for her short stature, Mother held the spoon high over her head. "Ten brothers! No wonder the porridge tastes like mud!"

"Mother!" Jo wrested the spoon from her. "I told you . . . the kitchen belongs to Cook. You are my guest." She shot Cook a look of apology over Mother's head. "And guests are to stay *out of the kitchen*."

One hour into the morning and Mother had created chaos. Her visit for a "day or two" had extended to a week and with it too much nosy imposition. It was time for Mother to return home. In these first months of managing the guesthouse, the most important thing Jo had learned was that a well-running kitchen was central to keeping the boarders happy. Interminable grocery lists. Exhaustive meal planning. Daily market trips. Three meals a day plus afternoon tea or coffee had to be delivered like clockwork. Her appreciation for Cook's command grew every day. Theo used to tease that he loved her despite the burnt toast. She could not afford Cook to be upset and leave.

Jo let go of Mother's elbow and eased her into a dining chair. "Now, Mother—"

"I don't know where you found this woman, Jo. That porridge was inedible. Like eating muck. Vincentje is a growing young man."

"Vincentje is a *baby*. He's fine. I told you before: please do not go into the kitchen."

Mother picked at the linen tablecloth, pinching it between her fingers. "I worry, you know. Vincentje looks unnaturally pale."

"It's a cool spring—that's all."

"You didn't see Theo's illness in time."

Shocked, Jo felt the blood drain from her face.

"You didn't notice. You weren't paying attention. A wife's job is to look after her husband's well-being. I remember how you took to your bed at the slightest ache when you were pregnant, how Theo hovered and worried about your health. Women are built to have babies. Do you think Theodorus hovered over *me* when I birthed six . . . no, seven babies?"

"Seven?"

"We lost our first son." Her voice broke. "Vincent."

"You *lost* a son?" Jo was confused.

"My first baby was Vincent. He died after a few days. We named our second baby Vincent to make up for him." She clenched the linen in her fists. "Women are born to suffer. We don't complain about it or ask for special favors. Grief is life. You can't afford to be spoiled anymore, Jo. Theo will never give me another grandchild. You must watch Vincentje."

NINE

AMSTERDAM

Jo

IT WAS VINCENT'S LAST SHOW. JO LOOKED UP AT THE SLOPED glass roof of Amsterdam's Arti exhibition hall. It acted as a mirror, reflecting swirls of blues and greens and reds from evening gowns like a living canvas.

She caught her breath. She was relieved to have found a little hiding space tucked behind one of the white columns regularly spaced along the walls. She needed a reprieve. For the past hour, she'd been passed from one ingratiating face to another—barely time to acknowledge each greeting or mentally file the name away before being whisked to another flustering exchange. She didn't want to be the center of attention. The evening wasn't about her. Tonight's standing-room-only commemoration was for Vincent. His final posthumous celebration.

And she hated it.

Her body felt tense, trapped. She wanted to be grateful—a part of her knew Theo would have been thrilled with this turnout—but she couldn't shake off a searing disappointment. Even though nineteen newspapers and journals had published complimentary articles about Vincent in the past year, she felt dismay. It was all a lengthy goodbye. The year was ending already. She hadn't done enough.

With only a handful of paintings sold, she'd barely made a dent in increasing the value of their son's inheritance. It was as though Vincent's artwork provoked a heavy headwind and she wasn't strong enough to push against it.

Even now, Jan Veth led a little pack of hangers-on around the gallery, no doubt punctuating his opinionated observations with labels like "bizarre" and "childlike," as he had in his newspaper columns. She'd thought her entreaties to examine Vincent's work more seriously would have won him over by now.

Well, they hadn't.

While her efforts had budged awareness of Vincent's art, his reputation as a loner and a nobody remained firmly intact.

Now safely tucked away from the crowd, she brushed back damp curls plastering her forehead. Despite the January cold outside, the room was stifling. With one hand, she flipped open an elegant tortoiseshell fan to wave in front of her hot face while she balanced a glass of untouched champagne in the other.

She should have done more. The bitter honesty brought a flush to her cheeks. She'd sold eight pieces of artwork in all, but only the sale of a drawing brokered by Director Maus had been smooth. The rest had been confusing, angry exchanges. Père Tanguy had claimed she'd meddled, even after he'd sold six of Vincent's paintings for twenty-two hundred francs—a price she'd insisted upon over his haughty condescension. After the sale, his sour reaction had disavowed any credit to her.

The friendly men she'd met at Theo's funeral were gone.

Émile Bernard, Paul Signac, and Père Tanguy . . . their stubborn friendship with Vincent and respect for Theo had probably tempered their rebuke this past year. Yet she'd rather smart from insults than experience what they actually did: they'd ignored her.

Now she wondered whether they were right.

She fanned harder.

Would Vincent's work have sold more in Paris if she'd backed off? Lately it seemed only Dutch art societies showed any interest in Vincent. Had her ignorance—no, bullheadedness—especially with her newfound knowledge from Georges Raulf—squandered this precious year?

She couldn't figure it out. If only Theo were here to tell her what to do.

A headache pulsed with bombarding thoughts.

She surveyed the mirrored ceiling, feeling the curls around her face lift and fall with each whirl of fanned air. Above her, the reflection revealed the entire exhibition hall. Around the periphery, spots of color from Vincent's paintings punctuated the plain walls. At the same time, clusters of guests huddled in laughing groups, talking louder and louder, lifting their chattering to deafening levels. She paused in mid-fan. Something was off. She stared. Something was odd in the picture above her.

"It's like herrings in a barrel in here."

She jumped at the voice close to her ear.

"Meneer Israëls." She smelled the wine on his breath. Unnoticed, the artist Isaac Israëls had slipped beside her against the wall. His shoulder brushed hers.

Blue eyes twinkling, he leaned closer, forcing Jo to turn her head away. His breath tickled her ear.

"*Isaac*, please!" he said. "May I ask . . . whom are you hiding from, Mevrouw van Gogh . . . Jo?"

She shifted, but they might as well still have been touching. She could smell the scent of sandalwood on his collar, a whiff of perspiration from beneath his coat. Warmth radiated off his body. She couldn't help the smile that crept to her lips. When she and Theo had been newlyweds, they'd spent a carefree night at a soirée in the Hotel Continental. Dancing and dining. Theo in his wedding suit, she in her wedding dress. They'd met up with Isaac and his father,

Jozef, and ended up staying out until half past one in the morning.

Isaac's shoulder nudged hers, bringing her back to the present. Out of the corner of her eye, she glimpsed his profile. Since that evening, she'd heard rumors of his reputation. Isaac was as well-known in Paris for his nighttime philandering in Montmartre cabarets as for his precocious painting talent. And now the soft padding of his suit's shoulder pressed her arm underneath the sheer fabric of her gown. When she shifted for the second time, the pillar's cold, smooth surface trapped her in place. Her safe corner had changed from a hideout to something else. Their corner—in an instant, it had become *their* corner—felt private, removed, somehow, from the crush of bodies a few feet away. The babble of voices receded.

"I had to hunt to find you." His eyes crinkled in their corners. A curl of brown hair fell forward onto his forehead. "I knew Vincent, you know. Painted his portrait."

Surprised, Jo turned to ask him more about the portrait, but before she could form the words, Isaac wrested her champagne flute from her hand, saluted, then took a sip from her glass, regarding her over the rim. His eyes flickered to her décolleté and back.

"Meneer Israëls!" Anna burst in front of them, eyes flashing, shoving Isaac back. Jo flushed, stupidly disappointed.

"Would you settle an argument?" panted Anna. "My husband needs your opinion." Her voice was steely.

Without waiting for a response, she grabbed his arm, twisting him away from Jo. At the far end of the hall, Jan's red face was visible, arguing with an unidentified man in a top hat.

Isaac surrendered and drained Jo's champagne. "Until next time, Mevrouw," he said to Jo with a wink and handed her the empty flute. Tipping his hat to both, he settled it at an absurd angle and weaved into the crowd.

"I've just met him," Jo protested, watching Isaac disappear. She didn't know why she felt defensive. They'd barely talked.

"I expected as much," said Anna, settling next to Jo. "You're the prettiest widow here, and you know what they say about widows . . ."

"Anna! Don't!"

"Lots of *experience* in bed. No one to share it with."

Jo's cheeks reddened. "I'm not interested."

Anna poked Jo playfully. "You better not be! He's hardly marriage material."

"Anna!" Jo said. Suddenly her recall of the sweaty hands and pressed cheeks against hers that evening fell under a different light. Had all of that fawning been *flirting*? At the outset, the painters Jozef Israëls, George Hendrik Breitner, and Willem Witsen had warmly pressed her hands, complimenting Vincent's style. Friends of Theo's she'd barely met had treated her like she was one of their own. Now repulsed, Jo's shoulders sagged. She was a fool. The fleeting feeling of belonging was a fantasy. Her loneliness had caused her to misread Isaac too. Without Theo, she didn't belong.

She saw herself as they did: widow of their deceased friend.

Theo was the love of her life. Isaac had distracted her and stirred her curiosity. But that was all. Her heart belonged to Theo, not some playful rogue. Jo looked at Anna. "I don't want this."

Anna slipped an arm around Jo's waist. "You're starting a new chapter. Jan and I were talking about it. It's almost a year since Theo's passing, and you've done so much. Villa Helma is quite the talk of the town! Little Vincentje is a cheerful, sweet little boy. And now your last show! No one could ask that you do anything more for Theo."

Jo leaned into Anna's arm. "It's strange, but I don't want it to stop. Tonight feels more like we're getting started. A beginning. Not an ending."

Anna chuckled. "It is! Thirty years old is not too old for your fresh start. Of course, not with a *playboy* . . ."

"I was talking about Vincent's work!"

"You needn't worry about that! Jan vowed to give Vincent a decent farewell show for Theo's sake. And he has."

With a burst of glee, Anna clapped her hands. Jo followed her eyes. Jan and his entourage had made their way in front of them. Isaac was gone. A red-faced stranger Jo had been introduced to earlier now pushed away from Jan and melted into the crowd. Anna grinned and cut a sideways glance at Jo. "I love listening to Jan win a good argument. He's quite thrilled with his success tonight."

Dumbstruck, Jo scrambled to process Anna's claim. She brushed a damp hand across her forehead. Jan had done nothing for this exhibit. She opened her mouth to object, then stopped. Certainly he'd publicized the exhibition by putting it in his column, and no doubt he'd write up a review for tomorrow's papers. But *she* had co-ordinated with the Arti, selected which paintings to show, and even found the right local carpenter to make the stretchers and frames for the paintings. She'd traveled to Amsterdam a day early to come to the hall and oversee the artwork hanging.

She hadn't thought of these steps as work exactly. Theo had always said details mattered. Each had been a small task, but it irked her that Jan would take credit for an evening in which he hadn't lifted a finger—or even spoken to her. She was the one who had curated the entire show.

As though a dike had burst, ideas flowed quickly as she gazed out across the room. Next time a smaller venue would be better. Invite a select group more focused on the art and less on the party. Perhaps a group of first-year art students? Loosen her focus on sales and instead allow the press to spread the word about Vincent's art. Approach other art reviewers instead of relying solely on Jan. Especially those who hadn't made their minds up on Vincent's style.

Vincent's work couldn't be appreciated in a single viewing. It was too different. If people had the opportunity to spend time with it, the art would speak to them.

At least, that was what Theo had said.

A wave of nervous excitement swept through her body. Isaac had distracted her for a moment, but now the strange edginess from earlier returned full force. A sudden movement in the mirrored ceiling caught her eye. She looked up. With a quick intake of breath, she saw what had been off earlier.

All around the hall, the mingling guests stood with their *backs* to the artwork.

No one was looking at Vincent's paintings.

To this group, this was simply another weekend party—an excuse to have fun. One more Dutch artist, never mind his name.

"I'm not done," Jo said softly. She stopped, surprised. The words had slipped out before the thought had fully formed. She could trust the art, have faith that it could speak for itself. As Theo had said, *Touch the viewer's soul.* Dealers and gallery owners had to give Vincent another chance.

Anna's fingers dug into her arm. Jo turned to explain, but her friend hadn't heard her. Her eyes glowed with pride. In front of them, the group around Jan had grown. They crowded close, clinging to his words. Jan's voice cut through the babble. "Vincent worked quite quickly. He raced from one canvas to the next. Sadly, far too many are unfinished. No depth. No atmosphere."

Jo straightened, protest bristling up her spine.

Jan continued, "He refused to blend colors. Instead, he wanted to leave impressions, though he could never master the style of the Impressionists."

A chuckle rippled through the men.

Jo's throat constricted. Jan was wrong. Vincent had not *failed* at imitating the Impressionists. He'd *chosen* not to follow them. As if a whisper, she heard Theo's voice again: *Vincent listens to his own inspiration, not the direction of others.*

She stood very still. Panic coursed through her body. She had to speak up. She had to defend Vincent. She had to give them Theo's message.

Jo opened her mouth, but no words came. Her mind seized, frozen. She stared at Jan and saw herself through his eyes. Through the eyes of the entire room. She was the Bussum guesthouse widow. The dead art dealer's wife.

The overly enthusiastic sister-in-law.

Sexual prey.

Not an art expert. She tried to swallow, but a painful lump blocked her throat.

Across from her, Jan crossed his arms across his chest and said, "It's a shame he died. Vincent had potential." His tone said *no talent.* Looking up, he caught Jo's eye and held her gaze. "God rest his soul," he intoned. His eyes flicked to Anna.

In one heartbeat, Anna's hands pressed on Jo's shoulders. "Come, Jo," she hissed.

Jo's feet had turned to lead. She had to say something.

"Jan wants us to move on," Anna begged. Her fingernails dug through the thin silk on Jo's shoulders. "He counts on me. I'm to head off any altercations with you."

Altercations? Jo swayed. She willed the words to come. *Theo, what do I say?*

But there was nothing.

Anna pulled, but Jo resisted. *Theo?*

Only an aching hollow silence. He had left her behind again.

"Jo," Anna begged. "Please move. Jan asked me to keep you under control."

"Under control!"

"Everyone knows you like to interfere."

"Interfere! You call taking care of my son's inheritance *interfering*!"

"*Please, dear—*"

"So, I can dress up," Jo spit, anger flaring. "Be doted on. Flirted with, but God forbid, not speak up. Opinions belong only to the experts."

"Honestly, Jo. No wonder you're scolded in the press. You are no expert."

"Are you quoting your husband?"

"I will not let you humiliate yourself." With a shove, Anna pushed, and Jo stumbled forward, deflated. Her anger receded as quickly as it had flared. She had not defended Vincent. The evening was no triumph. It was a defeat.

At the end of the hall, Anna stopped at the periphery of a circle of chattering women, who shuffled aside to make room for them. Placing herself behind Anna's shoulder, Jo hid.

Her palms felt damp. Moments ago, the idea had been so clear that she couldn't stop showing Vincent's work, then in the next instant, she'd allowed herself to be shut down.

If only she could feel Theo's permission again. She was sure she would know what to say, what to do.

Next week was the anniversary of Theo's death. He lay in a cemetery a train ride south in Utrecht. Jo took a deep breath. Wiping her palms on her dress, she looked back at the noisy crowd, tipsy with wine.

She was failing. She didn't know how to navigate this world. She would visit Theo's grave. Ask him for help.

Without him, she was useless.

UTRECHT

Jo

JO KNELT AT THEO'S GRAVE AND LAID A LIMP WHITE ROSE against the black dirt. The soft, delicate petals took her back to the first morning after their wedding, waking slowly, luxuriously stretching. Her relaxed body humming with the tingling aftermath of its delicious newfound ecstasy.

Ah-hem, Theo had cleared his throat.

Jo's eyes had fluttered open.

He'd stood ramrod straight beside the bed, hair like a mop, his hands tucked behind his back. Dressed only in a nightshirt, his white legs had stuck out below the wrinkled linen. With a rakish grin, he'd given her a bow. *To my little wife,* he'd said. With a flourish, one hand had sprung from behind, clutching a bouquet of white roses.

With a laugh, she'd pulled him into bed. Later that morning, she'd shaken fragrant white petals out of her hair.

But now, on the grave, the single rose looked forlorn. Standing up, she shivered against the sharp wind. The burly seller at the flower stand in the Utrecht train station had taken her coins and wrapped the rose in a newspaper in one efficient motion. An ordinary purchase on an ordinary day for him.

Not the anniversary of her darling's death.

All year it had felt like she'd marked events by his absence. Vincentje's first steps. Cooking her first perfect roast. Her very first sale of the drawing to Museé d'Art Moderne in Brussels.

For each one she'd yearned to hear Theo's laugh.

And the big events. Running a boardinghouse. Moving to Bussum. Taking all the paintings and drawings with her far away from Paris.

What would he have said? Would he have been proud? Would he recognize her now?

She hadn't unpacked his clothes from the moving trunks yet.

She was the one who couldn't move on.

Brushing away twigs and dead tufts of grass blown up against the curved gloomy tombstone, her eyes pricked at the chiseled epitaph: *Theodorus van Gogh. 1857–1891. Beloved son, brother, husband, and father.* She pushed back tendrils of ivy grown up around the gravestone and trembling in the wind. In a few years, the vines would encroach on the etching, trapping the words into a terrible permanence.

"I will never get over you," she whispered. "You changed me. Made me feel my ideas mattered."

It was Theo's fault that she was here. In the beginning, their nighttime conversations had come from his desire to unburden the day's worries. She'd loved smoothing the wrinkles from his forehead, bringing him tea or a glass of wine. But the discussions had gradually changed. His one-sided art instruction and questions had begun to draw her out. Theo had invited her into his world, seeking her opinions. With his encouragement, she'd felt safe to speak up.

But ever since the Arti night, tormenting shame had circled round and round her thoughts. What she should have said. How she could have responded.

How she had failed.

She didn't know what to think anymore. She was responsible for Vincentje's future. She was accountable for Vincent's art. Yet her role was also to be the bereaved widow. Women were not listened to in the world of art business. What was she supposed to do?

She stared at the tombstone. Closing her eyes, she reached out. *Forgive me, Theo. I'm failing. I can't do this work without you. Please tell me what to do.*

A part of her knew this was crazy. Another part didn't care. Concentrating, she bent forward, straining to hear something other than the rushing rise and fall of wind. Above her, oak tree boughs rattled. Undergrowth from a woodland grove whooshed in symmetry.

But no beloved voice.

A sudden icy gust licked down her neck, startling her eyes open. She yanked at her muffler. She didn't want a future without Theo. Crossing her arms across her chest, she hugged herself, shivering. Aching fatigue swept her body.

She was so tired. All the thinking and worrying about everything.

A convulsive tremor wracked her. A sliver of sunlight broke through the clouds, illuminating the grave and the lone rose. The sight—seconds before a symbol of grief—now held a strange serenity. An inexplicable longing washed over her, a desire to lie beside him on the dark earth.

My darling. Please . . . tell me what to do.

An icy grip seized her toes. Biting cold from the ground had seeped through the thin soles of her shoes. Stamping her feet, still, she lingered, longing, desperate.

The wind moaned through its branches.

Tell me what to do.

BUSSUM

Jo

IT WAS THE WORST DAY EVER AT VILLA HELMA. ON A TYPICAL turnover day, once Jo coaxed the departing guest to check out, the room would be stripped, the iron bedframe polished, the armoire wiped inside and out, cobwebs swept from the corners, and the floor mopped and dried before spreading broom-swept rugs. The last step was to spread fresh linens scented with lavender onto the bed. It took Marta a good hour to clean and prepare a single room.

Today all three guest rooms had to be turned over on the same day.

Nothing happened as planned. Cook burned the cinnamon rolls. Doctor and Martha van Eeden's son arrived late to pump buckets of water for the cleaning, hauling it from the back garden into the kitchen, only to get annoyed at Cook's running complaint that he sloshed water onto her floor. A boarder accused Marta of stealing her broach, which Jo then found in her underthings. The grocer dropped off someone else's order. Then Vincentje spilled an entire cup of chocolate down his shirt just as Jo had offered to help Marta with the mopping. Marta ended up dragging a hollering Vincentje in for a bath while Jo rolled up her sleeves, slogging buckets upstairs to mop the floors herself.

By the time she tossed the last bucket of darkened water outside, only an hour remained before the first of the new boarders arrived. Vincentje was about to wake from his nap. As she collapsed into the deeply cushioned chair in the salon, every joint in her body ached.

She had to get up and change her blouse. Make herself presentable. Growing up, Ma had always made running a household look so easy. Ordering maids here and there. She wouldn't be so worn out and tired if she'd gone back to Amsterdam with its housekeepers and nanny. Examining her coarse red fingers, she tried to imagine her sisters Lien or Mien mopping a floor. Impossible. No respectable household of Pa's stature would let the family women scrub.

She splayed her fingers. When was the last time she'd tended to her nails? They were chipped and torn back to the nubs.

A tear squeezed from her eye. Soiled blouse. Rough hands. Who had she become? Certainly not Pa's perfect daughter. The happy, young newlywed she'd been with Theo felt like a stranger too. She couldn't recognize herself anymore.

The front door squeaked open. *Oh heavens, please.* Jo quickly swiped her eyes.

Wil rounded the corner.

"Wil!" Jo laughed, relieved. She didn't have to be anyone other than herself with Wil. The last time she'd seen her sister-in-law had been Theo's funeral.

"Surprise!" Wil clapped her hands gleefully. "I've been dying to come! Mother chatters on so about your famous boardinghouse. I needed to see for myself. Oh, I like the sign over your portal: Villa Helma. 'Home of the Determined Protector.' Sounds about right."

"*You're* the determined one!" With delight, Jo held her at arm's length, feeling her self-pity whisk away before Wil's dancing eyes.

Yet, though Wil's cheeks glowed with two spots of pink and her thin hair was swept back in a charming chignon, she still looked frail. "You've never left my thoughts. Are you rested? How was the sanitorium?"

"You mean *asylum*."

"But Mother said—"

"I had a full breakdown. Completely embarrassed her. She shut me away."

"Oh, Wil! If I'd only *known*!"

"I never doubted you, dear sister. Even when I was confused."

"You're here now. Give me your cape."

"I'll give you my hat and gloves. Let's keep my cape until I warm up . . . *Vincentje!*" The toddler was teetering down the hall toward them at full speed. Wil pitched him up into a hug, swerving to catch her balance.

Vincentje screamed happily.

"Look how you've grown!" she crowed. Turning to Jo, she said, "Don't all babies look drunk when they walk?"

Jo laughed. "Some days I swear Cook slips a little wine into Vincentje's milk."

"Oh, I *love* that he has Vincent's name. Oh, Jo! Vincent's *art*!" Spying the artwork on the salon walls, she settled Vincentje on her hip. "Give me a tour?"

A half hour later, the women arrived in Jo's bedroom. While Jo changed into a fresh blouse, Wil rolled a ball back and forth with the toddler.

"Vincentje looks like Theo," Wil said.

"He's growing fast. Do you know I think there's an artist in him."

"Really!"

"He insists on drawing at my desk. He perches on his toes to reach it. He can concentrate and scribble for hours with a pencil, holding it perfectly straight."

"Oh, Jo . . ." Wil's smile faded. "I feel so . . . untethered without my brothers."

At the change in Wil's tone, Jo sat down next to her and gathered Wil's cold hands. The bones felt delicate. Wil shivered, even in her heavy cape. Jo started up. "Let's warm you by the fireplace in the salon."

"Not yet." Wil pulled away and reached into her deep cape pocket. "Before your guests arrive, I want to give you something." She held out a thick packet of envelopes. "These are letters Vincent wrote me. I found them again when I came home from the asylum. Vincent poured his heart and soul into these pages. They've given me such comfort, Jo. I thought maybe they'd do the same for you?"

"Are you sure? I have all the letters Vincent wrote too."

Wil nodded. "Take them. It's hard for me to hear his voice. You should read Theo's."

"I hadn't thought to read them. I only met Vincent a few times, you know."

"When did you meet him?"

"He came to Paris after we were married. He met Vincentje. I'll never forget the image of them standing side by side over the cradle. Then Theo and I visited him after he'd moved to Auvers-sur-Oise, but it wasn't a happy time." Jo remembered how angry Vincent had been after she'd innocently asked him about his paintings' sales. He'd always been so gruff; she'd no idea he could get so angry. Their peaceful afternoon picnic had dissolved into a shouting match between the brothers, and she and Theo had left for an early train.

It was the last time she'd seen him. She'd written him an apology letter afterward but received no response. Then he'd died and Theo had died, and she was left full of regret.

Wil's laugh startled Jo back to the present. "Not a 'happy' time? I can only imagine, poor Jo. But I'm sure it was nothing compared to the rows he had with Father!"

"I wish I could have said how sorry I was to him face-to-face."

"You can't know people from the outside, Jo. He wouldn't have harbored a grudge. At least, not toward you."

"He was so angry—"

"He was *fearful*, Jo."

"I upset him. I knew Theo felt financial pressure. He supported Vincent and Mother—"

"And me."

"And then when we married, Theo added Vincentje and me to his burden. I don't know what got into me that day. I think I made Vincent feel guilty."

"What are you saying?"

"I think I made him snap."

"No, Jo."

"If we hadn't argued. If I hadn't come between him and Theo that day. Maybe he wouldn't have—"

"It wasn't you, Jo."

"You weren't there!"

"I know my brother," Wil said firmly. She put a hand on Jo's arm. "He was scared he was wrong. After all that time with Theo supporting him, he was afraid he didn't have talent. He felt guilty that he'd been dependent so long." Tears showed in Wil's eyes. "Remember, *I know* what confusion feels like. It's . . . overwhelming. Like falling into a deep, dark well with no light . . . and just think." Her voice softened. "If he'd only known that you would be the one to sell his work. Look at you. You're selling the paintings. Something Theo never did."

She thrust the letters at Jo.

"You need these more than I do."

Later that night, Jo crept out of bed, turning back to pull the blankets over Wil's thin shoulders, and tiptoed out of the bedroom. Making her way through the shadowy house, she slipped into the salon. The house was still. No wind rattled the window frames. Only remnants of burnt wood glowed orange in the fireplace. Cook had closed the chimney flue too early; the smell of lingering smoke hung in the air.

Pulling an afghan around her shoulders, Jo sat down at the desk. She couldn't get Wil's words out of her mind.

Vincent poured his heart and soul into these pages.

She'd forgotten how Theo used to ask for the mail as soon as he'd come home every evening, how he'd torn open Vincent's letters even before removing his coat.

He'd treasured the connection with his brother.

Jo lit a gas lamp and jerked open the desk's sticky bottom drawer. It was stuffed. Yellow envelopes lay in careless stacks, jammed along the sides of the drawers, caught by crimped corners. She remembered cramming as many letters as possible into drawers and cubby holes to clear desk space months ago.

Scooting the chair closer to the desk, she picked an envelope off the top and slid out the letter. No date. The page was jammed with closely written lines, every available inch filled with ink. Scanning the scrawl, a sentence popped out: *The great doesn't happen through impulse alone and is a succession of little things that are brought together.*

That sounded like something Theo would say.

She pulled out another letter, flipping it back and forth, squinting at the tight handwriting. Again, no date. A phrase caught her eye: *Working with as much cold-bloodedness as I can muster, don't let myself be deterred by my mistakes.*

Again, just like Theo.

In the third letter, another line: *The weathercocks have no effect on the direction of the wind, so opinions have no effect on certain standard truths.*

Theo's voice read the line in her head.

It was strange to see Theo's words in Vincent's handwriting. All along, she'd assumed the brothers' relationship had been one-sided, responsible Theo always supporting the dependent Vincent.

That was the way she'd felt with Theo. It didn't take a genius to see that Theo was the teacher, she was the student. He'd been wiser than his years, able to stare down life's challenges and bolster others around him.

Now reading these sentences, she wasn't so sure. Who had uttered these encouraging phrases first?

Had Theo been the instructor she thought he'd been? If she couldn't rely on Theo, then who?

As the late hour wore on, Jo dug into the pile of envelopes, pulling out one random letter after another. After the first few, instead of skimming for phrases, she settled into reading the letters in full. When a dozen missives lay on the desk, she realized the notes held enough references to places that she could pencil in a date at the top of the letters—reading them out of order made her head spin. In one note, Vincent had recovered from his breakdown at the Saint-Paul-de-Mausole Asylum; in the next, he was in The Hague seven years earlier with his lover, Sien.

Meanwhile, an internal dialogue emerged between the two brothers.

I need to find my feet instead of going under, Vincent wrote as an art student in Antwerp.

Vincent hated traditional art instruction, Theo observed. His voice whispered in her thoughts.

So many days pass without my saying a word to anyone except to order supper or a coffee. And it's been like that from the start, Vincent confessed from Arles.

I didn't realize only government officials or soldiers would speak French. The local people only spoke the Occitan dialect. Theo's voice carried regret. *Vincent was terribly lonely.*

Vincent scolded: *Achieving fame is like sticking a cigar into your mouth from the lighted end.* Jo burst out laughing.

That's so like him. Theo chuckled.

The clock struck two o'clock. Jo looked up, blinking, tears on her cheeks. For a few exquisite hours, the weight of loneliness had lifted, replaced with companionship.

Jo straightened the letters and slid them back into the drawer. She would put the correspondence in order as she read. One thing was certain: she had heard Theo's voice through Vincent.

She had a way of finding the answers she sought.

TWELVE

BUSSUM

Jo

JO BROKE HER PROMISE ALWAYS TO BE THE ONE VINCENTJE would see if he called after tucking him in for the night.

For the third time that evening, Vincentje's plaintive wail reverberated through the house like a trapped ghost. Jo had resettled herself into a cushioned chair in the salon, a stack of Vincent's letters on her lap. What harm would come by letting him cry? She'd already trudged down the corridor twice to check on him. Each time, he'd been wide awake, standing on his cot. Jo grimaced, imagining her new lodger lifting her head and scowling at Vincentje's interruption to her peace. Again.

"Shall *I* see to him, Mevrouw?" Marta hovered at the edge of the pink lamp's rosy circle of light.

Why was it that the maid had boundless energy for her two-year-old but dragged her feet changing linens on a guest bed? Jo resisted answering for a second, irritated at the girl's knack for calming her son. Vincentje should've been obeying his mother, not the girl. Still, Jo nodded, noting the smug flash of satisfaction cross Marta's face as she turned to skip to the back bedroom.

Jo resented needing the girl's help. A mother's first duty was to raise a strong, healthy, good-natured son. It was up to her that Vincentje become the man Theo had wanted. Guilt tempted her to race after Marta, shove her aside, and hurry down the hallway a third time, but a wave of exhaustion sunk her deeper into the chair. It was late, and she had to get to Vincent's letters.

Jo picked at a loose thread on the chair cushion. An intermediary named Joseph Isaäcson had contacted her on behalf of two art dealers—Buffa in Amsterdam and Oldenzeel in Rotterdam—requesting to exhibit some of Vincent's paintings. If only the appeal had come a few months ago.

Pulling the thread gently, Jo unraveled a thin tear into the cushion. If Isaäcson's request had come in the fall, her answer would have been an immediate yes. That was before Jan had criticized Vincent's work in his *De Gids Nieuwe* column. Before, he'd paraded around the Arti ridiculing Vincent's paintings. If she took up Isaäcson's offer, wouldn't she be insulting Jan by openly defying him? Jan had been clear with his instructions to leave art decisions to the experts.

And in no uncertain terms, in his expert opinion, she was done exhibiting Vincent. One year was plenty of posthumous honor for an unsuccessful artist. Period.

If she went ahead and sent paintings for the exhibits, Jan would be infuriated. Anna would have to side with her husband, and Jo would lose her best childhood friend.

And if she accepted Isaäcson's offer, she would need to insist that *she* set prices for the paintings. If there was one thing she'd learned this past year, pricing created an impression, and impressions paved the way toward higher prices.

Higher prices meant a better inheritance for Vincentje.

But if her experience with Tanguy had taught her anything, Isaäcson would balk at the audacious idea that she could have any opinion on something as critical to business as price. So, when she insisted, Isaäcson would probably rescind the offer.

For days, she'd been torn with indecision, and this afternoon a telegram had arrived asking for a response by morning. She hoped to find an answer in one of these letters.

From the back of the house, Vincentje's wail abruptly stopped. Jo pictured him smiling dry-eyed as Marta approached him. Of course Vincentje responded to Marta. She indulged him.

Lose a friend. Be a bad mother. Confront angry art dealers. Like a relentless windstorm, her thoughts circled until a headache blossomed behind her eyes. Whom was she kidding? She couldn't untangle all of this. She could hear Pa's voice in her mind: *Your constitution is weaker, dear.* Jo rubbed the bridge of her nose between her thumb and forefinger. No wonder she was overwhelmed.

Still, she had to try to find the answers Theo would want. Jo set the stack of letters onto the floor by her feet, stood up, and turned the cushion upside down to hide the tear. She'd add the cushion to the mending basket later. For now, the promise of an hour with the letters beckoned. Hopefully tonight they would give her the answer she needed for Isaäcson in the morning.

It was Vincent's voice through his letters, of course, but, as Wil had promised, a different man than the intimidating personality she'd known. As Vincent's private thoughts unspooled each night, her memory of his gruff belligerence began to fade.

She turned her full attention to the first letter she'd plucked off the stack at her feet. The notes reminded her of Don Quixote. As if Theo and Vincent were lone warriors locked in a joint struggle to save "the art of the future." According to Vincent, it was a spiritual battle against a materialistic age run by greedy moneymen, hellbent on smothering all that was humble and pure in their pursuit of arrogant power. Unfailingly, Vincent's railing brought Georges Raulf to mind. How he'd boasted about clearing modern art from Theo's warm, inviting showroom on her last visit to Paris. The memory of that sterile, cold space brought a wave of regret.

Had the brothers' struggle all been in vain? She hated that in a few months Raulf had erased all signs of Theo in a gallery space her husband had carefully curated. It made her wonder if Theo's unwavering faith in Vincent—for ten long years—had been a mistake or a dream. Jo fanned her hot cheeks with the envelope. But there was nothing illusory about the physical rows and rows of paintings in the attic and the portfolios lined along the walls containing hundreds of drawings. She had the hard evidence of Vincent's effort as he'd written: *I am a bull about becoming an artist.*

How could she possibly counter attitudes against him like Raulf's and Jan Veth's?

Perhaps the next letter would have an answer.

The first she read was shocking. January 1882. Vincent had squirmed under the cruel ridicule of Hermanus Tersteeg, the manager of Goupil & Cie's art gallery in The Hague and a colleague of Theo's after Boussod had purchased the Goupil dealership. She'd met Tersteeg right after her engagement to Theo. She recalled his distant formality, his neat moustache and beard, but little else, even though he'd dined in their apartment and then hosted them for dinner at a lovely outdoor restaurant, Le Doyen, in Paris.

But in the letter Tersteeg told Vincent that looking at his drawings made him feel *a kind of opium daze you administer to yourself so as not to feel the pain you suffer at not being able to make watercolors.*

It felt like a slap across her own face.

She'd no idea he'd been so hateful to Vincent.

Had Theo known?

How had Vincent kept on painting when an art dealer had told him that?

No inspiration there. Jo shoved the letter to the bottom of the stack and reached for another.

July 1885. Jo searched her memory for Vincent's whereabouts. In his parents' home in Nuenen, having moved back from The Hague. She calculated quickly: Vincent would have been thirty-two years old. Had he been embarrassed to move back in with his parents? And Theo would have been twenty-eight and in his fifth year as manager of the Montmartre gallery.

Young men with no knowledge of the love and loss ahead of them.

She turned to the letter. *I often find the servant girls so much more interesting and beautiful than the ladies—the labourers more interesting than the gentlemen. And I find a power and vitality in those common girls and fellows . . . to express them in their singular character.* Jo smiled. She and Vincent were kindred spirits. She had never understood Pa's boast about being better than the lower class. As if money made an individual more valued in God's eyes. A worker's life was anything but simple. A few paragraphs later, Vincent agreed with her: *Seemingly there's nothing simpler than painting peasants or rag-pickers and other labourers but no subjects in painting are as difficult as those everyday figures!*

Vincent had visited soup kitchens, sat in third-class waiting rooms, and gone to the charity hospital. He'd been a fellow laborer in the working class; yet how ironic that today going to art exhibitions—where an entry fee equaled a loaf of bread—was a luxury no worker could afford.

"One day I'll get your paintings to everyone," Jo vowed to the empty room.

The clock chimed midnight. She stretched; her limbs felt heavy. She'd try one last letter for an answer to Isaäcson. May 1882, from The Hague. Lifting the closely written ink lines closer to the lamplight, she read:

My dear Theo,

Today I sent off a few drawings and sketches for you; what I want to show you above all else is that what I told you about doesn't mean that I'm easing off on my work, on the contrary. I'm literally engrossed in my work and take pleasure in it and am in good spirits. . . .

I must delve deeply into life and must get ahead by coping with great care and difficulties. I can't imagine any other way, and I don't ask to be without difficulties or cares, only that they don't become unbearable, I hope, and that doesn't have to be the case as long as I work and continue to have the sympathy of people like you. Life is the same as drawing . . .

A smile curved on Jo's lips. Vincent had loved to use metaphors in drawing and painting.

. . . sometimes one has to act quickly and resolutely, tackle things with willpower, take care that broad outlines appear with lightning speed. It's no use hesitating or doubting, and the hand may not tremble and the eye may not wander but must remain fixed on one's purpose . . .

Jo paused. Was the Biblical phrase a tongue-in-cheek poke at their father, the parson? *The hand may not tremble and the eye may not wander.* Her father-in-law had written off his oldest son as a failure by then.

What I wanted to say to you again is this. I don't have any great plans for the future. Though I may have a fleeting desire for a life free of care, for good fortune—*time and again I return lovingly to the difficul-ties, to the cares,* to a difficult life—*and think, it's better like this. I learn more this way . . .*

She reread the words. *I return lovingly to the difficulties.* He'd chosen a near-impossible way to make a living. Glancing up, Jo's gaze rested on *The Potato Eaters* over the fireplace. At the time Vincent had written this letter, he would work for three more long years before producing this masterpiece.

How had he kept at it?

She reread his scrawl. *It's no use hesitating or doubting, and the hand may not tremble and the eye may not wander but must remain fixed on one's purpose. . . .* She didn't understand. Why wouldn't he doubt? He'd failed in everything else he'd tried . . . art dealer, teacher, minister. His parents had been ashamed of him. Melan-choly had torn at him every day. He'd been desperately poor. Other than a few weeks here and there, he'd had no instruction, no teaching. And his age! He'd begun painting when he'd been twenty-eight years old. Hadn't he known he was too old? Hadn't he realized he was starting too late to be an artist?

Yet none of that had stopped him, nor had it mattered to Theo. Theo had seen something in his brother that had caused him to believe fervently in him when no one else had.

As he had with her.

Something caught her off guard. The phrases echoed inside her head. *No use hesitating or doubting. Must remain fixed on one's purpose.*

Did she have a purpose? Her heart thudded in her chest.

Ideas to improve the exhibitions came to her so naturally.

She had a knack for understanding that people bought paintings with the same uncomplicated motives they purchased clothing or bread. To make an impression on others. To reflect a value they wanted to claim for themselves. And sometimes to nourish their souls to feel a sense that existence was greater than one's small life.

Contrary to Raulf's political opinions, there was something about art that made it oblivious, even transcend narrow national interests.

Picking up the stack of letters, Jo shuffled them gently to straighten their edges. Bernard and Signac and even Tanguy only wanted to help. She could give them space, listen and learn from them. Jan: she would stop pressuring him so directly, figure out another way to gain his support.

I return lovingly to the difficulties, to the cares, to a difficult life—and think, it's better like this. I learn more this way.

Jo pressed the papers to her chest. *Stop turning away from the difficulties.*

She would agree to the exhibits with Buffa and Oldenzeel.

She would press on.

THIRTEEN

BUSSUM

Jo

THE MUTED SOUND OF A CRASH CARRIED UP THROUGH THE attic floorboards, breaking Jo's concentration as she flipped through the rows of paintings.

"No, Vincentje! No!" Mother cried out.

Jo's heart dropped. Was Vincentje hurt?

She flew down the stairs. Her mother-in-law had arrived for a visit from Nuenen earlier in the week. Around the corner, the accident came into view: An upturned table. Bits of glass from a broken vase. Limp pink tulips splayed across the floor. Vincentje furiously wriggled in the middle of the spreading puddle.

Mother stood over him, one hand clamped around his wrist, struggling to avoid his kicking feet.

"No! Mine!" Vincentje sobbed. His little fist clutched a handful of ink pens.

"Lord, have mercy," gasped Mother.

"Mother, let him go." Jo shook Mother's hand loose. In one motion, Vincentje rolled and scampered down the hallway, a trail of wet footprints disappearing into the kitchen.

"You . . . must . . . watch . . . him," panted Mother, both hands on her knees.

Marta appeared with a mop. Jo had a feeling the surly girl had hidden and watched the entire mishap. "Clean up, Mevrouw?" she grinned.

"Please." Jo rotated her mother-in-law away from Marta's smirk and walked her to an armchair, where the older woman collapsed. Jo rubbed her back, her slight shoulder blades like a bird's. Mother twisted to look up at her and offered Jo a faint smile.

"You're trying, dear, but it's not working. You don't discipline him." She sighed. "I found Vincentje at your desk. Drawing *with ink*."

Guilt shot through Jo. "I was only upstairs a minute—"

"Vincentje *especially* must be watched! You were gone far too long." Her eyes narrowed. "What was so important in the attic that you neglect your son?"

Ignoring the criticism, Jo leaped at the chance to share her news about Vincent's artwork. "Mother, I was selecting paintings for an exhibition in Paris!" That should impress her. "A friend of Theo's—Émile Bernard—arranged to show Vincent's work at Le Barc de Boutteville gallery. I need to get sixteen paintings on the four o'clock train. I picked the paintings last night, of course, but then this morning I thought to switch to *Flowers in a Blue Vase* for *The Night Café*. It will be more . . ." Jo's voice trailed off. A look of horror crossed Mother's face.

"Do you realize how you are babbling? Is everyone around me—"

"Mother, stop! You don't understand. Monsieur Bernard *asked* me for help."

"You let those dealers walk all over you. Those men should be coming *here* to get their own paintings. You're not their servant!"

Mother didn't understand. She wanted to be involved.

Mother sat up straighter. "Your poor boy doesn't have a father to discipline him. By the time my children were three years old—"

"Two. Vincentje's two years old, Mother."

Mother waved her hand. "My children were very well behaved, but I had to keep an iron hand. Their father was a leader in the community. His children could not be hooligans. No one knew what it took for me to keep them in line!"

Jo said nothing. Theo's stories of his father's cold ministerial disapproval had been heartbreaking.

"Vincentje needs more supervision. You need to watch him. Every second."

"I'll do better."

"You treat motherhood like a pastime." Mother folded her hands tightly in her lap. "I've been here one week. Your days are chaotic. You never sleep. You don't take enough time with Vincentje."

"Mother, Vincentje is the *most important—*"

"I'll take him. Wil can help me."

Shocked, Jo stuttered, "M-M-Mother!"

Her mother-in-law's strength had miraculously revived. Standing up, she faced Jo. "You need rest. Your boarders run you ragged. Your maid is *lazy*." She glanced at the doorway where Marta had disappeared. "You're up in the attic, doing who knows what, while Vincentje runs wild."

Jo searched for the words to explain.

Vincentje's muffled laughter rang out from the kitchen. Mother lifted her chin. She always made sure she got the last word.

"I won't let my grandson be raised by a *maid*."

Later that afternoon, Villa Helma settled into blissful quiet—one of the few lulls in a typical boardinghouse day between the luncheon's cleanup and the final rush to serve dinner on time. Both Mother and Vincentje were down for naps. Bouwman had just left with the paintings for Bernard safely crated, promising the shipment would make the train. The fragrant smell of fresh-baked bread floated through the house. Jo's mouth watered, but Cook had already handed her a steaming cup of hot tea and waved her out of the kitchen before Jo could steal a slice.

Settled at the writing desk, Jo wet her finger in the tea to rub away the ink lines Vincentje had drawn into the desk's wood. More ink lines scratched the outside of envelopes from her mail. She tried to concentrate, but Mother's angry words still rattled. Mother didn't know that Vincentje hadn't been misbehaving. Jo allowed him to draw on the envelopes. Better than ruining writing paper.

Still, Mother was right about her exhaustion. There were simply not enough hours in the day. Something had to give.

With quick efficiency, she slit open the envelopes with Theo's pearl-handled letter opener. If the letter inquired about lodging, she made quick notes, checking her calendar for vacancies. Villa Helma kept a roof over her and Vincentje's heads, and she would not neglect it. In short order, she'd completed her responses and set the notes in the mail basket for Marta to take to the post office in the morning.

Taking a sip of lukewarm tea, Jo noted the absence of any invitations for tea or cards from Bussum ladies who had come calling while she'd been out. Not that she would have accepted. She couldn't spare a minute. Even Anna had stopped coming by. Though she couldn't blame her, it hurt a little. With a shake of her head, she took a deep drink of tea. Vincentje's welfare was more important than silly outings.

The remaining few letters were her favorite mail: inquiries on Vincent's art.

Jacobus Slagmulder, a partner from the Buffa art dealership, reported back on the February exhibit. Jo's heart raced. Vincent's ten paintings had a mixed review. Younger clientele admired Vincent, but his typical patrons were wary. Jo reread Slagmulder's last line: *It has stirred the spirits, stirred discussions, and we are very grateful that you have given us the opportunity to bring a new sensation to ourselves and to many others.*

Stirred discussions! To hear that Vincent's work challenged people to see from a new perspective . . . felt exactly right. Her heart thumped wildly. And to think she'd wavered over the Buffa exhibit. She hummed a little tune under her breath. She'd save this letter. Press it into the scrapbook she'd begun of Vincent's newspaper reviews.

Refer to it in the future when she asked Meneer Slagmulder for another show.

The next letter wasn't as forgiving. Christien Oldenzeel—the owner of the Oldenzeel gallery in Rotterdam—demanded that she lower prices. Several paintings had arrived damaged with small holes and tears. Jo cringed and jotted a note. She would get Bouwman to add more wood shavings in the crates for better cushioning, but she wouldn't change the price. A newspaper clipping fell into her hand from the envelope. Reading it, she frowned. Oldenzeel should've been happier. The twenty paintings in his show got extensive press. He'd sold *A Corner of the Asylum Garden,* one of Theo's favorites.

Curiously, the next envelope had no postmark. Jo turned it over, searching for an address. It must have been dropped off at the house. Sure enough, the brief note was from Jan, characteristically curt. *I have a sale of* Cypresses *for 125 guilders.*

Who? Someone had reached out to Jan? Of course, after the Arti show everyone would assume he was an intermediary.

Well, this anonymous person would be disappointed. Jo closed her eyes, picturing *Cypresses*. Off the center of the canvas, majestic trees swirled with lifelike energy. The green brushstrokes of cypress branches stretched toward a sky swirling with the wind. The boughs jostled above a windswept golden field at its base. Circular gusts of wind battled with a boisterous cloud and sliver of sun. *No.* She opened her eyes. One hundred twenty-five guilders was much too low for this fervent, agitated energy.

Frowning, she drummed her fingers on the desk. Did this note mean Jan supported Vincent now? Lately, his stance against him had seemed to soften. But she couldn't afford to give in, not to Oldenzeel or to Jan. Lowering the prices now would open the door to dropping them in the future. She wanted prices to *rise* over time.

The next letter proved her point. Père Tanguy was characteristically blunt. He needed to clear the room in his shop. He planned to cut prices for Vincent's work to get rid of the   paintings. Hurt, Jo dashed off a note imploring him to hold them a little longer. Honestly, sometimes it was difficult to remember he'd wept at Vincent's deathbed.

The final note lifted her heart. The Vingt group was requesting two more shows—one in The Hague and the second in Antwerp. Vincent had complained about the conservative art school in Antwerp, but today's art students might be as open to Vincent's work as Buffa's young clientele were.

Jo glanced at the clock. Still an hour before Vincentje usually woke up. She couldn't get Tanguy and Jan out of her mind. What could she do to warm them to Vincent? What had brought Bernard around?

For one thing, he had a cache of Vincent's letters. No doubt they kept Vincent alive to him, as the letters had for her. Jo pulled open the bottom drawer. Theo's letters now ran in neat rows, divided by the year in which Vincent had written them, Next she'd planned to organize them by geography.

Perhaps Tanguy would be less churlish if she sent him a few of Vincent's letters. Remind him of the friend Vincent had been, the artist behind Tanguy's very own portrait. Jan too. He'd never met Vincent in person; all he knew was Theo's obsession to support him.

Jo's heart skipped a beat. Jan could get to know Vincent. The same way she had.

Hastening to her feet, she grabbed a stack of letters. She had just enough time before dinner preparations sprang to life to get down to the Veth house and back.

If Jan would read Vincent's words, he'd reverse course. Become Vincent's advocate.

Besides, she had a gentle but firm message for her prickly neighbor: she would most definitely not be lowering *Cypresses*'s price.

BUSSUM

Jo

JO SWUNG OPEN THE DOOR OF JAN'S ART STUDIO. "MENEER Veth, oh!" Riotous bright colors leaped from a painting in front of her.

"Mevrouw!" Jan exclaimed. He sidestepped to block her. "I wasn't expecting you."

"Are you painting, Meneer? May I see it?"

"Since you're here . . . I'm experimenting." He stepped aside to reveal the canvas. Compared to the somber-toned compositions around his studio, this painting's colorful outburst felt shocking. Jo drew in a quick breath. Was he imitating Vincent? It was a good sign. Perhaps Jan's icy resistance toward Vincent had begun to thaw.

"It's . . . it's . . ." She searched for the right words to encourage him.

"An *experiment*," Jan finished for her. "Why are you interrupting me, Mevrouw? Anna is in the house."

"I've come about your note."

"Excellent." Jan looked relieved. "That little painting of the trees."

"*Cypresses*. Meneer, I won't lower the price."

He flushed.

"Wait. Are *you* the buyer?"

Jan lifted his chin. "You should be grateful I'm willing to take one."

Delighted, she tried to keep a straight face. Jan wanted to buy a painting! He saw value in Vincent's work after all. But he mustn't see her reaction, nor would she be drawn into an argument. She'd come with an olive branch. Digging into her bag, she offered the parcel to Jan.

"Read these, Meneer Veth. They're Vincent's letters to my husband. He'll come alive to you."

Jan accepted the thick packet as if it was soiled. "You're meddling again. I've told Anna you've become a pest."

Now it was Jo's turn to flush. "The artwork is my son's inheritance. Theo would want me—"

"Why do you think I'm risking my reputation? For my *friend*, Theo. I changed the tone of my reviews to give Vincent some respectability, then found out you approached the Arti for another exhibit behind my back!"

"You needn't be concerned. They turned me down."

"Of course they did. I told them to! I had to turn down a show for Vincent at the Panorama because of you too."

The Panorama! She felt a sudden adrenaline rush.

One of Amsterdam's premier exhibition halls, the Panorama had a unique circular structure. With a flash, she visualized the mural of vibrant color and movement Vincent's paintings would bring if they hung on its walls. Her heart fell. Jan had turned it down? Exhibiting in the Panorama would be more than an amazing public display—it would have been a statement, an acknowledgment that Vincent's art was worthy and legitimate. Why hadn't the organizers contacted her? Jan should have asked her what she thought. She would have accepted the invitation in a heartbeat.

Alarm gripped her. "Because of me? I don't understand."

Jan smirked. "Of course you wouldn't. My reputation rests on recognizing serious art." He glanced at his painting. "Vincent's interplay of color doesn't work. I have an obligation to my readers to be honest in my endorsements. I reserve the prerogative to adjust my opinions when I see fit."

"You could have asked me about the Panorama, Meneer," she insisted.

"Asked you? Did you hear what I said? Others depend on *me* for my opinion."

Exactly. Enraged at his arrogance, she wanted to shake him. "*Promise me* you'll read the letters." Vincent could get through to him.

"You have to let this obsession go. It won't bring Theo back," he dismissed and turned away.

For a few seconds she hesitated, fuming at his back. Willing herself to retort something, anything to get his attention. Stubbornly ignoring her, he picked up his brush and dapped at paint. Eyes filling, she grabbed fistfuls of her long skirts and ran.

Jan's words followed her into the lane. He'd turned down the Panorama because of her.

The anger felt good. Swiping at her wet face, Jo could barely see the road. Her breath turned ragged, but still she ran. Jan and Tanguy were blind. They couldn't see her in any other way than Theo's widow. As if she was an annoying insect, they swatted at her.

What had Jan said?

You've become a pest.

If only she had the constitution to do this work on her own.

Gasping, she reached the boardinghouse and dropped her hands to her knees to take in deep gulps of air. She hoped no one had seen her unladylike dash.

She couldn't understand what she was doing wrong or how to fix these broken relationships. Jan turning down the Panorama stung. She had to figure this out and needed help. If only she knew someone who wasn't personally invested in Vincent to work with.

Someone like Georges Raulf.

Aloof. Indifferent. She pictured his elegant suit and arched eyebrow. Could she trust him? An uneasy feeling shivered up her spine.

Who else did she know?

He was the perfect man to help her.

———◇———

FIFTEEN

PARIS

Raulf

"I *TOLD* YOU VINCENT WOULD NOT SELL IN PARIS," RAULF SAID.

Madame van Gogh deserved to be taken down a notch. Her whining might have worked to cajole the partners into insisting he have this meeting, but he alone directed what hung in the boulevard Montmartre gallery. Her brother-in-law's art was out of the question.

The young woman was paler than he'd remembered, but she had a new composure about her. Or was it arrogance?

"Vincent's work would sell if I had the right partner to help me, Monsieur. I thought of you."

Raulf smothered a laugh out loud. Women and their flattery. "I made my opinion of modern art quite clear last time you were here, Madame."

"I've sold eight paintings since then. My brother-in-law's art is making money."

Raulf steepled his hands in front of his chin, feigning close attention. The widow couldn't see the pity in those sales. The Dutch were clearly making sentimental, parochial purchases.

"An interest in art is a pastime for you Van Gogh widows."

"Van Gogh widows?"

"Cornelia van Gogh is your aunt, is she not?"

"Theo's. But what—"

"No need to feign innocence, Madame! You made your aunt lean on the partners' sentimental memory of Theo's uncle Cent for this little meeting. Fine. I never met him, but the Boussod partners like to stick together, even in death."

"I don't know anything about Aunt Cornelie—" Eyes wide open. She was a terrible liar.

"Never mind. Why are you here?"

"I . . . well," she stuttered. It gave him a twinge of satisfaction to see her flustered. The woman kept hammering away. "That is . . . the Vingtistes are collectors. I've sold a few pieces of art to them already. They've asked for another show. The Panorama in Amsterdam wanted to do an exhibition. . ." She swallowed, evading something, and continued, "The art school in Antwerp—"

"Antwerp! The art school?" Raulf sat up straight. An image of rough brick walls and dingy-white columns flashed in his mind. Raynaud's school?

At last she had his interest. "Students are intrigued by Vincent's art. He went to school there himself, years ago," she said, a whisper of relief in her voice.

In an instant, Raulf returned to those stone steps. Reliving the sharp winter wind raking his scarf across his face. Flakes of dried gray paint scattered like snowflakes as Raynaud's chewed fingernails scraped bits of peeled paint from a cracked pillar. A dull yellow stain lined his cuticles. His brother was young for his age. Always too tender-hearted. God knew Raulf protected him from Père's fury, but now that Père was dead, Raynaud was his responsibility. Raynaud had to toughen up. Be more like himself.

"Only ten guilders, *mon frère*," Raynaud said softly, eyes concentrated on picking at the column's cracks. His thin wrist protruded from a sleeve too short even for Raynaud's razor-thin body. The knuckles on those long fingers, red and rough from the winter cold, were chapped.

"Absolutely not. This art school is nonsense." Raulf took a small step sideways to block Raynaud from the wind.

Raynaud raised his eyes, deep in their sockets, a faint smile on his lips. "You haven't seen my new work, brother. I found some friends who are experimenting and trying techniques outside the typical academic training. It's exciting."

"Exciting to be penniless?"

"Exciting to see the possibilities," Raynaud said. His eyes glowed. "There's this one older student—"

"No more, Raynaud! You're not listening to me. It's time to stop this daydreaming! Being an artist is an *unimaginable* career. You can't possibly be prosperous. I stood up for you over Père's objections. But I've indulged you too long."

"Don't say it!"

"I'm cutting you off. Don't call me until you've come to your senses. You can't live on paint."

"I'll live on *love,* then."

It had been the last time Raulf had seen him alive. Three weeks later a telegram had arrived from the school—Raynaud had died from pneumonia. Raulf had returned to Antwerp for his body and buried him next to their parents in the family plot.

Now he raised his eyes to the widow sitting across the desk from him. Her late brother-in-law had been the sort of irresponsible radical who had seduced Raynaud with false dreams of glory. If not for that influence—an artist like Vincent—Raynaud might've still been alive. Vincent's paintings were not only vulgar and an affront to art but dangerous, poisoning youth like Raynaud with deceptive hope.

The widow weighed her words carefully. "As you explained last time I was here, I need guidance. I can't sell paintings without help. I can offer you a ten-percent commission for every painting—"

"You're mad!" Raulf exploded out of his seat.

He'd picked the word deliberately. She jolted back.

"I've tried to tell you, Madame. Modern art is *nothing*. A passing fancy. Your husband was an idiot. Nothing you or his aunt can say will change that!"

"Aunt Cornelie? I honestly don't . . ."

"Please!" he blasted. "I'm not a fool! I know you connived together to get this meeting. You women play with folly! Modern art is a dangerous distraction. Especially for our youth. You have no idea of the stakes."

"Stakes? I am very clear on the stakes—"

"How could you possibly understand? It's my duty to look out for the next French generation."

"I have a duty too, Monsieur." The widow's eyes flashed. "I have a duty to my son, who deserves an inheritance earning more than dust in my attic!"

"I can't correct your husband's mistake—"

"Instead you've tried to erase him."

"Not *tried*, Madame. I *have*. The misshapen modern art your husband dealt in undermined Boussod's dignity." He looked over her shoulder into his gallery's pristine space. White-faced, she stared at him. A small part of him admired her for not collapsing into hysterics or running from the gallery. It rattled him a little.

He softened his voice. "Your son's inheritance is not my concern. What is my concern is how every time art like your brother-in-law's sells, it sows false hope in the young men tempted to follow in its footsteps." Raulf stared ahead, Raynaud's gaunt figure before him, reproaching him. "Your brother-in-law has *ruined* lives."

Madame van Gogh's cheeks flamed. "How can you say that? Vincent painted from the heart. If you only knew him, if you could read his letters." She pulled a parcel from her bag. "He was a true artist—"

"True artist! Your brother-in-law was a *nobody. A true artist sells internationally and hangs in museums.* Drop this . . . this . . . feminine *stupidity.* I've kept my obligation to the partners and met with you. Go back to Holland! Back to your son! Tell your aunt to take her hands off my gallery. You have no business here."

The girl snatched her bag to her chest. "Then I must do the best I can without you," she said. As if in one fluid motion, she had disappeared out the door.

His eyes burned at the empty chair in front of him. Van Gogh was no longer some misguided simpleton. He was a disease. A virus. Raulf was now on the lookout.

He would never allow Vincent van Gogh to get a foothold in Paris.

SIXTEEN

BUSSUM

Jo

ON THE FIRST DAY OF SPRING, THEO'S OLD FRIEND AND
art dealer, Piet Boele van Hensbroek, meandered in front of Vincent's paintings in Jo's salon. She eyed the portfolio he swung in
one hand. Inside was the catalog listing for the artwork she'd
handpicked to display at the Haagse Kunstkring exhibit in The
Hague next week. She suspected Van Hensbroek had brought it
more as a gesture than for her to review it. But last night a new
idea for the catalog had sprung out of nowhere. Tossing and turning,
she'd finally gotten up and spent the rest of the night in the attic
making out a list of paintings to give to The Hague dealer.

Now that he was here, she panicked.

She was out of her depth. How could she be sure her idea wasn't
a mistake?

On impulse, she grabbed the stuck window handle next to her.
Wrestling and straining, she banged the window open.

A bit breathless, she looked up to meet Van Hensbroek's stare.

"A little fresh air?" she offered.

"Humph." He lifted an eyebrow and tapped the portfolio with a
finger. "Let's get this over with, shall we?" They settled into arm-

chairs across from each other. She couldn't help feeling they were squaring off like two opponents. "Forty-five paintings, forty-five drawings, and one lithograph. It's all in order." He handed her the portfolio. "I'll take the catalog to the printer on my way back."

It was now or never.

"I have . . . an idea. An addition for the catalog."

"No, no dear," he tsk'd. "The art is already hung."

"Please take this, Meneer. It's a list of some masterpieces I have in the attic here." She unfolded a paper from her pocket.

He chuckled. "Madness creates a fever of work, doesn't it!" He held up his hand, refusing to take it. "You're getting ahead of yourself, dear. Let's see if *this* show is successful before we start planning a second one."

"Oh, these aren't for sale. I'd like you to simply list them in the catalog."

"The catalog? You don't understand, dear. One can't *tamper* with a catalog. It's *essential* to an exhibition. It must be accurate. We use it to calculate sales."

"I do understand," she said, ignoring his smirk. "Why couldn't a catalog show more of Vincent's oeuvre? By including paintings that are *not for sale*, it will increase the value of those that *are*."

"That's *not* the way it's done."

"Perhaps not—"

"Most definitely not! The Haagse Kunstkring may be new, but we *are* legitimate. A serious group. Our mission is to convert curiosity seekers into *collectors* of modern art. I expressly petitioned the group to exhibit Van Gogh. This isn't a frivolous vanity display for you. The works in the catalog must *all* be for sale."

Jo leaned forward. "Don't you see, Meneer van Hensbroek? People will appreciate the individual paintings more if they see their purchase is part of a big collection. Quite large, in fact."

"Theo never did this. My god, he was deathly persistent in his attempts to sell *any* of Vincent's work."

If only Theo were here, she thought for the thousandth time. Thanks to Vincent's letters, Theo's words about *art* had come back to her, but he stayed frustratingly silent on art *dealing*. Jo raised her eyes to meet Van Hensbroek's, searching for the right response. No one understood her balancing act. She wrestled with two contradictions. Theo had wanted Vincent's work to be appreciated as much as possible, and half the inheritance belonged to Vincentje. If she pulled half the paintings to save for Vincentje—keeping them out of the public's eye, hidden in the attic—then they weren't being appreciated. Nor could they rise in value.

Her catalog idea—list the paintings for sale and not for sale together—seemed like a simple solution.

"It's true. You knew Theo well, Meneer van Hensbroek." Jo picked her words carefully. "My husband was passionate about Vincent's work. He never gave up on him." Raulf's cold makeover of Theo's Montmartre gallery appeared in her mind. "But Theo wasn't able to make much headway in Paris. All the modern art in his gallery has been cleared out since he died. Modern art needs Haagse Kunstkring. It's on the leading edge of . . . of a new century."

"Exactly, dear!" he beamed. "It may be 1892 today, but the year 1900 is around the corner. We want to drive progress. We want to prove that modern art is *worthy* of being purchased." He chuckled to himself. "A *sales* catalog listing paintings *not for sale*? What would be the point?"

Jo forced her voice to be bright. "You've set aside three large rooms in the Café Riche for this show. So generous. Why not indicate that there are many, many more works—more than the three rooms can fill? Show how modern art is like a train."

"A train?"

"These curiosity seekers don't want to miss getting on board."

"Hmmm." Van Hensbroek swung the portfolio around to his chest, tapping one finger on it. "There have been quite a few articles about Vincent in the press lately," he mused.

"Jan Veth's columns have been complimenting Vincent." He must've been reading Vincent's letters. She pressed on: "Your visitors are intrigued. They've read the articles. Let them know there are paintings they can't have."

"But in the catalog—"

"As you said, it's the essential record of the show. Where better to show that modern art is a force to be reckoned with? And listing *three hundred* works of art would make quite an impression."

Van Hensbroek gazed over her head, bouncing the portfolio gently in his hands. He mused, "And if all goes well, Vincent could get to the Panorama."

"Get to the Panorama?" she repeated, not understanding. But Jan had turned it down. No one there had responded to any of her letters pleading to reverse the decision.

He nodded. "Roland Holst is trying to arrange it."

Jo was stunned. Writer and artist Richard Roland Holst hated her. He'd criticized her only a few months ago in *De Amsterdammer*, his words seared into her mind: *Mevrouw van Gogh is a charming little woman, but it irritates me when someone gushes fanatically on a subject she knows nothing about, and although blinded by sentimentality still thinks she is adopting a strictly critical attitude. It is schoolgirlish twaddle, nothing more . . .*

And now he had reopened a door into the Panorama that Jan had shut? She didn't understand Holst's change of heart. *If* it was a change of heart. Like Van Hensbroek, he might've believed she worked against Theo's wishes.

"Fine." He held out a hand for her list. "You're a woman." He slid the inventory into his portfolio. Sighing, he said, "I have a lot of explaining to do, but I'll get this to the printer first. The Haagse Kunstkring *is* a force to be reckoned with . . . I do like that." He started toward the door, then turned back. "I've heard about you, you know. 'The wife who fights so passionately for the new art.' I didn't expect your *scheming*. For all our sakes, I hope you're right."

Jo wrapped her arms across her chest as the art dealer hurried down the walk. A single trickle of sweat slid down her back. Her dress was damp under the arms.

Van Hensbroek had agreed, but it didn't feel like a victory. Her heart beat wildly. She'd no idea the Panorama was at stake.

What if the catalog idea created confusion? What if the Haagse Kunstkring exhibition received a hateful reception like the art students in Antwerp?

She'd be blamed if sales were few. Or nonexistent.

And now she might have jeopardized this unexpected second chance to show in the Panorama. She wiped her damp palms on her dress, watching Van Hensbroek's profile diminish as he walked down the lane. The Panorama's beautiful exhibition hall would be a sign of Vincent's legitimacy, proof that the prices she'd given his paintings were justifiable. Validation that Vincentje's inheritance could be realized. She needed the Panorama. She needed Holst's approval, and here she'd nearly ruined her chances.

She didn't know what she was doing.

SEVENTEEN

BUSSUM

Jo

JO FELT STUCK, SUSPENDED IN A DRAGGING MELANCHOLY, despite the hectic day-to-day activity in the boardinghouse. Word of Villa Helma's art-covered walls had spread. Artists, poets, and intellectuals arrived daily, tripling Jo's work, aggravating Cook, and prompting bickering between Marta and the new maid, Alene. Each day became a sweaty race to launder mountains of linens and dictate endless food-shopping lists. It wasn't until after supper that the house quieted, when the guests headed en masse down the road to Jan Veth's. He hosted evening gatherings for the Tachtigers, a group of supporters of his *De Nieuwe Gids* newspaper.

With the help of the Tachtigers, the publication had become a progressive voice dedicated to ideas for the new century. The Tachtigers debated nationalism and the artist's role.

One night Jo sank into her customary chair next to Anna at the very back of the Veths' salon. Every bone in her body ached from the long day, yet she hated the idea of missing a meeting.

The gathering reminded her of evenings in Paris when Camille Pissarro and his son, Lucien, would argue with Theo late into the night, draining bottle after bottle of wine in their salon. Sitting on the edge of their bed, Jo would slip her shoes off to run her toes along the curlicue pattern of the rug, easily eavesdropping through the paper-thin walls as they'd ranted against capitalism. Their ideas of equal rights for workers had appealed to an impulse in her own heart. She'd looked forward to the evenings.

Tonight, though, she almost hadn't come to the Tachtiger meeting. A devastating telegram from Holst had arrived as she'd been leaving Villa Helma. Her heart had soared—Holst had secured an exhibit for the Panorama!—and then plummeted, for there was one bitter condition: Holst would curate and manage the show alone.

Without her involvement.

She'd brought this on herself. She'd made too many mistakes.

The telegram crinkled in Jo's pocket. She could use her best friend's sympathy tonight. "Anna," she breathed.

But instead of responding, Anna sat stiff and upright, her eyes straight ahead. Following her gaze, Jo's heart flipped. Perched comfortably in the Veths' best leather armchair within the inner circle of men sat a woman.

Short, bobbed hair cut right to her chin. Black kid boots crossed at her ankles, visible because her skirts hung scandalously short of the floor. She wore a dark jacket over a white shirtwaist trimmed with small pleats and a high collar. A flat straw boater rested on her knee. But even more shocking, she looked perfectly relaxed, completely at ease—especially in contrast to Jan to her left, whose pinched face looked like he was sitting on knitting needles.

"Her name is Marie Mensing," whispered Anna. "She sat right down in front."

Marie Mensing. Jo recognized the name from her guest book. Marie had arrived at Villa Helma that afternoon when Jo had been in town paying the butcher's bill.

Something inside of Jo shifted, alert. She sat up straight. The day's fatigue lifted.

"We teach the girls algebra, geometry, history, and physics," Marie said, ticking the subjects off with her fingers. "English, German, and French, of course. And . . ." Marie paused, eyes dancing, and continued, "Business arithmetic and accounting." She beamed, dropping her hands in her lap.

Business arithmetic. Accounting. Jo held her breath and scanned the circle of hardening faces. A little thrill rippled through her. Girls did not learn business subjects.

"It's cruel to overwhelm the girls!" a faceless voice to Jan's left blustered. Another voice blurted, "Beyond their natural abilities!" Chairs creaked as bodies shifted.

Marie's amused voice rang out above the rustling. "I assure you, the girls are quite capable. And *interested*."

"In this part of the country, girls are delicate."

"The girls in north Kampen are the same as yours."

"Come, come," called out Jan. He clapped his hands to quiet the room. Forcing a humorless chuckle, he scooted to the front edge of his chair. "This discourse is a distraction. We have weightier matters to discuss—"

"Weightier than the future of Holland?" Marie asked brightly, her eyebrows arched. She fanned herself with the boater hat.

Jan's face reddened.

Marie declared, "Holland is falling behind England and France. The new century is upon us, and we're not ready. There's been a distinct decline in married women's work outside the home and—"

"Hold on!" Jan stood up, face angry. "This is not a women's meeting. *De Nieuwe Gids* is dedicated to art serving our national cause. The very future of our country is at stake. We are concerned with civilization in the next millennium."

"Exactly!" Marie's eyes blazed. "I *am* talking about the next phase of civilization! We are preparing our girls to play their part in Holland's future. Women have the right to advance in education, professions, *and the arts* alongside their fellow men. And gentlemen—we are in this phase right *now*." She looked directly at Jo.

Jo's heart flipped. In a second, oxygen seemed to suck from the room. For a beat, Marie's words hung in silence, until abruptly, shouts erupted. Jan leapt to his feet. Anna raced to summon servants for wine, while Jo barely noticed.

She had a *right* to be in business. A *right* to be in the arts.

It was as if she'd never heard the word before.

The rest of the meeting was a blur. Once servants arrived with armfuls of wine bottles and Jan could establish order, hot tempers cooled. Jo could hardly take her eyes off the young, poised woman who sat perfectly at ease at the center of tumult she'd caused.

When the meeting was over, Jo found herself strolling alongside Marie back toward Villa Helma under a deep blue blanket of winking stars. A slight breeze fanned their faces. She felt oddly alive, more energetic than she'd felt in weeks. After turning onto the dirt road from the Veth's house, in silent agreement they slowed their pace until the distance between them and the other boarding guests gradually widened.

"Marie, I was so scared when you were speaking! Weren't you frightened?"

"They're gentlemen." Marie laughed. "The worst that's ever happened to me is a bruised elbow from being hauled out of a meeting."

Jo stared. "I wish I could be braver, wish I could speak up like you."

Marie stopped, facing her. "But you do, don't you?"

Jo shook her head. "You don't know me. I'm not only running a boardinghouse. I'm trying to sell my brother-in-law's paintings."

"Oh, I know who you are!" Marie laughed again. "You *have* spoken up!"

Jo shrugged her shoulders. "I don't have anything to say. All the Tachtiger meetings are political. How art should respond to new industries and growing cities. How classical art is out of step with the times. Modern art must take on a moral duty, uphold Christian ideals . . . I'm the *last* person to voice any predictions about what makes art appealing."

Puzzled, Marie scrunched her forehead. "You're not giving yourself credit. You are *selling* artwork, aren't you?"

"Well, yes," she said. "In fact, earlier this spring Haagse Kunstkring in The Hague held a two-month show with Vincent's work. I sold one of my favorite paintings, *Wheatfield after a Storm* And Marie . . ." Jo's words spilled out, so happy to confide. "A Danish artist bought it. Johan Rohde. Apparently he was so captivated he never questioned the price—two hundred seventy guilders! That's almost *half* of my boardinghouse annual rent!"

Marie grabbed her hands. Jo laughed out loud. It was shocking.

She shrugged, thinking of her catalog additions. Van Hensbroek had made the edits but claimed her additions made no difference. "Every time I feel *certain* about an idea, I have no clue if I'm right. I create a huge fuss for nothing."

Marie kept hold of one of Jo's hands and tucked it into the crook of her elbow. The touch settled Jo's frayed nerves. Their strides fell into an easy rhythm, soft steps crunching a matched beat on the dry ground. "How do you know you're the one who's wrong?" Marie asked. "Perhaps it's the audience?"

"That doesn't make sense. I'm constantly trying to *win over* audiences."

"My *audience* tonight disagreed with me. Change makes people uncomfortable. It doesn't make me wrong. But it makes them think."

Holst's telegram crinkled in Jo's pocket. The Panorama organizers had more faith in Holst's curating than hers. Jo sighed. "I may not be the right person . . ."

Marie stopped, pulling Jo around to face her. "Who told you that?" she demanded.

"N-no one. *I* know—"

"Know what? That women don't have the business sense for art dealing? Or, better yet, we use our feminine wiles and *scheme* to get men to do our bidding."

"But . . ." Jo stopped. "I've been told as much."

"I hate those tawdry, run-to-heel comments!" Marie gripped Jo's arms. "The world is changing! Stop listening to what other people tell you about what you can and cannot do!"

"I'm not like you."

"What?" Marie laughed, surprised. "Why do you think I came to Bussum? I admire you. I wanted to find *you*. *You* are a role model for *me*. For the *New Woman*. You've taken control over your entire life— economic, social, personal."

Jo stared at Marie.

Marie shook Jo's arms. "Think about it. You are the *only* female art dealer in Holland. Perhaps in all of Europe! An industry decidedly run by men. I can't think of a better example of a New Woman *insisting* you're equal to any man!"

An equal.

Jo bit her lip. Could she really stand up to Holst?

"I suppose so. No one knows Vincent's work better than I do. I am the best representative."

"*This* is what I think of naysayers." Marie stepped back, hands on her hips, hocked up a wad of phlegm, and vigorously spat onto the ground.

Stunned, Jo stared and burst into laughter. Marie stood a second longer, doubled over, and howled in laughter too.

"Trust yourself," she finally gasped, wiping her eyes.

Trust myself. Overhead in the blue depth of sky, stars sparkled like spinning gems in a brilliant show. Jo took a deep breath. "I received an ultimatum today. A dealer named Holst has offered me a chance to show Vincent in the Panorama. Do you know it?"

"Of course. Quite the building."

"It would make a statement to hang Vincent's work there. I want it so badly."

"I expect they know that . . ."

"Their condition is that only Holst can curate it. Not me."

"And what do you think?"

"I could do something they don't expect."

"Something they'd never *imagine* a woman would do."

"Since I know the Panorama organizers are interested . . . maybe I can go to them myself."

"Set aside this Holst."

"Tell them Vincent and I are inseparable."

Marie grinned at Jo. "Two peas in a pod!"

"And I won't take no for an answer!"

"Absolutely not!"

Jo sobered. "But there's one more thing . . ."

"What's that?"

Jo arched an eyebrow at Marie. "Show me how you spit."

AMSTERDAM

Jo

SIX MONTHS AFTER JO HAD RECEIVED THE GO-AHEAD FROM the Panorama organizers, Holst still acted like she was a visitor when she entered the circular space.

"Why are you moving my paintings?" She pulled off her gloves and shook snowflakes out of her hair.

A guilty flush flashed across Holst's face as he smoothed his thick mustache around his upper lip. He approached her briskly, the impatient *tap, tap* of his hurrying step echoing on the rotunda's marble tile. A blue-smocked workman leaned inside the bare spot where Vincent's painting of *In the Café: Agostina Segatori in Le Tambourin* had hung.

Jo put her hands on her hips. "Not another change? It's the last week! The portrait of Agostina Segatori was painted in Paris. Don't tell me you're placing it in the middle of Saint-Rémy?" she said, spotting an empty space across the room.

"You see, *aesthetically—*"

"As I've said before, the paintings should be in the order Vincent painted them. I want to show how his work progressed from somber grayish tones to his exuberant color and strong brushwork, from peasants to street scenes to—"

"*You* want—"

"Landscape images of Auvers-sur-Oise."

"Mevrouw, curating takes a trained eye."

"You did agree to include me in the process."

"Yes, but—"

"In all decisions."

Scanning the walls, Jo hid a smile. Ninety-seven paintings and twenty drawings surrounded them, an impressive, beautiful evolution of Vincent's oeuvre. She wished the paintings could hang here forever.

Holst sighed noisily. "A *true* artist must be presented with utmost attention to the *overall* visual presentation."

Jo faced him. Why couldn't art aficionados speak in straightforward language? "Meneer Holst, we've been through this. Vincent *is* a true artist—"

"A true artist *suffers* for his work. We owe it to Vincent of all people to place his paintings in the best possible manner. Look carefully," he said, stepping to her side. He measured his words out with infinite patience. "It's a *minor* adjustment. Merely fine-tuning. Notice, *aesthetically*, how the blend of colors is much more harmonious."

"You gave me a *gentleman's* agreement, Meneer Holst."

Holst's eyes narrowed. "What was the sales tally from last week?"

"You know what it was. I paid you a commission."

"Six hundred thirty guilders."

Jo kept a straight face while watching his fingers smooth his mustache. She could still hardly believe their success. The sales amount was staggering. Equal to an entire year's rent for Villa Helma.

Holst tapped his chin. "From only two paintings and one drawing—"

"*And* a lithograph."

"And an etching . . ." Holst repeated. His eyes flicked to a nearby table where catalogs had been carefully fanned out, displaying the lithograph cover he had commissioned.

Irritation rose in Jo as she followed his proud expression. That catalog cover was a sore subject. He was implying that it had attracted sales, but she disagreed. Holst had designed the horrid illustration himself: A dead sunflower with dried-out leaves against a setting sun. The wilted flower was crowned with a halo. Holst had reproduced Vincent's signature below it. He was implying that the catalog cover had attracted the sales, but she disagreed. She loathed it.

For the idea of Vincent as a dying martyr was ludicrous. The image was a distortion of the lucid, hard-working, funny personality she'd come to know through his letters. For heaven's sake, he'd thought of himself as a laborer. She worried the catalog cover fanned exaggerated accounts of Vincent's mental illness, though Holst vigorously denied it.

Jo spun away from the tables and scanned the hall, fighting a familiar pang of regret. She should have been here when Holst had written her that he wanted to brighten the space before the exhibit's opening. Another one of her mistakes. Instead of brighter gas light as she'd assumed, he'd hired the artist Henry van de Velde to cover the Panorama walls with bolts and bolts of ugly blue-green fabric. Vincent had been so specific about white frames on a neutral background in his letters; she could imagine his blunt irritation if he'd seen it. And Theo's laugh.

She'd hesitated, distracted by Villa Helma business or Vincentje—she couldn't remember exactly. Just that Holst had slid the change in behind her back.

The worst part was she needed him. There was no way she could pull off an Amsterdam show and run the guesthouse in Bussum. It was all she could do to eke out a few hours of playtime with Vincentje as it was. Still, she had no one to blame for the sensational catalog and lurid fabric but herself.

Holst swished past her to the table. "My Dutch martyr," he moaned, picking up a catalog to admire the cover.

Jo cringed. Holst cared less about the individual paintings and more about making his own mark. This exhibition had been a chance for him to preen and prance around the gallery expounding on Vincent as if he was an expert. After Jo had spent two years defending Vincent, it was grating to hear his name spoken with such hushed self-serving reverence.

Vincent would have raked Holst over the coals. He'd been abrasively honest.

Earlier that morning, waking past midnight, a sudden fierce longing had seized her. She wanted to stand in the Panorama alone. She and Theo and Vincent with the artwork out in the open instead of closed in crates or hidden in the attic. Last week had been the second anniversary of Theo's death. Perhaps today they could have a reunion of sorts, even if bittersweet. For with every exhibit, every sale, the ache of Theo's absence magnified. After ten years of supporting his brother, neither he nor Vincent had ever experienced a reception like this.

Despite catching the earliest train to Amsterdam, she'd found Holst in the Panorama when she'd arrived. Did he sleep here?

Holst materialized at her side. "You have excellent timing this morning. I want to talk to you," he said smoothly. Out of the corner of her eye, Jo saw the waiting workman yawn and stretch his arms behind his back, then lean back against the wall. "I've been making arrangements for my next Van Gogh exhibit. Perhaps in Rotterdam—"

She looked him in the eye. "No, Meneer Holst. I want the next exhibit to be in Paris." She raised a hand to forestall his argument. "Vincent loved France. And Paris has more buyers."

"I have no contacts there! You need art dealers, my dear—"

"My brother lives in Paris. He's my intermediary." Dries lived in Paris, true, but he would be her intermediary in name only. He was much too harebrained for the art business, but at least she could convince him to do what she asked.

"The French are all money grubbers," grumbled Holst.

He was missing the point. Paris was the heart of the art world. She would never keep Vincent out of France, no matter how arrogant the art dealers were there, like Georges Raulf. She was beginning to understand how unique Theo had been in caring so much about the art. For the one thing Holst and Raulf had in common was that they were both out for themselves.

That and their grating, patronizing tone. On cue, Holst purred, "You don't know what's best, my dear. True art is idealistic. Vincent is appreciated by his own countrymen. We Dutch understand our own. Vincent is a true artist. He emphasized purity. Clear form. The French are obsessed with the past. We Dutch are the progressive ones."

Progressive. How was Holst progressive? He thought of Vincent as a tragic, romantic martyr from the past. Some sort of dead symbol of national talent. A true artist? Raulf had considered Vincent one among thousands of nameless mediocre artists. She knew better than both these men. Vincent had been flesh and blood, driven by an unquenchable impulse to create. An insatiable zeal to express energy, life, and love using only the awkward, limited tools of paint and brush and canvas.

He'd painted in all types of weather. His face had peeled from sunburn. He'd brushed away interminable gnats and sand stuck to his paint. Mistral winds would whip and rattle his canvas. Dogged by aching shoulders and gaunt hunger and hollow loneliness, he'd lived on coffee and bread and beer. He'd been a machine in his work, rarely satisfied. Every day he'd turned to a fresh canvas to try once more. *Working with as much cold-bloodedness as I can muster,* he'd written.

Those words barely captured it.

This was the Vincent she knew. Not a romantic martyr.

How could she help others see Vincent as himself? See the man Theo had seen?

Jo jumped as Holst's hand closed over her elbow. With a pull, they began walking along the Panorama's perimeter of paintings.

"Your *buyers* have all been Dutch patriots," he sniffed. "*I* cultivated them."

"I *am* grateful, Meneer Holst. I gave you a drawing—"

Holst abruptly halted. "Of course, I appreciate the *token*, but quite frankly, I assumed it was merely a gesture. Hardly an equal measure to all my efforts." His fingers slid down his mustache.

"I thought you admired the Arles landscape!" She could swear he'd been pleased when she'd surprised him with the drawing. He'd practically hummed.

He shrugged. "It doesn't fit over the mantel. And I can't have it hanging alone. It doesn't work aesthetically." Deliberately, he looked at the painting before them, then back to Jo. Her eyes followed his.

Golden oranges and greens glowed as if lit from within. Bold blue vertical lines sliced through the tranquil setting. Figures dwarfed by the landscape walked below. *Les Alyscamps*. Painted in Arles after Paul Gauguin had roomed with Vincent. Jo gazed at the colorful scene. She knew it well. One of three studies of falling leaves in an avenue of poplars. When she'd pulled it out in the attic, she could swear its lovely light had shimmered.

Jo looked sideways at Holst. His lip quivered, staring greedily at the painting. His avarice repelled her. The naked grubbiness of his want. And the worst part was she knew he would squirrel it away, granting permission only to a lucky few to see it. Using the painting to bolster his ego. His fingers smoothed his mustache.

Perhaps she could use his greed to her advantage.

"May I offer you this painting, Meneer Holst?" She added a veneer of modesty to her voice. Instantly, his face blossomed with magnanimity. "*With* your agreement that I may borrow it whenever I need it for future exhibitions?" He drew a quick intake of breath.

"Naturally, it would be labeled appropriately: on loan from Richard Roland Holst."

"From the *private collection* of Richard Roland Holst."

"Of course."

"A true artist," Holst repeated happily.

True artist. She gritted her teeth. There was that phrase heavy with judgment again. Raulf had sneered. *A true artist sells internationally and hangs in museums.*

Jo sucked in a breath. *Sells internationally. Hangs in museums.*

Of course. Enough of begging random halls to show Vincent. Enough of dealing with people like Holst making money by climbing on Vincent's back. She'd already proven that Vincent's work would sell. She'd already seen his exhibits fill with curious people. Why not aspire for more—get Vincent in front of many more people.

Jo eyed Holst's greedy stare at *Les Alyscamps*. It was up to her to ensure Vincent's work did not disappear into private homes.

"Meneer Holst, thank you for offering to manage more exhibitions. However, I don't want them right now."

"But—"

"You're wrong, you know. Saying I don't know what I want. I know *exactly* what I'm doing. Vincent's work needs to be sold overseas, not only in Holland. And I'm going to see to it that his art hangs in museums."

Holst's laugh barked humorlessly. "My dear little bereaved widow, you are both out of your mind and over your head. You have no idea how hard this work is—"

"I'm certain of this decision. International sales. Museums." The idea felt complete, neat, as if she'd been working on a puzzle and suddenly the overall picture emerged. The rest of the pieces could simply fall into place.

She spoke her next steps out loud, "The first step is to concentrate on Paris. Vincent's work needs that foothold among dealers to be able to introduce him to other galleries in other countries. Museums will take notice when his work becomes more visible." Her eyes met Holst's. "Paris is key."

"I *told* you. I don't have contacts in Paris. Vincent is from *Nuenen*. Full of backwoods and farms, for god's sake. No art dealer outside of Holland will care about him as we do. No one will listen to *you*."

"Maybe not to *me*." Jo remembered how close she'd felt to Vincent after she'd read the last of his letters. Even now, she could hear his voice inside her head. His notes had turned Jan into an ally. If she could get his letters into broad distribution, in a book or magazine, Vincent could speak for himself. Like a key, his words could open Paris's closed doors.

She turned to Holst. "I'm going to try to publish Vincent's letters. After reading them, I feel like I know him. The letters will open up people's hearts."

"Isn't that just like a woman? So emotional! Judging art is a *learned* craft. Not some sentimental mush."

"I am hardly sentimen—"

"No! Vincent deserves to be understood by his work alone. All of us who see the work *outside* of the person, admire the mighty rigor, the Old Testament strength in him."

"You're missing my point—"

"Vincent's dramatic power is so strong that even his most tender subjects, like the flowering orchards, become works of great intensity." He whipped the catalog out from under his arm and smacked the sunflower drawing. "Vincent should be elevated to the Dutch hero he is. I have the influence to do this. You have no one in Paris." Holst pressed his mustache. "Who would listen to a boardinghouse widow from Bussum?"

Jo looked Holst in the eye. "Émile Bernard is in Paris. He's spoken of publishing the letters Vincent wrote him into the *Mercure*."

"*Mercure!*"

"I have letters too. If Parisians read Vincent's words, they'll get to know him. I can get this done." With the literary magazine's help—and a little luck—Vincent would enter the hearts and minds of art lovers in Paris. She was sure of it.

SUNFLOWERS IN A VASE

———◆———

I'm painting with the gusto of a Marseillais eating bouillabaisse, which won't surprise you when it's a question of painting large SUNFLOWERS. . . . I work on it all these mornings, from sunrise. Because the flowers wilt quickly and it's a matter of doing the whole thing in one go. . . . I'd like to paint in such a way that if it comes to it, everyone who has eyes could understand it.

—VINCENT VAN GOGH, *August 21 or 22, 1888*

Spring 1893
to
Winter 1896

NINETEEN

BUSSUM

Jo

JO SHIFTED HER WEIGHT, WILLING HERSELF TO SIT STILL. SHE still hadn't mastered the knack of moving from polite chitchat to business topics. The art dealer George Seligmann had arrived all the way from Denmark to hand-carry paintings back with him to a show in Copenhagen. Now he was sitting in her parlor, munching on a square of Cook's honey cake.

Fiddling with the latest copy of *Le Mercure de France* on her lap, Jo searched for the right words to impress Seligmann. Den Frie Udstilling was her first international show outside Paris. He swallowed; Jo pounced.

"I'm so grateful to Meneer Rohde for bringing Vincent to the Danish public."

Seligmann slurped a sip of coffee. "Your brother-in-law's *Wheatfield after a Storm* created a stir. It's one of Johan's prized possessions."

"Meneer Rohde's purchase was the one sale I received from the Haagse Kunstkring a year ago."

"Indeed. It inspired Johan's vision. He wants Den Frie Udstilling to be a leader in Denmark's embrace of modern art."

"Theo always said the Danes' taste for modern art was a perfect fit to appreciate Vincent's work." Jo was delighted he'd picked up on her overture.

With a little finger, Seligmann picked a crumb from his teeth. He smiled and shook his head. "You ladies . . ." He chuckled and waved his hand as if swatting a fly. "No need to flatter me. I do have another *promising* topic to broach with you."

A second show. Jo could hardly believe it. Her plan for Vincent to be seen internationally was working. She knew Vincent was making a sensation by the Copenhagen newspaper articles Rohde had sent her.

Seligmann cleared his throat. "Johan is pleased that Vincent has generated positive reviews. Excellent discussion and debate as he hoped. But my dear, reviews are not enough. Debate is not enough. Art is *commerce*. Den Frie Udstilling is an artistic and commercial enterprise." He paused, and she felt a *but* coming. "As you know, we have no *sales*. And that's your fault," he added.

Jo blinked at the unexpected turn in the conversation. "My fault?"

He waved his hand. "You don't know the art market like we do. You've simply set prices that are too high."

"I've already corresponded with Meneer Rohde about this."

"You're scaring off buyers."

"I don't price in a vacuum." She patted the French and Dutch art magazines stacked beside her. *Le Mercure de France. De Amsterdammer. De Nieuwe Gids.* She read each one cover to cover as soon as they arrived in the mail.

He eyed the dog-eared journals. "*Reading* is not the same as *working in the trade*, dear. Vincent is *unknown*. Collectors expect lower prices."

Jo bristled. "Vincent is not like other artists."

"You make my point! His work is different. He creates conversation—we'll grant you that—but don't confuse being *controversial* with being *marketable*. He doesn't fit into the current market. You can't expect collectors to pay top dollar for an outlier." Seligmann sat back in his chair and reached for another honey cake. "We *know* Copenhagen prices." He raised his chin. "What's that on your lap? *Le Mercure?*" He gave a humorless bark. "Don't get me started on the Parisians! Snooty, arrogant crooks! The Danes are different, more discriminating. Honest. Frugal." He sniffed. "You're turning off Danish collectors. If you can't sell them in Copenhagen, you don't have a prayer in Paris."

"But I do know the Parisian market," Jo insisted. "Vincent is known in Paris." He hadn't noticed the *Mercure* articles on Vincent, she realized. So much for being an international scholar.

She flipped the magazine to the latest feature article on Vincent— she'd supplied the letters —all from Arles, plus Vincent's drawings to accompany his text. Tumultuous and tragic. As good as one of George Eliot's novels, but Seligmann waved away the proffered magazine.

Jo eyed him. How had their conversation turned sideways so quickly? She wanted to cultivate him and Rohde as allies, not anger them.

She needed this international show.

"No, no, dear. It takes years for a living artist to become noted in Paris. If he's dead, you need a century." He scooted forward. "It's one thing for you Dutch to honor Vincent. He's your own country-man. Perhaps you think he elevates the Dutch in some way?"

"I don't allow Vincent to be used as a political tool."

"No?" He brushed cake crumbs from his fingers. "Don't think I can't recognize manipulation. Can you deny that your catalog cover was . . . *sympathetic?*" He nodded at the corner of the Panorama catalog under her magazines.

"I didn't approve of that illustration." Her voice sounded small, even inside her head. She pressed *Le Mercure de France* to her chest.

Seligmann clamped his lips tight as if suppressing a laugh.

Honey cake crumbs glistened on the crest of his protruding stomach. "No one in Paris will give Vincent a second thought. That series will be forgotten by winter."

Confidence waning, Jo resisted handing him a napkin. If Seligmann hadn't bothered to read the *Mercure de France* series, Denmark was further away from the international outpost she'd hoped for Vincent.

Still, she couldn't afford to throw away her first international contacts.

Gripping the arms of the wicker chair, she forced herself to respond with calm. "About the pricing. As I wrote to Meneer Rohde, I'm willing to receive offers."

"Johan says—"

"And to consider discounting if a buyer wants to buy *two* paintings." Jo raised her voice. "Or a *combination* of a painting and drawing."

"I thought you wanted a second show in Copenhagen? You're being quite *argumentative* for someone who needs us."

The cords of wicker dug into her palms. She'd gushed in her letters to Rohde. He knew how much she wanted Vincent to be seen overseas. She hadn't dreamed they would hold it over her head to get their way.

She kept her voice low. "Give the show time, Meneer Seligmann."

"I'm done!" Seligmann set down his coffee cup with a loud clatter. "I'll deliver your refusal. As I warned him this would happen." He sniffed, glancing around. "You're a woman in a backwater Dutch town. You can't go it alone. You'll find out that in this business, you need friends."

TWENTY

BUSSUM

Jo

ON THE LAST DAY OF AUGUST, JO STROLLED THROUGH BUSSUM'S square with her neighbors Anna and Martha van Eeden. On either side of their path, local farmers stood behind heaps of tender carrots, round yellow potatoes, and limp spinach. Three-year-olds Vincentje and Saskia held hands, skipping ahead. For once, Jo had come to the marketplace without a shopping list for Villa Helma. Ridiculously, the small gesture made her feel like a girl again, with no concerns or responsibilities for a few hours. She linked her arm into Martha's and beamed at Anna, who cradled her latest baby swaddled to her chest.

"I found a silver hair this morning," Jo confided.

"At least you've kept your youthful figure," Martha said and patted her own thick waist.

"My feet are bigger!—thanks to this little one." Anna rested her hand on her baby's head. The three friends laughed.

"I can't see how women are expected to do it all *and* look like a French model. I do believe in women's equality with all my heart, but I can't deny it does my body good to be released from that devilish corset. Oh, look . . ." Martha stopped. "Those farmwives are chatting." Anna and Jo followed Martha's eyes and listened for a moment to the cheerful rise and fall of the peasants' chatter. "I'm so glad! For once, they're taking a break. Those women labor from dawn to dusk."

"All farmers are having a tough time of it now. And if their men have come to town to work, the women have twice the workload," Jo said.

"Women's work isn't recognized." Anna nodded. "Jan hasn't a clue about all I do. And look at you, Jo! You care for Vincentje *and* run a boardinghouse."

"And she's an art dealer," Martha added with a ring of pride. "By the way, how's that going?"

"Not as well as I'd hoped by now."

Anna frowned. "But Jan says the *Mercure* editor is brilliant. His articles must create new interest every time an issue hits the newsstand."

"They do," Jo said, deciding not to take credit for the articles. "Dries handles the inquiries."

"Are you getting sales, then?" Anna exclaimed. Jo felt a groundswell of love. Anna had come around to accepting that Jo should be selling.

"Not yet. The buyers always ask for ridiculously low prices. Dries tells me all I do is irritate them by refusing their offers," Jo explained.

"You don't do what your brother says?" asked Anna, surprised.

"The higher the prices, the better for Vincentje's inheritance."

"You are a New Woman!" said Martha. "You stand your ground!"

"I suppose . . ." Jo sometimes wondered whether she was right or simply stubborn.

"But aren't the paintings being sold overseas?" Anna persisted.

"Well, yes and no." Jo hesitated. "I had a show in Copenhagen in the spring, but there were no sales. Then Vincent got a write-up in a Flemish magazine, *Van Nu en Straks*. It was marvelous." She glanced at Anna. Anything she said would get to Jan's ears. She decided to boast anyway. "They were going to do a simple article, but I convinced them to devote the entire issue to Vincent. I sent excerpts from thirteen of Vincent's letters and three reproductions of drawings." She stopped and tested a melon at a stall. "I've been hoping for an invitation to do a show in Helsinki, but so far, nothing."

"I've heard of *Van Nu en Straks*," Martha said. "It's socialist, isn't it?"

"The editor believes that when the working class is exposed to high culture, differences in class can be reduced."

"This makes sense to me." Martha nodded vigorously. "I believe art can be an equalizer between classes. Why should an educated person be more moved by art than a poor one?"

"Jan thinks—"

"Anna! We don't want Jan's opinion. What do *you* think?"

Before she could answer, Vincentje's scream pierced the air. In an instant, Jo raced toward his voice.

Vincentje's small struggling body was lifted high in the air above a stranger's head. A threadbare jacket hung from the stranger's thin body. His face was half-hidden behind a mass of straggly black beard. Stumbling, he weaved toward the edge of the canal. Saskia screamed and pulled on the man's loose pant legs with her fists.

"Get rid of thish pest," he slurred. With a backward kick, Saskia was sent sprawling. He twisted, lifting Vincentje over the canal. Jo sucked in a breath, but before she could scream, two men tackled the stranger, one grabbing the man, the other yanking Vincentje out of his hands. Like a bullet, Vincentje tore to Jo. She caught him in a hard hug.

"Drunk in the middle of the day!" Martha scolded, raising her voice over the children's wails as they clung to their mothers' skirts. "We need to do something about this!"

"Do? What could we do?" Jo asked as she soothed Vincentje.

"Alcohol is evil. It tears apart families. Causes crime. Frightens children! If people were educated about this, we could build a society that gets rid of this blight. I'm going to put a temperance booth up in the square."

"A temperance booth in the middle of town? In broad daylight?" Jo looked at Anna.

"You'll be quite unpopular," observed Anna.

Martha put her hands on her hips. "Who will join me?" She looked straight at Jo.

TWENTY-ONE

LEIDEN

Jo

"FASTER! FASTER!" VINCENTJE'S DELIGHTED SQUEAL MADE JO laugh out loud at the New Year's Eve party.

Dancing wildly in a rocky circle with Cor's sweaty hand gripping Jo's on one side and little four-year-old Vincentje's on the other, they skipped and spun, mouths aching from laughter. Cor looked so much like his brother Theo. Tipsy, with half-open eyes Jo pretended that Theo danced with her.

"Freedom! Freedom! Long may it reign!" Cor sang at the top of his lungs.

"Shush, Cor!" Mother scolded with a smile. "The neighbors!"

"Freedom! Freedom! Long may it reign!" Wil's soprano cut through the air. She lifted her skirts up to her knees, revealing pretty white stockings, and danced a little jig.

"Wil!" Mother's voice rose an octave, stopping the dance.

"Don't you want me to dance, Mother?" A smile played on Wil's lips.

"Cor, control your sister."

Jo scarcely recognized Wil. Her cheeks glowed with pink. She'd tied her long brown hair back with a bright blue bow matching the trim of her dress. Marie Mensing stood next to her, tapping her foot to Cor's song. Catching Marie's eye, Jo mouthed, *Thank you*. Laughingly, Marie shook her head, but Jo was sure her encouragement of Wil to join a local women's group had something to do with the change in her.

"Vincentje's a little man!" Cor said, and they turned to watch Vincentje carrying a glass of lemonade to Mother. Jo could see him concentrating on not spilling a drop.

"He needs a man to look up to," she said.

Cor turned to her. "Not me, Jo. There's a fire in my belly. Have you heard? I'm going to South Africa!"

"So far away! Mother must be upset."

"Not really. When I told her I got an engineering job with the Cornucopia Gold Company, she said, 'Try not to fail this time.'"

"Cor—"

"Who could blame her? I can't seem to keep a job. Apprentice in Helmond, a half dozen jobs in London. That factory in Lincoln."

"There's nothing wrong with trying out different work."

"I wasn't trying it out. I hated it. I couldn't stomach being a boss man. The way I was expected to treat workers was appalling."

"I feel exactly the same way—ever since I was a little girl. I remember going to the docks one day with my brother Henry and crying when I saw men prodded and beaten for who knows what. When I pleaded with my father to do something about it, he only shrugged and said, 'That's how industry works.' I've never understood it."

"At least you're a woman. You're expected to have a finer sensibility. I swear my father turns in his grave every time I change jobs. Men are supposed to be providers. And I'm not doing much of that yet." He looked across the room at Wil and Mother. "But I will soon, Jo. I want to send money back home like Theo did. To Mother and Wil and you."

"Not to me, Cor. I'm doing all right." She seized his arm. "Let me be the first to say that Corn . . . wait, what's its name?"

"The Cornucopia Gold Company—"

"Is lucky to have you!" She lifted her glass.

"*Proost!*" They clinked glasses. "I do wonder what it will be like to work in a British Colony."

"Does this company practice forced labor?"

"Probably." Cor nodded. "I'm no fool. I hope the British are more open to new ways of doing things. All I know is I can't stay here working in jobs I dislike. I need to do something that makes a difference. Mark my words, Jo—South Africa is it. A new frontier."

"*It's just nonsense to say that there's nothing to be done.*"

"What's that?"

"Oh! So sorry! I'm quoting a sentence out of one of Vincent's letters."

"I like it. Fits my mind perfectly," he winked. "Now, where's that nephew of mine? I promised him some gymnastics!"

As Cor crossed the room to Vincentje, Marie sidled up to Jo and handed her a glass of whiskey.

Jo raised her eyebrows. Studying Marie's eyes, in unspoken unison they threw the shots back together. Jo sputtered as a trail of fire burned her throat.

"Your face is so serious." Marie poked Jo under her ribs. "You needn't be so worried. Cor's plan is admirable."

"Colonizing people in their own lands never made sense to me." Jo watched Wil sitting alongside Mother across the room, laughing as Cor swung Vincentje up onto his shoulders. She couldn't have imagined Wil bearing the news of Cor living halfway around the world so easily, yet here she was, enjoying herself. Cor grabbed Vincentje's wrists and somersaulted him onto the floor. The women burst into applause.

"Again!" Vincentje demanded, hopping on one foot after the other until Cor lifted him up.

"I'm so proud of Cor," Jo said to Marie. "He's standing up for what he believes in. He's trying to make the world a better place."

"Ordinary people can do extraordinary things. It runs in the family." She poked Jo.

"You don't know me, Marie. I'm a failure! I accomplished nothing this past year."

"I don't believe it!"

"It's true. I've made mistake after mistake." Jo felt the urge to make Marie understand, to confess all of her failures. "I had this crazy thought to try to get Vincent into the hands of art dealers overseas, in other countries. And someday have Vincent's work hang in a museum. This year I had some interest—or so I thought. I'd hoped Copenhagen or Helsinki or London would be receptive, but—"

"Why are you letting *them* decide?"

Jo stared back at Marie. "That's the way it works! Dealers are doorways to getting Vincent's work shown. I can't bypass them."

Marie raised an eyebrow. "Perhaps you're focused on the wrong things?"

"You have no idea. You're so confident about being a 'New Woman.' Well, I'm not. How can women be new when the rules remain old? How can women have new roles when the old rules remain set in stone?" Jo softened her voice. "I've learned since I saw you last, Marie. Men can agree with me and then turn around, *lie to my face*, and do exactly as they please."

"It's a new world—"

"Not for me. Not in Bussum. The old world is alive and well."

"Says who? You create the world you observe. If all you see are limitations and rules, then all you'll experience are limitations and rules."

"What do you mean?"

"You see doors shut. I see a public that's curious about Vincent because his name has appeared again and again in *Mercure*. Because of you. And not only his name—but his drawings. Images that Wil told me you hand-picked to tell the story *you wanted* about him. Along with excerpts from his letters. I read every issue when it comes out. I feel like I know him. His letters are intimate and revealing."

Jo pressed her lips together. This was the first time anyone had acknowledged how she had influenced the series.

Marie said quietly, "Vincent is one of us, you know."

"What?"

"A socialist. A rebel for the working class."

"No—" Jo shook her head, but she felt her body tremble.

"What you pay attention to is what will come about. The art dealers in Paris are only an obstacle if you give them that power."

"You're not being realistic. Of course art dealers have all the power. And it's all well and good that Vincent's name ran in *Mercure*, but if the dealers won't sell his art—at decent prices—then Vincentje's inheritance is no closer to being realized, and Vincent is still unknown."

"Tsk, tsk. Old rules. *You're* enforcing the obstacles, not *them*."

Irritated, Jo remembered how Theo had struggled to bring Impressionist art buyers into the gallery. "You don't know Paris as I do."

"Let me give you another example. Do you have a lover?"

Jo could feel her cheeks heat up. "Of course not! I'm a widow."

"Theo's been gone for three years."

"I don't want to remarry."

"Who said anything about marriage? I asked you about a *lover*. Don't you miss being touched? Feeling transported—"

"Stop!" Jo's cheeks reddened. "I told you! Not another marriage."

"*Who said anything about marriage?* We've been taught to view the world a certain way. Men make the decisions; women obey what the men say. Men think women should only be making love when they have a husband. Otherwise, she's a prostitute. But who wrote those rules? The ones who have everything to lose by allowing women more freedom."

Heat radiated from Jo's face. She felt conflicted—one voice in her head said Marie was scandalous. The other voice argued that Marie made sense. Across the room Mother was laughing with Wil. She'd be horrified to overhear them.

Marie leaned closer. "Have you ever felt invisible?"

"Only every day when it comes to Paris dealers. It's only when I disagree with a painting's price that I have any say-so."

"That's because widow-inheritance laws preserve that right for you."

"Those laws also make it possible for me to run Villa Helma."

"Yes! The law and our culture make it *acceptable* for you to run a boardinghouse. But recognize you've defied convention by choosing to do that instead of moving back under your father's roof."

"I'll grant it was unusual." Jo shuddered. "But you don't know my father. He would have run every detail of my life."

Marie's voice became gentle. "You have an entire life ahead of you. No man should be a barrier between you and what you want."

Even as Marie's words were unsettling, there was something about them that drew her in. If only Marie's view of the world was true.

Vincentje launched himself at Jo's legs. She stumbled back, breaking their conversation. She brushed her son's hair away from his sweaty forehead. Cor grabbed Marie's hand and twirled her into the center of the room, while Wil clapped to the music beat. Jo laughed and joined in. Marie didn't know what she was talking about. She was single, working for her sister at a girls' school. She didn't know what it was like to be in commerce.

Jo needed Paris. It was all well and good that *Le Mercure de France* readers knew about Vincent. She needed people of influence to back him too. Paris was her mark. Still, Marie's question intrigued her. If the Parisian art dealers were blocking the doorways, maybe she could find another way in? Given that Paris was the lynchpin to getting Vincent's paintings into museums and other countries, perhaps she'd been too impatient. Copenhagen had shown her that Vincent drew curiosity seekers but no buyers. She needed Vincent to be taken seriously. She needed him to be accepted by the establishment.

Marie could allow herself to be a New Woman from the safety of a girls' school. Paris's art world had more in common with Pa's hostile world of dockyards and warehouses and rough men.

She shouldn't have been surprised it was so difficult to gain entry.

But perhaps there was more than one way to get into Paris. If there was, she was determined to find it.

TWENTY-TWO

PARIS

Raulf

"MADAME TANGUY," RAULF SAID, SLIGHTLY OUT OF BREATH. He swept the bowler hat off his head and pressed it to his chest. "My condolences on the death of your husband." He dipped his chin.

News of Père Tanguy's death had flashed along the dealer grapevine. It was the break Raulf had been looking for. Tanguy had a large supply of Van Gogh paintings, and he was determined to relieve the widow—and Paris—of the stash.

His patience in waiting to rid the city of this vile art would be rewarded, assuming he could get through to Tanguy's little wife.

Carefully opening one eye, Raulf peeked down at the widow. As wide as she was short, the stout woman stared at him stonily with hands on her hips. A mop of salt-and-pepper curls spilled out from under a sloppily tied kerchief. His perfunctory solicitude felt a little flat, out of place after his harrowing walk from rue Laffitte's elegant storefronts to the Tanguy paint shop, dodging horse manure, packed wagons teetering with haphazard goods—stacks of boots, wheels of cheese—and throngs of running children, all on cramped streets lined with black snow. His boots would need a good cleaning.

If his visit was successful, it would be worth a little excrement. He resisted the urge to take out his pocket watch to check the time. His business with Tanguy's widow wouldn't take long. He held out his hand to give hers a comforting squeeze.

But Madame Tanguy didn't budge. His hand dangled in the charged air between them.

"I don't know you," she said. Her voice was flat, unemotional.

Raulf hastily fiddled with unbuttoning his overcoat to cover her snub. Inhaling sharply, he immediately fell into a coughing fit. Pungent odor permeated the Tanguy paint shop. He'd forgotten how pervasive turpentine could bite at one's throat. Peering out from his hastily applied handkerchief into the shadows behind the widow, he made out clusters of squared canvases stacked haphazardly against leaning easels and tall barrels of scattered paint tubes. In the shafts of light, he could make out how thick dust had settled onto disorderly shelves where paintboxes, palettes, and wood-handled brushes lay jumbled together. At their feet, a scuffed, unwashed floor bore the black marks of ground-in mud next to new puddles of melted snow.

No wonder modern art was so repulsive. This shop exactly reflected its appalling nature. A visual representation of how it dishonored his trade. With fresh resolve he determinedly removed the handkerchief from his nose. The sooner he got through his business in this hellhole, the better, and judging from the clutter of the shop, he was in luck. The widow could use money.

"Georges Raulf, Madame," he began again. "A principal of Boussod Valadon and Cie art dealers. Your husband and I were colleagues."

"I doubt that."

Raulf rubbed his hands together to give himself time to gather his wits. These damn hardened lower-class women didn't know how to speak to a gentleman. He sucked in his irritation. He'd schooled himself to be patient as Père had. Ever since the *Mercure* series had stirred up ridiculous curiosity around Van Gogh, he'd had to bide his time. Père had always promised patience would deliver.

"Let me be more accurate," Raulf conceded. "I knew *of* your husband. This . . ." He scanned the room, looking for the right word. "*Establishment* is known among art dealers as a gallery that carries a collection of rising talent."

"You mean *unsalable* talent?" The widow sprang to life. He'd struck a nerve. "Tanguy was a sucker for a poor artist's story. *I'm* the one that kept this place afloat. Not Tanguy."

Even better. No artistic sensibility here. Business sense. He warmed to her. They had common ground.

"Then I'm speaking to the right person. Let me get right to the point—I'd like to take some paintings off your hands. The ones by a Dutch artist. Vincent van Gogh."

"The madman? Why him?"

Raulf shrugged his shoulders, thinking fast. He hadn't presumed he'd have to explain himself. "I know . . . *knew* his brother, Theo van Gogh. He worked for me."

The widow blinked, waiting.

"I know his widow," he added.

"Pfft!" She erupted as if he'd kicked her. Chuffing for breath, she shook a finger at him. "That meddler! Doesn't know her place! Pestering Tanguy constantly with requests all the way from Holland. Couldn't leave well enough alone. It upset him! I told him to ignore her."

A smile tugged Raulf's mouth. He'd found an ally.

"Well, good riddance," she continued. "You can have them. Tanguy sold a few paintings right after Van Gogh's death, but not much since." She glanced over her shoulder as if the shop had eavesdroppers and dropped her voice. "I tried to get Tanguy to dump them, but he and Van Gogh were friends. Tanguy went to his deathbed, you know? That's when Theo asked if he'd take the whole lot painted in Auvers. Ornery man, that Vincent, but I still don't wish his death on anyone." She grimaced. "Gunshot wound to the gut. Lingered two days."

She grew quiet, her eyes distant and remembering. "He painted portraits of Tanguy." She looked at Raulf. "I'll keep them," she added quickly.

"Fine. Excellent." Raulf couldn't believe how easy his errand had turned out to be. He rubbed his hands. "You need to transfer all the Van Goghs you have to the Durand-Ruel Gallery."

"Durand-Ruel! Hoity-toity!" She examined Raulf. "Van Gogh's a curiosity—I'll grant you that. The *Mercure* stories have brought a few people into the shop. No buyers though. What is it that *you* know? Why do you want them?"

Raulf fought to mask his annoyance at her barrage of questions. "Madame, I—"

"Never mind. I don't care. But whatever you're up to, I want a piece of it." She turned. "Follow me and I'll show you to the attic."

"To the . . . attic?"

"You don't expect me to do your work for you, do you?" She stepped behind him and opened a door, revealing a narrow winding staircase. Sweeping aside threads of abandoned spiderwebs, she hustled up the stairs. Raulf sighed and followed, taking care not to brush his shoulders against the stairwell's coal-darkened walls.

Over the next hour, Raulf set aside painting after painting under Madame Tanguy's watchful eye. Even in the attic's dim light, he could discern these paintings were shockingly different from the few he'd seen. Intense, dramatic lines. Deep, strong brushstrokes in vivid color. The striking jagged outline of a church in Auvers. A wheatfield alive with wind rolling the golden stalks as black crows rise in flight. Van Gogh's style had evolved into an intense energy that seemed to reverberate off the canvas. Raulf tilted a painting of a man leaning on his hand, pensive and wistful.

"Van Gogh's doctor." The widow's voice came from behind him. She stepped up to his shoulder. "Paul Gachet. He fancied himself an amateur artist. Let's hope he was a better doctor."

Raulf took a few seconds more. He couldn't take his eyes off it.

None of the various blues competed with each other. Intermittent, forceful brushstrokes of other colors broke them up. Had he seen this way of applying paint before? And the image of the man himself. Pensive, melancholy, somehow complex. It was vastly different from the fine art he'd grown accustomed to.

Looking up, he caught Madame Tanguy studying him.

"Like what you see?" Her voice was low and calculating.

He shrugged his shoulder, feigning indifference. "As you said, Van Gogh's a curiosity. Nothing more." He looked at the number of paintings they'd dragged to one side of the attic. Forty, even fifty. For being a failure, the man had been a machine when it came to painting. He'd have to warn Durand-Ruel to clear space in his back room. "This about it?"

"Here, yes. There are others hither and thither in little galleries. No idea where."

He nodded. Lost among the thousands of failed paintings all through the city's back alleys. He wouldn't worry about those.

"And the ones in Arles," she added.

"Arles? In Provence?" He vaguely remembered the train station stop on his way to vacation on the Marseilles shore.

"Tanguy told me a café owner in the town has them. Another friend of Vincent's." She shrugged. "Unless he's destroyed them by now." She looked at Raulf sideways. "By the way, I expect my portion of the commission."

"Commission?"

She faced him, hands on her hips again. "I'm not my husband. Durand-Ruel has a different clientele up on rue Laffitte. There must be something to these paintings if *you're* concerned with them. I want my fair share." She sniffed. "Cover my storage fee."

Raulf grinned at her. "I can see you are a businesswoman, Madame." A sudden thought caused him to pause. "One more thing. I need you to get in touch with the widow's brother, Andries Bonger. I'll have my protégé come round with his name and calling card."

Handing her his own card, he continued, "Here's my information. You say the widow's a meddler? If the . . . *transport* . . . of these paintings is facilitated by her brother, I suspect she'll go along with it. Tell Bonger that Tanguy arranged it. We can get these paintings off your hands. You earn a commission without lifting a finger."

"Keeping your name out of it, I assume?"

"Let's say my name could cause questions."

Madame Tanguy studied him. "I don't know what you're up to, and I don't care. No skin off my nose, and since it clears this clutter out of the attic, all the better." She stuck out a grimy hand for him to shake. "Vincent was Tanguy's obsession. Not mine. Good riddance."

TWENTY-THREE

BUSSUM

Jo

"PAUL GAUGUIN!" JO BLURTED. SHE DIDN'T BOTHER MASKING her annoyance. She had enough to do on this blustery March day without the artist's unexpected visit. She knew he'd been back in Paris, having read about his irritating stunts on the society pages in more than one Paris newspaper. When he showed up in Bussum this morning without notice, acting as though his spur-of-the-moment stopover was a special favor, she was in no mood to tolerate a man who had wronged both Theo and Vincent.

At the very least his social exploits appeared to be keeping him well fed. His build had more in keeping with plump art dealers than a starving artist, though the elbows on his jacket sagged and had worn away into bald patches and his dark hair spilled over his coat collar. She doubted he remembered that they'd met before. Thinner, ill-mannered, he'd dropped in unannounced to see Theo at their apartment shortly after Vincentje had been born. While Theo had hastily put on a teapot, she'd disappeared into the bedroom to pace and sing nursery rhymes to keep the baby quiet.

Now as he circled her salon—pausing before each painting—her instinct was to make this visit as brief as possible. Towering before the artwork, he strolled with his hands shoved deep into his overcoat pockets—for Jo had expressly *not* offered to take his coat.

"Coffee, Mevrouw?" Standing in the doorway, Cook balanced a tray with a coffee pot, two cups, and a bowl of sugar cubes. She must have overheard their voices.

"Bless you!" Gauguin stepped forward.

Irritated, Jo grabbed the tray, swinging it out of his reach. She carried it to a side table across the room, away from *The Potato Eaters*. Oblivious to her irritation, Gauguin slung his coat on top of the sofa.

"I feel quite at home in this room." Gauguin smiled, reaching for a cup. "You may not know it, but Vincent and I were close friends."

"I know more than you think."

He blinked. "Theo too."

"I'm familiar," Jo cut him off. She hated that Ma's hostess drills overwhelmed her desire to throw Gauguin out. Instead she shoved the cup and saucer at him, sloshing the coffee over the rim. "Theo sold your work in his gallery. He paid you to be with Vincent while you delayed traveling to Arles. He paid you while you lived in Arles—"

"Hold on now! I paid Theo back in paintings."

"You were supposed to be Vincent's companion."

Gauguin flushed, surprised at her vehemence. "And I was! We painted each other's portraits!"

Jo remembered Isaac Israëls making the same claim and replied, "Many friends painted his portrait."

"I was not just any friend! We painted side by side for weeks."

"Sixty-one days." Jo savored a moment of triumph as Gauguin winced. "I am perfectly aware of *everything*. How Vincent dreamed of starting an art community. How lonely he was in Arles. How he longed for companions to paint alongside him during the day, debate art late into the night. Just like the circles of artists he joined up with in Paris. He was ecstatic when you agreed to come," Jo scolded.

She paused, recalling how Vincent's lonely letters made her heart ache, and dropped onto the sofa.

"I see Theo shared a lot with you—"

"And Vincent did too."

"Vincent? With you?" He eyed her. "I'm surprised." He sat down opposite her and dropped two lumps of sugar into his cup. "Your brother-in-law was difficult. He didn't discuss his feelings so much as yell them." He shook his head.

"That doesn't excuse—"

"No doubt, no doubt." He sipped. "Still, as a matter of business, I've come to claim the paintings Vincent gave me. There are three. Your husband was holding them for me."

Three paintings? Over her dead body. "I know nothing about this arrangement," Jo said coldly and stood up.

"Why would you?"

"You didn't pay for them." She knew their accounts inside and out.

"Pay?" Gauguin leaned forward. "Come, come, my dear. I *earned* those paintings. *I'm* the one who left a lucrative sponsorship to go to the south of France to be Vincent's nursemaid."

"You're the one who betrayed him."

The artist flushed. "Betrayed? *I'm* the one he berated in ridiculous arguments every single night. He was not an easy man to live with—I'll tell you that!"

"Apparently not, since you fled after he hurt himself!"

Gauguin leaped to his feet. "He was violent! He was waving a razor in my face!"

"He was ill! He cut off his ear! Nearly bled to death because you abandoned him!"

"*You weren't there.*" Gauguin hovered in her face, then dropped back into the chair. "You weren't there. Don't think I haven't relived that night over and over," he mumbled. He ran his hand over his face. "Everything you describe is right. I indeed stalled before going to Arles, but it's not what you think. Vincent was *intense*. His moodiness was legendary in Paris. It was exhausting being around him. Once he decided something . . ." With a humorless chuckle, Gauguin shook his head. "That man could argue and *would* argue, all night long. I remember one night I said that one could paint from imagination—one can be in nature and then paint one's recollection in the studio. I do it all the time! Oh, no, no. Vincent was adamant that one had to be *in the elements* to paint. The hours we spent under that infernal sun!"

"You couldn't see that he needed help?"

"There's a fine line between personality and madness."

"That's no excuse!"

"I guess I *expected* him to be difficult. I was in the middle of it. I had no perspective."

"'In the middle of it,' all right—he even bought new furniture for you. He decorated the walls with his sunflower paintings for you. He was so *happy* you were coming. He was so lonely." Her voice broke, remembering the yearning in his letters. It felt good to defend Vincent.

"In the beginning, it *was* marvelous," Gauguin admitted. "Vincent was so single-minded, so focused. Have you ever been around someone who inspires you to be better than you ever imagined yourself to be?"

Theo. She nodded.

"Vincent's intensity was intoxicating. I don't know that I've felt quite so alive ever since." He paused, running a finger around the rim of his cup. "Except maybe in Polynesia." He looked at her. "I need to get back there."

So, that was why he wanted the paintings. To sell them to raise funds.

She put her hands on her hips, feeling tall despite his height. "You want to sell Vincent's paintings, don't you? You need money. I know your show last fall didn't quite work out." She was being kind. The review in *Le Mercure de France* had been devastating. "Well, I don't believe you were promised any. Theo would have told me. So I'm not giving you any paintings."

"Oh, would he now?" Gauguin snapped. "Theo couldn't have told you *everything*. Vincent gave me three paintings in Arles. Your husband offered to store them."

"I wonder why he didn't leave them with the shop owner in Arles. Vincent's other paintings from that time are there."

Gauguin sniffed. "The three paintings are sentimental. I'm claiming them for personal reasons."

"You want the Van Gogh family to sponsor you again, don't you?"

"Vincent's work is hardly in demand."

"No? I just sold two paintings at the Durand-Ruel for five hundred fifty francs." She kept her eyes steady on Gauguin, enjoying the quick flash of surprise in his eyes. "Monsieur Durand-Ruel hosted your show last fall, didn't he?" she baited.

"You should feel fortunate that I want them. The word's out that Vincent's work is being passed around like a bad counterfeit coin."

"What does that mean?"

"Tanguy's widow is cleaning house. She sent all of her Van Gogh paintings to Durand-Ruel."

"I knew that—"

"Really? Looks like you paid a double commission for those sales—to Durand-Ruel *and* Madame Tanguy."

Jo was dumbstruck. No wonder Durand-Ruel's bill had been so high. First she'd had to read about Tanguy's death in the newspaper. Then Dries—with a decision completely out of character—had moved the Tanguy paintings to Durand-Ruel. On the one hand, the move to a top-tier dealer was wonderful, but on the other, it was mysterious. Why hadn't Dries explained it all? He was hopeless. She fumed. It was impossible to understand what was happening among the dealers in Paris. She needed better information. She was still on the outside; she needed someone inside.

You create what you observe. Was this what Marie had meant? She saw herself as an outsider, and so it was coming about. What if she could have an insider viewpoint—perhaps it could make a difference.

Jo took a sip of coffee to swallow her pride. She loathed Gauguin's narcissism, but that didn't mean he couldn't be useful.

"Monsieur Gauguin, tell me which three paintings Vincent gave you?"

Surprised, he blurted, "*La Berceuse*, *L'Arlésienne*, and *Wheatfield with a Reaper*."

Jo winced. Each one of Vincent's paintings felt like her own children. "*La Berceuse*, *L'Arlésienne*, and *Wheatfield with a Reaper*," she repeated heavily. "All right. You may have the three paintings on two—no, three—conditions."

"*You* have conditions?"

"You give me one of *your* paintings." Gauguin looked shocked. Jo quickly added, "The one of the woman on the riverbank." She'd seen it in *Le Mercure de France*.

Gauguin started to shake his head.

Jo raised her coffee cup to her lips. "*One* painting in exchange for *three* of Vincent's. I think that's generous, don't you?"

He grunted. "What else?"

"When I have an exhibition of Vincent's work in Paris, I'll expect you to loan me the three I'm giving you. The catalog will show that they're on loan from you. Showing it's part of your private collection will lend credibility to Vincent."

He grunted again. Jo doubted he would keep that promise. They'd probably be sold before then.

Gauguin tapped his coffee cup irritably. "And the third condition?"

"Write to me detailing as much as you can about Durand-Ruel's business. What paintings he's selling, and who his top clients are—especially those who are interested in Vincent's art. I need to fill in the gaps of what's been happening. Give me the news that's *not* reported in the newspaper." She took a piece of paper and pencil from her desk. "Where are you staying? I'll ship the paintings there."

"An apartment on rue Vercingétorix." He scribbled the address. "Do you know it?"

"Not far from where Theo and I lived," she said. "I'll send them as soon as I receive your letter on the dealers."

"*After* I write the letter?"

"Yes. Oh and . . ." With a sudden thought, Jo added, "Include any news you have about Boussod Valadon and Cie as well. Especially anything about Georges Raulf."

That night, Jo played with Vincentje long past his bedtime, tickling and tackling and playacting with his toy horse until he yawned and said, "Let's play more tomorrow, Mama."

She sat with him, listening as his breathing deepened into sleep while replaying Gauguin's visit in her mind. She still felt energized. Where had her anger come from? Standing up for Vincent had felt so good. Her ability to speak up like that with no second-guessing. Saying exactly what she'd thought. She'd scarcely recognized herself. Over and over, she replayed their argument, feeling an odd new satisfaction that she'd said everything that had come to her. She'd held nothing back.

What else?

A little idea crept on the outskirts of thought. Gauguin had reminded her that two years ago Isaac Israëls had told her he'd painted Vincent's portrait. She'd like to see it, she decided. But would he remember her?

He's a playboy, Anna's voice warned.

Jo stood up, silencing the voice. No more second-guessing. She would contact Israëls and invite him to come with the portrait to Villa Helma. This was exactly what she wanted.

She paused, glancing back at Vincentje's sleeping form.

Was this being a New Woman?

If so, she liked this New Jo.

TWENTY-FOUR

BUSSUM AND AMSTERDAM

HE CAME ON A SUNNY AFTERNOON WHEN THE AIR WAS HEAVY with the cloying weight of a thunderstorm brewing on the horizon. Isaac Israels was taller than she'd remembered, lanky, with dark hair tamed by a glistening pomade combed over a balding patch. He wore a fashionable dark suit with a white waistcoat and a dotted necktie she recognized from the pages of *La Mode Illustrée*. Now they stood in the hallway while he took in *Garden of the Hospital*, the last painting on their impromptu tour of Villa Helma's artwork.

"Your home is a museum, Jo." He smiled with his eyes. She was glad the corridor was in shadow. She didn't want him to see how her cheeks burned when he said her name. She scrambled to keep her wits.

"May I see the portrait?" she suggested. Marta had opened the door to his knock earlier. She'd been so flustered, so pleased to see him actually standing in her salon *in the flesh* that she'd instantly jabbered on about touring the paintings just to give her something else to look at. Now that she'd finally regained her equilibrium, she remembered her ruse to see him. Besides, she *did* want to see the portrait.

"I've been thinking of you." He placed his hand on the small of her back, pressing her to turn into the salon.

I've been thinking of you. His hand felt like fire.

She was enjoying this.

"Where is it?" Jo looked around the salon, expecting to see a rectangular parcel. She assumed Marta had placed it there.

Settling into a chair, Isaac crossed his legs and lifted his palms with a playful shrug. "I don't have it."

"You forgot it?"

"Never painted it, I'm afraid, but I wanted to."

"Wait, you told me at the Arti—"

"That brother-in-law of yours never stayed in one place long enough!"

Jo laughed and flushed again. She loved it that he'd lied to her. She wanted to hear him say it. "But then you came today . . ."

His eyes lingered. "To see you."

She shivered involuntarily.

He cocked his head, raising his eyebrows. "Should I go?"

She turned away, pressing her hands to her cheeks. They must've been flaming. *He's not marriage material,* Anna's voice echoed. She would be horrified Isaac had come to visit unchaperoned, let alone to flirt. Anna, Mother, Wil, her mother—their voices rose like a tidal wave of warning. Guilt swayed her. She might regret this later, but then again, he was here. In her salon. By her own volition.

Brazenly, she turned back to his grin. "Isaac!" His first name tripped off her tongue.

His eyes crinkled. "Yes?

"Come take a stroll with me in the back garden. Stay for dinner?"

His smile sent another shiver up her spine.

Nine months later, Jo stretched deliciously next to Isaac's warm body on his narrow bed. He lay on his stomach, tousled hair over his face, snoring.

The regular rhythm filled his small studio in Amsterdam. Soft footsteps vibrated through the ceiling. Was it the artist George Breitner again? Or Willem Kloos? Isaac's neighborhood was full of artists, coming and going. Sara de Swart had rented the upstairs studio for a while, but she'd arrived and left in between Jo's clandestine meetings.

Jo felt like one of them. Isaac's studio drew her like a magnet. For months she'd caught quick train rides between Bussum and Amsterdam, feigning errands, stealing afternoons. She loved the secrecy of it. The escape.

Now with her eyes closed and a blanket pulled up to her chin, the bed felt like a cocoon, safe and hidden. Isaac's body radiated heat—so comforting after three long years of scrunching blankets and pillows into a mound to fight off Theo's absence in her bed.

Isaac snorted. "Jo?" he muttered. His body shifted.

The light touch of his finger traced along her cheekbone. "Hmmm?"

"My beautiful, fragile, bad little girl."

Jo nipped his fingers with her teeth.

"Ouch!"

"No talking." She gave him a long, deep kiss. She was not a little girl. As for being bad, she wasn't sure. This bed didn't feel bad. It was the idea of Ma's or her mother-in-law's reactions that made her cringe. But Theo hadn't thought in such black-and-white terms, had he? Good, bad.

She suddenly wished she'd been more playful in bed with Theo.

"Women who know their minds are wildly attractive."

She pushed Isaac's hand away and traced a finger down his spine. He was wrong. She didn't know what she wanted. She knew she wanted to be in this bed right now—she *chose* to be in this bed—

but if she thought about it too much, their secret relationship became complicated. Too much on top of all her other roles: She wanted to be a good mother to her five-year-old. She took pride in Villa Helma's reputation. She was certain Vincent's art had to be before the public. It was hard enough to juggle those three without adding a *lover* into the mix. In Isaac's studio, she didn't want to think. She wanted to take a break. Suspend time and push her day-to-day life away.

It felt easy and lovely to simply give him her beautiful young body.

Isaac began to move around. With the flat of her hand, she pressed him hard, back onto his stomach.

"I can't get enough of you," he insisted.

This time, she let him pull her to him.

Jo giggled until Isaac's mouth silenced her. She was in this bed because she'd invited him to it. The idea made her feel breathless, dangerous, energized. She closed her eyes, enjoying the titillation of his touch. It was a new feeling to give her body over simply for the sensual enjoyment of it.

"Jo . . ." Isaac muttered.

His hands moved with gentle insistence. A trail of fire where he touched her.

Oh, she was fond of him. Not in love, but so fond.

This was nothing like the depth of certainty she'd had for Theo. But she knew when this morning's lovemaking finished, for a while, she would feel comforted, less lonely. Isaac gave her that.

She wished a thousand things. That she had been bolder with Theo and pushed forward the ideas she'd had to sell Vincent's work. He could have experienced the joy in sales for Vincent. Or that she'd insisted he start his own dealership as he'd wanted. She knew now that she could have been his business partner. She wished that she'd have been braver, stayed in the dining room with artists as they'd debated politics, learned to speak her mind, have her own opinions.

She knew now she'd only given half of herself and that now it was too late.

She was so sorry.

She would cherish Theo forever, but she had to keep living.

Isaac's fingers paused.

She opened her eyes. "Don't stop."

"You're crying."

Jo swiped wetness from her cheeks. "Old memories."

"Then let's make new ones."

BUSSUM

Jo

"PLEASE! PLEASE! *OH NO!*" JO LEAPED FROM THE CARRIAGE at the Bussum train station just in time to see the rear of the train bound for Paris accelerate away from her. She closed her eyes to fight back tears. She'd botched it. Ambroise Vollard—*the* Ambroise Vollard from the exclusive Vollard Gallery, no less—was putting on a special exposition for Vincent: *The Exhibition and Van Gogh*.

She'd only just read his request for twenty more paintings this morning. And then missed the only train that could have gotten the artwork to Paris.

"It always leaves on time, Mevrouw," Bouwman apologized. He tapped the back of the carriage where the cartons of paintings were loaded. "But I can store them at the station. Get them on tomorrow's train?"

She would not cry in front of Bouwman. Tomorrow's train would be too late. The show would open its doors in a few days. By the time the extra paintings arrived—in three days—Vollard would have already arranged and hung the show in his gallery. "No, thank you. Please take them back home." She turned away to hide her face.

"Jo!"

Martha van Eeden bustled toward her, hefting a bulky valise alongside her stocky body.

"What luck!" her neighbor puffed. "I'd planned to walk from the station, but this suitcase is much heavier than I thought. Mind if I catch a ride?" Dropping the suitcase, Martha drew closer. Her smile dissolved to concern. "What's wrong?"

"You are a sight to behold," Jo said, wiping her eyes. "Of course you may have a ride. Or, better yet, the carriage can deliver your valise to your house, and we can walk." She looked to Bouwman, who nodded and, in one easy motion, swung the suitcase up into the cab.

"Where were you?" Jo asked, intertwining their arms as they started off.

"In The Hague. Oh, Jo. I went to the first meeting of the National Exhibition of Women's Work. It was electrifying!"

"I read about that. You *went* there?"

Martha nodded. "The meeting hall was jammed. Every seat taken, women standing along the walls to get in. It was breathtaking. Marie Mensing spoke—"

"I know Marie!"

Martha's eyes glowed. "When she spoke, you could have heard a pin drop. It was as though she was pulling away a veil. As though the very structure on which I've built my entire life is a mistake, an illusion. Women *are* capable. We *are* worthy and have a right to have a voice and a say in our lives—in the world!"

"I do remember that feeling." Jo thought back to the New Year's Eve party and Marie's words: *No man should be a barrier between you and what you want.*

"Jo, suffrage is key. My eyes are open. To have the right to vote means having a say in the laws to help the poor, to improve education, to improve women's wages and working conditions. To protect those who are vulnerable in our society. To elect leaders who believe in what I believe. We're at the turn of the century. It's *our* turn."

Jo laughed. Her earlier frustration had taken wings. Thoughts tumbling, she asked, "But how does Doctor van Eeden feel about this?"

Martha laughed. "Oh, Frederik knew I was a firebrand when he married me!" She sobered. "Honestly, he sees firsthand how laborers suffer from living in squalor. He tries to spend at least one day a week doctoring among the poor."

Jo thought of Pa's indifference to the workers in the shipyard. As her father had advanced in his job, bringing home more money each year, there had been something about those who had been left behind that hadn't felt right to her.

"I saw your sister-in-law at the meeting."

"Wil?" Jo halted. It was impossible to imagine Wil's timidity among a hall of cheering women.

Martha grinned. "She was positively glowing. She looked like she's found her passion. Like you," she added.

Jo groaned. "Oh, Martha. You don't know. I may be passionate, but that's not everything. I've just made a stupidly careless mistake."

"Tell me."

With Martha's gentle invitation, over the next several minutes Jo told her about the morning's negligence. How she'd missed this chance to show more of Vincent's work. Gauguin had been as good as his word and loaned the three paintings she'd given him. Thanks to his letter, she knew the stockbroker Émile Schuffenecker and the late art critic's wife, Madame Gramaire-Aurier, had loaned their Van Goghs too. Those, plus the seven she'd originally sent Vollard, would be a decent selection of Vincent's oeuvre but hardly the big impact another twenty paintings would have had.

"This show was important, then?" Martha sympathized.

Jo nodded miserably. "The agreements I get to do shows are few and far between. Just this morning I received a refusal from London. I don't know what I'm doing wrong." The theatre owner's blunt rejection to display Vincent's work in the foyer had had no explanation. Why couldn't others see what was so clear to her? Didn't it make sense to pair an avant-garde artist with an avant-garde theatre?

Not to mention for her, a show in London would have been an international foothold for Vincent.

"Cheer up!" Martha shook her arm. "I refuse to allow you to blame yourself any longer on this beautiful spring day. Here, help me be lazy." They'd arrived at Villa Helma. Martha plopped down onto the front steps. "Let's sit awhile before I get home and have to face my chores . . . and the children!"

Leaning back on her elbows, Martha dreamily tilted her face to the sun. "If only you could have come to the meeting. Such joy and hope in that hall! Perhaps next time . . ."

Jo leaned back with a wash of guilt. She had been with Isaac yesterday. That was why she hadn't seen Vollard's telegram until this morning. This love affair came with a price. Why was it whenever he contacted her, she dropped everything, *everything*, to go to him? Jo glanced at Martha. She couldn't tell her about Isaac—not because she was ashamed of having a lover; it felt good to have him all to herself.

"Don't waste time ruminating on the past," Martha murmured.

Did she read my mind? Jo wondered.

"We need to place our energy on what we can do *now*," Martha continued and sat up. "Everyone has the opportunity in the *present moment* to affect change. That was one of the meeting's central messages." She seized Jo's arm. "And I don't mean standing at an abstinence booth passing out brochures. Something more. I was wondering what that could be the entire train ride back . . ."

What could Jo do to help? She had no spare time. Her life was a tedious, unending carousel of Villa Helma, art promotion, and Vincentje. That was why she ran to Isaac. He was an escape.

"You're wearing your worried face," said Martha.

"I guess I want to do my part, but I don't know how I can add one more thing . . ." Just then, a newspaper article popped into her thoughts. "Or wait . . ." Jo turned to Martha. "There's a little gallery in Haarlem named Maison Hals. I read about it in *De Amsterdammer*. The gallery claims to support artistic innovation."

"Yes? What are you thinking?"

"If I provided the paintings . . . I wonder whether they'd be willing to donate the show's entrance fees to benefit the poor?"

"Use your art to raise funds?" Martha hugged Jo. "Beautiful!"

Jo's spirits lifted. "Do you think so?"

"It's a statement. You're saying that art is meaningful. Art has an impact in more ways than one. In this case, it can put food on the table."

"Isn't that just female sentimentality?"

Martha arched an eyebrow. "Or innovation?"

Later that afternoon, Jo hummed a little as she sat at her desk with Vincentje drawing on envelopes at her feet. She noticed that she felt lighter and less tired than usual at the end of the day. Smoothing Vincentje's blond curls, Jo said, "I have to write one more letter, then shall we play out in the garden?"

"Five minutes?"

"Five minutes," she said with a laugh.

She pulled out a clean sheet of stationery. One of Vollard's wealthy clients, Lucien Moline, wanted a price break on some paintings. Last week he'd sent a note offering to pay two hundred francs each for three paintings. Now he'd changed his offer to eight hundred francs for seven paintings, effectively cutting his offer for each painting in half.

It was puzzling as well as insulting. Why would he discount Vincent's work by 50 percent in one week?

Jo reread the postscript: *Camille Pissarro has made concessions. He is not ashamed to sell his work for less.* For once, the name-dropping did not impress her.

No, she would hold the line on pricing and refuse his offer. Today she'd discovered Vincent's artwork could serve another purpose other than making money for her.

She had to have faith that this new idea to raise funds for the poor would not be a setback. That Paris and international galleries and museums would come calling when the time was right.

TWENTY-SIX

PARIS

Raulf

"YOU HAVE EXCELLENT TASTE, MONSIEUR," RAULF DECLARED TO
Moline as his fat client drained the last dregs of brandy. Raulf
snapped his fingers to get a server's attention and pointed to their
empty glasses.

The men's club was packed with the usual Friday-night crowd.
To the uninitiated, the crowd looked indistinguishable, but there
were subtle lines of territory. Talentless groups of young men
clung around tall bar tables and shot constant looks about them,
hoping to be recognized. Raulf ignored those who nodded at him.
He relished determining who to snub, who to acknowledge. The
next tier comprised men who had achieved a measure of successful
enterprise. They perched alertly at smaller tables like his own.
The highest tier of power carried on in a reserved seating section
in sumptuous leather armchairs toward the back where a permanent
server hovered to deliver drinks and to keep the riffraff away.
Raulf liked the clear lines of demarcation.

Raulf glanced up to the four Boussod & Valadon partners in

their circle. Heads together, their shoulders shook with private laughter. Raulf wet his lips and pulled down the edges of his new dark blue frock coat. He looked like the epitome of success. His entertainment of this fat cat Moline would not go unnoticed.

The leather armchairs were practically within his grasp.

"G-good evening, Monsieur Raulf."

"Bonger!" Raulf greeted Dries, noticing his rumpled suit and scuffed shoes.

"How do you do, Monsieur," Bonger said to Moline.

Horrified, Raulf stood up hastily. Had the idiot no propriety? Ever since asking the widow's brother to take care of the transfer of paintings from Tanguy to Durand-Ruel, the Dutchman had acted much too familiar.

"Not here," Raulf scolded. "We're in a private client meeting, Bonger."

"What? Oh, I beg pardon . . ." He flushed and retreated.

"Do you know him?" Moline asked, licking his finger after running it around the glass rim.

"Junior broker at Wehry's. He's taken care of some small tasks for me."

"I hire only the best—doesn't matter how little the job is."

Before Raulf could answer, a heavy hand fell on his shoulder. "Good evening, Georges! Won't you introduce me to your guest?"

Raulf hid his cringe at the gravelly voice. Paul Durand-Ruel. Rival art dealer. Double-crossing cheat.

"Lucien," he clipped through clenched teeth. "May I present Paul Durand-Ruel, owner of the Durand-Ruel galleries? Paul, my *client*, Lucien Moline."

Moline mocked. "*Another* art dealer! This club is swarming with commerce! Mine is much more genteel. Perhaps I should come here more often!"

"I'd be honored to invite you as my guest," Durand-Ruel said with a quick bow. He winked at Raulf.

"Come, come," Raulf inserted. "Monsieur Moline and I were just getting down to business."

Moline pointed at Durand-Ruel. "I know your name. Didn't you have that exhibit of haystacks a few years back?"

The tables turned. Raulf felt smug. Durand-Ruel had displayed fifteen paintings of the same haystack by the Impressionist Claude Monet. Such absurdity. He hadn't bothered to go.

"You're too kind. I sold out of those paintings in three days, two thousand to four thousand francs each," Durand-Ruel bragged. "They're worth more now."

Raulf felt the blood drain from his face. What kind of fools did Durand-Ruel cater to?

"That's what I want!" Moline banged his fist on the table. "To find a new artist before he's famous! To get in on the ground floor—"

"And that is exactly what we are doing," Raulf assured him.

"Are you?" Durand-Ruel's hand dug into Raulf's shoulder. "Let me go give my regards to your partners, friend." He tipped his hat to Moline. "At your service should you want another advisor."

They watched Durand-Ruel cross the room and greet the Boussod & Valadon partners.

"He's smooth," Moline commented.

"He's indiscreet." Fuming, Raulf watched Durand-Ruel signal the server to pull another chair into the Boussod & Valadon circle and settle in with the partners. Turning back to Moline, he plunged on. "He double-crossed us. Got his hands on a stockpile of Van Gogh paintings, and I asked him to hold the prices down. He's greedy. He refused."

"*I'm* greedy!"

"And I'm greedy for you!" Raulf signaled for another two brandies. "This is exactly why I've turned to Ambrose Vollard. He's Durand-Ruel's chief competitor. He's holding the prices down for you."

"Why aren't you handling this?"

"I told you. A relative owns several Van Goghs. She's a widow now, married an employee. She's...excessive. Quite emotional. Best that I direct affairs without her knowing."

"You know, Georges," Moline began. He held up his index finger. "That Van Gogh widow is stupid. I did what you suggested—made her an offer to buy *seven* paintings for eight hundred francs. She refused me!" Moline looked around the room. "Do you see any other buyers for Van Gogh's paintings in Paris? Anyone like me?"

"There's no one like you in *all of Paris*, Lucien. You have a unique, refined taste. You take your art collection seriously and understand the role it has in defining Paris's reputation on the world stage."

Moline blinked. He reached for a canapé from the tray on their end table and popped the entire cheese puff into his mouth. Chewing, Moline mumbled, "All I know is that Père Pissarro was reasonable. I did what you recommended, and he dropped the price of his painting to sixty francs."

"Père Pissarro knows his place. He understands the value of your patronage."

"Others own Van Goghs though. At Vollard's show, I saw paintings *on loan* from the stockbroker Schuffenecker, Madame Aurier, and that painter Paul Gauguin." Moline banged his fist on the table. "I want one too." He pointed a greasy finger at Raulf. "You'd better be giving me good advice."

"My strategy won't fail. Let's remember *she is a woman*. Her head is turned by the closest flatterer. *Vollard* needs to work harder for you. His Van Gogh exposition was pathetic. Your influence can pressure him to do more for you. We must hold down Van Gogh prices until you've been able to acquire your fair share. After that, we'll allow market forces to rise."

"I won't be patient forever," Moline complained.

Raulf bit back a retort while Moline wiped his greasy fingers on the edge of the tablecloth. These grubby aristocrats had grown so used to having money that they didn't realize the careful manipulation dealmakers like himself orchestrated to make it. He took a deep breath. The widow was a problem, but not an unsolvable one. Time was in his favor. The public was fickle. Already the *Mercure* series on Van Gogh was fading from people's memories.

"I suggest you do not let up pressure on the widow," Raulf said. "She'll succumb. I have it on good word that she's taken a lover, Isaac Israëls, and her brother-in-law's art is a mere distraction. She'll grow tired of it if she hasn't already. Lean on Vollard to keep the prices depressed. You want to buy low now. We want to protect the value of your investment until the right time."

"How do I do that?"

"Insist that he do more for you. Demand that the prices be lower temporarily. This is a woman he's dealing with. She can be manipulated if Vollard would do as you ask."

"Women can be flighty and unreliable. What makes you think she's different?"

"What's the one thing women care about above all else? *Their children*. She has a child. Those paintings are the only inheritance her son has in this world. She's told me herself that creating an inheritance is critical to her. We can use that."

"You're a good man, Georges Raulf."

"A good patriot, I hope."

Moline raised his glass in salute and drained it. With a shaky finger, he signaled for another. Old money. Raulf hid his distaste behind his tilted glass. Men like this Moline, men who inherited their daddy's wealth instead of building their influence and power, were not the ones to shape Paris's future. They were men to be used. To put their unearned plump purses in service to Paris. It was men like Père who deserved to be honored for their dedication to this fair city. It would take men like himself to protect and grow that heritage.

Not to mention reap his own reward.

TWENTY-SEVEN

BUSSUM

Jo

DRIED AUTUMN LEAVES BLEW THROUGH THE FRONT DOOR AND whirled in a circle on the rug before Jo could ease it shut behind her. Wincing as the door squeaked, she stood still, listening. The house was quiet. Just then, from down the hallway Cook's shadowy shape appeared, carrying a lit candle.

"It's me, Cook," whispered Jo. "Off to bed now."

"Whore!"

Jo jerked back. It wasn't Cook. Mother must have arrived while she'd been out. Her mother-in-law's face wavered like a ghost above the flickering flame.

"Mother—"

"Don't you 'Mother' at me!" she scolded. "If I was your mother—or your father, for that matter—I'd haul you home so fast you'd think a storm blew through these rooms! What do you imagine your neighbors are thinking? A whore among them? And don't assume your servants' tongues aren't wagging."

"Mother—"

Her mother-in-law leaned closer, the heavy licorice of absinthe on her breath. "No wine on your breath," she commented incredulously. Mother swayed on her feet.

"Should we both go to bed?" Jo reached for her arm.

"Where were you?" She side-stepped Jo's hand. "Not another women's meeting! You and Wil both. This New Woman business has gotten carried away."

"I enjoy the meetings," Jo lied. The crude reference to "whore" must have only been a passing thought. For in truth, she had just been at Isaac's. Could Mother tell? Jo smoothed the flyaway hairs around her face and pulled her coat collar up to cover the red bruise Isaac had sucked onto her neck. Her lips felt puffy from all their kissing. As Mother stumbled into the salon, Jo pressed the back of her hand against her lips to flatten them.

Villa Helma's rooms had been upgraded to gaslight for some time now, but her mother-in-law made no move to light the gas lamp. She preferred the "familiar old ways"—wax candles.

Stumbling again, Mother allowed Jo to steady her. She spied a photograph of Vincentje on an end table and picked it up. "It won't be long...Vincentje will be a six-year-old," she crooned.

"Yes, Mother—"

"He should be in school!"

"He can read, Mother. One of my boarders is a former teacher, and she gives him lessons every day. She's quite pleased with his progress." Jo paused, proud of Vincentje's enthusiasm for his lessons. Having Mevrouw Muller here had been a godsend for all of them. Vincentje received private lessons, and Mevrouw Muller received a boarding discount.

"He needs lessons in math, geology, history—"

"Music, French," Jo chimed in.

"No, Jo! Boys need *serious* subjects. As Vincentje gets older, a mother's responsibility only grows. He needs to be prepared for *life*. And without a father or older brother to show the way, things will already be more difficult for him."

"Mother—"

"Let me finish! I've stayed up late enough to speak with you, haven't I?" She lifted her chin. "You've done a commendable job with the boardinghouse. I'll grant you that. And dear Vincent's work is known far and wide all over Holland. I never thought I would live to see it. So why—why—must you be galivanting to Paris? If you must do what you do, can't you stay close to home?"

Jo hesitated. She hadn't been to Paris in two years, not since her disastrous meeting with Georges Raulf. Mother could be confusing her visits to Isaac with trips to France. Her mother-in-law was woefully ignorant about distances. She'd never traveled outside the country and only this past year had agreed to ride on a train. Paris was an obscure idea to her, not a reality. She doubted Mother would understand how important Paris was to artists. Better to assure her with an answer about her homeland.

"I'm not ignoring the Dutch, Mother. I sent a letter yesterday requesting that Vincent's work hang in the new Stedelijk Museum. It's going to focus on modern art. I am *proud* that Vincent is a Dutch artist."

Mother sniffed. "He was a simple country artist, dear. Wil and I used to have boxes and boxes of paintings he did before moving to Paris. Simple, rough drawings. Paintings. He drew *common* folk."

"Used to have?" Jo hadn't realized Vincent's early work would exist outside of sketches in his letters. "May I see them?"

Mother waved her hand dismissively. "Wil gave the boxes to a shop when we moved from Nuenen. In Breda, I think." She scowled and shook her finger at Jo. "Our branch of the family never put on these airs. Vincent and Theo come from a simple preacher's family."

"Vincent needs to be acknowledged *outside* of our country too. I think his work could hang in museums, Mother. Find a permanent place in Paris."

"I don't understand."

Jo stepped closer to Mother. "Succeeding in Paris will prove to everyone that Vincent's work stands shoulder to shoulder with other great artists. He worked so hard. Hasn't he earned that?"

"Vincent . . ." A glint appeared in the corners of Mother's eyes. She set down the candle on an end table and walked to stand in front of *Irises in a Vase* next to the chimney. The painting's slender stalks of purple blossoms were barely visible in the dim light. "We expected a lot from him. He had to live two lives—the life of his dead brother's soul *and* his own. The thing is he wasn't *meant* to be firstborn. He had the temperament for a second son, one who wanted to follow his own path. His father never understood that."

Mother shook her head, lost in memory, and continued, "Oh, Vincent struggled. Even as a little boy, he was so difficult. The more he acted out, the stronger Theodorus's hand. The rows they had! Oil and water."

She hiccupped softly, and a tear ran down her cheek. Jo glanced at the clock. Midnight. Fatigue swept through her. Theo had talked often about the fights between Vincent and their father. No one could change the past. Jo fought for patience. Could it only be a few hours ago that she'd lain in Isaac's arms? Of all the times for Mother to come unannounced. There was so much to do tomorrow. Jo took Mother's elbow to urge her to retrace her footsteps down the hallway, but Mother twisted away and returned to stand in front of *Irises in a Vase* again. Sighing, Jo started to shrug off her coat until she remembered the love bite, pushed her collar up, and jammed her hands into the coat pockets instead.

Mother rested her hands on either side of the painting.

"I couldn't see how serious Vincent was about being an artist. So caught up being the perfect preacher's wife." Mother pushed away from the wall with a sigh. "Vincent demanded so much attention—I didn't have it to give. What with four other children. And so many charity rounds visiting the sick or those who'd fallen on hard times. We were dependent on donations too, you know. I had to keep up appearances. Sometimes I wonder . . . if I'd been more attentive to Vincent. *Listened*. Maybe things would have turned out differently . . ."

Jo stepped up beside Mother and stared at the painting. The flowers bobbed a little as if the flickering firelight was a breeze moving through the stems.

Mother's face was streaked with tears. "I missed the signs! So caught up in me. Preacher's wife!"

Perplexed, Jo searched Mother's face. "The signs?"

"Are you *watching* Vincentje?"

Jo bristled. So this was it. Criticizing Jo's mothering again. She would not sit through another lecture on how she allowed Vincentje too much freedom. Drunk or not, Mother had no right to tell her how to raise her son.

"It's late," Jo said firmly. "There's a lot to do tomorrow. You're tired. I'm tired."

Mother's eyes narrowed into marbles, hard and mean. Jo drew back as Mother twisted toward her, exhaling absinthe. "Really? Tired? Do you think sneaking into the house at this hour may have something to do with it? Spending entire afternoons out who knows where?"

Jo flushed angrily. So Mother had been suspicious after all. The servants must have been talking.

"*You say* you're working with Vincent's art."

"I am—"

"Doing *Theo's* work?"

Jo flushed even hotter. The *Cypresses* painting unwittingly came to mind. Her scattered decision to let it go to that damn persistent horsefly Moline rankled her. Why had she given in? She'd been tired and not thinking clearly.

Mother wasn't done yet. She held up her hand with fingers spread. With the other, she ticked off the fingers one by one, "Off to Haarlem. Off to The Hague. Off to *Paris*, for lord's sake! Are you a floozy now? You're distracted! I refused to see signs of madness in Vincent when he was a boy. Don't make my mistake!"

"Signs that *Vincentje* has madness?" Jo's skin crawled. Doctor van Eeden had assured her that Theo's madness had come from untreated syphilis, not genetics. But she'd always wondered if it had been in Theo's blood, couldn't it be in Vincentje's? Or hers?

"Look at his uncle. His father."

"Mother, I can *assure* you . . ." Jo's voice petered out. What exactly was she sure of?

"I'm warning you, Jo." Mother looked up at the painting. "The Van Gogh mania is sneaky. It's in the blood. It appears and disappears . . . but it's never really gone."

The older woman sagged suddenly. Jo caught her under her arms. "Time for bed, Mother," she murmured. Then, holding her up with an arm around her waist, she led her to the guest bedroom at the end of the hallway.

Later, lying in bed and listening to the steady breathing of Vincentje across the room, Jo tried to quiet her hammering heart. Mother had been drunk out of her mind, but it didn't mean she was wrong. No doubt the absinthe had loosened her tongue, allowing unspoken fears to spill out.

Jo had to admit she was worried too. The older Vincentje grew, the more he looked like Theo. The image of Theo's wild, unrecognizable eyes in the asylum came to her, and she shuddered. Theo would never have passed along anything dangerous to his son. Not knowingly.

But if Mother was right and something was wrong with Vincentje, the earlier Jo noticed it, the better his chance for treatment. She couldn't keep up this breakneck speed while juggling all four roles—mother, guesthouse manager, art dealer, and lover...something had to give. She still cringed at missing the train that should have sent twenty more paintings to the Vollard exhibit. If only she hadn't given in to Isaac that time.

Turning to her side, Jo gently rubbed the mark Isaac had nuzzled onto her neck earlier. He was a nice distraction, but he didn't love her. She didn't love him. Like the bruise on her neck, their romance had to fade away.

Sitting up, Jo stared at Vincentje's shadow across the room. His breathing sounded steady, but Mother's words haunted her.

Is there something wrong with my son?

TWENTY-EIGHT

PARIS

Raulf

"THIEF! YOU'RE STEALING A CLIENT BEHIND MY BACK!" Ambroise Vollard's face puffed with rage. Hands on his hips, he squared off with Raulf in the middle of the Vollard Gallery's dim light. An early afternoon December snowstorm brought heavy clouds low over the city, casting a dreary pall into the gallery.

"You received your commission." Raulf kept his voice low, controlled. He'd anticipated the old coot's reaction to Raulf's interference in helping Moline buy *Cypresses*. The victory still glowed. The widow had cracked under their pressure. His job this afternoon was to mollify Vollard. Now that he'd seen for himself how persistent Raulf could be, he would come around to helping, instead of hindering, his efforts to rid the city of Van Gogh's art.

"A *lower* commission than if the painting sold at a higher price! You make no sense! You're taking money out of my pocket!"

Raulf clapped a hand on his shoulder. "No, no, no. I have your best interest at heart."

"You seem desperate."

"Not at all. Lucien Moline will *buy more*; the widow has broken her stalemate and will *sell more*. Just at a lower price—where Van Gogh's work belongs. Later—after time passes—you can raise the prices."

Vollard pressed his lips together. "You've thrown your weight around ever since your appointment to the Académie. Do your partners know what you're doing?"

"The Boussod and Valadon partners *recommended* me."

"We top art dealers have always had an understanding that we cooperate on pricing. You don't act like you're one of us."

"Just like Durand-Ruel did with Monet?" Raulf scoffed. This morning Raulf had heard that Durand-Ruel had found American buyers interested in Monet's work. His insistence that he be the exclusive sponsor of Monet's work would fatten his bulging pockets even further.

Vollard growled. "He got lucky. Still, no one can say Durand-Ruel hasn't been tenacious. He's never let up promoting Monet. Even during the lean years."

"Monet is a temporary fad. Durand-Ruel stumbled upon some Americans with no taste willing to throw their money at anything Parisian."

"I'd like to find some gullible Americans. I could be Van Gogh's sponsor. Introduce his work to some Americans."

"Regardless, Monet's Impressionism only has a narrow following. It won't last."

Vollard peered at Raulf. "What makes you the expert?"

"Commercial success, my good man. The men who are shaping this new century don't stand by waiting for the next faddish wave to wash over them. They take a stand and *command* the wave."

"I guess I'm too stupid. I've never thought art could be controlled. Which brings me back to you." Vollard shook his finger in Raulf's face. "Don't mess with Moline and his art purchases. He's my client. If he wants more Van Goghs, I am his dealer."

"Of course he's *your* client. Moline must have gotten his wires crossed. Listen . . ." Raulf drew Vollard aside even though they were the only ones on the gallery floor. "Now that I'm in the Académie, I expect to be able to do favors for my friends. Boussod and Valadon has a long history with you. We've always had an understanding."

A risky thought occurred to Raulf. If he played it right, Vollard would be in his debt and Raulf would have tighter control over the Van Goghs.

Raulf put a hand on Vollard's shoulder. "Tell you what, Ambroise. To prove my goodwill, let me give you a tip. You say you want to sponsor Van Goghs. I know where there are some more of his paintings. I don't know if the widow knows about them. The location's rather inconspicuous, but I know I can trust you." He dropped his voice. "In the south of France, there's a café owner, Joseph Ginoux, who has a stockpile of paintings."

"Where?"

"In Arles. Van Gogh lived there for a time. Tanguy's widow told me that Van Gogh asked Ginoux to store paintings he did there. No doubt they've been sitting in a dusty attic. Ginoux might be persuaded to sell."

"*Store?* Aren't they part of the widow's estate?"

Raulf shrugged. "She doesn't know about them."

"And I could get them for a steal . . ."

"The café owner wouldn't know the difference."

"And charge what I want here in Paris."

Raulf raised an eyebrow. "Now who's the thief? I dare say since Moline has *Cypresses*, he'll be eager for more. My involvement was never about getting in between you and your collector. My role is to protect art dealers. I have a duty to protect Paris. You have a patriotic duty to display and promote the very best of art. Why . . ." Raulf swept his arm, pointing out to the sidewalk where passersby hurried. "The rue Laffitte is a kind of permanent salon with all of its galleries and their exquisite window displays. Only the Louvre rivals it!"

Vollard eyed Raulf. "Look, friend, I'm a practical man. I didn't become a top dealer by being a patriot. What put Paris on the map for art are the artists. I already did my part in the Franco-Prussian War. We're a republic now. We could have a monarchy again, for all I know. I need to make a living while I can. And Van Gogh attracts a lot of curiosity. He could help me get there. But why are you so interested in this Dutchman? You act like this is personal."

"Don't be daft!"

Vollard's mouth tipped into a grin. "Seems like Madame Van Gogh has gotten under your skin."

"The widow? Don't be ridiculous."

"She's a woman, old man." Vollard clapped Raulf on the shoulder and laughed.

Raulf shrugged Vollard's hand off and stepped forward as if to study the gallery art on display. Working against the Van Gogh widow was like playing a game of chess. With Boussod galleries in each city, he'd been able to respond to each of her moves. He'd squashed her request to show art in a London theatre. Gotten her inquiry to the Stedelijk Museum denied. The widow was tenacious—he had to give her that. Which meant it was time for new tactics.

These rue Laffitte imbeciles were so short-sighted, each out for themselves. Now with Vollard as an ally—and his position at the Académie—he'd be able to move more quickly to rid Paris of this Van Gogh parasite and others like him.

If only he'd been in this position of power earlier, perhaps his brother Raynaud would still be alive.

Patience, son. He could hear his father's voice in his head.

He swore he could feel Père's arm resting across his shoulders.

TWENTY-NINE

AMSTERDAM

Jo

JO PACED THE FLOOR OF ISAAC'S APARTMENT. AFTER SHE'D decided to stop seeing him, he'd asked if they could meet in his chambers on New Year's Day to talk in private. Their "talk" had collapsed into wild play.

Now she halted before a mirror, pinning her hair back up into a chaste chignon.

Isaac perched on an ottoman behind her and wrapped his arms around her legs. "Let me mess that up for you again."

"What am I to do with you?" Jo shook her head, smiling. "This was the *last*—"

"Last time! You told me. But you still don't understand me. I live moment to moment, *chérie*."

"Perhaps," Jo said, inserting the final hairpin. She picked up her bag. "That reminds me. Here's something I don't understand. A rejection from the Stedelijk." She pulled out the letter and handed it to him. The Stedelijk Museum had refused her detailed proposal to exhibit Vincent's work.

She chewed her lip as Isaac read it. Vincent's work was attracting increasing crowds throughout Holland. Wasn't he the type of artist they were interested in?

Isaac shrugged a shoulder. "You're taking this too personally."

"You don't understand. The museum put out a request to show Dutch artists that exemplify modern art. Think of the fascination Vincent creates. I can't see why they rejected him."

Isaac put his hands around Jo's waist. "Come, come now. Don't make me scold you!"

Jo twisted out of his hands. "Don't treat me like a child."

"Fine. Get some perspective!"

"It's not just this. Dries told me he heard a rumor at his men's club that Vollard had some new paintings of Vincent's. He bought them from a café owner in the south of France."

Isaac scooted back into the armchair, stretching his legs onto the ottoman. "Yes, sure. My father mentioned it." Jo's heart sank. If Jozef Israëls knew about it, then the rumor was likely true.

"You didn't think to tell me?"

"We were going to break up! Then we got so *busy* when you arrived." Isaac's mouth curled into a smile.

Jo backed out of reach. "Isaac, *tell me—*"

He held his hands up. "All right! My father mentioned a rumor that Vollard picked up a few paintings in Avignon or Arles. One of those southern cities."

"Arles." She sighed. "It's true, then. It's my fault. I forgot about them. I remember Theo telling me Vincent had given some paintings to a friend, a café owner there. Still, I wonder why Vollard didn't tell me?"

"Why would he? I daresay he thought he'd make a quick profit."

"Dries heard he bought three for one hundred eighty francs, then sold *one* for one hundred eighty francs."

"Excellent return on his investment."

"Isaac! I want Vincent's paintings to go for at least *double* that price!"

"And I want *my* paintings to sell for more! Just because you *want* a price doesn't mean you'll get it."

"I wish you'd told me earlier."

"What would you have done?" he asked. "And why are you so upset anyway? Paintings change hands all the time. It's called the art *trade*."

Jo flushed but ignored his patronizing tone. She needed him to understand. "I need to be able to control Vincent's paintings. Their prices. Which ones are available for sale."

"No one controls the Paris art market."

"I need control in Paris."

Isaac stood up. "*No one* controls Paris. You think I wouldn't like to sell more? Even with my connections—and my father's—we control nothing! Look, Paris is a circus. A dog-eat-dog circus. Hasn't Dries told you that? It's no place for you."

How could Isaac not understand? Had he not been listening when she'd shared her dreams for Vincent's work? "Paris is *everything*. I need to have more than a foothold there. I need a *stronghold*. If Vincent is accepted in Paris, he'll be accepted everywhere."

Isaac's tone switched to soothing. "Listen, you've done a lot. Look at the *Mercure* series. Those articles created a lot of chatter. Do something like that again. Get Bernard to publish more."

Jo shook her head miserably. "Bernard's gone. Disappeared into Egypt. As far as I know, he took the letters with him." Jo closed her eyes. Such a stupid mistake. They were the original letters too. All from Arles when Vincent had been experimenting with light and landscape. When he had been lonely and dreaming of starting an artist community.

She sighed. "I can't have some dealer mess things up by acting outside my control."

Isaac raised his eyebrows. "*Control?* There's that word again." With a flourish, he presented the Stedelijk letter in the palm of his hand and bowed. "Proof of your control, Mevrouw."

Jo snatched the letter from him.

"Look, Jo." Isaac's face turned serious. "Paris is a jungle. This type of thing happens all the time. If anything, it's a sign of your success that Vollard sought out Vincent's work. Traveled to the south of France, for God's sake. Vollard's a businessman and an influential one. By all rights, the paintings belong to him, and he can sell them for whatever he wants."

"No, Isaac. *By all rights*, Vincentje and I own Vincent's *legacy*. I care about *all* his paintings. Regardless, I must see to it that Vincent's paintings appreciate in value."

"Vincent's practically a national hero in Holland!"

Jo shook her head. "He's still a curiosity. Not appreciated the way he should be." She sat down on the side of the ottoman. "Besides, I mean *internationally*. His work should hang in museums. In Paris and other countries."

Isaac cradled her face. "Be careful, love. Stir the pot too much and you could find yourself in the fire."

"I can't sit still, Isaac. I'm going to Paris to find out what's going on myself."

"I wouldn't . . ." With his finger and thumb, Isaac gently pinched her chin. "Look at me. You cannot go to Paris and confront these men. If you challenge them directly, they absolutely will tear you down and Vincent with you. You cannot confront one man in front of another one. You won't win."

Marie's words flashed through Jo's mind: *The art dealers in Paris are only an obstacle if you give them that power.* "Women need to stand up to—" Isaac pinched Jo's chin again, harder this time. She yelped in pain and yanked her head back.

"Don't be a fool, Jo," Isaac hissed. "You'll unravel all the work you've done." He let go of her chin. "Tell you what: bring your brother with you to your meeting."

Jo shook her head, rubbing her chin. "Not Dries. He has no backbone."

"Oh, I believe it! Around you! Still, if you want the conversation to turn to the business, you'll need a man there with you. I'd offer to go, darling," he said with a crooked smile. "But I value my career too much."

"Fine." Jo didn't want Isaac there anyway. Dries she could handle. "I'll bring Dries," Jo conceded. "But I'll do all the talking. I have to do *something*. If these dealers continue to discount Vincent's paintings, I'll never get to where I want to go and Vincentje will never get the inheritance he deserves." She crumpled up the letter from the Stedelijk. And no museum would accept Vincent's work.

If she was going to do all the talking, what exactly was she going to say?

She couldn't do anything about the Arles paintings Vollard had already sold. That wasn't the point of her journey. It was time that she did more than complain about their transactions.

She needed to be heard.

———◇———

THIRTY

PARIS

Jo

ONE WEEK LATER, DRIES RUSHED UP TO JO, WHO WAS HUDDLED in a doorway of a milliner shop opposite the Vollard exhibition on the rue Laffitte. Flurries of brisk January wind swept up the street. Passersby leaned into the gusts, holding onto their hats.

"Sorry I'm late, but this couldn't be a worse day." Dries panted. Pulling a length of his muffler out from his collar, he wiped his sweaty forehead. "George Wehry himself is coming by the offices this afternoon. I can't be caught away."

"We'll try to make this quick, then." Jo kissed one of his red cheeks, then the other. She pulled back to scrutinize his face. "You look tired! I haven't seen you in so long—"

"Annie can't bear to travel in the winter. Perhaps in the spring."

Jo nodded, hearing his defensive tone. She wouldn't press Dries about visiting her in Bussum. Annie made all the decisions in their household. Besides, she needed Dries now to help her confront Vollard. All during the long train ride into Paris she'd practiced her speech—how she and Vollard could work together and come to a mutual agreement on pricing, share information about sales. This meeting would be a turning point. Her patient work in Holland and Vollard's interest in Vincent could come together.

Pointing across the street to the gallery's lighted window, Jo said, "See those two paintings?" In the dim morning light, the bright yellow of a café scene and the undulating blues of a mountainous hillside gleamed. Jo felt an instant affectionate recognition. "Those are Vincent's. The colors are like *The Yellow House*. I don't know them, so they have to be from Arles."

Where else might Vincent have left his artwork? Could there be paintings at the asylum in Saint-Rémy? Suddenly, Jo was eager to talk with Vollard about his discovery, why he'd sought out the paintings, and what he saw in Vincent. She was sure that once they came to an agreement on pricing, they could form a wonderful partnership. In fact, in that light, she was happy he'd acquired the Arles artwork. "Monsieur Vollard and I can work together more closely now."

"Don't make a scene," Dries said. "You said this would be a short meeting. Let's get this over with."

Dodging vendors with pushcarts and horses snorting steam as they pulled lurching carriages, the two scrambled across slippery cobblestones and yanked open the shop door. In unison, the narrow silhouettes of two men advanced from the interior. Surprised, Jo recognized Georges Raulf. She hadn't expected him. But before she could make sense of why he was there, the second man advanced in front of him. Neatly trimmed mustache and beard. Three-piece gray morning suit cut fashionably shorter in the front and neatly tapered in the back. He looked like wealth. Success. It had to be Ambroise Vollard.

Jo's heart nervously skipped a beat. She'd read his name in *Le Figaro* and *Le Mercure de France* for years. It was surreal. Here were two of the top art dealers in all of Paris. They held the keys to hundreds, perhaps thousands, of artists' success, including Vincent's. She had to win them over. A nervous thrill ran through her. This was exactly the opportunity she'd hoped for. In a few strides, the men crossed the floor.

"*Enchantée*, Madame." Vollard took her hand and bent over it. Releasing it, he turned to Dries, holding out his hand. "Monsieur Bonger?" He grasped his palm with a sharp pull.

"Ple-pleased to meet you," Dries stuttered.

Raulf turned to Jo. He, too, was the picture of elegance with his crisply tailored black frock coat and black-and-white striped silk tie. She extended her hand, expecting him to acknowledge their past association. Instead, his eyes flickered from her to Dries, even as he automatically bent over her glove. "Andries Bonger!" he stated with a little smirk. "A broker from George Wehry, the importer."

"Monsieur . . ." Dries managed as they shook hands.

Jo saw a look pass between the two art dealers. Something was off.

Vollard rubbed his hands together. "Now then, Bonger. I don't mean to rush the pleasantries, but we are all busy men. I have an important collector coming . . ." He pulled a pocket watch out of his waistcoat and consulted it. "Very soon. What's this meeting about?"

"Ambroise! Manners! We are Frenchmen, after all," Raulf chided. "Your coat, Madame?" Even though his question was polite, his voice sounded odd. She couldn't put her finger on it.

"No, you're in a hurry . . ." Jo answered, but she could see Raulf was barely listening. A smile played on his lips. His eyes were fixed on her brother. Like a target. Or prey.

Dries glanced at her and cleared his throat. "This meeting . . . I wanted to meet with you. That is, my sister and I wanted . . ."

She had to take over. Quickly intervening, Jo said, "To discuss pricing. The price you charged for *Interior of a Restaurant in Arles* was too low."

Ignoring her, Vollard continued to Dries, "You're a broker of . . . artificial flowers, is it?"

"One hundred eighty francs was like giving it away!" interjected Jo.

Abruptly, Dries squeezed Jo's elbow, silencing her. Panicked, she could see his huge eyes meant he was intimidated.

"Not an art dealer, then."

Dries's ears turned bright red. With an audible swallow, he said, "Well, yes, no, but—"

Vollard said evenly, "You are on the rue Laffitte. One of the most prestigious streets in one of the most prestigious art galleries in all of Paris."

"Actually, in all the world," added Raulf.

"I don't tell you how to sell *flowers*," said Vollard to Dries. The polite expression carried an undertone of warning. "Why are you presuming to tell me how to sell art?"

"Monsieur," Jo interrupted, "*I* am the one who asked for this meeting."

"Ah, yes." Raulf placed a hand gently on her other elbow. "May I give you a tour of the exhibition, then?"

Jo pulled away. "There's some confusion. I'm the one—"

"Certainly, I . . . I am not advising you on any art decisions," Dries interrupted, swallowing. His eyes jumped back and forth between the two men. "But . . . Vincent's work can s-sell for m-more . . ."

Vollard frowned. "And your point is?"

Jo placed a hand on Dries's arm. She had to gain control of this conversation. "*I* own the bulk of Vincent van Gogh's work. Vincent was *my* brother-in-law; Theo van Gogh was *my* husband." Desperately, she nodded to Raulf as if she needed him to corroborate.

"Indeed, Theo van Gogh was my employee," Raulf affirmed, patronizingly.

"I have been cultivating buyers, setting prices, holding exhibitions—"

"Such a strain!" Raulf tsk'd.

"—in Holland," Jo continued firmly. "And I simply wish to collaborate with you, Monsieur Vollard, when you set prices. You were collaborating with me before when you held an exhibition of Vincent's work."

"The exhibition in which I sold nothing." Vollard scowled. "The exhibition in which you did not respond to my request for additional paintings."

Jo reddened. "That was a mistake . . ."

"I don't make my arrangements lightly, Madame. This is business, not a frivolous pastime you fit in between . . . dalliances."

Jo flushed. He meant Isaac. He thought she was some paramour. None of this was going as she'd imagined.

"Jo," said Dries. "It does look like these men should be in charge."

"*Dries* . . ." She needed his help, and he was already acquiescing.

"May I offer you a cup of tea, Madame?" Raulf sniggered.

Ignoring him, Jo pushed ahead. "Monsieur Vollard, my son inherited his uncle's paintings. I believe they will appreciate over time. I need to keep watch over the entire oeuvre, including the paintings from Arles. This would benefit both you and my son." She glanced at Raulf. "In fact, *all* art dealers who choose to show his work, if we can coordinate pricing."

"Is this conversation about *ownership*?" Vollard laughed. "The paintings from Arles belong to *me*. *I* bought them. For heaven's sake, why are you meddling? I am *representing* your brother-in-law. I stand to benefit from sales. I am not working against you or your son's interests, Madame." Taking a deep breath, Vollard turned to Dries. "We're finished here."

"You could have charged double for *Interior of a Restaurant in Arles*. At least four hundred francs," Jo blurted.

Vollard glanced at Raulf before responding. "Madame, you don't appreciate my position. I want to help your dead brother-in-law, but pricing is not as black and white as you think it is."

"You're not used to it in Holland," Raulf explained. "Dutch painters simply aren't as valued in Paris as they are on their home turf."

"Vincent is being appreciated overseas."

"Oh, is he now?"

"In Denmark."

Raulf raised his eyebrows in amusement.

Jo could feel the heat rise in her face. Turning to Vollard, she begged, "Would you like to represent more of Van Gogh's work? I have hundreds in other galleries in constant circulation in Holland." She nodded to her brother. "And with Dries's help, there are Van Gogh paintings in many smaller galleries here in Paris." She caught Dries's eye, daring him to speak. He reddened. Her brother hadn't been as helpful as she'd hoped in finding Vincent's dispersed paintings, and they both knew it. Determinedly, she continued. "Monsieur Durand-Ruel has some paintings too. Of course, we need to be careful not to flood the market."

"Who taught you all this?" Vollard asked bluntly.

Jo glanced at Raulf to give him credit, but before she could speak, he jumped in. "Doesn't matter. Your point is that you want Monsieur Vollard to be Vincent's sponsor so long as you can make exclusive pricing decisions."

"No." Jo shook her head. A part of her noted with satisfaction that finally both men were speaking to her. Dries had taken a half step back. "I own the bulk of Vincent's considerable work. The point is that *I* am his sponsor."

Vollard and Raulf burst into laughter.

Dries chimed in with a forced chuckle. She glared at him.

Vollard wiped his forehead with a handkerchief. "Enough! You are entertaining, Madame, but I regret I have to prepare for a collector arriving momentarily."

Raulf clapped Vollard on the shoulder as he said to Jo, "Frankly, Madame, you don't seem to appreciate that your *Dutch* brother-in-law is being sold in a top Parisian gallery. Stop interfering. Go back to your guesthouse. If you want your son's paltry inheritance to sell in this gallery, stay out of these affairs, Madame."

"I know how *you* feel about Vincent's art," Jo snapped. She faced

Vollard. Her mind teetered. She had the desperate feeling that time had slipped away. This was her last chance. Recklessly, she grabbed Vollard's hand with both of hers. He pulled back, but she couldn't let go yet. She felt lightheaded. Grasping his hand tighter, she babbled, "I'd hoped we could work together. I thought you might understand."

A flicker of sympathy crossed Vollard's face. His eyes blinked to Raulf and back.

This was her opening, her chance to have a direct say on Vincent's exposure in Paris. She could see a door open a crack before her. She saw how mistaken she'd been to think Raulf represented all art dealers. Vollard was empathetic. She could feel it. "Please, Monsieur. If we priced Vincent's artwork *together*—me from Holland, you in Paris—I could help you—"

"You? Help Monsieur Vollard?" Raulf laughed with sharp disdain. His hand locked around Jo's wrist, pulling her grip from Vollard's hands.

In concert, Dries took hold of her arm, pulling her a step back. Eyes wide, he barely shook his head at her.

Raulf's voice was taut. "You're appealing to the wrong man. *I* am the one with influence on this entire boulevard. I control the smaller galleries you boast about. Paris is a small world. We art dealers protect each other's interests."

Jo fought to respond. Raulf had moved to stand in between Jo and Vollard. His voice dropped to a whisper. "We've suffered you enough. Let me be even clearer: stay out of Paris, or your *flower* brother here"—he nodded at Dries's white face—"will suffer. George Wehry and I are longtime friends. You wouldn't want your brother's career to end because of your childish obsession to be somewhere you don't belong."

Dries's hand froze on Jo's arm.

Raulf hissed. "Be satisfied with Vincent staying in Holland." He stood up straight and with clear, careful enunciation said, "You're not welcome in Paris, Madame."

Jo looked at Vollard, standing half behind Raulf's shoulder, silently beseeching him to intervene, but he clamped his mouth into a firm line.

She scrambled, "But Monsieur—"

"But nothing! *You may never set foot in Paris again.*"

Jo's ears rang with the words.

Never set foot in Paris again. The cruelty repeated over and over in her mind.

Never set foot in Paris again. The words circled under her and fumbled her goodbye to Dries at the Gare du Nord station. *Never set foot in Paris again.* They tormented her again and again during the long train ride across France into Amsterdam and the local trip to Bussum. *Never set foot in Paris again.* The words haunted her as she pushed open the door of Villa Helma at 1:00 a.m. Hours earlier she'd left home with such high hopes. Instead, she'd ruined everything in one stupid, failed meeting.

Jo tiptoed down the corridor to her bedroom. Resting a hand on Vincentje, the gentle rise and fall of his chest brought tears to her eyes. She had failed him.

Slipping into the dressing alcove, Jo stepped out of her dusty traveling clothes and eased a nightdress over her aching shoulders. Pouring tepid water from the pitcher Marta had left into the dressing room bowl, she splashed water on her face.

Never set foot in Paris again.

She was banned from Paris, or Dries's career would be forfeit. All of her work was ruined. Now Vincentje's inheritance would gather dust in her attic, worth only a fraction of what it could have been. All the trust Theo had placed in her—betrayed. Without even thinking about it, she knew she couldn't hurt Dries. Since childhood, it had always been that way, and it always would be. She had to protect her brother.

Standing in front of the mirror, Jo pulled hairpins from her messy chignon. Long tresses tumbled over her shoulders. She stared at the shadow of her face. In the dim light, the worn lines around her thirty-four-year-old eyes were hidden. Her face looked like that of a young girl's.

When she'd been Theo's wife, she'd been so carefree. Safe under Theo's wing, she could spin dreams and play in the world of art. With him as her safeguard, she could be spontaneous and share ideas with abandon. She hadn't had to weigh the merits of her imagination. Hadn't had to second-guess. Theo had done all of that.

Jo stared at her silhouette. That naïve young bride was no longer the person in the mirror. There was no one here to rescue her.

She didn't know how, but she'd have to carry on.

Alone.

STARRY NIGHT OVER THE RHÔNE

———◇———

It does me good to do what's difficult . . . so I go outside at night to paint the stars, and I always dream a
painting like that . . . My only wish is that they could
manage to prove something that would be calming to
us . . . without having at each step to fear or nervously
calculate the harm which, without wishing to, we
might cause others.

—VINCENT VAN GOGH, *September 29, 1888*

Winter 1896
to
Fall 1901

THIRTY-ONE

BUSSUM

TRUE TO HER PROMISE, JO KEPT HER DISTANCE FROM Paris. No more telegrams spelling out pricing instructions. No more instructions on how to curate the paintings. Yet in the ensuing months, as George Wehry passed Dries over again and again for promotion and her brother angrily accused her of meddling in the dealer affairs, she wondered if her silence really mattered. The fact was she'd become nearly invisible. On rare occasions, a small commission check would arrive in the mail without an accompanying note. Even the telegrams she sent confirming receipt of a requested painting to Vollard shot into an unanswered abyss of silence. She was irrelevant. They didn't need her. She was simply a Dutch supplier, one among hundreds fighting for space on the rue Laffitte.

Then a change came to Villa Helma. Their energetic mascot, Vincentje, began primary school. The staff stood by as Vincentje rode his bicycle to the schoolhouse in Bussum's town square, insisting "I can go myself." His dinnertime chatter switched from imaginary pirates in the back garden to real boys racing each other in gymnastics. Trails of papers—nature-study drawings, arithmetic columns—fluttered out of his knapsack and lined the edges of Villa Helma's corridors. Sometimes, late at night, listening to Vincentje's deep breathing, a lump would form in Jo's throat. Vincentje was growing up. She was no longer the center of her son's world.

Without the art plans, without Vincentje underfoot, and only Villa Helma's relentless routine, the years stretched ahead, bleak and empty.

One afternoon Jo escorted a new maid, Bella, through the upstairs bedrooms, pointing out her duties. "Every morning the corridors and steps must be swept thoroughly. Every Monday it's your duty to strip all the beds in the house and remake them with fresh linens." She stopped outside a guest room, tapped on the door, leaned forward to listen, then swung it open to reveal a neatly made bed in the empty room.

"So, this bed would not be changed," the girl affirmed.

"*Every bed*. Made up or not. Mevrouw Muller is quite neat, but she still needs fresh linen."

"But *every week*, Mevrouw? What are the guests doing? Working in the fields?"

Jo fought back a retort and led the girl from the room, pulling the door shut behind them. Not for the first time, she wondered where all the hard workers were. Bella was the third maid Jo had hired this winter. So much for believing in an ideal society where intellectuals and workers could come together through art if she couldn't find any workers. "After the beds are changed, you'll launder the linens and pin them to the clothesline outside. They're usually dry by midday. You must fold and put them away in the linen closet before the evening cools."

"Wait," the girl wrinkled her brow. "Did you say *all* the beds?"

"The guests, mine, Cook's, Marta's, your own . . ."

"What? Not the other maid's bed!"

"We all work for each other," Jo insisted. "Next, let's go to the kitchen . . ."

"I don't like cooking!"

Jo looked at the girl's puckered face. She forced her voice to be calm. "You answered my want ad for a 'decent, quick servant who can cook well.' My cook needs an assistant. Tell me now if that's not you—and return the godspenning guilders I gave you." Jo waited. Asking for the spending money back usually did the trick. No girl wanted to return the first money she'd been given to use on her own.

Bella pouted, but before she could answer, the front door banged open downstairs.

"Hello! Hello!" bellowed a male voice. "Where's the woman of the house!"

Who on earth? Jo and Bella stared at each other, eyes wide. Cook's agitated chatter rose muffled through the floor. Heavy foot-steps thundered up the stairs. Bella grabbed Jo's arm. A tall, tanned man built like a barrel burst from around the corner of the stairwell. With a shock, Jo recognized him. "Cor!"

"Sister!" With one stride, he lifted her into a tight hug and spun her around.

"Cor!" Laughing, Jo pleaded, "Put me down! I can't believe it's you." Teetering, she caught her balance as he planted her feet back on the ground.

"I wanted to surprise you."

"You did, Meneer," interjected Bella, looking at him from under her lashes.

"Bella, please!" Jo scolded, embarrassed by the girl's cheek. Mother would have fired such impertinence from a maid on the spot.

Bella arched a pretty eyebrow at Cor.

"Bella! To the kitchen. Cook is waiting to give you instructions." Jo pointed toward the stairs. "And you." She grabbed Cor's arm with a sudden inspiration. "Come with me."

She pulled him out of Villa Helma and turned up the road toward town.

"Vincentje's school gets out any minute. I want his friends to see you with him."

"I've come to see him! But why the school?"

"I've overheard him brag about you. His 'brave soldier uncle.'"

Cor lifted an eyebrow. "So, I'm to play a hero?"

"Well, you *are* a brave soldier fighting in a far-off land."

A look passed over Cor's face. "Battlefields are not as romantic as I believed when I left. Nor working for a company that ignores its workers' conditions. In truth, I'm the lowest man there. No one cares what I think."

Jo nodded, taken aback by his sober tone. She knew what that felt like.

"But hey . . . according to Mother and Wil, *you're* doing great!" Cor said with enthusiasm.

"You've spoken to Mother? How is Wil?"

"I barely recognized Wil. She's *thriving*, Jo! I visited her first when my ship arrived in Amsterdam. Her bed is in a guesthouse, but I swear she lives for work with the women's group. Lectured me about women gaining the vote!" He laughed. "And then lectured me about women in general. Acted like a big sister. I quite enjoyed seeing the old Wil."

"Did you visit your other sisters too?"

"Briefly." He shrugged. "You know I barely remember them growing up. They were both married and gone while I was still in short pants. They have no need for a little brother. Their husbands take care of them now." He looked at her. "I feel closer to you than those girls."

"Just what I need! Another little brother!"

Their feet crunched in unison on the dry road. A contented feeling came over her. Perhaps it was Cor's similarity to Theo. He had the same laugh. She remembered how shy he'd been when he'd visited her and Theo in Paris. She'd warmed to him immediately. Her own brothers kept their distance. Her oldest brother, Henry, was like Pa—work came before all else, including marriage. Dries's wife, Annie, refused to travel to Bussum. Jo wished she could get to know her younger brother, Wim, but he was away at a boarding school the few times she'd traveled back to Pa and Ma.

"As your *little* brother—" Cor broke into her thoughts.

"Yes?" Jo had to look far up. Her head came to his shoulder.

"I've come to check on you and Vincentje."

"Check on us?"

"Least I could do. I am the man of the Van Gogh family now. Theo sent money home every month when I was a boy. Father counted on it. And Wil. And, of course, Vincent."

"I remember."

"Theo was a real man."

"And *you*—"

"Is that the schoolhouse?" He pointed his chin toward a brick building. As Jo looked up, the doors sprang open and boys began to pour out. Cor dashed ahead, sprinting up the street and into the yard. "Vincent! Vincent van Gogh!" he called.

Stunned, Vincentje stood in the doorway. Boys jostled around him.

"Uncle Cor!" He leaped off the steps. Cor caught him in a hug. Vincentje's face buried into his neck. Jo's hands flew to her mouth. Her son had hurled into his uncle's arms. He must've been longing for a man's touch.

"Now!" Cor's voice carried across the yard. Disentangling Vincentje's arms, Cor wiped his own eyes. "Now, Vincent. I've come all the way from South Africa to see *you*."

A cluster of boys gathered around Cor and Vincentje.

"Are you a soldier?" a voice rang out.

Cor nodded solemnly. "I am."

"I told you!" Vincentje exclaimed.

Another question called out of the crowd, "Have you killed anyone?"

"At least one hundred men."

The boys gasped together.

"But you weren't afraid, were you?" asked Vincentje.

Cor rested his hand on Vincentje's shoulder. "Brave men are always afraid. Fear is your friend because it makes you more alert." He looked at each boy. His face was grave. "When you're afraid, your physical senses grow a thousand times sharper. When I was afraid, I could see the barrel of a gun across the schoolyard. I could toss a cannonball from one hand to another, light as a feather. I could hear the faintest footstep in the town square. And I could smell the lye soap a man had used a week ago underneath his sweat."

"His stinky sweat?"

"His *very* stinky sweat. But you know what?" Cor paused. "*I* had the stinkiest sweat of all!"

Vincentje snickered with the rest of the boys.

"Where is South Africa?"

Cor sank onto his haunches, and the boys shuffled closer. Jo tiptoed unseen behind them. Cor looked out above the boy's heads, remembering. "South Africa is a strange, exotic land. Wild lions and elephants roam through the streets. The jungles are thick with snakes. When I looked out at the ocean from its cliffs, I could see the edge of the world. It's so far away my travels took three months through heavy storms to get here. One night the waves were so high they crashed onto the sea decks, and we had to tie ourselves to the masts to keep from going overboard. The winds howled so loudly you felt a thousand ghosts were right next to you. It was very danger-ous. More than once, I thought I would die."

"You almost died?" Vincentje choked. The emotion in his voice brought a sudden lump to Jo's throat.

Cor held Vincentje's teary gaze. "I'm here, aren't I? I've come to Bussum to see *you*, Vincent. We are Van Gogh men. Even when I'm far away . . ." He thumped his hand on his chest. "You're right here. In my heart."

Later that night, Cor came into the salon where Jo waited while he finished saying goodnight to Vincentje. Earlier that evening, Vincentje had banished her. They'd needed to talk man-to-man.

"He's a fine boy, Jo," Cor said. He headed straight to the claret decanter and poured two glasses. "I know Theo would be proud," he smiled, handing her a glass and settling into an opposite armchair.

"He's everything to me. Without him, my home would be empty."

"Your home is a respite for weary bones." Cor scanned the room, his eyes pausing at each painting. "Your Paris apartment was covered in art too. Do you remember when I came to visit?"

"Let's see. You would have been twenty-two or twenty-three. You were a little . . . awkward?"

He laughed. "I was such an oaf! First off, I was besotted by how beautiful you were. I thought, *Of course my brother would marry a beauty*. And completely impressed by all he was doing for Vincent. I don't think Father ever realized how much. He simply expected Theo to support the family. That visit was an eye-opener. I remember thinking I wanted to be like Theo when I grew up!"

"But you were already a young man!"

Cor shook his head. "Still a boy." He drained his glass. "I wish I could talk to Theo."

"If he was here, what would you say?"

Cor poured another glass. "Something idiotic, no doubt. But I do wonder . . ." He swirled the claret in his glass. "How to stand up to my bosses? The working conditions at the gold mine are horrific, Jo. Men are maimed. Men die in the mines. But the bosses don't care. There's always another worker standing by to replace a missing man. My bosses act as if colonized people are less than men because they're a conquered people. A Dutch colony. I've already been labeled a troublemaker. I told Mother I got a leave so I could check on her. But truth be told, I was fired."

"What!"

"I'm actually relieved. I left to get out of their crosshairs. Let tempers cool down a bit."

"All because you protested those worker conditions!" Jo felt a rush of love for Cor. He had the same soul sense of being pained by others' suffering as his brothers.

"I remember Vincent hated the idea of colonies. I suppose I'm trying to walk in his footsteps. And *yours* . . ."

"Mine?"

"Mother wrote to me about how you held an exhibition to benefit the poor."

"You mean Maison Hals in Haarlem? It's true I donated the entrance fees toward poverty relief."

"That's what I mean! You find a way to act on your principles."

"Oh, Cor. That opportunity came to me. It was unique . . . *although* . . ." An idea popped into her mind. "I did receive an invitation to hold an exhibit for a museum in Groningen."

"Up north? Near the coal mines?"

"Yes! Do you remember Vincent lived there for a time? Before he became an artist?"

"I do. He was studying to be a minister. One of the few times Father boasted about him. Following in his footsteps, you know. That is until he couldn't pass his exams. Then Vincent was a failure all over again."

"But he wasn't truly a failure, was he? His heart was touched by the coal miners' hard lives. I've seen the sketches he sent to Theo in his letters." The desolate inked drawings were haunting.

"I remember Father being so angry that Vincent gave away all his food and salary to the coal miners there."

"Their plight touched him. Some still remember his kindness. That's where you've inspired me!"

"*I've* given you inspiration?"

"The idea to *act* on my principles. Like you, I believe in equal opportunities for workers. Well, I'm going to ask the museum to allow the workers to come to the exhibit free of charge. Wait, not ask. *Insist!* They should be able to see an artist who thought of himself as their equal."

"You're riding a wave, sister!" Laughing, they clinked glasses and drank. Contentment settled in the room. Both stared at the fire in companionable silence, listening to the crackling of the burning wood. Jo closed her eyes for a moment, in awe as she recognized the malaise she'd felt for months had lifted. She felt lighter. All because of an idea and Cor's wonderful visit. She turned to tell him and saw he was staring at her.

"You and Vincentje have done me a world of good. I'm so sorry I need to head out tomorrow."

"No! So soon!"

He nodded. "I'll say goodbye to Vincentje at breakfast. I have a new job waiting for me." He saluted her. "Civil servant for the Netherlands South African Railway at your service!" A crooked smile crossed his face. "And there's a girl . . ."

"A girl!"

He blushed. "Anna Catherine Fuchs."

"Tell me about her!"

"Of course, she is the most beautiful woman in the world."

"Of course."

"And clever and not afraid to speak her mind. Like you."

"How does she feel about you?"

"Let's just say she's waiting for me to come back." He smiled to himself and sighed. "I do need to be a man and become successful at *something*, Jo. Mother is angry that I've moved so far away. She told me my duty is to my family *here*. Really made me feel guilty." He sighed. "And I'm not the hero Vincentje thinks I am. Or the men my brothers were. But it's the twentieth century, right?" His eyes glowed with intensity in the firelight. "A new world. A second chance. I have to get it right this time." He nodded to himself. Dropping his voice, he whispered, "I must get it right."

Jo let out a ragged breath. Cor was on his way to doing great things. She could feel it. A part of her wanted to go with him and escape Bussum too. Venture out into an expansive world and leave all these limits behind, like banishment from Paris. Her earlier lightness felt ethereal. The cold reality of being stuck in one place weighed her down again.

Would the Groningen idea be enough? Would it matter?

Jo's world felt small again.

THIRTY - TWO

BUSSUM

Jo

ONE DAY IN MAY 1897, JO ARRANGED TO MEET MARTHA OUTSIDE the bakery in Bussum's town square to make the rounds of shops to place orders for Villa Helma's meals.

"I've joined the twentieth century!" Jo greeted Martha, panting a little as she rushed up.

"Don't tell me—they've paved the road to Villa Helma!"

"Finally! Less dust. And easier for curiosity-seekers to get to me."

"You should charge admission."

"Except the visitors are usually artists, and artists have no money." She gave a rueful sigh. "Oh, Martha, while I do appreciate their interest in Vincent's paintings, the tours are tedious. There are strangers in my salon begging me to show them the art nearly every day. Cook complains she's interrupted by having to prepare coffee and tea all the time. I just had a maid quit. She claimed her work had doubled with cleaning up after the extra dirt tracked in."

"The new road will help with that."

"That's not the point. Vincent deserves a bigger stage. I feel trapped."

"You've never explained why you stopped going into Paris."

There was nothing to explain. Jo wouldn't share Raulf's threat to Dries. She was at an impasse. She couldn't risk hurting her brother.

She forced a smile. "Let's place our orders quickly. Reward ourselves with a cup of tea at the confectioner's?"

"And a sweet!"

Together, they stepped into the bakery.

"It's *time*, Jo," Martha said as they emerged a moment later, baguettes sticking up from their shopping bags. "You *promised*."

"The women's labor group? Martha, I don't have time for even one more thing."

"None of us will ever have more time."

"I'm telling you—running Villa Helma is unending. Between the visitors and the boarders and Vincentje, I have no time to myself." Just two days ago she'd refused to meet Isaac. One more obligation pulling at her.

"What are you afraid of? You put off forming our society all winter, and now it's spring."

Once again, fear held her back. Ever since the meeting in Paris, she'd felt hesitant to draw attention. She knew she was a coward, but she couldn't shake it.

"So, I've invited Marie Mensing—"

"*What?*" Jo froze.

Martha laughed. "Good! You look guilty! Well, she's delighted to come! And you know she'll help draw a crowd for our first meeting." Martha twirled. "Just think, our very own society for the National Exhibition of Women's Work—in Bussum!"

Jo stood stock-still, her thoughts racing back to the last time she'd seen Marie at the New Year's Eve party. Marie's impact felt like yesterday. Wil had written about her electric speeches at their Amsterdam meetings. She didn't see how she could ever get out of her current predicament, but she could use a lift in spirits. Martha had picked the one person Jo didn't want to disappoint.

"When is it?"

Martha clapped her hands. "Yes! Next Thursday. And don't you worry—I've organized all of it. Nothing for you to do but come."

"Will you invite Anna? I haven't seen her in ages."

"You know she won't come without Meneer Veth. Her entire focus is on him and the children."

"She's a good soul. Try anyway. I don't want to give up on her."

Martha shrugged. "Fine. No skin off my back. I'll send a note."

"I don't know whether you're my best or worst friend."

"*Definitely* worst friend."

Jo grinned at Martha, a little trill of nerves jittering in her stomach. She was nervous but also a little excited. Something was about to begin.

Despite her best efforts, Jo arrived late to Martha's house the evening of Bussum's first Society for the National Exhibition of Women's Work meeting. As she let herself in, animated conversation swelled from the small salon. Twenty or so women crammed together on chairs and the sofa. A few men dotted the crowd.

Next to the fireplace, Jo spied Marie Mensing, bent close in deep conversation with two women Jo didn't know. Jo scanned the group. Neither Martha nor Anna was there. Spotting an empty space along the back wall, she worked her way between chairs toward it. A man with a creased soiled hat scooted over to give her room.

"Ladies!" Marie's voice carried over the crowd, quieting the chatter. She wore the same straw boater hat Jo had seen when they'd first met but cocked at an angle. This time her outfit was one of the stylish suits Jo had read about, fashioned after menswear with a matching jacket and skirt. Immediately the babble in the room died down. "Instead of handing you a specific agenda, the national committee recommends you identify local issues right here in your own region."

"I thought we were here to talk about big changes," a woman in a floral dress objected.

"Change starts first in our own communities, in our own homes. The first thing we're doing is raising awareness of possibilities that exist right here."

"In Bussum?"

Marie laughed. "Absolutely in Bussum! In Gouda and Leiden and Volendam. Small towns carry as much wallop as Amsterdam or The Hague. Even more so."

"Hidden in plain sight?" Jo recognized the voice of the confectioner.

"Shown through our individual lives. Your labor is essential to your households. Women's labor should be valued as highly as men's work."

"This sounds selfish. I'm grateful my Aaron keeps a roof over our heads," a voice from Jo's left called out. She thought she recognized her from years ago when Anna had introduced ladies on afternoon calls to Villa Helma. "I'm proud of my home and children," she added. In response, a chorus of heads nodded.

She was missing the point. Jo was proud of Vincentje too and of running Villa Helma on her own. But it wasn't enough. It was about being listened to and having a voice.

"It's about more than pride." Jo's voice sounded loud even to her. Heads turned.

"What are you thinking, Jo?" invited Marie, smiling at her. "Come stand by me so everyone can hear you."

Jo's heart thudded in her chest. She pushed away from the wall. She'd only meant to listen tonight, not to speak. What did she have to say?

"I'm proud of my son too." Jo halted in front of the crowd. She'd never had so many people looking at her at once.

"Tell us about him," Marie murmured.

Vincentje's impish face appeared to her. "He-he's six years old.

I *am* proud of him. He can already do arithmetic from the older boys' class, but at the same time, he can't seem to keep his clothes clean for more than five minutes." A few nodding faces in front of her broke into smiles. "And I'm proud of my boardinghouse too. I'm a widow. Villa Helma is the name of my guesthouse." She gestured toward the front door. "Up the road."

"I don't know how you do it!" an anonymous voice called out.

"Thank you." Buoyed by the support, Jo looked up to see Martha, open-mouthed, standing in the doorway carrying a coffeepot and tray of cups. "When I was a little girl, I never imagined I would run a boardinghouse—*could* run a boardinghouse—but when my husband died, I couldn't face going back to my father. Being a wife and mother changes you." More heads nodded, encouraging her. "But what if my husband hadn't died? I don't think I'd know what I'm capable of doing. It's so easy not to question the limitations others give us."

"Exactly!" Marie addressed the group. "How many of us were raised to believe our brains were smaller than a man's? You know, there's absolutely no scientific evidence of that. Or that we have no upper body strength? Or that we couldn't handle strong emotions without taking to our beds?"

That had been her. With a shock, Jo realized the last time she'd taken to her bed was when Theo had been alive.

"When we grow up being told over and over that we're weak and incapable, it's no surprise that after a time we believe it. We accept restrictions. We presume that's the way it is," said Marie.

"Exactly," Jo said, nodding. "In hindsight, I can see now that I learned to be dependent. I was taught not to trust my own instincts."

"What do you mean 'instincts'? We're not animals!"

"I suppose 'intuition' is a better word." Jo thought of the Panorama exhibit and how Holst had worked behind her back. "In one of my early exhibitions of my brother-in-law's artwork, I knew a man I worked with had his own agenda, but I didn't trust my intuition. We women are told we have no head for commerce, and we believe it! Even though the evidence of our own skills in managing households and children is literally under our noses."

Marie put her hand on Jo's arm. "And then we pass on those same beliefs to our children. Our girls *and* our boys. Yet in your heart, don't you know how strong and capable and intelligent and worthy you are? This awareness is our first step. I want you to select another person to explore this topic with. Share with each other what you were told a woman's place is. What was emphasized in your upbringing? Not all of it will be bad! Your goal is to see how your world was shaped by being female. Let's take a half hour. Martha has coffee for anyone who'd like it. We'll reconvene, and those of you who want to can share what you discussed."

"Mevrouw van Gogh." The voice came from behind her shoulder as voices rose following Marie's instructions. It was the man with the creased hat she'd stood next to. He held out his hand. "Thank you for your comments. I've been wanting to make your acquaintance! I'm Pieter Tak, editor-in-chief of *De Kroniek*."

Grasping his hand, Jo noted how solid it felt compared to the limp Parisian custom of men bending over it. "It's a pleasure to meet you. *De Kroniek* . . . is that the magazine on socialism?"

"*Emerging* socialism. I personally feel we are on the cusp of defining a new society. Like in this meeting!"

"Are you covering it for the magazine?"

"I am. But listen, I've been wanting to meet you. I read about the socialist art exhibits you did with Maison Hals and in Groningen."

"Socialist?"

"Absolutely. You dedicated entrance fees to poverty relief. You invited Groningen workers to enter for free."

"*And* a local boy's academy too." Jo couldn't help feeling a pang of pride at having carried out this idea.

"Indeed! It is an outstanding example of using art for society's advancement."

"What do you mean?"

"Art can close the gap between the laborer and the intellectual, between the young and old. Every individual has the capacity to appreciate art in some way. I read in *Van Nu en Straks* that the Groningen program was quite large and very well received."

Jo nodded. "One hundred two paintings. Sixteen hundred paying visitors. Plus the workers and schoolboys. The organizers were very pleased. They seemed to feel that the term 'modern art' does contain something new and different."

"So, the show was a resounding success!"

"It depends on your definition of success. Groningen was less about sales, more about sharing Vincent more widely. Getting him in front of ordinary people. Vincent certainly thought of himself as a worker." She paused, then laughed. "His work is quite different. There's plenty of ridicule. But I don't mind laughter. It still means people are paying attention. And I'll take outrage over indifference any day."

"Bravo, Mevrouw! Well said!" Tak admired. An unreadable look passed over his face. "I have an idea of my own . . ." He straightened up. "Tell me, Mevrouw. Do you speak any other languages besides Dutch? I presume French?'

"English too. Why do you ask?"

He clapped his hands. "I need a translator. You would be perfect!"

"A translator?" Jo recalled translating a novel into Dutch for *De Amsterdammer* when she'd been a twenty-two-year-old schoolteacher. She remembered the thrill of earning her own money. The hundred fifty guilders had felt like a goldmine.

"I receive articles and serials from socialists in England, France, even Germany. I need them translated into Dutch by someone with intellect and empathy. That's you, Mevrouw."

"Oh, I don't know . . ."

"Please! Don't refuse yet. Let me send you an article. See what I mean. The deadlines are flexible, and I'd pay you, of course. And if you ever want to write an article yourself, I'd love to see it."

"Me? *Write* an article?"

"Your ideas should be heard."

Her ideas? Should she tell Tak that the success in Groningen had been followed by an outrageous bill—two thousand three hundred forty francs—for shipping paintings on loan to Groningen. The note had felt like a punch in her stomach.

And when Vollard had ordered her a commission check that month, he'd made it out in francs. Jo had had to hire a costly intermediary to convert it to guilders.

She glanced at Tak, who concentrated on eating a square of cake. Did he have any idea how little her opinions mattered in the art world? Could it be possible her written words would be any different?

———◇———

BUSSUM

Jo

IN THE WINTER OF 1898, THE MORNING AFTER AN ENERGETIC eight-year-old birthday party for Vincentje with four other little boys, Jo stepped out onto her front stoop to shake birthday-cake crumbs off the dining room rug. As usual, she glanced down the road toward the Veth house. On the horizon, a trickle of whitish smoke rose from their chimney. She hadn't seen Anna in months. Probably chasing one of her five children, or more likely serving breakfast to one of Jan's art students.

Jo heaved up the rug and spread it over the lilac bushes in front of the house. Picking up a broom, she began to beat the carpet. The steady rhythm warmed her muscles.

As little girls, she and Anna had been the closest of friends, sharing secrets and playing hide-and-seek with Dries. But now as adults, it hurt to think they had less and less in common. Martha had become her companion for outings.

Tomorrow night they planned to take the train into Amsterdam for a concert. Jo doubted Anna would ever dream of stepping out for an evening without Jan. But still, she missed her friend.

With every beat of the broom, dust and cake crumbs leapt out of the carpet fibers. The glistening bits of white reminded her of a sugary strawberry tart—a favorite of Anna's that Cook was baking today. Jo would bring a plate over. Sort of a peace offering.

Invite Anna to go to the concert.

Ten minutes later, Jo paused to catch her breath, panting out puffs of steam at the Veths' back gate. Smoke still rose from the Veth studio behind the house. Anna must've been inside straightening it up. She lifted a corner of the linen napkin and took a deep breath. Her mouth watered from the fresh-baked aroma. Pushing open the gate, she marched up the path and yanked open the studio door.

"What the deuce!" A thin man standing before a wooden easel whipped around as a blast of frigid air shot into the room. Jo caught sight of a mustache and neatly trimmed goatee before he pressed a pale handkerchief to his nose. "Influenza!" He frantically waved his free hand pinched around a paintbrush. An arc of blue paint droplets spattered in a thin circle.

"Who are you?" The question fell from her lips before Jo could take him in. Balancing her plate with one hand, she used her hip to shove the door closed. There was no sign of Anna.

"You've ruined it!" The stranger grimaced at the blue drops splayed across his sketch of a bowl of apples.

"I'm so sorry, Meneer!" Eyes on the canvas, Jo stepped closer. The blue arched across a yellow background. To the right of the easel, orange-red apples had been piled high in a kitchen bowl. A still-life arrangement. She wondered how often Jan pilfered their root cellar for his painting lessons.

"It's a catastrophe," the man moaned.

"Perhaps it can be salvaged." She studied the sketch. Vincent had explained color combinations in his letters. "Blue is complimentary to orange. You could make the background blue and soften the apples into more of an orange."

He picked up his paint palette, where several colors of paint blotted the surface. Pointing with his brush, he said brusquely, "*I know that*. Actually, I was going to *mix* the blue with the orange—"

"Oh, you can't mix them. They'll destroy each other."

"What?"

"Colorless gray."

The man scowled at her. "What do *you* know about painting?"

Jo ignored his question and studied the drawing. "You could try—"

"*Don't tell me!* If I put orange and blue *next* to each other . . ." He gingerly added a stroke of blue next to an apple.

"Yes! They'll complement each other. The apples will pop off the canvas!" She beamed at him as the man dabbed more blue.

After a moment of silence, Jo asked, "Do you know Georges Seurat's work? Your brushwork looks like pointillism."

"Hardly." He squinted. "I saw a Seurat painting at an Indépendants show in Paris a few years ago."

"*Bathers at Asnières*."

"You know it? It was monumental!" Their eyes locked. Jo noticed his were a deep blue.

She shook her head. "I've only read about it."

"The farther away I stood, the more solid the colors appeared. Luminous, even."

Jo nodded. "That's pointillism. No need to blend the pigments. Your eyes and brain blend the hues and create color. You have a nice systematic pattern going. Try a little yellow?"

"Your turn." He handed her the paint brush.

After a second of hesitation, Jo dabbed it in the smudge of yellow paint.

"If you get closer . . . and paint even smaller dots . . ." She concentrated on nicking the canvas. "You're like Seurat!" She handed him back the brush.

"Hmmmm." Closing his eyes into slits, he pricked the canvas. "Perhaps this is it . . . I saw a demonstration by Signac in Paris."

"Paul Signac?" The last time Jo had seen him had been at Theo's funeral. Tousled brown hair. Red-rimmed eyes.

The man straightened up. Older than Jan's typical student, but not too old. Perhaps early forties. "You know Signac's work?"

"I haven't seen it in an exhibition. Through the *Mercure*. But I did meet him a few times when I lived in Paris." Jo remembered one night when Theo and Signac had stayed up well past midnight debating in their dining room. She'd fallen asleep listening to the rise and fall of their voices down the corridor.

"From Paris to this small town. Off the beaten track." He smiled.

Jo returned his smile. "Bussum is small, but the train runs to Amsterdam several times a day. We're not *quite* at the end of the world," she said and laughed. "In fact, I'm going to a concert in Amsterdam tomorrow night. Have you heard of Fanny Flodin?"

He shook his head.

"She's Finnish. Gorgeous pianist. You should join us!"

He reddened, cleared his throat, turned back to the canvas. Jo stiffened and stepped back, embarrassed. What had gotten into her? She didn't even know this man's name. Sharing her personal plans? It was their conversation. It felt comfortable, *normal*. She looked at the stranger sideways. She had an odd feeling she knew him already. She studied his face. Had they met at the Arti in Amsterdam?

A burst of cold air blasted them. The man skipped to the side, holding his brush up in the air. "Not again!"

"Meneer Gosschalk! Jo!" Flustered, Anna stopped in the doorway. Something flickered in her eyes, and she rushed forward. "Jan will never forgive me allowing your work to be interrupted," she said to the man, then frowned at Jo.

"It's my fault, Anna," Jo said. She picked up the dessert plate and folded back the napkin, revealing a corner of the golden tart. "I came to bring you this and thought you were here. Peace offering?"

Anna ignored the plate. "I saw you cross to the studio from the kitchen window. Jan has very strict rules about protecting his students' practice. You shouldn't have barged in," she scolded.

"No, I shouldn't have . . . you're right," Jo fumbled, taken aback by Anna's agitation.

Anna turned to the man. "I *apologize* for the interruption, Meneer Gosschalk! My husband teaches an excellent program."

"The interruption was not . . . It was pleasant." He glanced at Jo.

"But what is *this*?" Anna stared at the canvas, littered in dots. "This is not the lesson on still life. Meneer Veth will be *so* displeased."

"Anna—"

Anna whirled at Jo. "*You* wouldn't understand with all your meetings and visitors and exciting life."

"What?"

"It's my *responsibility* to maintain the students' schedule, Jo. Jan *depends* on me. *I'm the one* who keeps his art instructions going while he is out visiting exhibits and writing his columns." She glared at both of them. "I *protect* his reputation for serious art."

"Of course you do," Jo soothed. It was strange. All this time she'd thought Anna was content, caring for her home and children, when she carried this awful weight for her husband's success. "Let's start over, shall we? We hadn't gotten around to introducing ourselves. Perhaps you could do the honors?"

"Oh?" Anna blinked away tears. "We're not bohemians in Bussum. You must forgive my eccentric neighbor, Meneer Gosschalk."

"Not at all. I, uh . . ."

"Well . . . Meneer Gosschalk, this is my neighbor and friend, Mevrouw van Gogh. Jo, this is Meneer Johan Cohen Gosschalk— staying with us for a fortnight to take art lessons from Meneer Veth." Anna held out her hand for the plate of pastry. Her manner softened. "We'll enjoy these today. Jo, perhaps you'd like to return for our afternoon coffee?"

"Did you say Van Gogh?" Gosschalk stared at Jo. "The proprietor of the boardinghouse with all the art?"

Jo nodded. "Up the road on the right as you head toward town."

"Your reputation precedes you, Mevrouw. I understand you have several works of art hanging throughout the house. Like a museum."

"Reputation?" Anna frowned.

"I often have visitors come to the boardinghouse to see the artwork." Jo looked to Gosschalk. "You're welcome to come by to see them."

"Of course." Anna's hand slipped through Jo's arm. "In the afternoon. When you serve coffee to *all* the guests?"

"Cook's baking does make it a full house."

Gosschalk cleared his throat. "I've never met a woman who could talk about art technique. You must have quite the dinner conversations! I would enjoy meeting your husband and seeing the paintings."

"Then you'll need a séance." The words came out before she could stop them.

"Jo!" Anna gripped Jo's arm. "What my neighbor means is—"

"I'm a widow."

"Oh . . . I'm sorry." His neck reddened. "And the concert in Amsterdam tomorrow?"

"I'm going with a friend."

"Of course. I didn't mean . . ." He ducked his head. "And now if you'll excuse me. Veth is quite the taskmaster, and I'm afraid I'll need to . . ." He glanced at Jo. "Start over."

A few moments later Anna and Jo were outside at the back gate. Anna hugged herself against the cold. "I'm sorry I was so frantic. It's that Jan counts on me to keep his students on task. And Jo, for heaven's sake! No private liaisons in his studio! You were quite *tête-à-tête*."

"It's not what you think. We simply slipped into a conversation.

It was so natural talking about painting with him—I didn't think about the fact that we were alone." That wasn't quite true. She'd been keenly aware that underneath his artist smock, he'd smelled of lye soap.

"Don't artists come to Villa Helma all the time?" Anna's question had a note of envy. "I imagine it must be so diverting. No two days are the same?"

"Sometimes. But the artists can become tiresome, and we never talk about technique."

"I see." Anna nodded without conviction and shivered.

"It's cold, and you have no coat! Anna, you need to go inside! I should be going."

"Wait! One thing . . . what did he mean about a concert tomorrow evening? I don't remember any notices at church."

"It's in Amsterdam."

"Amsterdam, goodness!" Anna's teeth chattered slightly.

"Martha van Eeden and I are taking the train. Back at midnight."

"Just you with the Van Eedens." A little twist of sly amusement crossed her face. "With whom? What escort? I *wondered* if you had a secret consort."

Jo hesitated, eyeing her friend. They had some catching up to do before she revealed Isaac. "Dr. van Eeden won't be going, but there will be a large crowd. We'll hardly be alone."

"No escort!"

"Do you want to come too?"

"Oh, no, I couldn't! Jan . . ." She bit her lip. "I've missed you. No one can stop you when you put your mind to something, can they?"

Jo's heart yearned toward her friend. "I've missed you too."

Anna's eyes widened. She nodded to herself. "Tell you what. I *will* go with you!"

"What about Jan?"

Anna lifted her chin. "It's only one evening,"

"And we'll come straight back."

"Home before midnight."

Jo nodded. "Nothing will happen to us."

She was sure of it.

THIRTY-FOUR

AMSTERDAM

SITTING BETWEEN MARTHA AND ANNA, JO FOUGHT TO STAY focused on the music. The concerto's melody swirled around her, but as soon as Jo closed her eyes, Gosschalk's crooked smile insisted on popping into her imagination. On her left, in place of Martha's plump presence, she pictured his angular body seated beside her. Long fingers resting on the armrest. Leaning toward him to mur-mur, *Wasn't that movement lovely?*

He wasn't as rakish as Isaac. It was the absence of pretense she'd felt. Without any formality—even an introduction—they'd slipped easily into conversation. She giggled under her breath at the image of his paint-spattered smock.

Glancing to her right, Jo noted Anna's wide-eyed absorption in the music. What did this small step of liberation mean to Anna? She hadn't said much about Jan's reaction, only that he'd grumbled something about his morning coffee being ready on time. The old surge of affection for her dear friend swept over Jo like a wave. Anna was more capable than she'd given her credit for.

Perhaps she could ask Anna for help with meeting up with this Gosschalk again. If Anna had one talent Jo envied, it was orchestrating flirtations. She squeezed Anna's hand. It felt wonderful to sit between her two best companions.

After the concert, the three friends moved along with the crowd, spilling into the lobby and pushing toward the ornate front doors of the theatre, flung open to the dark night. A cluster of guests formed a buzz off to the side. The performer Fanny Flodin accepted thanks from the concertgoers. A man with curly brown hair like a bushy halo stood at her side.

Jo grabbed Anna's arm. "I want to thank Mevrouw Flodin for her performance. I'll be quick."

"The train leaves in half an hour." Anna's eyes skittered to the large clock in the foyer.

"I'll be back straightaway." Jo made a beeline toward Fanny and her male escort.

"Mevrouw Flodin, thank you for tonight's performance. I especially loved the Bach concerto. I heard a similar performance in Paris on a harpsichord. Your keyboard concert was wonderful."

The pretty woman raised her eyebrows. "I'm so pleased! But I'm from Finland. My husband knows the Parisian musical landscape better than me." She turned to the man with the bushy hair talking animatedly to another concertgoer. "Julien, this lovely guest heard a Bach harpsichord concerto in Paris. When was that?"

"I beg your pardon!" Jo interjected. "It wasn't recently. I lived in Paris seven years ago."

"Seven years is nothing! After all, art is eternal." His eyes danced as he grasped Jo's fingertips and bent over them. "Julien Leclercq, at your service."

"Johanna van Gogh-Bonger."

"Van Gogh? I knew an artist named Van Gogh in Paris. Vincent van Gogh. Tragically, he died a few years ago."

Jo caught her breath. "Did you say *Leclercq*? I know you, sir. You wrote an obituary for Vincent in *Le Mercure de France*. I was married to Vincent's brother, Theo van Gogh."

"Theo's widow?" Leclercq bowed deeply, surprising Jo. "I'm honored, *delighted* to meet you." He turned to Fanny. "The Van Gogh brothers are revered in the art world—at least among modern artists."

Jo was startled. She hadn't heard such a compliment in ages. "You're a dealer?"

He laughed. "A dealer, a poet, an art critic."

Fanny pressed his arm. "My husband is a Renaissance man. Limited, I'm afraid, by my frantic schedule."

"I wouldn't have it any other way."

"Do you see what I mean?" Fanny said to Jo. The couple beamed at each other. Jo's mouth hung open like a rude child. She'd never heard a man so openly admire his wife's accomplishments. She felt like this concert hall belonged in another world.

A woman with hair piled high like a coiled white snake stepped up, and Fanny turned to address her.

With a friendly smile, Leclercq focused on Jo. "Fanny's concert schedule is relentless. Tomorrow we leave for Rotterdam. Then off to Sweden. Stockholm. Gothenburg. Then Berlin." He shrugged. "So I write art criticism. An occasional poem. Best I can do on the road."

Jo drew in a sharp breath. Stockholm. Gothenburg. Berlin. All international cities. And here was a man who was an art critic *and* enthusiast of Vincent. She remembered the obituary he'd written: *Vincent was a talent.* Before she could rationalize it, an idea clicked in place. Could Leclercq bring Vincent to the art communities in those foreign cities? Could he get Vincent in front of dealers and museums? In a few seconds, the invisible constraints locking her down felt lifted.

Was this the opening she'd been waiting for?

A tall man's shoulder jostled Jo, shoving her back. Leclercq lifted his eyebrows as a goodbye when the black tuxedo pressed between them. An anonymous elbow pushed her farther away.

She couldn't ask Leclercq. He was a stranger. How could she

trust someone she didn't know to represent Vincent? So many of her other so-called partnerships—Holst with the Panorama, Rohde in Copenhagen, even Dries in Paris—had been disasters. She had to learn from those mistakes.

Dismay flooded her. How could she forget her expulsion from Paris? Lately, Vollard's notes had sounded more cordial, but Raulf's cold eyes still haunted her. *Never set foot in Paris again*. Would she ever get that awful voice out of her head? He would not hesitate to retaliate by hurting Dries in some way. There was no point wishing Dries could be different. He was no match for Raulf.

Jo was jostled again. Another couple pushed themselves forward. A feather on the woman's hat brushed against Jo's face, and she sneezed. It had been so long since she'd allowed herself to dream of Vincent's work being shown overseas. Things were good in Holland. Vincent's name had only just begun to circulate among workers as well as the art community. She had more work to do right here at home. Why disrupt the routine she'd carefully constructed? The local National Exhibition of Women's Work was still so new. Judging by tonight, her friendship with Anna was beginning to bloom again.

She couldn't do more alone.

Could she trust a stranger with her dream?

Jo glanced over her shoulder toward Anna and Martha hovering at the concert hall front doors. Through the crowd, Anna caught her eye, jabbing her finger toward the ornate clock. Ten forty-five. Fifteen minutes before the last train left for Bussum. Jo's heart leapt to her throat. She'd run out of time.

"Monsieur Leclercq!" Jo elbowed the woman with the feathered hat. "Monsieur Leclercq!"

Leclercq cracked a surprised grin at the turmoil. "Madame van Gogh?"

"Does your wife's tour stop in Paris?"

He raised his eyebrows. "No, not again. We were there last month—"

Good. "I have a proposal," Jo interrupted. There was no time for politeness. "I've been looking for an opportunity to show Vincent's work to overseas dealers. Get his work to other countries. Outside Holland."

"But is he not on the rue Laffitte?"

"He needs to be seen in other countries *besides* France," she insisted.

Leclercq's eyes lit up. "Vincent branched away from the Impressionists. Had his own style."

"His paintings speak to people's hearts."

"He was a unique character."

"He's either loved or reviled, but he deserves to be *seen*."

"At least to those of us who think of the future instead of protecting the past," Leclercq beamed.

Jo glanced back. The crowd pressed in behind her. Anna and Martha were waving frantically now. The clock showed ten fifty. It was now or never.

"Would you be willing to bring a few of Vincent's paintings with you on your wife's tour?" Thinking fast, she added, "And a catalog. Show the range of his work. Introduce Vincent's art to dealers in each city. Go to museum directors. You know his background."

"Ask for meetings with dealers? Take around a few paintings as we travel?" Leclercq tapped his finger on his chin. "Why me?"

"You wrote such kind words about Vincent in his obituary."

His eyes widened. "You remember it? That was years ago!"

"I remember it gave Theo comfort to feel as though Vincent had been understood—at least by the art community. Vincent's work transcends national boundaries. He wasn't a political man. He was an ordinary, common man whose work speaks to everyone. He's known here, in his own country, and to a few collectors in Paris. But other countries should know him too."

"It's been a few years, but it's true his work has stayed with me."

"He has that effect."

"And if he isn't received well?"

"If we don't try, we can't find out."

Leclercq grinned. "*We*, heh? I suppose I could make room in my luggage for a few paintings."

Jo bit her lip. She had to tell him about being shut out of Paris. He had to know she'd ruined Vincent's advancement there by bungling her interactions with Vollard and Raulf. That representing Vincent could be dangerous. "There's one thing I must tell you. Vincent's paintings have been rejected by some Parisian dealers."

Leclercq smiled. "The old guard, eh?"

"I guess you could call them that."

"The status quo likes to protect its own interests. I'm not worried about them. Shall we work together, then?"

Relieved, barely believing his response, Jo jumped onto the balls of her feet and grabbed his arm with both hands. "Yes! Yes!"

"What's this, darling?" Fanny asked.

Leclercq put his arm around his wife and winked at Jo.

"Your Renaissance man has a new quest."

THIRTY-FIVE

BUSSUM

Jo

FOR THE FIRST FEW MONTHS AFTER LECLERCQ AND FANNY had left on her concert tour, Jo's heart skipped whenever a letter with a foreign postscript landed in her mail basket. Each time she spotted Leclercq's thick, loopy handwriting, she ripped open the envelopes with her fingers instead of digging around for Theo's letter opener. His notes carried hope.

An art gallery in Finland was excited, a gallery owner in Stockholm intrigued. She would crush the notes to her chest. She'd known this would happen. Her dream of seeing Vincent's artwork appreciated across the world was coming true. Getting Vincent in front of art lovers in other countries would become a reality. She could feel it. Soon Vincent would be as familiar overseas as he was among his own Dutch countrymen.

Yet as one month became two and two months turned into four, Leclercq's cheery reports slowed to a trickle so that when they did arrive, each missive's disappointment felt like one of Cook's collapsed soufflés. Initial interest, but no next steps. No exhibition offered. No requests for more paintings. No sales. Maybe she should have sent different samples? Or changed the pricing? She looked at her notes a dozen times. *Bed at Saint-Rémy* at five hundred, *Park at Arles* at eight hundred, and *Jardin* at twelve hundred. Maybe she should have given Leclercq more background on each one? He could be saying the wrong things. Being an art critic didn't mean he knew how to sell.

Wracked with second-guessing, Jo couldn't help but feel this chance was slipping through her fingers.

Six months after Leclercq had left, Jo sat at Theo's writing desk, chewing the end of her pen, annoyed at a news article spread out in front of her. Maria Barbera Boissevain-Pijnappel, a senator in Holland's parliament, had been interviewed on women's rights. In the article, she was quoted as saying the women's movement was "an ugly, natural growth of our fin de siècle civilization and development."

Jo groaned.

"Mevrouw?" Cook stood in the doorway with concern on her face.

"Oh, Cook. I'm reading about our very own female parliament member, Mevrouw Boissevain. You'd think she'd be an ally for women. Instead, she's repeating the same old argument against our women's movement—that it distracts women from their number one priority: taking care of the home."

"I wonder if she has children? She must have a maid."

"A woman in her position? Absolutely. She's making the mistake of thinking *privilege* gives her the right to consign her household to servants. And if she has children, it wouldn't surprise me if she's relegated their upbringing to maids and nannies. My mother did, and she had no work. The servants were a sign of her status—and my father's growing wealth."

"So, your mother would agree with the senator?"

"I think so. Taking care of the home has always been her only priority. But the women's movement has never claimed that women should neglect their homes. Rather, that they should have a choice in how they conduct their lives and duties. And those choices shouldn't be limited to certain roles and jobs."

"Some of us can't choose. I started cooking from my mother's knee. It's all I know."

"You're a brilliant cook. Your meals are renowned!"

Cook smiled but then bit her lip. "Never went to school past ten years old."

"The right to an education for all is a principle of the women's movement too."

Cook rubbed her eyes. "Well then, Mevrouw, best you put your education to work and write that MEP back! She's got the facts all wrong. You need to tell her!"

"Write to her? My thoughts?" A letter would be nothing like translating someone else's ideas.

"Right now! While you're angry!"

"Oh . . ." Jo looked down at the open newspaper. "Or a letter to the editor?"

"You *choose*." Cook grinned and held out her hand. "But first, I came in for the menu plan. I need to send that lazy Bella to the market."

Chuckling, Jo slid the menu plan across the desk to Cook. With a deep breath, she pulled a blank sheet of paper from a drawer. Ready or not. She dipped her pen into the ink and scratched out a response: *I am utterly unable to find the case of the woman who needs a housekeeper as foolish as you make it appear, I think, on the contrary, that it is a very wise and sensible woman who would prefer to spend her time with her children, rather than always washing up the cups, mending and doing the laundry. A person can only do one thing at a time and sadly I know a lot of women who put their house before their children.*

Before she could change her mind, she shoved the letter into an envelope, addressed it to the newspaper editor, and dropped it in the basket for outgoing mail.

Two days later, when she saw her letter printed in the paper, fear jolted through her body. What had she been thinking? Her private thoughts criticizing the government on display for everyone to judge. Each time the front door opened, she expected some faceless accuser to waggle his finger in her face.

But the following day two more letters appeared in the column agreeing with Jo's sentiments. The next day, letters appeared on both sides of the argument. It was as if Jo's comments had broken open a dam, and debate on the women's movement roared. Within a month, MEP Boissevain-Pijnapple backtracked. She'd never meant to attack the women's movement and had been misjudged. *What it is: a protest based on emotion.*

The day after the apology appeared in the paper, Jo opened a note from Pieter Tak. *Are you ready to write for me now? I need an article on the relationship between the women's movement and socialism.*

Her mind spun with ideas even before picking up her pen.

That fall, an exhibition of Vincent's work in the Arts and Crafts Gallery in The Hague earned an astounding fourteen hundred fifty guilders. *Field with Poppies* alone sold for four hundred guilders. Prices for his paintings were increasing, yet Jo couldn't help feeling a twinge of disappointment. His fans still remained firmly entrenched on Dutch soil.

Months passed into another year. Leclercq's sporadic letters were brief and routine. Fanny's concerts were going well. Travel was fatiguing. No interest yet in Vincent. It was clear that her spontaneous idea to partner with Leclercq had been childish. Another failed attempt. She pushed him to the back of her mind.

Another year passed.

THIRTY-SIX

BUSSUM

Jo

ONE MORNING IN EARLY FEBRUARY 1900, JO HAD RETURNED from walking down to the market when she discovered a visitor in front of *The Potato Eaters*, both arms outstretched with his hands on the fireplace mantel.

"Good morning, Meneer." Jo suppressed a wave of exasperation at another visitor stopping in without notice.

He approached her with hands open wide, cupping her hand in two of his, pressing it. "Mevrouw van Gogh, it's a pleasure to finally meet you. My name is Pieter Haverkorn van Rijskwijk. Do you remember me?"

"Of course, Meneer van Rijskwijk. Director of the Boijmans Museum! I wrote an introduction of Vincent for your catalog."

"You were too kind. I know our display was quite small in comparison to your typical requests."

"Every display is equally important," she insisted. "Please. Let me hang up your coat. Would you like some coffee?" As she spoke, she picked up a little bell.

"No, no! I'm not staying . . . I simply had to come in person to give you the most exciting news." Perched on the edge of an arm-chair, he squeezed his hat, crumpling the ribbon band. "The people of Rotterdam have bought a Vincent van Gogh painting."

"The *people*?"

He nodded giddily. "The *people*. Our visitors. We're a small museum. Especially for Rotterdam. Our funds are limited, but Vincent's painting created such a stir . . ."

"What do you mean?"

He sprang to his feet. "His work is quite distinct. A buzz such as I haven't seen or heard . . . really *ever*. It was an experience of what art should do. Reach and connect with people. Challenge them to view the world differently."

"And so, a group of collectors bought—"

"No, not exactly. That did occur to me, but it didn't feel right. Vincent's paintings feel like they belong to everyone, don't you agree?"

"I do, but I'm still not clear on who the 'people' are."

"That's it! I don't know either!" He chuckled. "I put out a notice in the museum. In the lobby. In a spot all museum visitors could see. We asked for donations of any amount so we could purchase one of Vincent's paintings for the museum's permanent collection." He began to pace. "Twenty-six people. All museum visitors. Once I saw the collection, I had another thought: give the *visitors* the opportu-nity to select a painting. Oh, I assure you," he added, "only from the paintings you had not identified as reserved."

"Which one did they choose?"

"*Poplars near Nuenen*."

"*Poplars near Nuenen*," Jo repeated, picturing it instantly. A lovely fall scene with golds and browns and reds in the treetops. An individual in blue walking beneath the cheerful trees passing a couple walking in the opposite direction. She'd always felt such peace from the painting. She beamed at Van Rijskwijk. Now others could enjoy it too.

This sale felt different. She loved it when individuals bought paintings, but for a group to do it scarcely felt possible. Instead of one person owning it, the painting was shared by many.

Jo grasped Van Rijskwijk's hand in two of hers. "I'm speechless."

Several hours later, after lunch and one of the most genial conversations that Jo had enjoyed in a long time, she waved goodbye as the director's horse-and-carriage taxicab pulled away. She crossed her arms across her chest and leaned against the doorjamb. Only then did the thought strike her: Vincent finally had a painting in a permanent museum collection.

One of her goals for Vincent to be recognized as a true artist had been met.

Marveling, Jo walked by the writing desk and noticed a telegram. It must have arrived during her luncheon. This was a day of good news. Perhaps a breakthrough from Leclercq? Jo tore it open.

She froze.

Cor killed. Funeral Saturday. Mother.

In an instant, memories flooded her thoughts. Playing the hero for Vincentje. Dancing a jig on New Year's Eve. Their last conversation by firelight and his words: *You've inspired me!*

Jo's eyes filled. *Oh, dear Cor.*

THIRTY-SEVEN

AMSTERDAM

Jo

TWO DAYS LATER, JO AND VINCENTJE SAT IN SILENCE ON a train trundling across the countryside. The bright blue sky and fresh green buds blurred like a painting as they sped through the fields dotted with farmers and oxen. On earlier trips, Vincentje would press his nose to the glass giving a nonstop ten-year-old's commentary on what he saw. This morning they sat in silence.

Abruptly, Vincentje scooted close to Jo, tucking his chin into the top of his coat. She pulled him closer.

"Cor was my favorite uncle." Vincentje's voice was muffled.

"He loved you too."

Vincentje looked up at her. She brushed his tousled hair back, revealing a bluish mark on his temple. Another bruise? She ran her thumb across it lightly. Her boy had been coming home with more and more of these marks. Grasping his chin gently between her thumb and forefinger, she turned his face. A yellowish mark faded on his other temple.

"You play too rough, Vincentje."

He slipped to the side, creating a little gap between them. Jo bit her lip. At least he hadn't pushed her hand from his shoulder.

"Don't worry." His voice quivered. "I'll take care of you."

Startled, Jo blurted, "You're ten, Vincentje. I'm taking care of *you.*"

He sniffled and swiped his hand under his nose. "Cor is dead. Uncle Wim is in school. Grandpa and Uncle Henry are always working." Jo felt a pang of guilt. It was true that Vincentje rarely saw her family.

"Uncle Dries cares about you."

His narrow shoulders shrugged. "He lives in France."

Jo combed her son's hair with her fingers. She'd no idea he cared about seeing her brothers. She felt a well-worn worry rise: Vincentje needed more men in his life. Male role models. Despite her belief in equality between women and men, the reality of day-to-day living meant he still had to know how men functioned in society. It was a fine line: teaching her son to respect all and still be a success in a man's world.

She sat bolt upright. Could the bruises have come about not from rough playing but fighting? With a light touch, Jo took hold of one of Vincentje's small hands and pulled it from his coat pocket. His red knuckles were rough and raw.

"Vincentje! Have you been fighting?"

"I *hate* art." Vincentje's voice was low and angry.

"You do not!"

"Do too! Wilhelm told me sons have to do their father's work."

"Wilhelm?" Jo pictured a sturdy dark-haired boy. The blacksmith's son.

"Wilhelm doesn't play after school anymore. His papa needs him in his shop. Wilhelm says it will make him grow bigger and stronger than us." Vincentje stole a glance at her. "I'm strong *now.*"

Jo looked at her son, small for his age. She remembered the lectures Pa had fired down on Henry and Dries when they'd been children. The only way to get ahead in this world was to outwit and outwork every man ahead of you. *There are winners and losers,* he'd said. *The Bonger men are winners.*

Henry worked incessantly and Dries felt like a failure. And Wim? She had no idea. He'd been a boy when she'd left home.

She couldn't rely on her own family to be role models for Vincentje. All he had was her.

"Yes, you are strong." Jo closed her eyes so he wouldn't see her emotion.

"What's wrong, Mama? Don't worry about me! I'm tough."

"You don't have to be an art dealer, Vincentje."

"Yes, Mama, I do! That's what Papa was."

"Yes. Papa was an art dealer, but—"

"If I'm an art dealer, you won't have to do it. You can be a proper mama."

Proper mama? Those schoolboys had been taunting Vincentje about *her.* Jo pulled his hands into both of hers and held his gaze. "Listen to me. Remember what Uncle Cor said? You are a Van Gogh man. You carry the Van Gogh name. And I know exactly what the Van Gogh men—Papa, Uncle Vincent, *and* Uncle Cor—would say to you right now."

"You do?"

"You must *not* follow in *their* footsteps. You must discover what *you* love and follow that. *That's* what being a man is. *That's* what Papa would say. And don't think that following what you love is easy. Papa believed in the artists he had in his gallery. He never gave up on them. Even when bad people"—Raulf rose to her mind —"said he would fail and never sell any paintings. Especially when it came to Uncle Vincent . . ." She gently squeezed his hands. "Your uncle Vincent was one of the toughest men I have ever known. He loved what he did so much that he wouldn't give up even when everyone told him to, told him he was difficult or silly or a failure . . ."

She loosened a hand and brushed Vincentje's hair back from his forehead. "Your uncle Vincent wrote in a letter . . ." She screwed her face to remember his phrase. *"The greatest and most energetic people of the century have always worked against the grain."*

"'Against the grain'?"

"It means it's very, very hard to stay faithful to what you love when everyone else tells you you're wrong. And *that's* what being a man is. Your uncle Vincent wrote something else: It's just *nonsense to say, there's nothing to be done.*"

"What does that mean?"

"It means when we see something we don't like, we're not stuck. You thought you were stuck being an art dealer. That's nonsense. You can choose to do something else. Tell me, son. What do you love?"

Vincentje held her gaze. His eyes widened. "I like math."

"You are *excellent* at math."

He frowned. "But I don't know exactly *what* I like about it."

"Then you'll have to find out!"

"How?"

"We could visit the shops in town. Talk to the shop owners to see how they use math to run their stores."

"Do you use math?"

"Of course. Every day."

"It's not a man's job, then," he said and sighed.

"Math is a tool for *everyone*. Men and women. It's used in all sorts of work. That's why it's wonderful you like it."

"Did Uncle Cor like math?" His eyes filled with tears. "I never asked him."

"I don't know. I didn't ask him either." There were so many things she'd never asked him. More about the girl he'd loved. More about why he'd been willing to fight. What it had been like to grow up with Vincent and Theo as older brothers.

She'd thought she'd have more time. A lifetime with her last Van Gogh brother.

The funeral procession seemed to happen in slow motion: Mother's haggard face behind a black veil, the nickering of the carriage horses on their way to the cemetery, Vincentje's cold hand tightly grasping her own, the incongruous smell of fresh spring air.

At the gravesite, Mother, Jo, and Vincentje stood in a tight row. Jo circled her arm around Mother's waist; Vincentje angled against her on the other side. Cor's two older sisters, Anna and Lies, stood ramrod straight next to Mother. With no husbands or children with them, Jo surmised they'd left their families at home. Wil had not yet arrived.

Behind them a small cluster of dark-cloaked women had gathered. They chatted in low tones. Probably women from the local church called on when the deceased had few attendees.

"Is this everyone?" the pock-faced minister asked, shifting his feet back and forth at the head of the open grave.

"Yes." Mother's voice was strangled.

"But Mother, what about Wil?" Jo whispered, looking over her shoulder.

"She's not coming," Lies answered for her mother. Her mouth was drawn into a grim line. "She's—"

"*Ill.*" Mother blurted. "Get on with it, Father."

Standing before the grave, opposite the coffin on the other side of the rectangular hole, Jo noted how the ladies ignored the Bible verses, satisfied with doing their Christian duty by showing up. They didn't know Cor.

Jo bent her head and said in her mind, *Thank you for your kindness to Vincentje. Thank you for believing in me.*

A steady formation of birds flew high above them, headed north. Jo watched their faint shape recede into the distance. Was their flight like the journey after death? A being who still existed but had moved out of sight?

Was Cor with Theo and Vincent now?

She'd been left behind again.

That evening, Jo pulled a chair close to the fire in the salon of Mother's tiny home.

"Come, Mother. You're chilled." With one arm around her mother-in-law's waist, Jo led her to an armchair. Mother's knees buckled, half falling into the seat.

"Where's Vincentje?" Her eyes were wild.

"In the guest room, Mother, already asleep." For once, Vincentje hadn't protested going to bed. Jo felt the exhaustion of the day too.

Jo took the older woman's cold hands in her own. She wished Anna or Lies had come back to the house from the graveyard, but she didn't know them well enough to insist. It was odd that they'd rushed back to their husbands instead of staying to comfort their own mother.

And Wil. She must've been beside herself. Jo promised herself she'd visit Wil in Amsterdam next week.

Jo busied herself assembling fire logs, scratching a flint until a flame sparked, and blowing on the kindling until it caught. She scooted Mother's armchair closer to the warmth, then knelt at the foot, welcoming the flickering warmth on her face. Slipping off her mother-in-law's slippers, she massaged her feet. It was probably only the reflection of the flames, but in this light, Mother looked haggard and more aged.

They sat in exhausted silence, listening to the crackle of wood. Jo tucked a blanket around Mother's feet, then reached up and took the older woman's cold hands to rub them.

"Lean closer, Mother. You need to warm up."

She jolted upright. "Where's Vincentje?"

"In bed, Mother! You know that." Jo pressed her back into the chair. "You should go to bed soon too."

Mother's hands clamped onto Jo's wrists. "I'm being punished."

"Mother!"

"The Van Gogh *curse* killed Cor."

The hair stood up on Jo's arms. "Cor was killed at the Battle of Brandfort." She kept her voice at an even keel. The morning edition of *De Amsterdammer* had carried a front-page article about Cor. "He fought in the Boer War. He was a hero, Mother."

Mother shook her head. Her voice broke. "He died by his own hand."

Jo's skin felt prickly. How could this be? Cor had been so cheerful when he'd visited. "But Mother—"

"Shot himself with a rifle. His commander saw him do it."

Jo shivered. *Like Vincent.* What had happened? No wonder Wil hadn't come to the funeral.

As if reading her thoughts, Mother shook her head. "Wil doesn't know."

"Wil doesn't know what?"

"I had to commit her."

A wave of nausea washed over Jo. Another mental institution. Was it the same one she'd been sent to after Theo had died? Her poor, fragile, dear sister-in-law. *Three brothers dead.*

Mother began sobbing. "My *babies.* My *sons.*" Blinking up at Jo through a tear-streaked face, panting the stink of wine into Jo's face, she grabbed her sleeve. "Save Vincentje!"

Jo wrestled to catch the clawing fingers. "Mother! Let go!"

"*I warned you.* First Vincent. Then Theo. Now Cor and Wil. Don't you see, Jo? They've all been cursed. Madness." Sobbing, she covered her face with her hands. "Vincentje is next."

A shiver ran up Jo's spine again. "Stop, Mother!"

The old woman wailed.

"Mama?"

Jo turned. Her stomach dropped. Vincentje stood in the doorway,

"What does Grandmother mean?" His eyes were wide. "I'm next *for what?*"

In a second, Mother's and Jo's voices collided.

"Vincentje, you are *safe*—"

"Child, you must hide!"

"Mother, *please!*"

"Mama, I'm scared!"

"The Devil's in this house!"

"Mama, *where?*"

"Come!" Jo commanded, opening her arm. Vincentje hurled himself onto her body. "Mother, *hush!*" Jo pulled the old woman to rest against her other shoulder. Her own heart thudded wildly. "Hush, hush," she repeated. "Breathe."

She felt the bodies on either side of her relax a smidgeon. The thin bones of age and youth pressing in on either side felt precarious. As their breathing steadied, her heartbeat quieted too.

"Today was terrible," Jo said. "We will miss Cor so much. But he was *not* cursed. *No one* is cursed." Mother stirred as if to say something, but Jo hurried on. "Though we do need to find out more about why Cor died."

Mother's voice was tired. "You can't argue with death. We have madness in our bloodline."

Jo loosened her arm so she could pull away and look at Mother's tear-streaked face. Jo's eyes smarted from unshed tears. "All right, let's talk about the deaths. Vincent died of melancholy. He went in and out of depression his entire life. Theo . . ."

She looked at Vincentje. She hadn't ever told him the facts of his father's death, but he was old enough to know at least some of the truth. "Your father died of a brain disease. Before he died, he had terrible headaches and could be confused." Her voice broke. "But one thing he was never confused about was how much he loved you."

"Jo, dear—" Mother's voice held a note of warning. Whether it was to reveal or to hold back on telling her son about his father's

illness Jo didn't know, but she wasn't going to give Mother an opening. This was not the night to explain the symptoms of untreated
syphilis.

"Not now, Mother. Let me finish." She turned back to Vincentje,
but her words were for Mother too. "That's why you and I have annual
exams with Doctor van Eeden. He treated Papa when he was sick.
Doctor van Eeden knows what to look for when it comes to being
healthy."

She and Mother exchanged a look of understanding. Now
Mother knew that she was not ignoring the risk that Theo could have
passed along the disease to her and Vincentje.

It was as though the electric energy had dissipated from the
room. The bodies on either side of Jo felt heavy. Vincentje was the
first to clamber to his feet. "I'm going back to bed."

"I'll come tuck you in again in a moment," she promised. "Now,
Mother—"

"Wait." She put a hand on Jo's arm. In contrast to moments
earlier, her voice was quiet. "I was so hard on Cor. So strict. The
last time he was here, I scolded him for going so far away. I don't
remember the last words I said to him, but they weren't kind, Jo."

"Deep down he knew you loved him."

"I've always been strict with the children, so concerned that our
family looked like an ideal minister's family that I couldn't see how
precious each one was. What rot!"

"It's not too late. You have daughters."

"*I have daughters.* Yes. I can try to make amends . . ." She lapsed
into thought. "I can reach out to Anna and Lies. Try . . . but Jo, Wil is
in a bad way."

"I'll go to see her."

"Good." The old woman rose unsteadily from her chair. "May I
lean on you?" she reached for Jo.

"Of course." Jo wrapped an arm around Mother's narrow shoulders. They shuffled forward.

"You must think I'm the one who's going crazy."

"It's been a long day."

Mother sighed. "I do worry about Vincentje. I'd hoped Cor could be the man in his life. He needs a man to look up to."

"I'm worried about it too," Jo admitted. This trip had alerted her to how much he struggled without a father. But she wasn't close enough to any of her friends' husbands for them to assume that role. All the other men she knew were stuffy art dealers like Jan. And Isaac. He was no role model.

The only other man she'd met was Johan Cohen Gosschalk.

She wondered if he remembered her.

It would be untoward of her to write to him, but what had she told Vincentje this morning about following intuition? Go against the grain.

BUSSUM

Jo

A STUBBORN CHILL CLUNG TO THE SPRING AIR, A STARK contrast to the promise of the season. Fat, ghostly clouds hung heavy, muffling the sun and casting a long shadowy chill over any hope of summer's warmth. Jo had just put another log onto the fire in the salon's fireplace when she heard the front door bang open.

"The time is ripe!" called an excited voice.

Leclercq burst into the salon. With a wide flourish, he swept a huge bouquet of tulips—pink, orange, peach—from behind his back and bent into a deep bow.

"Monsieur Leclercq!" Jo exclaimed. "Is it truly *you*?"

It had been two years since she'd seen Leclercq at the concert hall in Amsterdam. Still the same wild halo of hair and a young face only slightly more lined than she'd remembered.

"Mevrouw van Gogh!" He danced a jig, the flowers dipping in time to his feet.

He could've been a young playmate of Vincentje's. "Thank you!" She accepted the flowers, laying them carefully on her desk. "I'll give these to Cook—"

Leclercq dumped his coat onto the nearest chair. "The master!" With two strides he crossed the room and stopped before *The Potato Eaters*. "Your time has come, old man!"

"What are you talking about?"

He clapped his hands. "When Fan and I got back to Paris last week, I couldn't believe the changes. The Impressionists are everywhere."

"Claude Monet?"

"He's the king, but also Pissarro, Signac, Renoir, Degas, Lautrec. All the men who were rebels when I left Paris are now thriving! We must get Vincent into that mix!"

Jo's heart surged. To be in Paris. Vincent absolutely belonged with that group, but she couldn't possibly. Dries's situation was still precarious. She had no reason to believe Raulf would not carry out his threat.

"I don't—"

"Hear me out." Leclercq leaned one hand on the doorjamb. "In meeting after meeting with art directors and dealers these past two years, there has always been initial interest in Vincent's work—even excitement—but in the end they were too damn conservative. His work is radical. I know—*know*—that with a little Parisian endorsement, those fellows will line up for Vincent's work."

"I don't disagree. I've always known Paris is critical for Vincent, but—"

"Excellent! Right now, there's no better place than the Grand Palais to give Vincent visibility."

Jo heart flipped. "The World's Fair?"

Leclercq beamed. "Exactly."

This idea was too ambitious, far bolder than adding more paintings surreptitiously to a few more dealers in Paris. A presence at the World's Fair would be like screaming Vincent's name from the rooftops. Raulf would take any excuse to cut down Dries. And this wasn't an excuse—it was an invitation. Dries would be ruined. Pa would never forgive him. Dries would never forgive her.

Jo shook her head. "It's too . . . public."

"If you're thinking of that old idea that Parisians think the Dutch are has-beens, you're wrong. Do you know of Jozef Israels? He's a big deal in Paris now."

Isaac boasted about his father all the time. She knew Jozef's work well.

Leclercq continued, "I've been through the booths. They're all the old generation of Dutch artists. Gray-toned canvases. Landscapes with sheep. Seascapes. It all looks like Dutch painting is stuck in the past." He whirled around to face her, grinning. "Vincent would pull them ahead. Put them all to shame."

For a moment, Jo was transfixed. She'd always pictured Vincent's work in a large exhibition room with a full luminous effect of color and movement and power. Out from the attic, removed from the back storerooms of galleries, breathing like a life force. In spite of herself, she felt excited.

Leclercq continued, "Think of it. Vincent in his own booth. A small one, but still a space dedicated entirely to him. In the Dutch Pavilion, but separate from the Dutch old timers. Let's show them!"

"You already have the space, don't you?"

His smile tilted up on one side. "I knew you'd agree!"

Dread instantly dampened her enthusiasm again. "The World's Fair is one of the most public exhibitions in all of Paris."

"Exactly."

"I have an . . . enemy." There was no other word to describe Raulf. Her anxiety deepened. "My husband's former employer. It's a long story, but he's blocked me from promoting Vincent in Paris."

Leclercq shrugged. "You're not doing it. I am."

"He's no fool. He'll know I've agreed. That we're working together. And he's powerful. He's threatened to ruin my brother, who is an importer in Paris, if I so much as take one step back into the city."

"Who is this man?"

"Georges Raulf." Saying his name out loud made the hairs on her arms stand on end.

Leclercq burst out laughing. "Raulf! He's a has-been!"

"What?"

"One of the cranks who tried to control what Parisian art is or some such thing."

Could this be possible? The image of Raulf's belligerent face rose in her mind. She couldn't imagine that he didn't wield influence any more. She wanted to trust Leclercq, but how could she be sure? The truth was she couldn't. He'd been out of the country for two whole years. She couldn't be certain that he truly knew the inner workings of that tight-knit dealer group.

"I need six paintings." Leclercq broke into her thoughts.

The booth must've been very small. "Only six . . . ?"

"Six more to add to the three I traveled with. Nine paintings will make a nice splash."

"You've done this without my agreement!"

"Yes, but see how that protects you. It's my name on the chopping block, not yours."

"Why are you doing this?"

"When I travel with Fanny, I have a lot of time to myself during the day when she's practicing or rehearsing." He glanced up at *Irises in a Vase*. "I know it sounds nuts, but Vincent and I are companions. In reading the letters you shared with me and in introducing him to so many dealers and museum directors . . . I owe him." He laughed.

"Owe him? How?"

"I failed him. I think I can do better."

Jo knew exactly how he felt. Once he got under their skin, Vincent had that effect on people. She chewed her lip, torn with indecision. The idea of putting Vincent on display in the World's Fair, one of the most visible public venues in all of Paris, made her palms sweat.

And it was bad timing. Cor's funeral had only been one week ago. She'd vowed to pay closer attention to Vincentje, especially his fighting. Her son was her priority, beyond anything else.

She scrutinized Leclercq, who now stared up at *The Potato Eaters*. She'd relied on him for two years without any result. He'd been absent so long that she'd forgotten how he radiated energy in person. His enthusiasm brought a smile to her face. Perhaps it was a good thing that she was so occupied with Vincentje. She was still sure that for Vincent to be acknowledged—honestly recognized as a true artist—that acceptance had to come from Paris. Leclercq had said so himself. With success in Paris, the rest of the world would open its arms.

"What about time with Fanny? The World's Fair opens early and closes late . . ."

He shrugged. "Same hours she spends planning and rehearsing her next tour."

Jo took a deep breath. "I'm trusting you."

"Yes!" Leclercq grabbed her hands and danced a jig.

Jo laughed and pulled her hands away. Her heart lifted in spite of the fear trembling in her stomach. So what if Leclercq's overseas tour had been unsuccessful? He was still determined, and it felt good to have a partner who believed in Vincent.

When Leclercq grabbed her hands again to jig, this time she joined him. The chilly spring day felt warmer.

Vincent was returning to Paris!

—— ⚬ ——

THIRTY-NINE

BUSSUM

Jo

"HE REMINDS ME OF A CHICKEN, MAMA!"

"Shhh! He'll hear you!" Jo scolded Vincentje, then saw Cook cover her mouth to chuckle. Despite herself, Jo giggled. Johan Gosschalk tended to bob his head when he talked. It had taken him just one month after receiving her letter to arrive in Bussum for another art lesson with Jan. Although he boarded at the Veths' home, he'd fallen into a comfortable routine of coming to Villa Helma for supper each evening. That morning at the market, Anna had teased Jo, *Is my cooking that bad?* Even now, the question made her blush.

Balancing a platter with a rissole filled with meat and spices and a bowl of tender peas and carrots, she shoved open the dining room door with her hip. Gosschalk and her current boarders, three German brothers who understood only a few words in Dutch, were already seated at the table. The room was unusually dark for an early evening. A storm that had threatened all day felt closer.

"Shall I help you?" Gosschalk scooted back his chair. In unison, the three brothers followed suit, hastily sliding back their chairs. Vincentje slipped into the seat next to Jo and giggled.

"Thank you, *everyone.* I'm fine." Placing the dishes on the table, she exchanged a grin with Vincentje and Gosschalk. She noticed Gosschalk's blue eyes looked nearly black in the dimmer light. "Meneer Gosschalk, it's gotten darker. Would you mind turning on the lights?"

"You are indeed a modern woman, Mevrouw," Gosschalk responded as he lit the gaslight. Jo couldn't help noticing his hands. An artist's hands with long fine fingers. His coat fit so neatly over his wide shoulders and slender frame. She wondered how he had the money for the custom suit.

Unless this was his best suit? At that moment, Gosschalk caught her eye and reddened a little. She passed the rissole to him. He peered at the dish and cleared his throat. "I beg pardon. Does this have any salt? My stomach is sensitive."

"We've left it out as you requested."

Vincentje handed the saltshaker to the German next to him, gesturing at his food.

Thunder rolled in the distance.

"Oh, my!" Gosschalk scooted back his chair again.

"What's wrong?"

"The rain! I do beg pardon . . ." He was out of his chair in a flash. Jo heard the front door open.

"He runs fast for a chicken," Vincentje said under his breath.

Before she could reprimand him, they all turned toward a clatter in the corridor. Dumbfounded, they watched Gosschalk struggle through the doorway, carrying a bicycle.

"Mevrouw," he panted. "A gift."

"A gift?" She shoved back her chair.

The Germans shoved back their chairs.

"No, no, sit down. Eat." Jo gestured while Vincentje spun out of his chair to investigate.

"A bicycle!" crowed Vincentje.

Still panting, Gosschalk leaned a shiny black two-wheeler against the wall.

Vincentje ran his hands over it. "It's like mine, but bigger," he examined. "Is this for Mama?" His eyes shone at Gosschalk.

Just then, the rain erupted outside, sending slanting silver streaks through the darkened sky. Jo pushed the front door closed and turned to Gosschalk, who was gazing at her, looking sheepish.

"I . . . I couldn't think of what to bring."

"You didn't need to bring anything!"

"I was so pleased you wrote to me. I didn't want to come empty-handed. Then I remembered how you said you loved the outdoor air. Bicycles are an excellent exercise." His voice trailed off. His ears were pink. "I know it's not a normal gift."

"It's wonderful! Perfect, actually, Meneer Gosschalk."

"Could you . . . Would you . . ." His ears had brightened to red. "Call me by my familiar name, Cohen?"

"Cohen." Jo beamed up at him. His eyes softened. And the gift was perfect. The sort of unromantic, practical gesture that showed he paid attention to her. Perhaps even cared a little? She ran her fingers along the bicycle handlebars. Perfect.

PARIS

Raulf

DISCREETLY, RAULF PRESSED THE STARCHED HANDKERCHIEF TO his mouth to hide his grin. Before him the massive central hall of the Grand Palais overflowed with larger-than-life marble statues. Streams of morning sun poured through huge skylights to shine on commoners scurrying like ants between gallant soldiers brandishing swords on horseback, imposing scholars bent in concentration, and virginal country girls gazing in permanent wonder.

The perfect society.

His selections, of course.

He'd outdone his wildest dreams.

The 1900 World's Fair covered an immense one hundred twelve hectares with forty countries showcasing their idiosyncrasies by outlandish structures on either side of the Seine. It was rumored that fifty million visitors had already traversed the grounds. No doubt titillated by curiosities like the moving sidewalk or globe-shaped planetarium or tanks of exotic marine life. Frivolous distractions.

In contrast, of all the exhibitions and pavilions boasted by the

World's Fair he knew the Grand Palais at the center, his masterpiece, was nothing less than a triumph.

He chuckled. Père would have been giddy.

"Ah, Madame." Raulf intercepted two women — a plump matron
arm-in-arm with a shapely young woman—perhaps her daughter?—
from entering the south wing. "The *finest* art is down the opposite
passageway," he directed, tipping his top hat.

"*Merci,* Monsieur!" the dowager exclaimed, turning obediently.
The daughter giggled, looked over her shoulder and winked. His
face immediately reddened. *Ah, discerning girl.*

Confidence squared his shoulders. He had never felt more
alive.

Every morning, since the exhibition opened in April, he'd
relished starting the day by standing in his customary spot near
the Grand Palais entrance discreetly prodding passersby toward
the north wing where paintings by the very best French artists
hung. His curation would have been immaculate, if not for the
pressure to include Claude Monet, Auguste Renoir, Camille Pissarro and the like. In the end, he pandered to the requests but
when the art arrived to be hung, he stuck the Impressionists into
an out-of-way alcove.

The ridiculous arguments had wasted so much time that the
south wing's arrangements had proceeded without him. No matter.
They were all non-French artists anyway. Except for an occasional
walk through the booths, he'd wasted no time on them.

He had a clear goal. Use the Grand Palais' prestigious north
wing to his advantage. This had to convince the Boussod directors of
his command. The last rung on the ladder to being named partner.

An animated group of dark-suited gentlemen approached,
laughing and talking as they walked. "This way," Raulf said,
sweeping his hat to the north, but they pushed past, jostling him,
and strode up the stairs toward the south wing without a backward
glance.

"Imbeciles!" he muttered and took the steps two at a time after them. He had to know what idiocy attracted them.

Huffing as he rounded the corner of the staircase, Raulf arrived in the Dutch artist section. Covertly, he followed the gentlemen toward a group of spectators crowded into a corner booth. Irritated, Raulf drew near.

"Wasn't the artist mad?" a voice from the crowd asserted.

"You mean as mad as the men who invented the moving sidewalk?"

"Or talking films?"

"Or that engine running on peanut oil?"

The crowd's chattering and laughter surged. Raulf couldn't see the speaker.

"I think he's a fine artist." Raulf shoved aside a man in front of him. The voice belonged to Vollard. Stung, Raulf drew a breath to snap a rejoinder, then stopped in shock. Nine paintings by Vincent van Gogh hung on three sides of the booth.

Anger bubbled up his throat. Vollard was a traitor. Seething, he watched as Vollard vigorously shook the hand of the young man in the booth. *Turncoat!* Encouraged, the fellow pranced about, gesticulating at the paintings, his clownish antics drawing chuckles from the smitten crowd. And Vollard was *grinning*. The sight pained him. It wasn't the first time his peer had betrayed him. He'd noticed how the dealer had continued to sell the Dutchman over the years. All these damn Laffitte dealers were the same. Greedy. Valuing the almighty franc over patriotic honor.

He watched the young man laugh with Vollard. He reminded him of Raynaud. Another victim of this obsessive Impressionist movement.

He would not stand by.

Several weeks after the World's Fair had shuttered its entry gates and the exhibition grounds were well on their way to being dismantled, Raulf raised his fist to bang on the rue Vercingétorix apartment door. When it swung open, the young man from the Van Gogh booth, Julien Leclercq, jumped back, startled.

"Monsieur Raulf!" Leclercq exclaimed.

One arm was half swallowed through his coat sleeve; he was headed out. Raulf lifted an eyebrow. He was pleased the young Leclercq knew who he was. A single discreet inquiry had gotten him the man's name and address. Raulf had dressed to intimidate with even more fastidiousness than usual. It had taken him three tries this morning to get the new cravat tied just so.

He stretched out his hand. "Monsieur Leclercq, I presume?"

The young man hesitated. Overwhelmed, no doubt, by Raulf's presence. No need for the young man to know that ever since his discovery, he'd been drawn like a magnet to the Van Gogh booth every day to spy between the staircase balusters.

"I was headed out, but your visit takes precedence, of course. Come in, come in. It's all in the front room." He stepped back and gestured for Raulf to walk ahead of him into the sunny apartment.

The corridor, the boxing room to the left, the salon to the right. It came back to Raulf in a rush. He'd been in this apartment before. The arrogant upstart Paul Gauguin had rented these same rooms five years ago, hung his own paintings on the walls in a makeshift display. Raulf had come by one afternoon—he'd made it a point to keep an eye on up-and-coming artists getting traction with their destructive ideas—and had been pleased to find Gauguin alone. Despondent. Raulf chuckled to himself as he remembered. The artist had practically groveled to get Raulf's attention since the Parisian public had had more sense than to buy his paintings of savages.

Leclercq was lucky. Raulf had decided to put his irritation aside and help this misguided young man with a little instruction. Give him the benefit of his own experience. If Raulf read the young dealer correctly, he might even make him an offer he couldn't refuse.

Entering the salon, Raulf sucked in a breath. Van Gogh's paintings hung on every wall of the sunny room.

"Your coat, Monsieur?" Leclercq buzzed around him like an annoying bee.

Raulf shook his head. Turning on his heels, he took in the span of color around the room. His heartbeat quickened. There must've been twice—no, three times—the number of Van Gogh paintings here than in the World's Fair booth.

Not only were there more, but the variety was dizzying. Van Gogh had painted more subjects than he'd ever imagined. Landscapes and parks. Seascapes. Still lifes. Portraits. Splashes of color alongside two-toned drawings. The total effect made him lightheaded.

"Spectacular, aren't they?" Leclercq grinned like a child.

"You only had a handful of these at the booth."

"You've been there? How did I miss you?" He nodded. "The paintings in the booth are a sample. I have more room here."

The widow had sent them. Raulf seethed. She was *using* this poor young man.

"They're an excellent investment." Leclercq was like a little boy—his feet wouldn't stop moving. "Prices are rising fast."

Leclercq was selling to him! A humorless laugh rose in Raulf's throat. He swallowed it back. The widow thought she could work behind Raulf's back. She had no morals. She'd enticed this naïve young man to do her bidding. This poor boy was beguiled just as his brother was.

He would not stand by and do nothing. He had to save him.

"Leclercq." Raulf tightened his jaw.

"Do you see something you like? Do you want to make an offer?"

Raulf put a hand on Leclercq's shoulder. "I have another type of offer to make to you. An *exclusive* offer."

It pleased him to see he had the young man's full attention.

"I could see at the World's Fair booth that you are a young man of high energy and intelligence. In my role as a partner in Boussod and Valadon"—*almost* a partner—"I am always on the lookout for new talent. Every year we take on one or two young men to teach the art-dealing trade. It's a highly sought-after position. Very competitive. There are so many young men pursuing art dealing, it's extremely rare to acquire a sponsor."

"It is indeed an honor, Monsieur." Leclercq took a discreet step back so that Raulf's hand fell from his shoulder. "In fact, Monsieur Vollard has already asked me."

Raulf was stunned. Why didn't he know this? The fool had become more secretive lately, but he could forgive this omission. In fact, he felt relieved. Vollard might have beaten him to hire Leclercq, but at least Raulf knew they were on the same page. And a sponsorship with Vollard was coveted almost as much as Boussod & Valadon.

Nodding at the room, Raulf said, "You're starting soon, I assume? This can be dismantled right away."

"Oh, I refused the offer."

"Refused!"

"I prefer trying to make a go of art dealing by myself."

Raulf's blood boiled. He sounded like Raynaud—always wanting to go his own way, go to his own school, to leave home when he and Père had known how to grease the right palms to bring him success. He would not let this ignorant young man make the same mistake. Raulf clenched his fists behind his back to try to release tension. He had to switch gears.

"Fine. Good. Good for you! Then let me give you access to some more *established* artists. If you really want to make it as an art dealer, then you need to take care to set your reputation right away."

"I think I've started—"

"Hear me out!" A vein throbbed on Raulf's forehead. He *knew* this business! The boy had to understand, had to listen.

"Becoming an art dealer takes education and training. Apprenticing with me will give you the chance to develop an eye. Distinguish the good art from the amateur, the lasting art from the temporary."

Raulf shoved by the boy and began circling the room.

"Dutch art has its place. In the seventeenth century, the Dutch Golden Age was stunning. Rembrandt, Van Ruisdael, Van Ostade. Vermeer before them. Everyone agrees that their paintings are sublime."

He whirled around to face Leclercq. "And all agree that Dutch painting has been in a widespread *decline* ever since. In fact, Jozef Israëls—who lived in *Paris*, by the way—is the only Dutchman who's made any effort to return Dutch art to its true national tradition. Windmills, herds of cattle, sheep on hillsides . . . bucolic, idyllic scenes of country life. His work sticks with what the Dutch do best."

"And what's that?"

Raulf relaxed a bit. The young man was listening.

"Everyday themes." Raulf shrugged. "He's shown that the life of a Dutch fisherman has a certain dignity and splendor."

Leclercq's face looked dubious.

"The Dutch have a natural superiority in the handling of seascapes due to the country's geographical position and natural environment."

"You mean like this?" The young man pointed to a bright painting nearby.

"Like what?"

"A seascape."

The painting's white caps were roughly drawn. Raulf peered closer. Were those granules of sand stuck in the oil paint?

"Vincent van Gogh painted several seascapes when he visited Les Saintes-Maries-de-la-Mer."

Raulf stared at the painting. He remembered when Père had taken him and Raynaud to a beach on the Mediterranean Sea one summer. After toiling all afternoon, they'd showed off their town sculpted in sand. Father had laughed—amateurs. Raulf had kicked and smashed the houses while Raynaud had cried.

"I have a collector interested in this one," said Leclercq as Raulf stared at the painting. "But you could make me an offer."

"What collector?"

"Émile Schuffenecker."

"I know him. His interest is only passing—"

"Actually, he likes *eight* paintings." Leclercq's voice had an irritatingly triumphant tone.

Raulf made it his business to know all the top buyers. Schuffenecker was a fool to part with his money on passing fads. Vollard had sold to him too. But had this young man not been paying attention? As if he, Georges Raulf, would buy something so inferior. He paused. Should he feign interest, get more information, abuse his naïveté? "What do these paintings go for? The drawings?"

"Depends on the artwork, of course; one thousand to sixteen hundred francs."

Raulf gawked. The widow had no morals. Her fleecing had worsened.

"*La Gazette* is sending a reporter to do an article tomorrow. If you're interested, now is the time to buy. The paintings will be worth more after that runs."

Raulf clenched his jaw. He'd heard enough. So young. He felt an overwhelming sense of needing to save him. He yearned for Leclercq to understand this surge of interest was nothing but a publicity stunt. It would be over soon, but the young man's future would be tainted forever by being associated with it.

Raulf had been in this business a long time. He knew how it worked.

Impulsively, he put a hand on Leclercq's arm. "Listen to me, young man. You're in the wrong camp. You can't be in this business alone and survive."

"I made lots of friends in the Grand Palais."

"Paris is a cutthroat business. You need connections."

"I'd be honored if I could be connected to you."

Raulf choked. Nobody *asked* for his connection. Georges Raulf deigned it. He dealt only with the very top echelon of dealers. He tilted his chin up and fought for calm. Young people were so impatient.

"Under normal circumstances, *we* would never be connected. There are *hundreds* of little apartment setups like this"—he flicked his hand—"across the city. And what do all these young men have to show for it? Initially, a little flurry of visitors. A sale if they're lucky. Then these curiosity-seekers and tourists move on. What do you intend to do? Live off your *wife's* income?"

He'd insulted Leclercq with the biggest insult he could muster. But the kid didn't have the decency to blush.

"You know Fanny's work?" Leclercq's smile had the slightest smirk.

Damn. Raulf had given away that he'd investigated Leclercq.

"Her music is transporting, isn't it?" Leclercq looked across the room and laughed. "Like these paintings."

Heat rose up Raulf's neck. "I'm done playing with you, boy."

Leclercq straightened his narrow shoulders. His grin disappeared. "Haven't you heard? The new republic means the old ways are dying. France is a country where *all* men who choose to do the work can make their own way, not just the elite. I *want* to do this. Madame van Gogh and I have a partnership. This is my chance to make my mark."

"A *partnership*!" Raulf seethed. The widow had her fingerprints all over this farce.

"We're equals. We sell, we exhibit. We're writing an article on Vincent together right now."

Raulf felt sorry for him. "You're a foolish boy."

"And you, Monsieur, are a has-been."

Unbelievable. Raulf's face reddened as he stared at the kid's belligerent frown. Madame van Gogh had no qualms. She'd truly corrupted him. His heart thudded. How dare she ignore the instructions he'd given her and his explicit threat to her brother.

She'd been warned.

Without another word, Raulf turned on his heels and stalked out of the apartment. He would waste no more time.

FORTY-ONE

BUSSUM

Jo

"YOU PROMISED ME." COHEN PUT HIS HANDS ON HIS HIPS. "*TWICE.*"

Jo couldn't quite get ahold of her thoughts. Everything from wondering why she was marrying this man to remembering he'd asked her about the appointment yesterday. Outside, the January flurries had picked up in intensity, whipping through the air, adding to her disorientation.

Cohen coughed and banged his chest with his fist. "I *need* you to come to my doctor's appointment with me, dear. This could be diphtheria."

"Last week you thought you had smallpox."

"I had the symptoms! And *this* . . ." He hacked a cough. "This cough isn't fake!"

She steeled her voice to be soft, persuasive. "Cohen—"

"Jo! I know that tone. I'm important too!"

"And my commitments aren't? Henriette Holst is coming over to discuss founding a new youth organization. And I promised Leclercq I'd have more letter translations done for the book. I can't always drop everything at a moment's notice. People are counting on me, Cohen."

Cohen reddened. "I should think I could count on my fiancée!"

Jo sucked in a long intake of air and exhaled to stay serene. It was so much easier to write about equality of women and men than to actually experience it in a relationship day-to-day. She'd assumed Cohen was a more liberal man and understood that her obligations were as serious as his. After all, he'd been willing to sign a prenuptial agreement.

Cohen threw his hands behind his back, jutted his chin forward, and paced. His head bobbed a bit. "You're always busy, Jo. It's too much! Don't complain to me when you take to your bed!"

"I doubt I'll take to my bed," she said. The last time she'd "taken to her bed," she'd been married to Theo. She shook her head slightly. She'd been such a self-absorbed child bride.

"The boardinghouse is a full-time job," Cohen lectured. "Ever since I came to Bussum, I see how annoying guests can be. Interrupting your days. Leaning on you for every little request."

Jo lifted an eyebrow.

"When you're not dealing with the maids, you're at your desk, scribbling away at god-knows-what."

"You know I write book reviews."

"Twaddle!" he snorted, then bent over, coughing.

Jo rubbed his back in a circular motion, fighting to calm her irritation. George Eliot was nonsense? She was not going to be drawn into an argument on literature. He wouldn't understand what it meant to her to see her name beneath an opinion, whether it was a book review or an essay. It made her feel that she wasn't hidden away in a small town, that she had something worthwhile to say.

She kept her voice at an even keel. "It's not only book reviews. You know I'm translating Vincent's Dutch letters into French." Cohen whirled around to face her. Her heart sank. Wrong topic.

He threw his hands up. "The letters! Always the letters!"

"This is art business—you know that," she snapped. She and Leclercq were making headway on their book about Vincent, but since many of the letters were in Dutch it was up to her to translate them.

As if reading her thoughts, Cohen threw up his hands. "You have *Leclercq*! He's not an employee. He's a *man*. You told me he's an answer to your prayers. You have a man solely dedicated to Vincent in the most important art capital in the *world*, and yet you insist on tying his hands!"

"This translation is deeper than simply exchanging one language for another. The right meaning has to be put on the page." She knew Vincent better than anyone else. She added, "Leclercq only speaks a little Dutch. I know what I'm doing."

"Actually, you don't. What about Bernheim-Jenue?"

She grimaced. The renowned art dealer was on the same level as Vollard, Durant-Ruel, and Boussod & Valadon. Without her knowledge, Leclercq had approached Bernheim-Jenue and gotten their agreement to fit in a show. Leclercq had asked her for seven or eight salable canvases. She had wanted to send the paintings, but the haunting vision of Raulf's ominous threat kept her from it. Thankfully the World's Fair was so large, apparently Raulf hadn't noticed Leclercq's little booth. It was one thing for Leclercq to be selling from Gauguin's small flat. Quite another to stage Bernheim-Jenue's proposal to exhibit over one hundred works in a major art gallery. In the end, her indecision had caused her to miss the deadline and Leclercq had been forced to borrow paintings owned by the collector Émile Schuffenecker and Albert Aurier's widow.

Cohen continued, "If you knew how important Bernheim-Jenue is, you would have rushed paintings onto the Paris train! Instead you were too distracted. And with what? Writing socialist book reviews? Going to social committee meetings? More women's work? You squandered a once-in-a-lifetime opportunity, and now those same paintings are gathering dust in the attic."

She'd never confided in him about Raulf's threat. Cohen wasn't the type of man to stand up to a bully. She tried to justify her decision.

"The Rotterdam Kunstkring exhibit did well. Three paintings sold for four hundred fifty guilders. And now the exhibit's traveled to Zwolle."

"Both are in Holland! You've missed another chance! Leclercq's secured Paul Cassirer's interest. Cassirer is—"

"I know who Paul Cassirer is."

"Only the foremost art-gallery owner in Berlin."

"I said I know who he is!"

"You've insisted over and over your goal is for Vincent to be sold outside Holland."

"You don't know everything, Cohen," she said brusquely. She didn't want to admit that it had worried her when Leclercq had said Cassirer only wanted to deal with him. Was Leclercq protecting his own interests by keeping Cassirer from her?

"Nor do *you*, dear," Cohen shot back. "You tell me your art negotiations are off-limits, but I'm about to be your husband. It's my duty to make decisions on our property."

"Cohen, we've been over this! Our marriage property does not include the paintings." She grabbed his hands. She took a deep breath. "You know the paintings are Vincentje's inheritance."

"I'm not trying to meddle in your work—I'm trying to help you." His voice softened. "I may not be the kind of man Theo was, but I do love you. And I love your son as my own." He shook his head. "Jo, you're not letting *anyone* help you. You shut Leclercq out. You shut me out. You can't possibly know *everything*, dear. What about that odd box of Vincent's paintings that sold for a single guilder?"

Jo scrambled to remember the rumor. Gossip had it that a widow who had inherited her husband's art gallery in Rotterdam had sold several of Vincent's paintings for pennies. Simply hearsay. It meant nothing. Over the last few years, as Vincent had become more known, claims by people wanting to sell his art to her had kept popping up. But Cohen wouldn't know that.

Now he collapsed onto the edge of a chair, twisting his hands. "I worry about you. I gave you the bicycle so you'd get more fresh air. You've hardly used it."

Her heart softened. Her dear chicken was trying. She knelt in front of Cohen and took his hands. "I do love riding it," she assured him. And she did—the rush of air against her face. The steady pumping of her legs made her feel strong, reminding her of gymnastics class as a girl. She loved her bicycle suit, with its hidden bloomers underneath the skirt. He was trying, and she didn't give him enough credit.

She regarded him. How she hated the idea of canceling her plans to go on a useless doctor's visit. She could ask Henriette to meet on another day. And she could always stay up late tonight to work on translating the letters.

"All right. I'll go with you, but it means I'll have to spend the evening translating the letters."

Cohen squeezed her hands. "I don't like you reading those letters. They bring up unsuitable memories."

Unsuitable meant Theo. Well, of course she thought of Theo as she read the letters. How could she not? But he had been gone for ten years, and she'd had to learn that life was more than what a husband thought or wanted. When she finally stopped wondering what Theo would say or do, she'd learned that no decision he'd made had ever been certain or safe. It hadn't stopped him from having faith in Vincent and the other artists he represented in Montmartre and doing his best to sell their work. "Certainty" and "safety" were false prophets. There was no such thing.

She had no illusions that Cohen was her knight in shining armor, and frankly, she didn't want one. Cohen had turned out to be the steady male presence she'd wanted for Vincentje, and she loved the conversations she and Cohen had over art. Long ago, she'd felt like

Theo's pupil, but with Cohen she was his intellectual equal. She loved that he wasn't threatened but genuinely enjoyed their talks.

She kissed his knuckles. "Theo was my past. You are my future."

Down the hall, the clock chimed eleven. An hour before lunch and Jo still had the grocery list to write out with Cook and her correspondence. She was done talking about this.

Her voice was businesslike. "I can go with you *today* if you reschedule your appointment to later in the afternoon."

"Sometimes I wonder if you truly want to marry me." As he spoke, he picked up a painting leaning against the wall and turned it around.

Astonished, Jo stared.

A swirling mass of light spun in a cobalt blue night sky. In the right corner, a golden half-moon pulsated with a lemony white aura. Magnified stars punctured the firmament, dwarfing the darkened sleeping town below. In the background, a mountain range gradually ascended.

"Leclercq found the painting in a small gallery in Paris and snatched it up. The owner had had no idea he'd owned a painting by Vincent," Cohen said softly.

Jo stared at the painting, transfixed. "I remember this."

"You've seen it before?"

"Not exactly," She stared at the painting, searching her memory. "Vincent wrote about doing a study of a starry sky. The difficulty of doing blue *in* the blue." She bit her lip and crouched in front of the canvas, studying it. "Was it this one? Cobalt blue. I think the other blue is more of an ultramarine? Look how thick the impasto is! That swirl is going to engulf those mountains!"

"The stars look drunk!"

"They do." Jo laughed, and stood up. "It's such a departure from his other work there."

"There? Where is 'there'?"

"The asylum near Saint Remy." She pointed. "That mountain

range would be Les Alpines. The cypress in the foreground too. He painted other paintings with similar scenes." Delighted, she clapped her hands. "Just think, Cohen! There could be more surprising paintings like this hidden away. Forgotten in Paris!"

"So much of Vincent's work is still scattered. I wonder why Leclercq isn't searching for more."

"He offered."

"Leclercq needs a freer rein, Jo. Give him license to make his own decisions on Vincent's art. He's on the ground in Paris—you're not. I wonder why you don't trust him."

"It's not that. His time is limited. Fanny has another international tour booked." With a start, Jo realized it was touring that made her hesitate to give Leclercq independence. "He's only in Paris until her tour starts."

"Then he'll be gone, what, six months? A year?" Cohen was angry. "And what about setting our wedding date?"

"I can't, Cohen. Not with Leclercq gone."

"That's an excuse. You don't want me."

"But I *do* . . ." And she did. She glanced back at the starry painting. How many more of Vincent's gems were hidden away in Paris? An idea dawned. "You're right. I need to treat Leclercq as my full partner." She took a deep breath. "I'll ask him to stay on in Paris. Not go on Fanny's tour. If I'm to treat him as a partner, he needs to be there for me. As you said, it's time I give him a freer rein." She smiled. "Our marriage is important. *You* are important to me."

Cohen folded her into his arms.

From here on out, she vowed, she would welcome Leclercq as a colleague. Would Raulf object? *Never set foot in Paris again.* He'd warned her to stay out. The well-worn worry surfaced—could Dries be threatened? She would have to take a chance. She doubted Raulf had ever imagined she'd take on a partner.

She could let go a little. Set a wedding date. Be a newlywed. Pay attention to her new husband.

She'd been too conservative. For all she knew, Raulf had moved on and forgotten her. Hanging on to an old threat had been ridiculous.

Nothing would happen now.

————◇————

FORTY-TWO

PARIS

Raulf

"YOU'RE *ALONE* ON THIS, RAULF." VOLLARD SWIPED A damp handkerchief across his forehead.

"Not alone if you stand with me! When we are on the side of right, we only need a few to hold the line."

Vollard ambled over to his desk in the back of the gallery where a full cup of tea rested alongside books and papers. Raulf ran a finger around the high collar of his heavily starched shirt. Fashion dictated a three-inch collar these days, and he still had to force himself not to pluck at it. He tugged the edges of his linen suit coat down to avoid wrinkles before taking a seat opposite Vollard. Picking up the cup of tea, Vollard tasted it, made a face, and set it down.

"Listen, Raulf, my tea is cold. You've set me off my routine. I have a lot of paperwork to attend to."

"I fear we are losing the upper hand. There's too much encroachment on our art!"

Vollard pressed his fingers to his forehead. "We've been over this before—"

"Hear me out! For years we've had to keep an eye out for the artists who are insurrectionists. There's a strong undercurrent of radical anarchism that runs through the art community. A virus. The combination of social art and artistic freedom and the departure from traditional painting techniques have attracted radicals. Camille and Lucien Pissarro. Paul Signac. Their influence is growing."

"You mean their paintings are selling."

"It isn't *sales* I'm worried about. Sales are short-lived. *Tourists* have no discrimination." He spat it like a bad taste in his mouth. "It's how our next generation is attracted to the group. Turning away from serving France."

"*Patriotism* is that what you're worried about? *Pure France!*" Vollard mocked. "Just think of the money patriotism has caused me to leave on the table!" He pointed his finger at Raulf's chest. "And you! You steered me the wrong way! You think that true patriots honor only the past. Wake up, brother. You're missing what's going on in front of you. What's *been* going on for the past decade!"

"You mean this Impressionist fad? I understand *exactly* what's happening. Art should not be ordinary, some dull mirror of dull lives. It should be uplifting, visionary, aspirational to the viewer so that they are lifted up and transformed. Grand symbols that speak to the pinnacle of progress our civilization has brought to the world. We have thrown off a king. We have birthed a new nation. Our art plays a critical role in maintaining these self-evident truths. Leading the way into the next century!"

Raulf gave his friend a moment to let his words sink in. Père had taught him that he could both honor French tradition and still drive progress. Few understood this balance. When Père had financed the renovation of the Champs-Élysées, he'd had to shut down arguments that the avenue was displacing poor people. He'd told stories of how he'd stood alone in creating the shimmering gemstone Paris had become. "You're wrong, Ambroise. I'm not missing what's in front of me, but I'm looking at what our *vision* is."

Vollard sighed. "And what is this vision, Georges?"

"Perfect France. First in republics, first in culture. Setting the standard for civilization in the new century."

"That tall collar is choking all the sense out of you! New techniques by Gauguin, Seurat, Signac, others. They've taken hold. They're not amateurs."

"Gauguin!" Raulf ground his teeth. His visit with Leclercq and the exhibit he'd set up in Gauguin's former apartment still irked him. "His influence still reeks long after he's slipped out of the city with his tail between his legs."

"I'd hardly call traveling to Tahiti on a sponsor's money 'slipping out.'"

"You're blind! I'm telling you—it's like poison, seeping in gradually without recognition." Raulf charged across the gallery, pointing at each painting as he pranced around the perimeter. "Signac! Seurat! Gauguin!" He stopped in front of a brightly colored oil canvas. "Van Gogh! Van Gogh?" He whirled around. "You have it on display? We agreed—"

"We agreed I'd use discretion when it comes to Van Gogh paintings."

"You and now Bernheim-Jenue."

"Bernheim-Jenue," Vollard growled, bristling at the name of his competitor.

"Don't worry. The mongrel got poor reviews."

"And by 'mongrel' you mean Vincent van Gogh? An artist who has already begun to pay back his space on my gallery walls and more?" Vollard's face flushed red. "You know, *I* could have done that solo show six years ago if Madame van Gogh had sent me more paintings." Vollard slapped his fist into his hand. "I saw that he had talent, but no, you insisted—*pressured me*—to doubt my own instinct. As it is, I've been trying to make up for lost time."

"What do you mean?"

"I was totally wrong about Van Gogh. I thought he had no future at all."

"You haven't been selling him?"

"About twenty-five works so far."

Raulf sputtered.

Vollard stepped inches away from Raulf's face. "There's a mongrel in this shop all right. An old one, past his prime, so intent on serving his own interests that he's missing how the world is changing."

"The only way we can allow for change is to ensure France stays on top!"

"You're the one holding us back, not allowing our artists to lead France into new ideas. No wonder . . ."

"No wonder what?"

"You haven't been named a partner yet."

"You don't understand!" Raulf thought of Leclercq's young face in Gauguin's apartment. He thought of the hundreds of pimple-faced art students he lectured at the École des Beaux-Arts. He wasn't a barrier preventing the good. He was a fortress against the bad. It was what Père would have done. It was what would have saved Raynaud.

It was the woman. The widow. Society depended on predictable divisions of labor. Women were assigned responsibility for children and households. Why he remembered as a child how newspapers had been full of headlines about the patriotic duty of women to bear children after the devastating Paris Commune.

This was what happened when people didn't play their part. This was what happened when the foreigners wanted to take on roles that didn't belong to them. Art dealing belonged to men.

Raulf took a deep breath. "Look at us. We're arguing. It's her doing. Van Gogh's sister."

"Sister-in-law," Vollard corrected. "You know, I won't admit it outside these walls, but she does have a certain knack. Six years ago, she insisted on pricing the paintings higher. I was so angry I washed my hands of her." He looked out into the gallery. "But today his paintings are selling at those higher prices and more." He turned back to Raulf. "There's rumors that Paul Cassirer is interested in Van Gogh."

Raulf's heart dropped into his stomach. Cassirer controlled Berlin's art trade through his network of galleries. He ran his hand over his head, messing up the pomade he'd carefully applied that morning. "Cassirer is simply looking for a splash, a temporary sensation."

"I don't agree."

"For God's sake, Berlin isn't Paris!" The grimace on Vollard's face alerted Raulf. "Wait, there's something you're not telling me. The Germans aren't influence-makers. You've kept the Van Gogh paintings in the back room as much as possible. Why this push now?"

"I know a young man trading Van Goghs on the rue Vercingé- torix."

"It's nothing."

"You know about him?"

"He's arrogant, thinks he can make a name for himself on his own. "

"I don't know, Georges. I tried to get him to work for me, and he refused. The cheek! But then I realized two things. I admire him. He reminds me of myself when I was young. And he's creating a stir. I can capitalize on it. That's what we do on the rue Laffitte, right? Control the market." Vollard sighed. "Come to terms with the truth, old man. You missed the Impressionist wave completely. You don't want the label of *has-been* to stick, do you?"

Has-been? Raulf's face reddened. Leclercq had called him a has-been too.

Vollard's face softened. "It's tough getting old, friend."

Raulf closed his eyes. In his mind's eye he could see his vision for the boulevard Montmartre and rue Laffitte's storefronts. Window after window of stately, dignified French fare. Like having the Louvre accessible to all the passersby, it would attract hundreds to Paris. The brilliant gems on the city's crown. Raulf punched his fist into his hand. "Don't you see? I'm doing this for you. For us. It's for the greater good."

"But why make it about Van Gogh? Why so personal?"

Raulf scoffed. "It's not personal."

Has-been. He'd prove them wrong. Like his father with the glorious Champs-Élysées.

He had to stop Leclercq and the Van Gogh movement.

It was time for more serious measures.

FORTY-THREE

BUSSUM

Jo

"WELCOME HOME, MEVROUW *GOSSCHALK*! HONEYMOONER!"

Jo spun in her new pale green dress. "Do I still look like a newly-wed?"

Cook cocked her head, a smile playing on her lips. She put her hands on her hips and said, "I don't know that I've ever seen you in anything other than a dark color."

Jo arched an eyebrow. "You won't recognize me anymore, Cook. No more dowdy Dutch clothing for me! I'm a married woman now and must keep up appearances!"

"Appearances? For as long as I've worked here, you've never cared for fashion, Mevrouw."

"I'm not sure I recognize myself, Cook! An entire month off to honeymoon!" She glanced at her desk and lowered her voice. "I do love my work. But"—she held up a finger—"I'm learning. All work, all the time isn't good, and I kept my promise to Cohen. I took a complete break from the art business. Instead, I was a proper tourist and newlywed."

"I'm glad. You deserved finally taking a holiday. Still, when you're ready, I sorted the mail so that all of Monsieur Leclercq's letters are on the top."

Jo smiled at her coconspirator. The thought of Leclercq taking care of requests for Vincent's work had given her comfort again and again on her trip. Cohen had been right—she'd needed to loosen her control and trust that Leclercq was making the right decisions for Vincent. When she'd sent him the telegram, he'd responded the same day. *I won't let you down, Jo.*

She'd left on her honeymoon with a light heart.

Cohen clambered into the salon, carrying fat valises in both hands. Dropping the cases, he winced, hand on his chest. "What did you pack in these? I swear they're heavier."

"Jammed with garish Parisian fashion, of course. You said you wanted a proper wife."

He patted his forehead with a handkerchief and placed a hand on his chest. "I'm sweating. My heart is racing. That nasty draft on the train—"

Jo skipped forward and silenced him with a light kiss, then she pressed forward to deepen it. Pulling apart, breathless, she placed her hand on top of his on his chest and looked into his eyes until he blushed. Then she turned to Cook and laughed. "I'm afraid my husband is still getting used to my public displays of affection!" She turned back to him. "One of the many nuisances you'll have to put up with from your *wife.*"

"Let me organize a hot cup of tea for you, Meneer," Cook said. "It's good to see you both home."

"Mama!" Vincentje jolted into the room.

"Son!" She pulled him into a tight hug. One month had been far too long to be away from him. His head came past her shoulder. He must've grown a foot. "I've missed you!"

But Vincentje pushed away from her, and when she pulled back his face was pale, his eyes wide with fear.

"What is it?"

"Look!" His voice trembled, thrusting a newspaper at her. Folded in half, *La Marche* newspaper had a prominent headline: *Art Dealer Murder*. And in smaller script, *Julian Leclercq found dead in rue Vercingétorix apartment*.

Stunned, Jo reread the words: *Julian Leclercq found dead*. No. It couldn't be. She looked at the envelopes on her desk with his telltale curly writing. It was a mistake.

Vincentje babbled, "I wanted to get your newspapers earlier today and went to the telegraph office. Meneer Westerhof pointed out the headline. He asked me, 'Isn't this the man your mother worked with?'" His face crumpled. "Oh, Mama, I'm so sorry."

Jo's throat constricted; her heart hammered. She'd received a telegram from Leclercq two days ago. He'd promised to come out to Bussum this week. He'd teased he'd had news to tell her. Big news. She pulled her son toward her, pressing her body into his shuddering thin frame, looking for stability from somewhere, anywhere.

Cohen patted her shoulder and gently pulled the newspaper out of her hand to scan it. "It says here the investigation's ongoing. They don't know who did it yet or why. It wasn't a robbery or a break-in."

Jo took a deep breath. She pulled away from Vincentje. "I have to go."

Cohen nodded rapidly. "Of course. How about the back room? More privacy to rest."

"I mean to Paris."

"To a *murder* scene? Preposterous!"

"I have to find out what happened. Decide what to do—"

Vincentje caught her arm. "No, Mama! There's a murderer over there!"

Cohen's voice boomed. "No, Jo. You will not. That's no place—"

She whirled on him. "For a woman? Don't you see? *I caused this! I'm* the reason Leclercq was in Paris. I asked him to do *my work*. Encouraged him to make inquiries into the art trade when all along . . ." Raulf's image rose before her. Her throat tightened. Choking, she swallowed. "I ignored my warning."

Cohen shuddered, his face red. His voice was steely. "What I meant was that a murder scene is no place for *my wife*."

"Wife? Oh, my heavens, *Fanny*!" In fresh horror, Jo covered her face with her hands. Fanny Flodin was a widow now. Jo remembered the shock, the terrible surreal feeling of being in an alien place when Theo hadn't come home. And *she was the one* who had asked Leclercq to stay behind on Fanny's concert tour. If Jo hadn't asked him, he'd be safe. Alive right now. It was her fault he was dead, her fault Fanny was a widow.

Cohen pulled her hands from her face. "You're upset. You've had a shock. You need to go lie down."

Wrenching away, Jo spoke through clenched teeth. "When have you ever known me to need to lie down?" She picked up her suit-case, stumbling back a few steps from its weight. "I need to repack."

"No!" Cohen pulled the bag out of her hand, and it fell over.

"Mama!" Vincentje pleaded, crying.

Jo drew Vincentje into the crook of her arm. Her voice turned cold. "Look what you've done, Cohen! My son is scared! Instead of upsetting him more, be a role model. Be a *man*. My *husband*. Don't stand in my way."

"Stand in your way! Are you joking?" He threw up his hands. "You never let me close enough! You're like a one-way train. I could never be anywhere *near* standing in your way."

"What I have always cared about is—"

"Vincent's art. I know. *I know.* The worst part of it is that I actually think you believe that."

"You are unbelievable! I have been working with Vincent's art for *ten years*! Theo entrusted me with Vincentje's inheritance—"

"I don't want it, Mama! Don't blame me!"

"Blame you, Vincentje? Your inheritance is your *birthright*." She whirled on Cohen. "You've confused Vincentje!"

"Me? You're the one setting impossible goals!"

"Not me, Cohen. *Theo*. He believed in Vincent. I've done so much work to bring his artwork to light—*Vincent* would be proud of me."

"So, I'm competing against dead men. Vincent. Theo. Now Leclercq. Even though I'm alive, *married to you*, you value what *they* think over me." He heaved his suitcase up to his chest, crossing his arms across its front. "I thought our honeymoon would change things." He lifted his chin. "You lied to me."

"What?"

"You told me things would be different."

"Why are you talking about our *marriage*? A man's *dead*!"

"The worst part about it is that you lie to yourself."

Vincentje's tear-stricken face stared at Cohen's suitcase. "You're not leaving?"

"I'm sorry, *son*," Cohen choked. In seconds, the front door banged behind him.

FORTY-FOUR

PARIS

Raulf

RAULF SAT IN THE DARK OF THE BOUSSOD & VALADON Montmartre gallery. Open newspapers were strewn on the floor around his chair and on his desk. He stared into the empty arcade. Ghostlike images from the rectangular shapes of paintings wavered in the shifting wan light.

He leaned his head against his hands. How had his simple warning become a nightmare? The cheeky, lively young man dead. He could still see his smirk the last time they'd met when he'd offered to sponsor his progress in the trade. There'd been a time when Raulf's word could make or break a career. Yet Leclercq had laughed at his invitation. Scorned him.

Still. He hadn't meant for him to die.

Balling his hands into fists, he silently tapped his forehead. *Remember, remember.* He'd met the thug in the middle of the alleyway between rue La Fayette and rue Saint-Georges. Shadowy figure. Collar turned up. A floppy cap's brim pulled down. When he'd seen a circle of pipe smoke curled around the man's head, Raulf's stomach had churned. Outside the gas circles of light on either end of the alley, the man's face had been a dark mask.

"Here's the address." Raulf had handed him a slip of paper.

Grimy fingers had snatched it and stuffed it into a deep coat pocket. "Description?"

"His name is Julien Leclercq. He's attempting to be an art dealer. *Junior* level. One of the thousands of young upstarts who—"

"*Physical* description?" The voice had dripped disdain.

"Oh, of course." The man hadn't cared who his target was, Raulf had realized. Who had he been trying to convince that this was the right course of action? Himself? It had been too late. He'd pushed the thought away. Something in the air had shifted, as if he'd been the hireling and not the employer. He'd scrutinized the man in front of him. "Well, about your height. Very unruly hair." He'd patted his shoulder. "Down to here. Dresses rather sloppily too. Not befitting a serious dealer . . ." His voice had petered out, unable to see into the shadow of the man's face. Was he still listening?

The man had punched his fist inside the coat pocket where he'd shoved the slip of paper. "You have the apartment number on here?"

Raulf had nodded.

His voice gravelly with tobacco spittle, the man had asked, "Rough him up?" The pipe had dipped from the corner of his mouth. He'd held out a hand.

Raulf had reached into his breast pocket and pulled out a fat envelope containing one thousand francs. Enough to buy a Boldini painting. This had been an investment of a different nature. "A good thrashing." He'd thought of the beatings Père had given him and Raynaud. They had gotten their attention. At least, his. Raynaud had responded by escaping. That would work too.

"He's young. Not too harsh."

But now, a week later in this gallery, he strained to remember. Had he said those last words aloud?

Leaning into his hands, Raulf swore he could still smell the man's pipe. *Not too harsh*. Surely he'd said it. But what had happened?

Leclercq must have fought back, the fool. Hadn't he seen the man had meant business?

Raulf pounded the desk. Why hadn't he been more careful? He had a wife, for god's sake. Friends. A promising future, if only he'd listened to reason.

When Raulf had first read the headline about Leclercq's murder, he'd immediately gone to the Dutch Pavilion to see for himself, certain Leclercq's high energy would be there, chattering with other artists among the emptying stalls. Instead, he'd seen a somber cluster of men talking quietly. Someone had tied a black ribbon across the entrance to his vacant booth.

At least no one knew Raulf had hired the hooligan.

With a jolt, he sat up straight. Vollard! The last time he'd seen him, he'd gone on and on, complaining about Leclercq. It wouldn't take much for Vollard to suspect and call the police.

He jumped to his feet. Gathering up the scattered newspapers, he stuffed them into his valise. He needed to take a holiday. A little break from his work. Hands shaking, he straightened the remaining papers on his desk. Squaring the chair neatly up to the table, he stared down at his white knuckles. He could go to Rome. Or London. He'd stop by his apartment, throw a few clothes into a bag. Buy a ticket at the Gare du Nord for the next train to a large metropolis. Didn't matter where. He had lots of friends, other art dealers, everywhere.

He pulled a sheet of paper in front of him and grabbed an ink pen. He must leave a note for Antoine. Suddenly his weak-kneed assistant felt dear to him. He'd leave some kind of explanation for his absence. Something plausible. Leave a few extra francs in the envelope for him.

He was sweating, his heart racing, the ink pen poised above the page.

A bubble of ink dripped. The blot gradually widened.

His hand shook.

His mind drew a blank.

He'd never taken a holiday. What possible story could explain his leaving town so quickly? He was *fleeing*, for God's sake. His absence would have guilt written all over it.

Maybe he could explain himself to an empathetic ear, like the other top-tiered dealers. They understood each other. Durant-Ruel? Bernheim-Jenue? Vollard? He took a jagged breath and wiped the sweat from his hairline with his fingers.

But no. Whom was he kidding? He had no friends. His influence had come from the authority of his position, not him. He used to have allies, but the group had dissolved. No one cared a fig anymore what he thought.

He dropped the pen into the inkwell, splashing ink across the desk. Stumbling back, he hit the wall behind him and slid to the floor. Somehow everyone had turned in one direction, while he'd held out for the other. Could it be that all this time, they had been right and he had been wrong? Clinging to Père's ideals felt strangely thin, like trying to grasp the wispy strands of a spiderweb. How could they have held him so tightly? And where had they led? A death. *A murder.* Raulf dropped his head into his hands.

He was a failure. No savior of France.

He was a murderer.

Pushing himself off the floor, he fled.

FORTY-FIVE

PARIS

Jo

IT WAS A HOT AFTERNOON, UNSEASONABLE FOR OCTOBER; THE
air in the Paris church was close and cloying. Jo sat in the middle of
a pew, invisible in the middle of the assembly. She ducked her head.
Over and over her thoughts circled as if on a mad carousel. It was
her fault Leclercq was dead. Her fault for putting him in danger. She
didn't accept the newspaper account that he was the victim of an
attempted robbery when nothing had been taken from the apartment.

"The robber was scared away before he could take anything,
Madame," the blue-suited gendarme had explained. She'd waited all
day at the police station until an exasperated officer had agreed to
speak with her.

"This doesn't make sense! Julien Leclercq wouldn't hurt a fly!"

"Really? There's evidence he fought back." The police officer
had frowned. "Do you know something about this, Madame? What
did you say your association was with the victim?"

The victim. That was exactly what she'd set up Leclercq to be.

"A clue?" the officer had pressed. "A suspicion that could help
us solve the murder?"

Raulf? Had he seen Leclercq at the World's Fair? She had no idea. She had no evidence. "No, no . . . I'm useless."

It was all her fault. She'd known the risks and still asked him to stay in Paris. She might as well have placed the target on his back herself.

The groundswell of voices within the church buzzed louder. It had become packed with people in black mourning clothes. It didn't surprise her that Leclercq's funeral would fill the church. She was sure it wasn't only the salacious newspaper coverage either. Leclercq had been a friend to everyone. His energetic enthusiasm and antics drew people to him like a magnet.

Used to draw people to him. Jo's eyes filled with tears.

A stir in the crowd caused Jo to turn. Fanny Flodin walked up the center aisle, a man and a woman on either side, grasping her elbows, holding her up. Fanny's chestnut hair was coiled underneath a veiled, wide-brimmed black hat hiding her face. Her black dress slack against her thin frame. All eyes followed her to the front, where she slumped into the first pew and out of Jo's sight. Fanny was a widow too now. Jo remembered the helplessness, the gaunt hole of a husband's empty spot. The raw yearning for a love that was gone forever.

Tears ran down her face.

And now what was the result? She let loose a sob. Leclercq was gone forever. Her marriage was over. *Good. I don't deserve happiness,* she thought. Leclercq's work—all gone. Oh, God. She looked up in a blur. Leclercq's contacts, his agreements with Paul Cassirer, the plans for Paris he was keeping as a surprise to unveil to her. Gone.

Her mistake had brought her back to the exact spot she'd been in before Leclercq had come to Paris on her behalf. She'd returned to the beginning. Only her kind, joyful, energetic friend was now dead. The idea to make Vincent known overseas and hang in museums felt worn out and tired. She'd dragged other people into believing a dream that would never come to pass.

It wasn't worth it.

JOSEPH ROULIN

———✦———

I have . . . a head, and a bust with hands, of an old postman in a dark blue uniform. He has a Socratic head that's interesting to paint. . . . I always feel confidence when doing portraits, knowing that that work is much more serious . . . but rather is the thing that enables me to cultivate what's best and most serious in me.

—VINCENT VAN GOGH, *August 3, 1888*

Fall 1901
to
Fall 1904

FORTY-SIX

BUSSUM

Jo

THE DAY AFTER THE FUNERAL, JO ENTERED THE DINING ROOM. She'd retuned from Paris late the night before. Vincentje sat at the head of the dining table, spooning large gulps of porridge into his mouth. Crumbs from Cook's coffee cake sprinkled the tablecloth.

Vincentje paused, his spoon in midair. "Morning, Mama. You look tired."

"Late train." Jo took a seat, nodding thanks to Cook, who appeared with the coffee pot and poured her a steaming cup. She took a sip, peering at Vincentje over the rim. He looked more grown up somehow. Composed.

"Did you find out what happened?"

She shook her head.

"Don't worry about anything here, Mama." Vincentje gripped the table edge in front of him. "I'm keeping an eye on the mail."

"Oh. Yes. Thank you." Boardinghouse business was the last thing on her mind.

With a quick glance, Vincentje rushed on, "I already reviewed the guest list and talked with Marta about cleaning the north bedroom once Meneer van Buren leaves. We have a new guest—" He scrunched one eye closed. "A Mevrouw de Bruijn? Coming in this afternoon. Schoolteacher." He pushed the bowl of porridge toward her. "Eat something?"

"I'm not hungry." The idea of food made her nauseous.

"I asked Meneer Bouwman if he would seal the window in your bedroom too."

"Good," she nodded, absent-minded. "Wait, what?"

"Remember how Cohen complained about the draft?"

Cohen. Her heart caught in her throat. Sadness bloomed inside of her. She couldn't think about her husband now. She'd destroyed their marriage before it had even begun.

"Another thing, Mama," Vincentje inserted into the silence. "I'm changing my study focus. I want to be an engineer."

"Oh?" Jo blinked at Vincentje. "I thought you wanted to be a mathematician?"

He shrugged and bit into a piece of toast. "More practical."

Look at that. Eleven years old and already a young man. Her son was growing up in spite of her. Her eyes watered. *If only I'd been able to improve his inheritance,* she lamented to herself.

"My teacher told me there are lots of companies that need engineers," Vincentje munched, his mouth full of toast. "Except I'll have to go to engineering school."

She couldn't help staring. Where had her little boy gone? Who was this composed young man? Her old dream to get Vincent's work acknowledged overseas and into museums now felt paper thin. Right here—in flesh and blood—Vincentje was a priceless legacy.

"You're unhappy about me being an engineer?" Vincentje eyed her serious face.

"I'm sorry! Didn't mean to give you that impression." She smiled at his seriousness. His resemblance to Theo was uncanny. She should have noticed this before—seen how his plump little boy face had given way to the markings of a young man. The time had passed so quickly. Recognition rushed in, tightening her throat. Vincentje was taking care of her. Asking her to eat. Conducting boardinghouse business. He was stepping into Theo's shoes.

"I'm not unhappy," she assured him, smiling. "I'm proud of you! And you're . . . growing up so fast." A sudden thought came to her. "Do you know what?"

"What?"

"I think it's time I called you *Vincent* instead of *Vincentje*. You're a young man now. Look at the decisions you're making."

He laughed. "Mama, *you're* the one who first gave me the idea. Told me to follow what I really like." He took her hand as his voice became earnest. "And I know what you're thinking. Engineering school will be hard. Harder than the regular secondary school. But Uncle Vincent said, *Nonsense to say, that there's nothing to be done!*" He grinned at her.

Her smile widened at her favorite quote.

"You used to say that all the time to me!"

"It's true I was pretty obsessed with quoting Uncle Vincent for a while."

"*A while?* More like every day!" Squinting his face, he concentrated. "*Scratching around . . .*"

"*Scratching around in that indifference and that apathy,*" Jo recited. "*It's just nonsense to say that there's nothing to be done, but one has to work all the same with aplomb and with enthusiasm, in short, with a certain fire.*"

"Certain fire!" Jumping out of his seat, Vincentje pranced in a little circle. "I used to imagine hopping around *on* fire!"

Jo laughed out loud. Her little boy wasn't completely grown up. "*Imagine?* Hopping is what you *do!*"

He stopped and threw his arms around her shoulders. "You're on fire, Mama."

Tears sprang to her eyes. Jo hugged him back hard.

"I love you, Mama."

"I love you too."

Jo pressed her face into his blond hair and breathed in the smell of wood smoke. Cook had probably given him the task of stirring the porridge over the stove earlier. She drew in another deep breath of the woodsy odor. She had walked through fire with Leclercq's tragic death, and she would never forgive herself for that. She had pushed Cohen away, though she hoped he would return and allow her to explain how desperate and scared Leclercq's death had made her feel. Even this morning, her anguish had tempted her to give up art dealing for good.

But it wasn't in her to truly quit. She knew that. And it wasn't because she'd been art dealing for so long, but rather because she was sure—in fact, certain, in the depths of her being—that she was drawn to Vincent's work for a purpose. Deep in her heart, his work and his words carried a clear entreaty to be heard. She was the messenger. His helpmate, his partner. She was irrevocably linked to the fulfillment of his destiny.

No one got through life without suffering or betrayal or loss. If there was more fire ahead, so be it—she couldn't be deterred now. The work would go on.

She gave Vincentje a final squeeze. He pulled away.

"Mama?"

"Yes?"

"Everyone already calls me Vincent but you."

"They do? How have I missed that?"

He laughed. "But you can still call me Vincentje if you want."

Not everything had to be different.

FORTY-SEVEN

BUSSUM

Jo

OVER THE NEXT SEVERAL WEEKS, JO KEPT UP HER DAILY routine: Breakfast with Vincentje before he dashed out to school. Checking boarders in or out. Seeing to the meal plan and cleaning schedule. Answering correspondence and updating expenses in her worn brown leather housekeeping ledger. Some afternoons she bicycled to an abstinence meeting in town. On others she met Martha to plan the next Society meeting. And each evening she and Cohen—who had slipped back home after a two-week absence—met in the salon and answered art correspondence together.

All the motions looked the same. Yet beneath the surface, interwoven throughout the day, ideas for selling Vincent's art slipped into Jo's thoughts, and without hesitation she simply did them.

Before when she'd reached out to dealers and art gallery owners, she'd tried to align with the gallery owner's prejudices, pointing out how Vincent's work could bring them sales or enhance their reputation. But now her approach changed. Vincent's art was good. He deserved to be shown. Her letters no longer apologized. Plain and simple, she offered others opportunity. Instead of pleading for space, she presented them with a chance to take a turn at showing Vincent's work.

The second-guessing and worrying were gone. She was confident Vincent had an audience. If she persisted in keeping the artwork accessible, they would come.

One evening Jo and Cohen and Vincentje sat around the kitchen table for a simple supper. The carpet in the dining room was still drying from a thorough scrub earlier that day. Jo ladled mounding spoonsful of fragrant brown bean soup into their bowls while Cohen broke chunks off of *tijgerbrood* from the local bakery.

"I like eating in the kitchen, Mama. Less stuffy." Vincentje leaned forward to inhale the rich aroma.

"It is cozier, isn't it?"

"No separation between the workers and elite."

Cohen laughed. "Another socialist in the family!"

"It makes *sense* to me though. Everyone should be equal," Vincentje insisted. "Like your exhibit in Zwolle, Mama, where you set it up for the poor to get in for free."

Jo reached for her glass of water. "Folks who can afford it still have to pay the twenty-five-cent admission fee. But that's the cost of two loaves of bread. The poor could never afford to see the show otherwise."

"That reminds me," Cohen interjected. "The five paintings are back from Charlottenburg. Bouwman picked them up from the train this afternoon."

"Charlottenburg?" Vincentje sat up. "Isn't that in Germany?"

"Yes," Jo grinned. "Ever since the Berlin show—"

Cohen raised his glass. "The first solo international show outside of Paris!"

"I've started to hear from a number of exhibitors in Germany." She clinked her glass to Cohen's, but her smile eased. It didn't feel right to celebrate. The credit for the event belonged to Leclercq. He had made the connection to Paul Cassirer, paving the way for the Berlin exhibit. Her true artist had finally broken through international borders, but achieving the goal felt bittersweet.

Watching her face, Cohen observed brightly, "Wasn't it the Charlottenburg exhibit that introduced Karl Osthaus to Vincent?"

"Who is he?" asked Vincentje, reaching for bread.

"The director of the Folkwang Museum in Hagen," Jo answered. "In western Germany."

"He's written that his goal is to uplift people by means of art," added Cohen.

"Yes, I saw the letter. I've decided to send *Reaper*."

"And the Utrecht show needs sixteen paintings. I'll pull some out tomorrow. Bouwman's coming at noon to pack them up."

"I'll look them over before then," Jo said. "Oh, don't pull *Field of Flowers under a Stormy Sky*. Willem Leuring has asked me to set it aside for him. He wants to buy it someday."

"Wasn't he the director for the Maison Hals show?" asked Vincentje.

"Now how would you remember that? You must have been five years old!"

Vincentje shrugged. "I remember the socialist ones."

Cohen looked at her. "This is something new. Setting aside paintings on the *promise* to buy it in the future."

"It is, isn't it? But Meneer Leuring is a friend. And he needs time to save up one thousand guilders." A thought struck her, and she said, "Set aside *Landscape with Snow* too. It would pair nicely with *Field of Flowers*."

"Speaking of good friends, Willem Steenoff wrote in *De Amsterdammer* today that an entire museum should be comprised of Van Gogh art alone."

Vincentje's eyes were wide. "Who is he?"

"Another good friend. Assistant director at the Rijksmuseum."

"The Rijksmuseum! Would Uncle Vincent hang next to Rembrandt? Vermeer?"

"No, no." Jo and Cohen chuckled at his wide eyes. "He meant a *separate* museum," Cohen explained.

"It would be amazing though, wouldn't it?" Jo mused. "A 'true artist' hangs in museums." Her goal had always been to see Vincent's work in a museum's permanent collection and had imagined his work hanging in city cultural institutions like the Boijmans. Was it possible the time would come when Vincent would have his own museum?

"It's what you've always said," Cohen affirmed.

"Doesn't seem like we're doing this all on our own anymore," observed Vincentje.

Jo looked at him and smiled. No, it didn't. Not at all.

The next afternoon, Jo breezed into the salon as Cohen pushed away from her desk. "I had a marvelous bicycle ride, Cohen. It's a gorgeous day—clear blue skies, beautiful brisk breeze. You should go out. The fresh air would do you good."

"You know I always sneeze in the spring," he grumbled. "You could have had a maid deliver your letter."

"I wanted to mail it myself." Jo was particularly proud of the translations she'd done for the feminist magazine *Belong en Recht*. She loved using her language skills to spread the word on women's equality.

"I took care of the boardinghouse mail. Left art business for you on top." He patted the mail basket, moved to the sofa, and picked up the newspaper.

"Thank you." She settled at the desk and picked up the first letter. "Meneer Thijm. Oh, yes. I need to send him some notes for his lecture," she muttered. He'd agreed to give a talk on Vincent at Amsterdam University.

"When is that?" asked Cohen.

"Two weeks," Jo said, scanning the letter. "Wait!" She stared at the note. "He's changed his mind! No explanation. How will I find someone now?"

Cohen looked up from the newspaper. "I bet it's the Breda boxes again."

"What? No. Couldn't possibly be," Jo dismissed. Cohen would not let go of the "Breda boxes" rumor, but it had to be a myth. Mother had told her Wil had left boxes filled with Vincent's drawings and rough paintings with a shopkeeper in Breda near Nuenen. But when she'd asked Wil about them, her sister-in-law hadn't remembered. As the value of Vincent's paintings had increased, ridiculous false claims about Vincent's work had begun to circulate, including the Breda boxes. It peeved her that Cohen would not let this falsehood go.

"It's all hearsay anyway!" Jo snapped. "This is nothing new. People are always making outlandish claims about Vincent's work. Breda is no different." The fortune hunters were annoying, even dangerous. In fact, Mother had complained about a stranger knocking on her door to ask for paintings.

"Maybe . . ." Cohen shrugged a shoulder. "It's weird is all. I've heard that someone is hunting down Vincent's early work left somewhere in the Dutch countryside and selling it for next to nothing."

"*If* it's Vincent's work. They're probably fakes." Still, a niggling doubt gnawed at her. Usually the imposters asked for more, not less. This must've been a new tack. People were poor, desperate to make money any way they could. Perhaps they weren't aware of how the prices of Vincent's paintings had risen so dramatically.

Vincent would have been astounded that people thought him worthy enough to be faked.

Cohen harrumphed. "Well, *I think* the tactic undermines the art's value. Everyone loves a rising star. No one wants to associate with a falling one. You are wrong to ignore this!"

Irritated, Jo shook her head. "It's nothing. And it has nothing to do with Meneer Thijm." She had to admit that it was odd he'd canceled his lecture though. The man loved an audience.

Suddenly from the desk, the telephone jangled, causing them to jump. "That damned contraption," Cohen wheezed, coughing. Jo had had the new-fangled telephone installed only a month before, and Cohen still wasn't used to it.

"Hello," Jo answered.

"Jo, it's me."

"Mother! What's wrong?" If her mother-in-law had placed a call on this awkward mechanism, the news must've been distressing.

"Don't blame me!" Mother's voice broke. "I've sent Wil to the madhouse."

"Madhouse!" Jo blurted. For a second, she'd wildly thought Mother had called about the Breda art. She scrambled to focus. "But . . . I thought she was doing better!"

"I couldn't handle her! Shouting, biting, scratching. *Hitting* me." Mother's voice receded. "Then the next day she'd sit perfectly still. Hours at a time. Wouldn't eat a morsel."

Shocked, Jo pressed the receiver to her ear. "Mother, say that again. *Biting? Scratching?* Hold the phone closer." The image of timid Wil hitting anyone, let alone her own mother, was surreal.

"She left me no choice," Mother whimpered, her voice still tinny. "I'm too old for this."

"Mother, there must be . . ." She struggled, at a loss for an explanation.

"Jo, wait!" exclaimed Mother, suddenly loud. "How is Vincentje? How are you?"

She meant *madness*. Jo tensed. She'd grown so tired of these insinuations. She took a deep breath. "We are *fine*, Mother," she affirmed as much to keep herself calm. Vincentje's annual examination was next month. Doctor van Eeden would let her know if he saw anything amiss. Could this call be another overreaction? Mother's description scared her. She would go to check on Wil, find out for herself about her state of mind.

Quickly taking charge, she hid her worry, briskly got the name of the hospital, and, with a promise to report back, hung up the phone.

Cohen stood waiting next to her. His breathing scraped with a small rasp.

"Wil is in that home for the neurotically ill in The Hague." She would not say *crazy*. "I need to go see her." Unsteadily, Cohen pulled her into his arms. She buried her head in his shoulder. Wil had just turned forty years old. Her voice was muffled. "I wish you'd known Wil in the old days, Cohen. She was so sensitive and kind. Made me feel welcomed into the Van Gogh family."

"I wish I could have known her then too."

Sadly, Jo realized in the time they'd been together, he'd never known her sister-in-law to be healthy. And here she'd assumed that no news had meant that Wil was better. She felt guilty. Why hadn't she visited? She should have been checking in on Wil. Abruptly, she pulled away from her husband.

"Cohen . . ."

With kind eyes, he gave her arms a squeeze. "The train schedule is in the paper. Let's see if you can get on one this afternoon."

FORTY-EIGHT

THE HAGUE

Jo

AS JO ALIGHTED FROM THE HIRED CARRIAGE, THREE STORIES of tall sooty brick walls with narrow windows rose before her. She looked up at the engraved sign, *Home for the Neurotically Ill*, hung above the double door entrance. A blast of dust and wind blew soot into her eyes. In seconds, she'd pushed open the massive door where a sickly odor of bleach and urine immediately assaulted her.

The last time she'd been in an asylum was visiting Theo. This entrance hall was nothing like the intimate hospital where Dr van Eeden had treated patients. Here vacant-eyed women lined the walls, slumped in wheelchairs. With rising panic, she scanned the figures for Wil. She felt sick with guilt. She should have been following up, asking Mother more questions.

"Patient name?"

A short woman with a long white bib and apron briskly walked toward her. Her hair had been pulled tightly up and under a white cap.

"Wil van Gogh?" Jo half hoped this was all a horrible mistake.

But the nurse wordlessly turned, and Jo hurried after her down the acrid corridor, their strides out of step, striking the floor with a sharp clip like the relentless advance of a clock. Glancing into rooms, Jo saw only the ends of beds where white sheets shrouded the bump of feet.

Reaching the end of the corridor, the nurse paused outside a closed door. "In here, Mevrouw." Her eyes were tired.

Wil sat ramrod straight in an upright chair at an angle, half facing the window, half into the room. Thin sunlight banked through the window in a weak attempt to brighten the air, but outside the light was blocked by a tall cheerless wall. Wil gave no sign that she was aware anyone had entered.

"Wil? Wil, darling? It's Jo." She kept her voice low. She didn't want to startle her.

Wil made no response.

Holding her breath, Jo tiptoed closer. Wil's lustrous chestnut hair looked limp and dull in the poor light. Her skin was sallow. Half-open eyelids hid her gaze. What was she looking at? Jo looked in the direction of Wil's stare, but there was only the cinder block barrier.

"Wil." She raised her voice. "Wil, it's Jo!"

She remained motionless.

Wil needed fresh air. Didn't this asylum have a garden? A hidden sanctuary bright with a final burst of color before winter? A crisp breeze to carry the earthy scent of fallen leaves? There was nothing outside her window but this ugly barricade.

Nothing inside but this stale air.

She whipped around to scold the nurse, but the attendant had vanished.

Pulling up another chair, Jo rested her hand gently on Wil's bony shoulder. In a flash, memories engulfed her. Wil—happy, dancing, laughing, singing joyfully in her sweet soprano at New Year's. Wil—eyes glowing, delightedly recounting the progress the National Exhibition of Women's Work had made opening up new occupations for women. And Wil—tenderly pressing the packet of her own letters into Jo's hands, insisting she take them. The letters that in turn had led her to the brothers' correspondence that had brought Vincent to life and returned Theo's beloved voice to her.

"Oh, Wil," she choked, a lump in her throat. "Please come back to me too."

She grasped Wil's hands, her fingers closing around bandages. Startled, Jo rotated her wrists. Wil's fingers were covered so completely they resembled claws. Dirty dressings were wound in a crisscross pattern, torn, with loose threads at the edges. Jo stared horrified, indignant. What kind of care was this? These rags must've been days old.

"Wil, what happened?" She touched Wil's exposed wrist. "Are you in pain?"

Her face stayed blank.

Jo used her thumbs to massage Wil's bare wrists. "Wil, it's Jo. Look at me, dear."

"She can't hear you." A voice chided behind her, making Jo jump.

A white-coated doctor stood in the doorway, his hands shoved deep in his pockets. A stethoscope dangled around his neck. "She doesn't respond to touch nor smell nor sight nor sound. I daresay she's shut down all her senses." He strode forward, stopping to tower above them.

"What happened? Why are her hands wrapped? Did she hurt herself?" Jo demanded. Tenderly placing Wil's hands back into her lap, she stood up, shoving back her chair. "Those bandages need to be changed! They're filthy! Torn! This is neglect!"

He shrugged. "Your sister did not hurt herself."

"Look at her hands! How can she eat? Dress herself?"

"The bandages are for our nurses' protection."

"*Nurses'* protection?"

"Your sister scratches and claws at the staff."

Jo looked back at her motionless, gentle sister-in-law. It seemed impossible, yet Mother had said the same thing. She took a deep breath. She needed this doctor's cooperation no matter how much she wanted to hit him.

"How long will she be like this?"

He shrugged again. "Some patients wake up after weeks or months. Some never do. If your sister has experienced a trauma so shocking or sorrowful that she cannot face it, then she's escaped by withdrawing. You may never get her back."

Never get her back. Jo stared at Wil's listless face, willing her to make some sign, give some flicker of recognition. She wanted to shake her. *Don't give up.* Vincent and Theo and Cor would never want her to end up like this. *Don't give in.* Hadn't the women's society made a difference? After she'd found the group, the glow on Wil's face had been real. Jo knew it was.

She blinked back tears. "I won't give up hope."

"That's what they all say." He turned to leave.

"Wait!" Jo looked around the narrow room. The only furnishings were the bed and the two chairs. The walls were empty. Meager light. Wil was sensitive. She needed color and beauty and sunlight around her. This room would depress anyone. "Is there another room Wil can be moved to? Something brighter?"

"All the rooms are the same."

Jo felt desperate. "What about making the room more cheerful. A pretty blanket! Or I could hang some paintings. Yes, *paintings*!" With sudden inspiration Jo touched the wall. "Her brother was an artist. I'll hang one of his. One that she'll recognize." *The Bedroom.* Vincent had painted the cheerful still life with its bright yellow bed in Arles before his breakdown, before Paul Gauguin's stay. With a rush Jo recalled Vincent's letter to Wil about being in Arles. *I can live and breathe, and think and paint.* She remembered the painting's quiet scene of a large bed, spotless floor, clothes hung along neat hooks, paintings and drawings hung on pretty violet walls, To

Theo he'd written, *looking at the painting should rest the mind, or rather, the imagination.* Perfect. With glowing eyes, Jo turned to the doctor. "I know just the one!"

The doctor's eyes held pity. "Mevrouw, please. No personal items are allowed."

"But it could aid in her recovery—"

"It won't matter."

Jo touched Wil's hair. "You don't understand! Wil is sensitive—"

"Are you a doctor?"

"What? No-o, but to Wil, a *painting*—"

"I've already explained her condition to you." He jutted out his chin. "This is not a hotel, it's a *hospital*. No personal effects. We can't encourage theft."

She clenched her fists. "*I* would be depressed in this room—"

His eyes glittered, annoyed again. "Visiting hours end in thirty minutes. Best get to your . . . *visit*." Turning on his heel, he left the room.

Infuriated, fists clenched, and helpless, Jo stared at the closing door. How dare he shut her down? She blinked back tears. He had no idea how much of a difference a painting by Vincent could make, how it could break through to wherever Wil had withdrawn.

"I'm getting you out of here," she said to Wil. Drawing up the chair again, she sat on the edge and took Wil's hands in her own. "Darling, you must get well." And if she didn't? What if the doctor was right? At only forty years old, she might need institutional care for a long, long time. Mother had no money. She doubted Wil's sisters would help.

She squared her shoulders. It was up to her.

She would sell a painting. Wil blurred as Jo gazed at her through a veil of tears. Of course. She'd sell paintings to pay for Wil's care for as long as she needed it. Jo looked around at the blank walls. "You're getting out of here," she repeated. "Moving to a better place." She squeezed Wil's wrists gently. "Vincent will take care of you."

FORTY-NINE

BUSSUM

Jo

COHEN'S COUGH RUMBLED. "OUCH!" HE WINCED. SWATHED like a mummy in blankets, he laid back against the sofa. Before him, a fire burned, warming the room so much that Jo sat in shirtsleeves at her desk.

"Breathe shallow, dear," she said but didn't look up. The postman was due to arrive, and she had to finish this letter.

For the next few minutes, Cohen's wheeze joined the scratching of Jo's pen in the room. After a moment, he shimmied into a sitting position and watched Jo. "You're overreaching this time, approaching the Stedelijk Museum," he commented.

Without looking up, Jo continued to write and said, "Meneer Steenhoff is a friend."

"You shouldn't ask him to risk his reputation."

"I'm not."

"He was only *just* made assistant director of the Rijksmuseum—"

"I know that."

"You shouldn't press him—"

"Honestly, Cohen! I hate it when you become whiny," Jo retorted.

She put her pen down. "Willem Steenhoff *told me* he admired Vincent. Asking him to propose an exhibition at another important museum like the Stedelijk is not an overreach. Vincent deserves to be there. Meneer Steenhoff's endorsement will make all the difference. I can feel it."

"Are you *sure* Vincent is quite the caliber you claim?"

It was true she didn't typically wait for others' help, but the Stedelijk Museum was different. Jo couldn't tell him that she'd written to the museum six years ago and been turned down. He would use logic to support his point of view, but what she felt was intuition. That rejection from the Stedelijk committee had set off the sequence of events that led to her argument with Raulf, which led to her being shut out of Paris, joining forces with Leclercq and, ultimately, to his death. She wasn't usually a superstitious person, but she felt a little nervous about the Stedelijk. As though she could taint her impulse to exhibit in the Stedelijk in some way. Ruin the chance again.

And the Stedelijk felt important. It was now renowned as a major museum, a gatekeeper for significant modern art. An exhibition in the Stedelijk would seal Vincent's reputation. He would be acknowledged as a true artist, even a genius.

As if he read her mind, Cohen said, "Can't you be satisfied? Your dream of Vincent being known overseas has come true." He pulled his hands from under the blanket and ticked his fingers. "Berlin, Munich, Vienna."

"Don't forget the little museums. Kaiser-Wilhelm Museum in Krefeld, near Düsseldorf." She could feel the stress drain away at the thought of Vincent's artwork displayed in small towns by local art societies. Their reception to Vincent felt less political and more heartfelt.

Cohen scrunched his face. "And the Wiesbaden Society for Fine Arts in . . ."

Jo grinned. "Central Germany. I do love the small venues. Vincent always loved—"

"*Laborers*, I know!"

Jo laughed aloud. "I'll turn you into a socialist yet, Cohen." She sealed the letter and dropped it into the mail basket. Moving over to Cohen, she planted a kiss onto his forehead.

He caught her hand. "You haven't truly told me why the Stedelijk is so important."

There it was, the question that had needled her in quiet moments, the same doubt she heard in Cohen's voice now. She dropped onto the sofa beside him.

"It's not enough," she answered softly, surprising herself. "Every time a painting is crated and shipped to the next exhibit, I feel a little as though it's Vincentje going off on his own. Far off to Germany. To Paris. I want the paintings to go, of course. That's the point of my work. It's just . . . I have this silly sense that each painting is almost alive. I wish it well. And when eight or ten or twenty are shipped off together, a part of me whispers, *Take care of each other*."

She glanced at Cohen. He wasn't laughing at her.

Encouraged, she walked up to *Irises in a Vase* and gazed at the painting. Its tangle of blue and purplish blossoms looked cheerful in the light. "I just have this feeling. Wouldn't it be marvelous for all the artwork to be seen altogether? A grand reunion. Like a *family* reunion when the members haven't seen each other for ages, even years. And invite as many as possible. Bring back paintings on loan that I've sold too. And not just a room or two in the museum." She turned to Cohen, her eyes shining. "Four or five rooms at least. Perhaps more. Wouldn't Theo have loved that? And Vincent! It would be grand, wouldn't it?"

"It would be impressive!"

"I know the art speaks for itself," she grinned. "I want to hear them *roar*."

Later that morning, Jo shut her account book and stretched a kink out of her back. Ever since she'd opened Villa Helma, she'd kept daily track of its income and expenses. Balancing the accounts always gave her a tug of satisfaction. Pa would never admit that she was a success in business, but in all these years, she'd never run short and some months could even build up a surplus. Jo eyed Cohen's balding head on the sofa, motionless in his nap. Lately, those extra funds had gone to doctor bills.

"How are the accounts?"

Cohen's voice startled her. He must have been waiting. She still wasn't used to his inserting himself into her finances.

"Our expenses are higher now that we pay for Vincentje's school."

"You never should have paid for Wil's move."

"It's worth it. Vincent would have wanted me to," she said, cutting him off. The image of Wil in her bright room in the psychiatric hospital in Ermelo comforted her. Mother had brought a pretty rose-colored blanket from Wil's bedroom at home to spread across the foot of her bed. She and Jo had added pillows to the two straight-backed chairs set in front of a large window overlooking a garden. Wil continued to be unresponsive, but Jo hadn't given up hope. Ironically, it was the sale of *The Bedroom* for five hundred guilders that had paid for Wil's admittance. Worth every penny.

"Important to save for extras," Cohen harrumphed behind her.

She bit back a retort. She supposed Cohen's pronouncements were his way of attempting to counsel her on financial decisions. She didn't need his help.

Plus, she didn't tell Cohen about every bill. There was one she intended to keep secret from him for a while longer.

Doctor Paul Gachet, she wrote on the check. They'd only met a few times in person, but Vincent's former doctor from Auvers-sur-Oise had kept in touch with her. Last month he'd written that the fifteen-year lease for Vincent's plot was nearing an end. He'd proposed that she consider buying not only a new plot for Vincent's grave but another for Theo too, suggesting that one day the brothers' remains could lie next to each other. Even though Theo's grave in Utrecht was nearer to Bussum, she liked the idea. It felt right that the close bond the brothers had in life could be continued in death. She didn't know when or how, but one day she'd transfer Theo's grave next to Vincent's.

Cohen made a strangled sound, holding back a cough until it broke out. With a wince, his hand flew to his chest.

"I'll have Marta fetch the doctor."

Hurrying down the corridor to find the maid, Jo felt more determined than ever. It made no sense to waste time. She needed that museum exhibit. She needed demand for Vincent's work to rise and give her room to raise prices.

She was so close. The time was right for the Stedelijk. She needed it.

It didn't work out. A week later, Willem Steenhoff took the train to Bussum to tell Jo in person. Perched on the edge of a wicker chair in her back room while his untouched cup of tea grew cold, he shook his head, puzzled.

"It all came down to one board member. Jan Six. He was *most* adamantly against Vincent, said he'd heard from reliable sources that Vincent's artwork is overpriced. That you've driven up prices like the tulip mania."

"Ridiculous." Every Dutch child grew up learning about the tulip mania. A crazy, risky rise in the price of tulips in the 1600s had escalated so high that many people had sold their valuables to buy them, even purchasing houses by paying with tulips. "I can assure you, Meneer Steenhoff. No one is speculating on Vincent's paintings."

"Meneer Six said you're charging higher and higher prices here while Vincent's work is selling for a pittance in the south of Holland."

The Breda boxes. "I've heard rumors too," Jo conceded. "But there's no proof those paintings are Vincent's."

"Meneer Six says otherwise. Said someone has found a cache of paintings and is undercutting you. The Stedelijk's reputation is at stake, Mevrouw. Even if the criticism is coming from the south."

Suddenly, Jo chilled. Tersteeg. The two-faced manager of the Goupil art gallery in The Hague. He had mentored Theo as he'd been learning to be a dealer yet had been so cruel to Vincent when he'd lived in southern Holland. The vicious taunts Vincent had quoted in his letters came back to her: *You started too late. You should start thinking about earning your bread. I'm absolutely certain you're no artist.*

Could that animosity still be alive after fifteen years?

"I'm getting to the bottom of this," Jo declared. "I'm hiring a private investigator." She felt a throb of regret. Cohen had been right; she could have stopped this long ago. Tersteeg had been against Vincent at the beginning of his career, and here he was still barring Vincent's way even after death.

Steenhoff took a sip from the cup, made a face, and set it down. He stood up. "I've overstayed my welcome. I should be getting back."

"Wait." Jo wracked her brain for something to detain him. She didn't want him to leave with any doubts about Vincent's worthiness. "There's an art book coming out that includes Vincent. It will back up his value."

"Tell me more."

"It's by Julius Meir-Greafe."

"Greafe! The art critic."

Jo nodded. "He saw Paul Cassirer's exhibit of Vincent in Berlin." She paused, but Steenhoff's frown remained. How could the Berlin show be old news already? She rushed on. "Earlier this year Meneer Greafe approached me about producing a book on Vincent. I've been selecting Vincent's letters and translating them into German."

"How far along are you? Books take a long time to be published."

"Yes," she conceded. "But in the meantime, he's working on an article named 'The History of the Development of Fine Art.' In it, he claims the founders of modern art are Cezanne, Gauguin, and *Vincent*! *Modern art*, Meneer! Which makes Vincent perfect for the Stedelijk!"

Steenhoff sighed. "That's something. I'll try to work with that . . ." He threw his coat over his arm; his face resumed its frown. "But you must find out what's going on in the south. Someone is undermining your brother-in-law."

---◆---

AMSTERDAM

Jo

A MONTH LATER, JO PERCHED ON THE EDGE OF HER CHAIR, impatiently waiting for Johan Jolles, her private investigator, to find his notes among scattered papers on his desk. His scraggy salt-and-pepper goatee beard and moustache could use a trim.

"Ah, here it is!" Triumphantly, Jolles waved the paper above his head. He squinted at it and leaned back on his chair legs. "I can't confirm or deny that it's that Tersteeg. Whoever it is never identifies himself, but he's left a trail of sorts. It looks like he's systematically searching in every hovel and town in and around Nuenen."

"Systematically?"

"There's a method to his madness. Like a dog that won't give up digging for a bone."

"What happens after he finds a drawing?"

"Talks whoever's got it into giving it to him, or he pays a few coins. I didn't find a single person who knew the name Vincent van Gogh or even cared about art. Times are hard. People care more about getting the next meal on the table."

Jo nodded. There were pockets of Holland secluded and untouched by industrialization. Vincent loved the countryside. She needed to do a better job of reaching out to that area. Find a gallery to propose doing another exhibition with free admission.

"After Tersteeg finds the artwork, then what?"

"As I said, I can't confirm that it's Tersteeg. But whomever it is drops it at a gallery in Rotterdam." Jolles pulled out a pocketknife and picked at some dirt under a fingernail. "A widow inherited the business. Doesn't concern herself much with it. The name's Oldenzeel."

"*Oldenzeel!* I knew her husband. Christian." She pictured Christian Oldenzeel's bushy eyebrows and handlebar mustache. They'd hid a kind heart. He had been among the first Dutch dealers to show Vincent's work after all the Arti's fuss about being the final posthumous exhibit. His rough appearance had hidden his empathy. Early on, he'd been the dealer to warn her that the shipped paintings were arriving with small tears and holes, but he hadn't demanded any concessions for the damaged paintings and had simply returned them.

"She's typical. Doesn't concern herself with commerce. When I interviewed her, she was a bit dull."

"Dull? What do you mean?"

"She's never seen Tersteeg's face. Told me herself she doesn't understand how business works."

"*Or . . .* she's shrewder than you're giving her credit for, hiding behind the myth that women aren't good at business."

"Humph," he dismissed, annoying Jo. "At any rate, she's hired a boy to keep the shop open. She tells him when to leave a guilder out on a table. Tersteeg—or whoever—waits until the sun's down, delivers his package, and pockets the coin."

"So, it's true that the drawings are selling for one guilder? That's ridiculously low."

He shrugged.

"So, what happens next? Are the drawings gathering dust in the back of her shop?"

"The widow got really coy and clammed up when I asked her

that." Jolles folded his knife and shoved it into his pocket. "So, I sniffed around. Turns out she waits until she gathers a sizeable number, then sells them to Frederick Muller and Cie."

"The auction house in Amsterdam?"

"That's the one." He tipped his chair forward with a thud. "I went to see Muller. They've held three auctions."

"*Three* auctions! But Meneer Muller is a bookseller. I had no idea he dealt in artwork. Do you know how many have been sold?"

"I judge about forty or so."

"Forty!" So many more than Jo had realized. No wonder rumors had started to float. No wonder the strange behavior had chipped away at Vincent's reputation. "Who are the buyers?"

"Muller was tight as a drum on that question. Said only that the sales are private."

Who were these collectors? She'd had no idea an entire enterprise of trading Vincent's old work was going on right under her nose. Incensed, Jo's head spun. This exchange was cheapening Vincentje's birthright. This so-called market had to be shut down.

"Do you know when the next drop-off is?"

"Tomorrow evening. Always after sunset when the shop's closed."

"You said there's a boy there?"

"He goes but leaves the gallery unlocked. Don't worry. I'll catch the scoundrel."

"Tersteeg was so hateful to Vincent fifteen years ago. It's hard for me to imagine him carrying a grudge for so long."

"Resentment is a patient bully. The thing is . . . the longer it lasts, the crazier it makes a man. And the more dangerous."

Jo placed a stack of bills on the desk between them. "Thank you for your investigation. I don't need you anymore."

"But tomorrow—"

"If what you say is true, your confronting or threatening Tersteeg won't stop this nonsense. I need to find out why he still resents Vincent after all this time. This is *my* fight."

FIFTY-ONE

ROTTERDAM

Jo

THE SUN'S LAST BURNT-ORANGE RAYS SHIMMERED BEHIND the dark shapes of buildings outside the window of the Rotterdam gallery. Arriving earlier, before the gallery closed, it had been easy to convince the bored young attendant that the widow Oldenzeel had agreed Jo could stay inside the gallery past its closing time. She'd barely finished her fictitious excuse of meeting the widow later before the young man had been halfway out the door.

Now Jo hid in a back corner of the dark shop. The shadows of passing pedestrians became sporadic as she waited. Somewhere in the back room a ticking clock relentlessly counted the seconds, propelling her closer and closer to this confrontation.

Jo wiped her sweaty palms on the front of her dress. She was close—so close to Vincent receiving the recognition he deserved—a bully from the past was not going to deter her now. She remembered Tersteeg's cruel taunt when he'd written Vincent that he'd needed . . . *a kind of opium daze . . . so as not to feel the pain you suffer at not being able to make watercolors.* No wonder Tersteeg was vengeful; she'd sold Vincent's watercolors for handsome prices time and again.

The thought of him had the feeling of an old wound. Resentful. Petty malice from a bully whose victim escaped or, worse, continued to fight back.

Outside the shop a lamplighter ignited a streetlamp, spilling a halo of pale light onto the floor of the gallery.

The room's shadows darkened as the last rays of sunset disappeared. The walls felt closer. The shop was blacker than she'd realized it would be.

Spying the door to the back storeroom, Jo darted across the gallery. In a step, she twisted the storeroom gas lamp on and lit it, then plunged back out into the dark gallery again, leaving a narrow shaft of light on the floor behind her. Backing into the far corner, her heart thudded wildly. At least now she could try to see the old man before he saw her.

What if it wasn't an old man?

Too late, she saw herself as another might: a slender, defenseless woman. Alone. Fresh fear swept through her.

She hadn't thought this through.

The gallery door opened with an eerie squeak. A gust of stale air swept the stink of manure and gasoline into the shop. Holding her breath, she froze as a shadowy figure stole across the exhibit space toward the storeroom with noiseless steps. A bulky shape protruded from Tersteeg's hip. Her heartbeat pounded in her ears.

Leaning forward, Jo strained to make out his face. In seconds, he was at the table where Mevrouw Oldenzeel had left the guilder. In the crack of light from the backroom, the dark shape of an arm detached from the shadow to finger the coin.

"Is that you, *garçon*? Mevrouw Oldenzeel?" the gruff voice called out, irritated. Tersteeg moved toward the storeroom door.

Licking her dry lips, Jo stepped out from the corner.

"Meneer Tersteeg," she croaked.

He jumped. "What the devil?" Fumbling with his bundle, he cried out, "Who's there?"

Shaking, Jo rushed to the storeroom door and flung it open, flooding light into their corner. Stunned, she froze.

This was no stranger. Behind a thick grizzled beard and long stringy hair the face bore a remarkable resemblance to Georges Raulf.

Shock shifted to recognition in his eyes.

"Well, I'll be damned. The little widow," he sneered.

Jo gawked. The last time she'd seen Raulf had been eight years ago when he'd chased her from Paris. Back then he'd been every inch a man of elegance with his European-cut suits and spotless cravat. But now his overcoat was smudged with a dark border of dirt along its bottom edge. It hung from his shoulders as if he'd bought it a few sizes too big. His pant cuffs were dirty and threadbare. Instead of polished fine leather, his shoes were scuffed, shabby.

And his eyes were different. Instead of the aloof cold glare he'd paralyzed her with so long ago, these eyes burned feverishly.

What had happened to him?

"Monsieur Raulf." She felt ill. Georges Raulf was the culprit. What did he care about Vincent? He had dismissed him, called him a nobody.

"I remembered you taller," he blurted, clutching the burlap package to his chest.

"And you're so . . ." Changed? Filthy? Crazy? Instead, she pointed. "Is that Vincent's work?"

Smirking, he dropped it onto the table, leaning against the edge to block her from it. With grubby fingers, he tossed and caught the guilder. "Alone *again*? Someone should teach you that's not how business is done."

Her mouth went dry. In the back of her mind, she calculated how far away the doorway was, noticed how the street outside had emptied out of passersby.

As if holding a tortoise-shell comb, he delicately smoothed oily hair back from his forehead. "Tsk. Tsk. Such surprise on your face! I knew I'd stop you."

"You're the one?" She felt stupid.

He grinned, triumphant. "Only doing what *you've* been doing. Fleecing your buyers."

"I've always known you didn't like Vincent's art. But . . ." Her thoughts tumbled, astounded at the network he'd created. Madame Oldenzeel, The Muller auction house. Jolles had said the dealing had been going on for three years. "You've been at this for *years*! Why? You told me Vincent was insignificant."

"You never suspected me, did you?" Raulf grinned, revealing a missing tooth. "At first, finding these odd paintings was a little joke. I left Paris . . . for a holiday. Wanted to be alone, so I decided to go to Holland. No one would expect me to come here; I've belittled your provincialism so often." He laughed, proud of himself. "Came across a fellow who had a painting. I saw your brother-in-law's signature. One word: *Vincent*," he said with a scoff. "Told the codger it was only worth a guilder. He took it! Poor bugger probably needed to buy bread."

He chuckled again, then the mirth drained from his eyes. "I almost burned it, of course. But then I thought Vincent must have left dozens of drawings and paintings scattered all through this area. I'd never find them all. Idiot wouldn't quit . . ." He shook his head, tossing and catching the guilder as he paused.

He was right about Vincent living in this area and leaving behind so much of his work. He'd been practicing then with barely enough money to buy food let alone mail all his drawings to Theo. Her promotions were working. Jo sensed a trace of satisfaction. Apparently Jolles hadn't dug deep enough. Even in these outlier rural areas, word of Vincent's talent had spread.

"Then I realized I could do better." Raulf's voice jolted her back. Incredulously, she realized he was *boasting*. "If I sold them for next to nothing, I could *devalue* them. Attack his reputation. I know all about this. Little by little, all it takes is a *suggestion* here and there, sowing seeds of doubt, to ruin a man." His hands shook as he tossed the guilder and caught it. "In time, I knew my scheme would call Vincent's talent into question. No one likes to be swindled." He looked out from under heavy lids. "Especially by a woman."

Thijm's refusal to lecture. Six's refusal to accept an exhibition in the Stedelijk. Jo had to admit it—the strategy had worked. Raulf had damaged Vincent's name more than he knew.

Three years of collusion and secrecy. How much damage had he done?

Who else had been influenced by this lie?

But there had to be more to this story.

She eyed Raulf's filthy clothes, his unshaven face, and how he leaned against the table as if he hadn't the strength to stand. He tossed the coin again. A single guilder for one drawing? It was crazy. His transformation from fastidious polish to bedraggled neglect was surreal. There was something more here than a simple dislike for Vincent. It drove him. Consumed him. He had something to prove. She had to find out what he was up to and put a stop to it.

She remembered her visit to see him after he'd transformed Theo's gallery. He'd been driven then too. Perhaps it held a clue.

She kept her voice low. "Do you remember when I came to visit you in Montmartre after Theo died? You'd converted that gallery from Theo's vision to your own. The paintings were perfect. Beautiful children. Victorious battles. A bucolic countryside."

Raulf stilled. "Do I remember it? I *burn* with that memory. I had Montmartre under control back then. The other art dealers walked in step with *me*. We had a common vision, a united goal." He glared. "Then *you* came along. Flirting. You with your dainty questions, your pretty face."

"Me?"

With sudden strength, in one movement he stood inches away from her, rising to his full height. Shocked, heart in her throat, she couldn't move. She forced herself to look up, holding his gaze, steeling herself not to back away from foul breath. Or faint.

"I know you now," he said softly.

Her throat was dry. "Know what?'

"*Know what?*" he mocked. "How dare you disobey. Step out of your place. Come into my world."

"Your—"

"I could have been the one! I *was the one* until you ruined everything. People followed me. I was on my way. I *owned* Montmartre."

"No one *owns* art—"

"I did! I was the gatekeeper. I dictated what sold and what didn't," he spit. "I *defined* taste, defined style. People are ignorant. People need me to tell them what perfect art is."

"Perfect art? There's no such thing."

"Of course you wouldn't get it. Perfect art inspires a perfect society. Controls it."

Jo's skin prickled. "A society free of poverty? A civilization where all are equal?"

He raked his hair back. "When I think about it now, I'm *dumbstruck* at your tricks. If you weren't a woman, I'd admire you! Cunning. Plotting behind my back. Never had any intention of obeying me, did you? Willing to sacrifice your idiot brother. And I could have buried his career, you know. Easily. You fooled and manipulated and used unsuspecting people."

"Used? Used who?"

"Ambroise Vollard, for one."

Jo laughed. "Monsieur Vollard is hardly intimidated by me."

"Julien Leclercq."

Leclercq. Her laugh cut off.

"That's right," he nodded, watching her closely. "You used that poor young fellow. *You're* to blame for his death."

Sudden tears pricked her eyes. She'd never forgiven herself for Leclercq's death. The police investigation had led to a dead end, finally concluded Leclercq must have fought off a thief. Regardless, she couldn't change the fact that she was the one who had asked him to stay in Paris. He could have been far from harm, safe on his wife's tour if it wasn't for her.

His voice rose. "And all to make yourself rich."

"No!" Jo blinked, refocusing. The money had never been for her. It was all about Vincentje. "All I've done is work for my son's inheritance."

"Liar." He cocked his head, looking her up and down. "So cunning. An enchantress. You fooled others. You fooled me. But now I see through your playacting."

"Playacting?" Jo swallowed. The Raulf she'd known in Paris was back. His voice dripped arrogance. Threat. Her nerves jangled. He leaned too close.

"You've played the martyr. *Poor widow,*" he mocked. "Yet you wouldn't give up. Leave well enough alone. *'My husband died.'* You broke the rules. Your role was to move to your father's, go back to Holland, *disappear.*" His eyes caught the light from the storeroom and glittered. "But you refused. You went behind my back, and for whom? The obscene scratching of a madman. A dead man! A *nobody*!"

"*Not* a nobody, Monsieur." The words leaped from her.

"For God's sake! Let me show you." Turning to the table, Raulf ripped away at the twine around the package and yanked out the canvas.

Curious in spite of her pounding heart, Jo stepped to his side.

The painting was of a woman.

An oil portrait.

With a practiced eye, Jo took in the canvas. First the eyes. Tired but steady. She was a countrywoman, her face enclosed by a traditional Dutch hat. Its flowing fabric fitted around her brow and cheeks. Greenish gray-and-white brush strokes drew her back to the eyes. Dropping to the familiar white collar, it too drew her back to the face. Dark luminous eyes gazed out over a thick nose and full lips.

"So ugly!" Raulf broke her reverie.

"Wait." She tugged at his arm. "Look again."

At first glance, the peasant's dark eyebrows appeared stern, yet within seconds a softness around her lips and sagging cheeks lessened the severity. Jo imagined Vincent studying this tired model. No doubt she had modeled to earn a few guilders after a long workday. "She was a worker. Perhaps a wife. A mother—"

"*You?* Instructing *me*?" Raulf's face had twisted to an ugly scowl. "I see a haggard *peasant*." He spat the word. The painting swung, dangling from his hand.

"Hold on!" Jo caught it. "First of all, there's nothing wrong with working for a living. Vincent would have adored how she lived and worked. Second, you're looking at her outward appearance. Try looking from the inside out."

"*Inside* out?"

Jo studied the woman's face. "She *is* a bit haggard, tired. And a little worried. She carries responsibilities, doesn't she? You can see that on her face. I think she takes care of others. Her family. Her neighbors. And children. Yes, most definitely, at least one child." She could feel a mother's deep yearning for her child's welfare.

Raulf made a slight sound next to her.

Jo tilted the painting toward him. "She has dignity. See how her clothes are smooth? She cares about herself. She knows who she is. I suspect she reaches out to others. Hers is a patient, long-suffering love . . . beautiful."

She glanced at Raulf. He was staring at the canvas. If nothing else, she'd won his focus for a moment. "You're making all of this up. You can't possibly know what Vincent intended."

"I'm not sure it matters. Theo used to say the painter can only tell us about what the world reveals to him. And if he is a great artist, he does so in a way that moves and affects us. Even connects us to something greater. Or to each other." She paused, then added softly, "But I do know a lot about Vincent. I think we can see he appreciated this woman. Tried to express something of that feeling through his paintbrush."

"Bah! I don't see it!"

"Look again," she insisted. Her hands tingled. "Why so few people understand painting is because they rack their brains and want something that pleases the eye, and so they miss what's most exalted. I used to think paintings were all about what I found pleasing to the eye and not much more than that, but I've changed."

"I don't remember her." He took a step back.

Surprised, Jo turned. "Her?"

"My mother." Raulf's eyes were defiant.

"Oh—" She reached out a hand.

He jerked away. "There you go again! You and your feminine wiles! I learned everything I need from my father. And you're wrong. I have *no* connection to you! Foolish woman, you think you know so much. Don't forget: I've *stopped* you!"

With a flash, Jo saw he was wrong. In fact, every encounter with Raulf had spurred her on. How when he'd answered her naïve art-dealing questions at their first meeting but turned to disdain on their second, she'd gone on to make her first sales. How when he'd scathingly defined a true artist, he'd unwittingly given her a compass to direct her work to promote Vincent's art. And when he'd banished her from Paris, the painful setback had ultimately forced her to dig deeper to trust herself and to find that she could marry two passions—Vincent's art and her desire to help those less fortunate. Instead of discouraging her, Raulf's relentless opposition had goaded her on to do more than she'd ever dreamed.

Raulf flipped the guilder, caught it, and jammed his hands deep into his sagging coat pockets. He was so wrong about her. They were a world apart. Could he ever understand her? Understand Vincent? She had to try.

Jo placed the painting carefully on the table.

Raulf shook his head. "A true artist sells overseas—"

"And hangs in museums," Jo finished. They stared at each other. The words felt hollow.

She turned back to the painting. The peasant seemed to gaze back at her through time. When Vincent had painted this portrait, he'd had no idea Jo would see it today. She hadn't met Theo yet. Vincent had had no inkling of the role she would play in the future. Instead, he had focused on this subject and painted her the best he'd known at the time. Yes, he'd drawn her facial features and costume. But more, he'd caught something of her essence. An impermanent, timeless aspect that connected this woman from the past to her at this moment. She felt a prickling recognition, and with it, a new thought dawned.

"You've taught me something, Monsieur."

Raulf snorted. "What's that?"

"All this time I thought I needed to prove Vincent could meet your definition of being a true artist for him to be recognized, to be considered legitimate."

"He is *not* legitimate!"

"His legitimacy is not about those *external* measures. How many collectors he has. How much his paintings sell for. Even what museums he exhibits in." She sighed. "And here I thought Vincentje's future was dependent on money."

"What are you talking about?"

She shrugged. "Rodin touches the viewer by causing us to reflect on the meaning of death. Monet touches us by celebrating life." She struggled to find the words. "Like a life force. *This* is what Vincent tried to paint. In people, in nature, in their own portraits. A *true artist* awakens this essence in our hearts."

"But rules must be followed!"

"I guess I used to think that too . . ." Jo thought of society's rules she'd mindfully broken. Raising her child alone instead of in her father's house. Choosing to run a boardinghouse instead of seeking to marry and bear more children. Pushing her way into art exhibitions and bumping heads with so many men who'd patronized and lied and colluded to keep her out of the art world. All this time she'd wrestled with an incessant sense that she'd had to break rules to give her son an inheritance that would have monetary worth because that was what Theo would've wanted her to do.

She recalled a line from one of Vincent's letters: *The greatest and most energetic people of the century have always worked against the grain.*

But rebellion wasn't the reason she'd broken the rules. Not at all.

Death had torn away Vincent just as he'd been breaking through to a new form of expression.

Death had stolen Theo from a marriage and family they'd just begun. She would never understand this cruel turn of events.

But she had come alive because Theo had died. In the depth of her being, she knew that the very force of nature that had ripped away her husband also had given an opening to a buried identity she'd carried, hidden, all along. She had to accept her gain from the loss.

Looking up, Jo saw that Raulf had slipped to the door.

"I kept your brother-in-law out of the Stedelijk," he boasted.

"For *now*," she admitted.

Raulf hesitated at the door. Somehow he'd changed from an intimidating bully into a sad, bedraggled man.

"Aren't you tired, Monsieur? It's late—where are you going?"

"None of your concern." She saw a flash in his eyes and wondered if he had money to buy a meal, stay at an inn. That single guilder wouldn't buy him much. It felt wrong for him to disappear into the night like this.

With sudden inspiration she said, "Wait, Monsieur! I want to take the painting. Let me buy it from you." She dug into her satchel and held out some bills. "Just between us."

Wordlessly, he snatched the bills, jamming them into his coat pocket. Something struggled on his face until he burst out, "No one will remember you."

"I want people to remember Vincent."

"*You're* the nobody!"

"Not quite." She smiled, softly. "I'm the one who's saved him."

SOWER WITH SETTING SUN

———✦———

At the moment I'm really in the shit, studies, studies, studies, studies, and that'll go on for some time yet— such a mess that it breaks my heart . . . From time to time a canvas that makes a painting, such as that sower . . . If we can withstand the siege, a day of victory will come for us, even though we wouldn't be among the people who are being talked about.

—Vincent van Gogh, *December 1, 1888*

Summer
1905

FIFTY-TWO

AUVERS-SUR-OISE

Jo

A YEAR LATER, ON A BEAUTIFUL FALL DAY, JO AND COHEN watched as a lumbering gravedigger hacked and dug into the plot bearing Vincent's casket in the Auvers-sur-Oise cemetery. Overgrown with shrubbery, a yucca plant, and two tall thuja trees whose narrow green columns marked the hidden headstone, the camouflaged grave had hardened into packed dirt. The digger paused, wiped his sweaty face with the dirty kerchief around his neck, then resumed digging again. Remembering how Theo had waited a day after Vincent's dying to tell her of his passing, Jo felt peaceful. It may have taken fifteen years, but she finally would have her turn to pay respects to a man who had defined her life.

A September wind swirled golden leaves in circles, settling onto the mounds of earth tossed to the side of the grave. Across from the cemetery, a field of white buckwheat blossoms rippled like frothy whitecaps as if an ocean beach stood by to take up castaway coffins and sail them out to an earthy sea.

Breathing in the aroma of fresh grass and dirt, Cohen murmured, "Smells like the dunes, doesn't it?"

"It would make a Dutchman feel at home," Jo agreed and crooked a hand through his arm.

"Interesting meeting Doctor Gachet," Cohen said softly, glancing off to the side where the doctor and his lanky thirty-year-old son stood at a respectful distance. "I wonder if he feels guilty?"

"Guilty?"

"Strange to me that he claimed to be a homeopathic doctor and declared Vincent cured only a week before Vincent killed himself."

"It doesn't matter now," Jo said. The doctor had been a keen friend of Vincent's. Whatever his motivation, she was glad he'd quickly accommodated her request to buy two new adjacent plots instead of one.

Just then, the sharp thud of the shovel hitting wood rang out.

With a quick step, Cohen retreated, but Jo stood still. Carefully, deliberately, the gravedigger picked and scooped away dirt until the cracked shape of Vincent's rotted coffin emerged. Thick white roots from the thujas entwined around and into the casket.

The Gachets stepped forward. Kneeling beside the grave, they worked in unison with the gravedigger, gently loosening the skeleton from the vines. Unable to see, Jo drew closer just as Doctor Gachet carefully lifted the skull out of the box.

In an instant, Jo recognized him.

Vincent.

The dozens of Vincent's self-portraits she'd studied over the years sprang to mind. Staring at the skeleton's forehead and high cheekbones and jaw, she saw Vincent's face. His elongated nose. The high eyebrow arch. The reddish hair and beard. His intense blue eyes.

Vincent's face was as familiar to her as Vincentje's.

Here was the man who had driven her life's purpose. Here was the man whose words were as familiar to her as her own from reading and rereading his letters.

He had called her to reach deep inside of herself. Insisted she fight against others' agendas and obstacles and, ultimately, her own fear.

In gratitude, her heart swelled.

"*I seek, I pursue, my heart is in it,*" she quoted Vincent's words back to him.

Then, as Doctor Gachet handed the skull to his son, who carefully placed it at the end of the new coffin, she whispered, "Me too, Vincent. Me too."

FIFTY-THREE

AMSTERDAM

Jo

"NERVOUS, MAMA?" ASKED VINCENTJE. HIS DEEP VOICE WAS soft as he patted Jo's gloved hand. She curled her fingers around his and squeezed. After four years of his studying at the Roelof Hartplein school, she'd gotten used to him returning home inches taller each holiday, but on this quick visit—granted by special permission for her July event—he'd surprised her with his voice's deeper timbre. It shocked her that he'd grown so fast. And at fifteen years old, he looked more than ever like Theo. Though with just a sketch of a mustache.

Before she could answer her son, Cohen laughed. "Have you ever seen your calm-and-collected mother anxious?" He took his eyes off the road for a second to wink at Jo before turning back to peer through the windshield at the slow traffic. The sunset's rosy-tinged hue over Amsterdam's downtown streets glowed on his face.

Sandwiched on the front seat between her husband and son, Jo breathed a noncommittal "Hmmm" in response, for the truth was she did feel jittery. It was a good excitement though, unlike the old Jo who would have been battling an undercurrent of panic.

Tonight's art exhibit had been a long time coming—nearly fifteen years since Theo's death—but there was a part of her that knew intuitively that it was occurring at the exact time it needed to, that she could trust the instinct that had helped her create the bulwark of collectors who would endorse Vincent and spur new visitors to come and see his paintings.

Never had so many of Vincent's works been displayed at the same time in the same space. She desperately hoped that the impact of doing a full exhibition—four hundred eighty-four works, seven large exhibit halls—would create the impetus for visitors to feel the essence he'd tried to convey in his work. Impatient, Jo shifted in her seat. Traffic was sluggish, and she didn't want to be late. She wanted to catch people's first reactions herself.

The car inched around a corner. Up ahead, the cause for the delay came into view. A man wrestled with a skittish horse, caught in the tangled reins of an overturned carriage next to an idling car.

"Ahhh, accident," breathed Cohen, then glanced at Jo. "They're sorting it out. Just a few minutes."

Jo pressed her lips together and said nothing. In the distance, the tall, dark silhouette of the Stedelijk Museum was a deep shadow against the reddish sky. She remembered the first time she'd seen the brick building, nine months ago when she'd sold Villa Helma, and she and Cohen had moved from Bussum to Amsterdam. Thanks to the art sales, she could finally put managing a boardinghouse behind her.

Up ahead, the Stedelijk suddenly lit up from lights placed along the base of the building. The traffic sat at a standstill. Jo glanced at Cohen's profile, his eyes straight ahead, watching the accident cleanup. She couldn't sit any longer. Tonight was the high point, the ultimate achievement after all these years of work, and whether Vincent's reception would be good or bad, she was anxious to find out. She wanted to be in the hall. Turning to her right, Jo instructed,

"Vincentje, open the door. Be careful." Then to Cohen, she said. "I can't wait. We can walk from here."

He threw her a quick smile. "You're the star. Meet you inside."

A burst of noise erupted when Vincentje pushed open the museum's front doors. A grand staircase led up to the main exhibition hall. Two exhibit rooms were on this ground floor, the other five were one story higher. Large bouquets of flowers were dispersed throughout. Waiters circled with trays of champagne. A moving sea of crisp black tuxedos and beribboned elegant evening gowns swirled in the vestibule and up the staircase. A babble of voices swooped through the waiting area like a wave.

"Jo!" a voice called, but from her short height, Jo couldn't see who had shouted. Hanging on to her son's arm, she made her way toward the staircase, noting with satisfaction that several people already referred to their open catalogs.

Vincentje leaned down and spoke into her ear, "I'll find you some champagne." Then he disappeared between the shifting bodies.

"It *is* a night for celebration," a voice behind Jo declared.

Turning around, Jo came face-to-face with a friendly smile from a stranger who sported a neatly trimmed mustache and beard. He held out his hand. "Pleased to finally meet you, Madame van Gogh. Émile Schuffenecker, at your service."

"Monsieur Schuffenecker! All the way from Paris!" Jo grasped his hand. After nine years of his buying Vincent's artwork, this was the first time she'd met the art collector.

As they kissed each other's cheeks, Jo marveled that he'd traveled from Paris, nearly five hundred kilometers away. "I'm honored that you've come."

"Actually, a group of us came by car," he said.

Jo stepped back, astonished. It was expensive and unusual to travel such a distance by automobile, but she was delighted word of the exhibit had spread.

"It was my idea," Schuffenecker said. "I couldn't resist. Besides, I noticed Vincent from the very beginning, remember? Bought my first Van Gogh at Vollard's. Can't miss this triumph."

"Smearing my name again?" another voice injected. Schuffenecker laughed as Jo spun around to see who had teased.

"Monsieur Vollard!" Jo exclaimed.

His hair had receded since the last time she'd seen him nearly a decade ago. A few more wrinkles, but the bright lights from a chandelier overhead sparkled in his eyes. He raised his eyebrows and laughed. "Thank God I came to my senses. Tell me, is that scoundrel Cassirer here?"

"Berlin's a little too far, but he did rush five crates of Vincent's paintings so I could include them in my show."

"Don't give all the good ones to the Germans. Remember you have friends in Paris."

Jo laughed out loud. How times had changed. As if reading her thoughts, Vollard quickly asked, "If you don't mind my question, how many paintings and drawings have you sold?"

"Ninety-nine since Theo's passing."

"You've come a long way," he said with admiration

Yes, she had. Like looking at a photo of herself as a little girl, she felt a rush of compassion toward that young widow fumbling about years ago. That girl was far removed from the art dealer she was today. Jo followed Vollard's eyes as he took in the full room. His arrival made her think of Raulf. He'd disappeared since their confrontation in Rotterdam.

As if reading her mind, Vollard said, "Have you heard about Georges Raulf?"

Pressing her lips together, Jo shook her head. No need to degrade Raulf any further by divulging his strange behavior a year ago.

"Well, he's in jail. A good twenty years, I guess. Caught stealing the paintings of a new up-and-comer—Pablo Picasso." He barked out a laugh. "Given Raulf's track record, I'm thinking of giving Picasso a solo show."

Jo imagined Raulf in a coarse prison jumpsuit. She could almost feel sorry for him.

Looking across the crowded exhibit hall, she realized she hadn't thought of Raulf in months. In fact, forgetting him seemed like the perfect revenge. She'd fought against Vincent disappearing into anonymity all this time. Letting Raulf fade from memory seemed like the perfect payback. He no longer had any hold over her.

Vincentje appeared, pulling a waiter with a full tray of champagne flutes along with him. "Right here, sir!" They each took a glass. Vincentje threw a questioning look at Jo.

"Your son, isn't he?" Schuffenecker asked, catching the exchange. He slapped Vincentje on the back. "What a sound young man! Let him celebrate with us!"

Jo laughed and nodded as Vincentje, grinning, took a glass. Her son was indeed sound. Despite all those years of worry, not a glimmer of mental turmoil had shown up in her son. She was grateful.

"Cheers!" said the men in unison, raising their flutes.

"And congratulations, Madame van Gogh," added Vollard.

"Cheers!" Jo sipped the champagne, enjoying the tickling bubbles. She should correct him. Her name was Mevrouw Gosschalk now, but being called Madame van Gogh, for tonight, seemed appropriate. Theo would have loved being here with her.

The night's hours seemed to slip through her fingers. A steady stream of people flowed through the museum doors. Cohen came and went, hovering near Jo's elbow to see if she needed anything, then fading away again. Although Jo's role in promoting Vincent's artwork was well known—thanks to the press—society still searched for a nearby man to pin acknowledgment to, so Cohen determinedly kept his distance from her. She overheard him modestly accept his own congratulations for the thoughtful introduction he'd written about Vincent and Theo in the exhibition catalog, but when their praise shifted to the show, he firmly redirected people to her.

Stationing herself between the staircase and a display hall, Jo intended to thank the collectors who had loaned paintings for the exhibition. She tried to hear the first impressions of guests entering the room, but instead of eavesdropping, she got caught up in welcoming common Amsterdammers. She was thrilled when she spied a plain jacket or dress, for it meant the visitors had taken advantage of her lower-priced "continuous admission ticket." It was especially designed for working people to visit the exhibit multiple times over the course of the show. As art critic Albert Aurier had asserted long ago, simple and illiterate people understood Vincent's work the best. Unencumbered by elite education and culture, they responded to the emotion in his work without pretense. Jo grasped hand after calloused hand. Vincent would have loved to see them here.

Martha and Anna broke through the crowd.

"I'm so glad you've come!" Jo pulled both into a hug.

"You are a sight for sore eyes." Martha stepped back. "Bussum isn't the same without you."

"I've missed you both!"

"I'm so sorry about your parents, Jo," Anna said.

Anna, alone, knew how Jo had finally reconciled with her family after a decade of distance. Then Pa had died in April, and Ma had followed him to the grave in June. Ever since the beginning of the year, they'd heard about her intention to hold a major exhibition. Though they hadn't lived to see it, in the end, they'd finally understood why she'd chosen to live apart from them.

It was a bittersweet blessing.

"Thank you," Jo said. She did a double take at Anna. Were those laugh lines around her eyes? "Oh, Anna, you've changed!"

Anna stood taller with a confident glow. "I am changed. I keep Jan guessing!"

Visitors streamed into the galleries on either side, jostling the women as the crowd pressed forward to climb the staircase.

"We're in a busy spot," said Martha as a man approached with his catalog open. "Let's leave Jo to her hosting for now."

As they moved off, Anna turned back and squeezed Jo's arm. "Your parents would be so proud."

Jo felt as though her cup was full. The people who believed in her, those she loved most had come to support her on this special night.

Over the next few hours, Jo moved from room to room, making notes in her catalog of actual sales and the interest of prospective buyers.

Rounding a corner, Jo saw Cohen lean in toward a gesticulating silver-haired matron. He held a handkerchief in one hand pressed to his side. He abhorred germ-laden social situations, so her heart swelled watching his valiant acting. It had taken months for Jo and Cohen to talk about why he'd fled. After their reconciliation, the honeymoon-like feeling had bubbled up again, and Cohen had been quick to apologize once he'd realized he didn't need to compete with Theo to win her love. She could love them both.

Cohen caught Jo's eye from across the room. She watched him give the matron a short bow. He strode to her. "Please. Save me."

She laughed and took his arm.

He pressed her hand. "It's almost closing time. Let's do a round upstairs."

She'd been through the exhibit halls several times, of course, while the paintings had been delivered and hung. Workmen had scurried around, and Jo had had her hands full with decisions about how to organize the paintings and where to place the cashier and how many servers to hire. At the top of the staircase, Jo dropped her hand from Cohen's arm. For a few minutes anyway, she wanted to walk into an exhibit room without a list of details clamoring in her head. Simply enter and watch and listen and absorb how Vincent's paintings were being received.

Jo circled unseen behind the onlookers. *Madhouse.* The word stung. *Intriguing.* Her heart lifted. *Trash.* That was offensive. *Heartbreaking. Passionate.* She walked along the paintings, listening in on the conversations, pausing to look around a viewer's shoulders to see which piece they were gazing at. She clung to the comments offering a glimpse of how Vincent's paintings spoke to them. The framed oils and watercolors were like family, as familiar to her as dear friends. It hurt when they were criticized and made her heart soar when they were admired.

"Ready, Jo?" Cohen called in a low voice.

"In a moment. You go on."

He slipped out the doorway. As the last group of guests followed him, Jo heard the shuffling of their feet on the stairs. Relieved, she slipped off her shoes. Dangling them in one hand, she drew a long, slow breath and began a final stroll through the exhibit hall.

Hello, *Starry Night.* Its swirling light glittered back. Hello, *Yellow House.* Such an essence of peace and comfort and home. Hello, *Almond Blossom.* Closing her eyes, she could smell the almondy scent on an imaginary breeze. Opening her eyes, the room blurred a little from the tears.

She entered the next room. Pausing before *Wheat Field with Cypresses,* she heard Theo's voice: *Do you see, dear? Look closely. The wheat field has eight colors. Tell me which ones you see.*

"Yellow, brown, orange, green, gold, black, white, gray . . ." Jo counted. Always the teacher.

In silent bare feet, Jo walked backward from the painting into the center of the room. Drawing in her breath, she pirouetted until the paintings flashed by in a blur of color. Little reflections of light glinted from the paintings. For a moment, it seemed as though they were alive, breathing. After all those years when the paintings had lain cramped in her attic, after all those years of covering them up in muslin and shipping them back and forth in packing crates, it was surreal for so many to be out and seen together. No longer hidden. A joyous reunion. All in the open.

Jo stopped spinning. It was the same for her. Though Vincent had painted the artwork and Theo had tried to sell it, she felt as though all along the paintings had been there for her. Despite how society or family or culture had tried to belittle or dictate her life, she had found who she was. Who she had always been.

Vincent, Theo, and her.

We've worked against the grain, haven't we?

Nodding, Jo closed her eyes, tears on her lashes. An inner voice had been here all along. Guiding her, creating the next step on a path full of bumps and tragedy. But a journey of joy too. Like Vincent and Theo, she'd kept on despite the setbacks. Learned by doing. Learned by following what she loved.

It was always only about love.

Jo looked up. One of the *Sunflowers* hung directly in front of her. She walked up to the mass of golden blossoms and lightly grasped the sides of the frame. The bright, bold flowers—as familiar as old friends—seemed to bob cheerfully.

Jo smiled.

"Well boys. We did it."

THE END

It was on a trip in 2016 to Amsterdam at a visit to the Van Gogh Museum that I first learned of Johanna van Gogh-Bonger. On that day—after two hours reveling in Vincent van Gogh's artworks and brimming in awe of him—I remember my surprise when I read a display about Jo's quest to save him from obscurity. As I stared at her solemn face in the black-and-white photo, wonder flooded my thoughts: *If not for you, we would not know Vincent. If not for you, none of this would be here.* Little did I know then, but that moment struck a spark that would ultimately set alight a new direction for my life.

Two years later I had closed a corporate-career chapter to take up the new endeavor to become an author. The work would take me seven years. I studied story craft and read accounts of Jo's life. I noticed a trend. Most tended to praise her obedience to Theo's vision for his brother. It struck me as odd. Didn't she have her own reasons? Why wouldn't her individual agency be recognized? And so, with these questions, I sought to notice the ways in which she took initiative, even as she was single parenting and managing a busy boardinghouse. And above all, I wanted to understand why she persisted despite hostile backlash for being "blinded by sentimentality" for Vincent.

With these questions in mind, I wrote Jo's story, threw out the first version, then began again. I read all nine hundred two letters of Vincent's correspondence, nearly one million words, not only to follow the trajectory of his career but in a small way get to know him as Jo did, since she only met him three times in person. Vincent's correspondence was critical to Jo's marketing strategy. Over the years, as she shared an array of Vincent's letters—intermittently cajoling, desperate, angry, funny, vulnerable—she would build curiosity and ultimately admiration for her volatile, talented brother-in-law. In 1914 Jo would publish a comprehensive three-volume compilation of Vincent's letters in original Dutch and French. Over the years, other authors' selections would follow. Happily, my husband gave me the 2009 six-volume letter collection from the Van Gogh Museum in 2019 for Christmas. Interested readers can now find this definitive work online at www.vangoghletters.org.

Through reading the letters and learning about Jo's life, I chose to focus this story on the first fourteen-and-a-half years following Theo's death when she fought to save her brother-in-law from obscurity. At that time, Jo inherited around four hundred paintings and many hundreds of drawings, representing about half of Vincent's surviving oeuvre. With her decision to keep and promote the paintings as the starting point for this story, it felt right to end the novel in 1905 at the breakthrough moment when Vincent "arrived"—Jo's orchestration of a massive retrospective of Van Gogh's work in the Stedelijk Museum—with four hundred and eighty-four works of art on display. The exhibition ran for seven weeks and is estimated to have attracted four thousand five hundred visitors.

Over the course of the next twenty years Jo would continue working with art dealers, lenders, museum directors, collectors, art critics, editors of newspapers and other publications, artist friends, and writers. She would offer works exclusively to British and American collectors to expand interest in these markets. In collaboration with Jo, art dealers Gaston Bernheim, Paul Cassirer, and Johannes de Bois would attract attention to Van Gogh as well as wealthy German collector Helene Kröller-Müller. Throughout this period, Jo actively negotiated and sold works even up to a few days before her death on September 2, 1925.

This book references worry that Jo and Theo's son, Vincent

Willem, could have inherited mental illness from Theo's syphilis, but this concern never manifested itself. In later years, medical science would determine that there can be no direct infection once the disease is in a later period of latency. After a successful career as an engineer, in 1962, Vincent Willem spearheaded the establishment of the Van Gogh Museum in collaboration with the Dutch state by donating the family collection.

In the book, I refer to Jo and Theo's son as Vincentje. By attaching the Dutch suffix *je* (a Dutch endearment) to his name, I could be sure the reader knew when the text referred to Vincent the son rather than his uncle Vincent, the artist. Similarly, for the sake of clarity, I chose to address Jo's second husband by his middle name, Cohen, since his first name, Johan, is so like Jo's name.

This research-infused novel follows true events when citing places, people, timeline, exhibitions, and art. As a work of fiction, I filled in gaps where information was missing and on a few instances, deviated slightly from the facts for the sake of the emotional arc of the story.

One such fiction is Georges Raulf, Jo's nemesis, who is completely imaginary. He is an aggregate of the opposition Jo faced from an art-dealing status quo hellbent on protecting their influence and stature. Near the turn of the century, and especially in Paris, the commercial world of high-stakes art dealing had little room for women, much less a young Dutch widow. It was a confluence of an emerging nationalism, new economic advancement due to industrialization, age-old power struggles, and resistance to challenging the status quo. Before it took hold, many thought of modern art as impetuous, dangerous. Within this quagmire, Jo had the audacity to attempt to elbow in recognition of an artist some deemed radical and ugly. I pictured Georges Raulf as the epitome of this criticism.

You can see how rewarding it was for me to trace the downfall of these misogynistic attitudes and Jo's triumph. For triumph she did. Her dedication, marketing skills, and belief in Vincent's genius kept steady pressure on the art world's gatekeepers to get Vincent's work in front of not just the elite but ordinary workers, a group to which Vincent himself felt he belonged. By 1905, she had sold ninety-nine works. Twenty years later, at the time of her death, she had sold an additional one hundred and forty more.

Jo took a collection of art that was virtually unknown to establish a genius ranked alongside such great painters as Leonardo, Michelangelo, Rembrandt, Monet, and Picasso.

When Jo insured her inheritance in 1891, it was valued at about six thousand guilders, including works by other artists. In November 2022, Van Gogh's *Orchard with Cypresses* alone sold for a breathtaking $117.2 million. And the second most expensive painting, *Portrait of Dr. Paul Gachet*, sold for an astounding $82.5 million in 1990. Jo took a stockpile of paintings worth nearly nothing and drove it to becoming a body of work worth billions of dollars.

That's an intuitive genius for what we now know is marketing.

For those readers who wish to know more, I recommend beginning with the Van Gogh Museum website (www.vangoghmuseum.nl). In addition, I found the following books immensely helpful:

Bailey, Martin. *Van Gogh's Finale: Auvers and the Artist's Rise to Fame.* London: Frances Lincoln, 2021.

Jansen, Leo, Hans Luijten, and Nienke Bakker, eds. *Vincent van Gogh: The Letters: The Complete Illustrated and Annotated Edition.* London; New York: Thames & Hudson; Amsterdam: in association with the Van Gogh Museum; Brussels: and the Huygens Institute, 2010.

Jansen, Leo and Jan Robert, eds. *Brief Happiness: The Correspondence of Theo van Gogh and Jo Bonger.* With introduction and commentary by Han van Crimpen. Amsterdam: Van Gogh Museum, Zwolle: Waanders Publishers, 1999.

Jonkman, Mayken, ed. *The Dutch in Paris: 1789–1914.* Leicestershire, England: Thoth Publications, 2017.

Luitjen, Hans. *Jo van Gogh-Bonger: The Woman Who Made Vincent Famous*. Translated by Lynne Richards. New York: Bloomsbury Visual Arts, 2022.

Jo once wrote to art critic Jan Veth: *When I came to Holland—completely sure in myself about the great—the indescribable height of that solitary artist's life—what I felt then, faced with the indifference that met me on all sides where Vincent and his work were concerned. [I felt] . . . the burning sense of injustice of the whole world against him . . . I felt so abandoned—that I understood for the first time what he must have felt—at those times where everyone turned away from him and it was as if "there was no place for him on earth." . . .I wish I could make you feel what Vincent's influence on my life has been. He helped me to order my life such that I can find peace in myself—serenity. . .*

Rest well, Jo. Your time has come.

ACKNOWLEDGMENTS

Jo van Gogh once wrote, *Humanity as a whole only benefits when each of us tries to do good in our own small circle*. So many of my "own small circles" have lifted me up in writing this book. Let me joyfully share them with you.

First, the small circle of the daily Early Bird Writing Group founded by the late Amy Sue Nathan has seen me through first, bad, and finished drafts. The circle of pros who inspired me include Jennie Nash, founder of Author Accelerator, book coaches Sheila Athens and Jill Angel, developmental editor Kim Blakemore Taylor, and Gabi Coatsworth for her insightful beta reading. Two larger author circles welcomed me in: the HistFic Group with our weekly Zoom of historical fiction know-how/fun and the Women's Fiction Writers Association whose community is boundlessly generous.

Outside these author circles, I will be forever grateful for expert advice: Hans Luijten, senior researcher at the Van Gogh Museum in Amsterdam, whose caring stewardship for Jo's legacy is palpable; women's studies professor Dr. Sally Steindorff, who met up with me at a Starbucks to give me rich resources on patriarchy and its nuances; and when the pandemic shut down access to research, Annelies de Bruijn painstakingly translated Dutch into English through the fall of 2020. Since then, my path to publication was made a reality thanks to the innovative She Writes Press circle with publisher Brooke Warner, project manager Lauren Wise and the fantastic SWP team.

There's a small band of girlfriends who were with me on that fateful Amsterdam getaway weekend when I first learned about Jo van Gogh: Asma Usmani, Linda Bannister, Robin Diedrich, and Stephanie Hoff (with us in spirit)—girls, who knew? I am beyond grateful for unflagging friends Joyce Serben; author buddy Deborah Lucas; and my intrepid sister, Meg LaRue. Your never-failing faith in me made this novel a reality. Katarina and Oksana, you know what you did!

For the deep and wide circle of book lovers—readers, teachers, librarians, booksellers, and book clubs (like the Villa crew!)—I am humbly grateful.

And finally, in my immediate family circle, Cristina, my bold dear daughter, I adore and am thankful for you every day. To Eric, my indefatigable son, you are in my heart, and I am forever in your corner. To Jay and Angela, you did good marrying my kids—I love you. And lastly, above all, my love and gratitude to Juan. He has been my anchor, my confidante, my foodie chef. Through his unwavering support, he has made my book adventure possible. I love you.

1. After only twenty-one months of a marriage, Jo's husband, Theo, died, leaving her with a one-year-old baby to care for. If you were Jo, how would you feel?

2. While Jo inhabited a woman's world in the late nineteenth century, she aspired to function as an art dealer, a realm reserved for men. Discuss the spheres available to women at the time. What factors led her to realize she could be a participant? In what ways is the idea of "women's work" the same or different today?

3. The novel takes place at a unique time in history—the turn of the century—showcasing Europe on the cusp of change with newfound nationalism, a rising middle class due to industrialization, and a developing consciousness of women's and workers' rights. How does the setting affect the characters? What role, if any, does it play in shaping their lives? Does it provide them with opportunities they wouldn't otherwise have?

4. Jo felt a strong duty to ensure her son would receive a valuable inheritance. How does this commitment motivate her decisions and actions? If you were Jo, what type of commitment would drive you forward?

5. While the world of Jo is grounded in fact, Georges Raulf is a fictional character, an aggregate of the attitudes and objections Jo faced in her pursuit to promote Vincent's work. How did you feel about Raulf? Did those feelings change over the course of the novel, and if so, how?

6. Compare and contrast Jo and her nemesis, Georges Raulf. In what ways are they similar? How are they different?

7. Vincent van Gogh is one of the most recognizable names in the world. What was your understanding of him before you read the novel, and how did your understanding change, if at all?

8. Did Jo's metamorphosis from a timid young mother to confident marketer surprise you? If so, how? If not, why not?

9. What is the importance of female relationships in Jo's story? Name the women who had the strongest influence on Jo and why.

10. The title of the book could be interpreted several ways. What meaning do you glean from the title? Did your interpretation change from the beginning to the end of the novel, if at all?

11. What benefits do we gain from rediscovering and giving credit to historical women like Jo whose stories are untold?

12. In the dedication, this biographical novel is called a historical fiction parable. Since parables are stories with the purpose to convey greater truths, what principles do you believe Jo van Gogh's story illustrates?

ABOUT THE AUTHOR

Credit: Elisabeth Wiseman

JOAN FERNANDEZ is a novelist who brings to light brilliant women's courageous deeds in history. In 2018, she retired from a 30+ year career as a senior marketing executive to be a full-time writer. In April 2020, she founded a historical fiction affinity group within the Women's Fiction Writers Association that grew from a handful of people to nearly two hundred authors. Her short story, "A Parisian Daughter," is published in the anthology, *Feisty Deeds: Historical Fictions of Daring Women*. Joan is a sought-after public speaker, most recently presenting "Top 10 Secrets for Forming a Vibrant, Lasting Author Community" at the Historical Novel Society UK (digital) Conference in May 2024. She also presented "How to Portray the Past Truthfully without Harm" at the Tenth Anniversary Conference for the Women's Fiction Writers Association in September 2023.

Y O U ' R E   I N V I T E D ...

... to please leave a review—even a few sentences—for my book on
Amazon. Reviews will help other like-minded readers discover
Saving Vincent, A Novel of Jo van Gogh.
... to discover insider background info on this book and writings
on my website www.joanfernandezauthor.com.
I hope to see you here!

Looking for your next great read?

We can help!

Visit www.shewritespress.com/next-read
or scan the QR code below for a list
of our recommended titles.

She Writes Press is an award-winning
independent publishing company founded to
serve women writers everywhere.